From
Sacred Ashes

by

Lloyd R. Agee

Benjamin Timmons Mysteries

From Sacred Ashes

Cover Art by *Kim Mendoza*

The Wild Rose Press, Inc.
PO Box 708
Adams Basin, NY 14410-0708
Visit us at www.thewildrosepress.com

Publishing History
First Mainstream Thriller Edition, 2020
Print ISBN 978-1-5092-2998-7
Digital ISBN 978-1-5092-2999-4

Benjamin Timmons Mysteries
Published in the United States of America

In the blackness he identified the shape of a raccoon moving in the underbrush. Downwind, the animal suddenly gained his scent, spun and scurried into cover. He put the weapon away, and turned back to the wreck.

The cold grew more intense, so he lit a cigarette. He knew he shouldn't, but field stripping and taking it with him removed the risk of detection. How long had he been standing on this spot? Too long! The reflective dial of his watch showed 10:42 p.m. in Powhatan, Arkansas—11:42 here in Elkton, Indiana. He shuffled as he got colder, but it didn't help the numbness in his feet, hands, and face. At his age, getting into the ravine to confirm the results had been difficult, and it'd be doubly hard to get out. He didn't know why he delayed. Maybe he felt he owed it to Timmons.

Another signal from the cellphone brought him back to his situation. He texted *Merry Christmas* and put away the instrument. One more second confirmed the night remained silent and unaware. A final glance at the dead man, and he turned to leave. He drew comfort knowing God would forgive him this sin, as he'd been forgiven so many times in the past. Before beginning the journey up the bank and out of the hole, he wondered why God hadn't given Jackson Timmons the same consideration.

Praise for *FROM SACRED ASHES*

At the 2014 Florida Writers Association Royal Palm Literary Awards in Orlando, *From Sacred Ashes* won First Place in its genre and a few minutes later was named Book of the Year.

~*~

In 2015, *From Sacred Ashes* was named a Finalist in the Pacific Northwest Writers Association contest.

~*~

In 2015, *From Sacred Ashes* was named a Finalist at the Tony Hillerman contest.

Dedication

To my wife, Marilyn,
who always believed in me—even when I didn't

~

To my son, Layne, my real-life hero

~

To Dr. John Toth, who inspired and motivated me
when I was a college student, remained my friend since,
and whose hand assisted throughout with the creation of
From Sacred Ashes

Prologue

The car's somersault down the steep terrain had shattered the driver's side window, allowing easy access to the victim. Removing his glove, he felt the sting of the Indiana winter on his bare hand. Leaning against the wrecked vehicle he pressed two fingers on Jackson Timmons's carotid artery. Pressure on the neck for several seconds confirmed the death. The lighter from his pocket revealed the stare from the blue eyes and the frozen look of surprise on the dead man's face. The job done, he felt the need to hurry with his exit plan, but he delayed.

Until a few days ago, such tasks were in his past. Not many in this work had retired, so he'd counted himself lucky when he walked away several years back. Earlier in the week, when the woman called with this mission, he tried to turn her down—pretended he had that option. But she knew too much about his history, wouldn't allow him to avoid her demands, and forced him to agree.

The cold numbed his fingers, but he kept the lighter burning and looked at Timmons's face, partially hidden by a deflated air bag and shadows of the night. He wanted to close the eyes, but his training wouldn't allow such an amateurish move. At nineteen years old, he learned to handle explosives in Vietnam, and even after forty years, he hadn't lost his touch. Earlier in the day, he'd placed a small charge under the vehicle, and it'd performed perfectly. From a carefully selected vantage point overlooking the narrow, lightly used stretch of county road in Northern Indiana, he'd triggered the controlled explosion at just the proper moment. The disabled front suspension on the Pontiac Grand Am caused it to veer sharply to the right and disappear into the steep ravine. He'd listened as the vehicle rolled twice before coming to rest at the bottom of the gorge.

Now, as he looked at Timmons's face, he remembered his first kill. Twelve days into the first tour in Vietnam and four days before his nineteenth birthday, his platoon humped a recon patrol to Phu Duc, a nothing village of just a few abandoned hooches on the edge of a nowhere jungle. His lifetime's nightmare happened in an instant, but now his mind replayed it in slow motion. As he surveyed his field of fire, a gook appeared out of the jungle and startled him. He couldn't recall pulling the trigger, didn't remember the sound of the M16, or feel the recoil. But he remembered the surprised look on the man's face when he clutched his chest and fell. While he bent to examine the body and received his first death stare, the others in his unit came running. Without words, the sergeant signaled for the men to spread out, and they found a patty tended by the gook's wife and three children. Goddamned rice farmer!

The cellphone on his belt vibrated, but he ignored the signal. She wanted an update. With Timmons out of the way, he'd just become her biggest liability, and she would have plans to remedy that risk. He'd have to take care of her before she did the same to him.

He put aside future problems, concentrating on the remaining tasks of the evening. He listened, but still no activity from the surrounding countryside. He'd picked a perfect location, and the job had gone unnoticed. Falling snow, heavy enough to hide his footprints, might cover the signs of the wreck, even in daylight. With any luck, he'd be back to Arkansas before anyone found the vehicle.

At a noise from behind, he pulled the Makarov from his jacket pocket, and squinted into the darkness, ready to repel any threat. In the blackness he identified the shape of a raccoon moving in the underbrush. Downwind, the animal suddenly gained his scent, spun and scurried into cover. He put the weapon away, and turned back to the wreck.

The cold grew more intense, so he lit a cigarette. He knew he shouldn't, but field stripping and taking it with him removed the risk of detection. How long had he been standing on this spot? Too long! The reflective dial of his watch showed 10:42 p.m. in Powhatan, Arkansas—11:42 here in Elkton, Indiana. He shuffled as he got colder, but it didn't help the numbness in his feet, hands, and face. At his age, getting into the ravine to confirm the results had been difficult, and it'd be doubly hard to get out. He didn't know why he delayed. Maybe he felt he owed it to Timmons.

Another signal from the cellphone brought him back to his situation. He texted *Merry Christmas* and put away the instrument. One more second confirmed the night remained silent and unaware. A final glance at the dead man, and he turned to leave. He drew comfort knowing God would forgive him this sin, as he'd been forgiven so many times in the past. Before beginning the journey up the bank and out of the hole, he wondered why God hadn't given Jackson Timmons the same consideration.

Chapter One
The First Step

Dr. Helen Epstein, head of the Stern School of Business at New York University, worked in her sixth floor office, seated at her desk. Just two days before the commencement address to be delivered by a popular former president, and as chair of the welcoming committee, a hundred tasks summoned her. So many groups needed her time, but this one student's record interrupted. As she turned the pages, stopping occasionally to highlight an entry, her thoughts honed in on the pending discussion with the subject of the file waiting in her outer office.

Prior visits during his three years at Stern were for academic awards, student committees, and several athletic recognitions. He'd built a reputation as one of NYU's best and brightest. Earlier that morning he'd completed his third year with a final exam in Global Economic Perspectives.

She pushed the folder to the middle of the desk and moved her left hand to the intercom button. "Violet, send in Mr. Timmons." As she waited, she thought about her need to convince the young man to change his mind. After a few seconds, the left side of the teak double doors opened, and in walked the dark-haired young man whose name appeared on the folder before her. He smiled as he entered.

She wanted him on the defensive and susceptible to her recommendations. His intelligence would make it difficult to dissuade him from his course, or gain any strategic advantage. Immediately, she realized the error in her strategy. They weren't enemies, and he avoided the vulnerability of the average student intimidated by a visit to the dean. She gestured toward the chair in front of her desk, and as he approached, she saw his eyes go above her head to the diplomas hanging on the wall behind. She knew his gaze rested on her undergraduate certificate from Vanderbilt, always his primary focus.

"How are you, Mr. Timmons? Yes, it's still there."

"I'm great, Dr. Epstein." He eased into the chair with the casual manner of someone much older. "I see it. Nice diploma you and my mom have."

"And how is Connie?"

His bright eyes on the framed document, he asked, "Haven't you two talked? Isn't that why I'm here?"

To the point and she liked that. At the same time it confirmed the error in her approach to the problem. He was not like most twenty-one-year-olds. "I spoke with her this morning at the Indiana state house."

"No doubt to discuss your college reunion," he interrupted. "Thirty-five years ago, I'll bet you never thought it would lead to this."

Now, his eyes looked directly at her, confident and relaxed. In her role at Stern, she'd encountered some of the best minds on the planet. The financial district lay just ten minutes south, and she'd seen that confidence all over "the street." Decision-makers shared qualities similar to his—decisive and cocky. But she had to convince him to change his mind.

"Your mother left an education committee to chat.

We talked about several matters." She knew the lie hadn't fooled him. "Why are we here, Ben?" She pulled the student record closer and pretended to examine a key point. "So many problems this time of year, but I hadn't expected this one."

She studied his face. He'd removed the grin but not the self-assurance. "Mother disagrees with my decision to take the summer off."

"Seems like she'd enjoy having you home. Dr. Agbetheatha called about your project in his economics class. Your work impressed."

His brow wrinkled as he stroked his chin. "Not just my work. The whole class labored in the research and construction of the model."

"But he realized your leadership drove the task. He told me the work's been presented to the graduate school and in several econ classes at Columbia."

His relaxed manner did not change. "We gained some attention, but still have much work ahead of us."

"What is this premise that so impressed our head of econ?"

"Well, it's involved, and I know you're busy."

Her irritation increased, but her voice remained calm. "Humor me," she said. "I'd like to resolve this issue and knowing more might assist."

"I didn't mean to condescend," he said. "I thought we were discussing my summer internship."

She accepted his apology. "Tell me about the course. We'll get to the internship."

"As you know, Stern econ is not just a class. More like a religion." He shifted forward for emphasis. "At the end of last year we started prepping for the third year project, bouncing ideas. The activities leading up to the anniversary of the 9/11 tragedy and the chaos around The Freedom Tower construction got us thinking. I spent the fall in London, and I missed the city's observance."

"I assume your team coordinated the work online?"

"Dr. Agbetheatha laid out the parameters. At the beginning of this class year, the group discussed the Capital Asset Pricing Model—the calculations behind the discovery of backdating stock options. We combined that with a report about the economic impact of 9/11. That discussed negative consequences, but someone asked about the benefits on certain economies and industries. Oil came to mind, the defense industry, and next, we added coal liquefaction. With the international conflicts created by the event, we looked at the military supply industries, and decided to construct a model to evaluate the economic benefits from the attack."

Listening intently, she stopped tapping the file, "There were some good minds in that class."

"Several," he answered. "Suni Yaniff, Abraham Greenstein, Janet Sharpton, Narayan Patel." More of Stern's finest, she mentally noted. "Different nationalities, different economic backgrounds, all with strong opinions and nothing came easily. Everyone had to be convinced, and we had more than a few doubters. Janet cited a work from the '80s discussing the relationship between power and public approval combined with the media. As a nation, we've been conditioned to fear, and we've spent a lot of money in pursuit of safety. The devastation from 9/11 ruled the nation's conscience, but not everyone suffered. We thought a model might look in the shadows. With so many conspiracy theories surrounding the attack, we didn't want to be labeled paranoid groupies."

She heard the excitement in his voice. "With the construction of The Freedom Tower on the site, the huge controversy over the location of the mosque, and everyday remembrance of the tragedy for New Yorkers, we attracted some attention. It would be disingenuous of me to pretend we'd not considered it, especially since the Navy Seals killed Bin Laden just a few months before. A few weeks ago, Dr. Agbetheatha told me he approved the project while convinced we'd fail. He didn't think we could construct and sustain such a model. To be totally honest, I had doubts, too. I still have doubts."

His modest attempt to share the credit impressed her. She knew too Abdelle Agbetheatha could not be easily impressed. "Your group's model identified an economic relationship to 9/11 similar to stock backdating?"

"Attempted to identify," he corrected. "At this point it's too soon to tell. We looked for economic movement before the event which could show prior knowledge. We looked for positioning after the event not specifically random. Nothing's been proven. We're talking about access to data beyond NYU's library. The professor contacted several of his colleagues in academia and government. Many have offered assistance. I've had several discussions with Dr. Preedlin, Columbia's Nobel recipient."

"Yes, I know Morris. I understand he's arranged a television interview."

"The interview is tentatively scheduled, but I'm not attending." She frowned, but said nothing. "Dr.

Preedlin and I talked and emailed, and yesterday, we met for coffee. Well, okay, I had ice tea. He sends his regards."

Her thoughts drifted. Morris's wife died last year, and since she'd separated from her husband in January, they'd enjoyed several dinners. She must remember to ask his impression of Benjamin Timmons.

"We're continuing the work next year. The model's inconsistent, and the processes haven't been stabilized. With access to the correct data, we could narrow the variances, refine the parameters. But the information we're seeking from governments, military services, and industries won't be freely divulged, especially to an undergrad class."

She offered, "I'm participating in the interview in my capacity at NYU. Dr. Agbetheatha will explain the work." She waited for his response, but he didn't seem surprised by her involvement. "Sure you won't attend?"

"The interview won't miss me."

"I assume you're being modest?" He didn't reply. "My two esteemed colleagues must believe they can access the data."

He hesitated, and appeared to choose his words with care, "The model has a direction and some very disturbing trends. Some in the group are ready to indict governments, industries, companies. I'm from Indiana, a conservative region. New York City's very liberal and full of conspiracy theorists—some in our group." A look of enjoyment lit his face.

"Explain the direction."

"I apologize in advance for the racist inference." He hesitated. "The terrorists were primarily Saudis, so we looked at their country's economy, oil production prior to the event."

"Let me guess," she injected. "The sheiks decreased production prior to September, preparing for the spike in price?"

"Actually, Russia increased production several months before—stockpiling. The Saudis responded by decreasing their production. Interesting, because the world's economy slowed afterwards."

She frowned to hide her stunned expression. "Are you saying OPEC?"

"You asked about the direction," he answered. "There are some interesting trends with money movement, market positioning, stock purchases on a large scale. The project needs work, and I don't want to indict the world. It's hard enough identifying the good guys in this economy."

She took the opportunity to address the matter. "NYU is one of the most prestigious universities in the nation. We work hard to maintain that standard. Every student has the right to take time away, as needed. However, with such promising, challenging work and the internship, you have many reasons to stay in the city this summer."

"I know."

"You've built an impressive record in three years, Ben. You have the third highest cumulative grade point in NYU, some impressive athletic achievements, the Brademas scholarship at the end of your sophomore year, and now the forty-second Haulbarth recipient— the reason we're here." The Wall Street firm and a major contributor to NYU recognized the top third-year business student with one of the most-desired honors in the country.

Leaning forward, he said, "Look, I'm proud to be chosen, and I don't wish to embarrass the University, or you. I interviewed in February, and at the time, if selected, I planned to accept. Haulbarth has been a dream since I arrived."

Sensing a weakness, she pushed. "You are embarrassing me. You need to change your mind. Your mother wants it. In the past forty-one years, no student has declined."

"I didn't decide this lightly but I need to go ahead with my plans. I'm sorry to stress you, or tarnish this school. I enjoyed my time with Haulbarth's CEO, Mr. Reezak, but I don't imagine I'll be in their employment plans after this."

She controlled her exasperation with a softened tone. "With all you're giving up, I need an explanation. Your mother mentioned the death of your father over a year ago. I'm sorry for your loss, but you must move on." He looked beyond her, not at the diplomas, but at the bookshelves. "Your father died in a car accident. A tragedy, but what does it have to do with this? Why are you passing Stern's greatest honor?"

He turned his gaze back to her. "My mother divorced my dad when I was seventeen. They'd fought for a couple of years. Mom's political career surged ahead, but my father struggled in his."

"He was an accountant?" Dr. Epstein knew the answer, but wanted his reasons.

"A good one. He'd done turnaround work for a dozen years, or so."

"That's a tough market."

He shrugged. "Helping small businesses emerge from the verge of bankruptcy destroyed his career. He told me companies got into trouble over bad management. His job required him to identify those deficiencies and correct them. My father excelled at the work, but his talents didn't include diplomacy, and he offended many managers. The past dozen years he'd been fired ten times." He paused, and she waited. "Initially, the owners or managers listened to him because they heard the wolves at the door. But, as things improved and human nature being what it is, they wanted to go back to bad practices. My father resisted the fall back to old habits, and he didn't sweet-talk his explanations. He could piss me off, and I loved him."

"Did that have anything to do with the divorce? His professional struggles, not the fact he pissed you off."

"It didn't help, and his drinking increased. He'd gone off the deep end by that time. My mom said bi-polar, and they argued money. I never understood fully. My grandparents had money, but my dad remained independent—wouldn't touch their money. It infuriated my mom, especially with her political aspirations." The dean watched him reflect. After a moment, he said, "I never thought so at the time, but looking back, my relationship with Dad had deteriorated by then." He turned his head and looked out the windows. "The last time the three of us were together, they dropped me here for freshman year."

Dr. Epstein followed his gaze for just a moment. From the sixth floor of the Stern building looking north, they could see the top of The Empire State Building.. Every time she looked out her window uptown, she thought of the Twin Towers absent on the south end of the island. "Where's your mind?" she asked. "I have to

13

understand to communicate to the others involved."

"In my younger days, my dad rocked. Respected in his profession, he and mom were great. My friends told me how fun he was, but to me he was just Dad. My first bike hangs in the garage back home. He taught me to drive in the car he died in. My mom wanted to crush it, but I purchased and stored it."

"Why would you do that?" She imagined it an unhealthy reaction.

"A wreck didn't cost too much, and I didn't want it destroyed without some thought. My cousin, a police officer on the Elkton force, bought and stored it for me."

"I hate to push you, but I need to know where we're going with this?"

"I know your time's short. I'm sorry to put you in the middle of this." She watched him frowning. "While home during Christmas, I found a file of my father's under the front seat. It detailed a family matter dating from his youth in the '60s. His favorite uncle died in Arkansas, shot by a woman. Apparently, he'd sexually assaulted her, and she had a pistol. The courts ruled it justifiable, but my father never got over it."

"I'm still not following." She hid her displeasure that her best student sat in her office, turning down an opportunity of a lifetime over a forty-year-old legal case.

"The file had a lot of detail, but it's incomplete. My father put many hours into the investigation. He'd hired an attorney in Arkansas to get around freedom of information, but he died before the attorney got all the public records. It meant a great something to my dad, and I want to finish."

"Why? What do you hope to accomplish?"

Barely audible, he said, "I want closure over my dad's accident. I know what I'm giving up. Next year I graduate, and if I don't go to law school, or grad school, I'll be working. If this is going to get done, it has to be now."

"I'm going to break a confidence, Ben. You need to know everything." She removed an envelope from her desk for emphasis. "You're being considered for NYU's Rhodes nominee. Going this path will not help your cause."

She noted the delay as he considered, "I appreciate the information and the vote of confidence, but it doesn't change my decision. This summer is my only opportunity. My mother is opposed. Other family members, my sister, all my friends think I'm crazy. Haulbarth and the NYU econ project are important, but I need to do this for my father."

"I don't think you're crazy, but I think it's a huge mistake." She glanced at her watch. "Is there any relationship between your father's accident and this case from '67?"

His expression turned solemn, and for the second time, she realized he chose his words carefully, "See how conspiracy theorists gain status. The Elkton coroner ruled my father's death an accident—a single car slid off an icy road into a steep ravine, and he broke his neck. My goal is to finish his story, and that task takes me to Arkansas. Nothing more."

Not the straight-forward answer she'd expected and she knew he'd left something out. She made one last attempt, "Maybe a delay? Would a week or two give you enough time?"

His display of gratitude offered little comfort. "Thank you for the offer, Dean. I am so grateful for your guidance. It wouldn't be fair to Haulbarth, you, or the University. I'm sure other worthy candidates can start immediately, just as I'm sure the delay would be viewed as an insult." He rose from the chair.

"You're putting me in a terrible position, and I feel compelled to voice my displeasure. Still, I appreciate the explanation." She had no argument left. "Your mother will be disappointed I could not dissuade you. I can't imagine people in Arkansas are going to embrace and appreciate your involvement in such an old case."

"It's crossed my mind. If I get in trouble, I will call." The easy look of confidence had returned. "Good luck with graduation and the reception for the president."

"Are you staying for commencement?"

Now at the door, he turned and nodded, "I have several friends graduating."

"Catch my attention," she said. "I'll introduce you to the former president."

"Thanks," he said. "I will. Goodbye."

She watched him walk through the door toward what? Such a waste.

Chapter Two
Commencement

Wednesday, May 18th, dawned clear and cool in New York City. Traditionally, NYU's graduation took place on campus, but Washington Square Park's renovation necessitated the move to Yankee Stadium. As Ben Timmons traveled via the 4 train from lower Manhattan to the Bronx, the extra time on the subway allowed him to relax.

Forty-five minutes later in a good seat on the second deck down the first base line, he relished the bright sunshine and the grandness of the new stadium. Janet Sharpton, the newly-named Haulbarth intern, sat beside him and chattered about their graduation day, still a year away. "Will this be the site? There are rumors of its move to Central Park? Who'll be the speaker? The University will have to work to better a former president. How many tickets will I get? How many did graduates get this year? My family will be there. I get dibs on your extras!"

Janet had one of the best minds Ben had encountered, and from freshman year, they'd become fast friends. Early in the relationship, Ben learned when she got excited, as she was at this event, the best course was to relax and listen. "Why'd you blow off Haulbarth?"

He'd hoped to duck the discussion. "I'm touring

with The Stones."

As they watched the right field crowd throw a beach ball, she said, "Go to hell! You're not really going to Arkansas?" He did not answer. "You are going!" she almost shouted. "That's so lame! Are you crazy?" Other spectators looked their way.

"Calm down." He patted her arm. "You were meant to be Haulbarth. As you say, it's kismet. I've known since freshman year."

"Bullshit! And don't go Yiddish on me. You're a Midwestern goy. The origin of kismet is Arabic." He watched her wave her arms at all the onlookers, dismissing them.

Ben pretended to be absorbed by the stage positioned on the infield around second base. "How many secret service agents can you identify?" He tried to divert her. "I count at least ten."

"You're so full of shit!" Ben had seen such performances, and he'd learned to watch and admire "Answer my goddamn question!"

"Okay, *plotz*." His amusement increased. "Do you like that one?"

She smirked. "How can a religiously obsessed atheist know Yiddish for chill?"

"I can read," he answered. "And my nature's logical. When accepted canons don't make sense to me, I try to understand—Buddhism, Christianity, Islam."

"Judaism?" she interrupted.

Ben chuckled, "Especially, your faith! As soon as you convince me, I'll convert!"

"I will schedule the bris tomorrow!"

Below them, the faculty filed into the VIP seating area. Former President Maxwell would be arriving soon.

"Okay, Janet!" Ben conceded. "You win the Yiddish contest!" Pictures of the graduates, faculty, and various crowd images flashed on the scoreboard screen. He recognized several faces. "Hey, I think a picture of us just crossed the screen." He pointed to a disappeared image.

Again, she waved her hand at the distraction. Then, she sat. He felt her fingers on his knee, and he looked back. She whispered, "Haulbarth is everything. I'll never spend my family's wealth. It doesn't mean as much to me."

"You could give it back."

He felt her pressure on his knee increase, "You know I want it. Everyone in Stern wants Haulbarth, and no one turns it down."

He put his hand on hers. Ben trusted her more than anyone at NYU. At various times they were dorm mates, classroom rivals, debate competitors, teammates, and over the past year they'd worked closely on the structure of the economic model. Ben cherished her friendship, and sometimes, wished for more. They'd considered dating, talked about it several times. Both recognized the bond, the physical attraction. Somewhere in their relationship, they'd discovered a connection stronger than romantic involvement.

Both understood, accepted, and had grown totally comfortable with each other. "I might prefer rock 'n roll, and you might prefer acting, but we both know what we have to do." He sensed the crowd still watching, but ignored them. "You deserve Haulbarth. My heart wouldn't be in it, and I'd make a mess of the summer. Somehow, I believe finishing his work will make the loss of my dad easier."

Janet continued to press the matter. "What do you have? Notes on an old, settled case, compiled by an obsessed, possibly disturbed, family member—your father. It's not worth it, not this."

He grimaced at her statement. "I have a dead uncle, killed by a prominent, wealthy woman in Arkansas. His death was ruled justifiable because of a physical attack upon her. However, rumor had Uncle Josh and the woman involved in a relationship. Such stories troubled my dad his entire life, and at the end he tried to find answers. Now, it's my turn to give them to him."

He saw her exaggerate another grand gesture to the powers above, "That's it? Rumor! Your father, no doubt, destroyed his life! He's dead, asshole." She looked at the infield "I don't think he should drag you down, too. It's stupid! If you prove anything, and that's unlikely, aren't they all dead?"

Faculty, graduates, dignitaries, and guests hurried to their seats. "Not all dead, but many are. Several key figures are around, and I hope to talk with them." He leaned close to her, feeling her breath on his cheek. "It meant a great deal to my father, and it should be important to me. Maybe, it'll help me understand his state of mind in his last days. I don't know."

She rolled her eyes at him. "My grandmother used to tell us that after five thousand years, many Jews realized some deserved such suffering. Your father's fate might—"

"I'm not looking for justification or redemption for my father," Ben interrupted. "There are some holes in the case. He recognized them and sought answers. Right now, that's more important to me than Haulbarth.

It bothered my father for years and caused a rift between him and my grandfather. The two of them argued about it most of my life, and probably longer. Maybe, it's the embarrassment of being driven from Arkansas by the scandal. I don't know. Toward the end—before the accident—my dad became more obsessed. Something drove him, and I intend to find it."

As she watched the activity on the infield, Janet said, "Your father would not want this for you. He'd want you to fulfill your potential."

"Oh, that unrealized potential. Such a burden and I'm a failure at twenty-one."

"Dammit, Ben!" She paused, as if considering her words. "When are you leaving?"

"Tomorrow," he answered. "I rented a car."

"Are you coming back for our television interview?"

He shook his head. "You can handle it." He saw her look of disgust.

Over the speaker system a voice announced, "Ladies and gentlemen, please stand and give an NYU welcome to former President of the United States—"

As they rose from their seats, he said, "My dad's information is good. The facts of the case are weak, and the account is not substantiated by my mathematical calculations. I'm not a forensic scientist, but I can calculate angle, trajectory, and velocity. The official file with interviews of the involved parties remained sealed, and after so many years, that seemed strange to me. To gain access my father hired an attorney in Arkansas for freedom of information. And, an interesting fact, the young prosecutor on the original case was someone of note."

"Who?" she shouted above the noise.

As the New York crowd started to shout and cheer, he put his finger to his lips and winked as the voice on the speaker said, "Andrew Pritchard Maxwell!"

Chapter Three
Welcome to Arkansas

Former President Maxwell's commencement speech cited post 9/11 accomplishments under his leadership, and three years out of office, took credit for the recent death of Bin Laden. He challenged NYU's graduates to take up the cause of freedom and reshape the world. After a standing ovation, he received an honorary NYU doctorate, the key to the city from New York's mayor, and an endless stream of praise from a chorus of lesser speakers—members of Congress, diplomats, celebrities, and even Dean Epstein got in a formal thank you.

Ben considered making his way down, perhaps catch Dr. Epstein's attention and get her offered introduction to the former president, but the crowd overwhelmed the infield area. Hundreds pressed the stage area, and secret service elevated their aggressiveness to maintain security.

Still, a glorious celebration, and afterwards, outside the stadium in an endless exchange of shared photographs, Janet Sharpton offended practically everyone by demanding a better ceremony for the next year's class.

After an hour of handshaking, back patting, best wishes, and talk of future plans, Ben escorted Janet to her chauffeured car, bade her farewell, and started toward the subway for the journey back to the city. Janet had offered him a ride, but a trip back to Ben's apartment on Water Street in the financial district would've taken her twice as long as the subway. Besides, Ben looked forward to the solitude to clear his mind before the task ahead.

As he walked toward the elevated platform, a handsome, Middle Eastern man in an expensive silk suit stopped him. With a British accent, he said, "Excuse me, Mr. Timmons."

"Do I know you, sir?"

The man did not introduce himself. "You intend to leave New York on another task, and my associates are concerned. I've been dispatched as a liaison to offer assistance, hoping to retain your efforts here. Many think the greater potential lies with your economic model."

Instinctively, Ben withdrew a half-step. He didn't feel threatened by the approach—just confused. He looked for any telltale bulge in the expensive jacket. Thankfully, the precision taper on the garment appeared unaltered by any foreign objects. "How do you know about our class project?"

"We live in a world with few secrets, young man." An NYPD uniform walked within a few feet, and Ben noticed the man allowed the officer to go beyond earshot. "The inquiries of your class drew attention in my country and others. My colleagues learned your group's achievements and believe it borders on greatness with some additional effort."

"In the fall we'd love to talk with your group. How can I contact you?"

"Oh, we'll talk before next school term. I do not

wish to detain you. I am just delivering a message." Ben turned back toward the subway platform, and the man fell in beside him. "Even if you solve your forty year old mystery in Arkansas, what good does it do you?"

"How do you know about my trip to Arkansas?"

"As I said, no secrets." Now at the base of the steps going to the elevated deck, the man stopped. "You desire to uncover secrets hidden by rich and powerful people. There can be consequences to your actions in Arkansas, and my friends are alarmed."

"What do you mean by consequences? Is that a threat?"

The man studied Ben from head to toe. "Stay with what you know, young man. Arkansas is another world, and you are needed here."

****

Just past mid-afternoon, he walked into his empty apartment. Semester over, his roommates had gone home for a few days before beginning their own internships. In the middle of the floor, his packed bags waited for the trip. He closed his window blinds on the New York sun and fell into bed.

Just after midnight, he exited the Holland Tunnel into New Jersey—the start of his journey. The day before he'd rented a Ford Taurus, two hundred twenty-nine dollars per week plus tax, power windows, power driver's seat, cruise control, and unlimited mileage. He disliked the color, charcoal gray, but it wasn't a purchase. It would get him to Arkansas and back. In the back seat, a bag of clothes, a laptop computer, his father's file, and additional information he'd accumulated over the past four months accompanied him. The sleep had done him good—refreshed him for the night drive. The trip ahead involved some twelve hundred miles, and he wanted to get a healthy portion out of the way during the quiet Thursday morning darkness.

He enjoyed driving. Living in New York the past three years, he'd driven very little—mostly on visits home to Indiana. Night driving relaxed him, and when he did tire, he'd stop and sleep. He hoped to make it well into Ohio before stopping. His open schedule could be adjusted at his own discretion. So many in New York were upset with his plan, but those in Arkansas seemed unaware and unconcerned. He wondered about the Middle Eastern gentleman. Which group did he represent?

Thirty-six hours later, Friday afternoon in southern Missouri on US Highway 67, he passed a sign that read Powhatan, AR 43 miles, and his iPhone sounded the iconic march from a favorite space fantasy. Janet programmed his ring tones, and he'd not changed that one. "Hi, Mom."

"Don't 'Hi, Mom' me! Where the hell are you?"

Her voice sounded strange, more nasal. "Nice talking to you, too. How have you been? How is the Indiana statehouse? Any new political scandals brewing? It's been a long drive, and I might be entertained by the gossip." He regretted the sarcasm. He knew it would only incite her.

He wished he could respect her chosen profession, but the economist in him prevented it. Since his father's death, his relationship with his mother had declined. As her political ambitions grew, so did the emotional distance between them. His rejection of Haulbarth had not helped, and he'd been forced to avoid her calls for the past weeks. She seemed to blame him for any qualities like his dad's. The death of Jack Timmons had amplified her resentment, and his attempted humor had missed.

Her "Go to hell, Ben!" confirmed his hunch. He attributed her temper to the stress of her current position, and he knew the upcoming campaign consumed her. "I've been calling for two days," Connie Timmons said. "Are you stopping in Indianapolis?"

Another conversation he'd tried to avoid. "I didn't answer, because I knew the topic. I'm past Indianapolis."

With the driver's window down and the car traveling at sixty miles per hour, the Missouri air streamed into the Ford. May brought weather already warm and crops growing in the fields. Raised in Indiana, Ben recognized straight rows of corn and soy beans. Relaxed, left hand on the steering wheel, right arm draped on the passenger seatback, he listened.

"Just because NYU thinks you're shit smells of lilacs doesn't mean you're not my son. Dammit, you know why I'm calling. If you change your mind immediately and return to New York, we can salvage this!"

Tightly, he squeezed the steering wheel, "Thanks for putting Dr. Epstein on me."

He heard her shuffling papers in the background, and she uttered something to one of her interns. "It did little good. You're still pissing away your life, just like your father."

"Love you, too!" He started to hang up, but then, "Who else did you talk to about this?"

"No one!"

"There had to be someone else," he pressed her. "Did you persuade others to get after me about Haulbarth—besides Dean Epstein?"

"I only talked to Helen, professionally. Why'd you ask?"

"No one, else?"

"Where are you going with this? I needed help from Helen. Do you think I'm proud of this move?"

A hint of regret tinged his voice. "Sorry I've embarrassed you. Good-bye, Mother."

"Wait!" she demanded. "Powhatan is home to Maxwell. He still carries great influence on the national scene."

"And the point?"

"My gubernatorial committee is seeking his support. Consider that before you offend the ex-president and his friends."

"I thought you hated him and his administration?"

"Dammit, it's politics, Ben. I haven't talked to him, but if I do, it would be wonderful if the subject didn't include your trip."

"So, you still don't like him, but if he can get you a few votes, you'll compromise your principles. He'll support your opponent, so why're you concerned?"

"He might not be a friend, but I don't want you making him an enemy."

"You've convinced me, Mom. Politics is definitely my calling." She didn't respond, but he could sense her anger through the phone. "From what I understand, he was a year out of law school on one of his early ADA cases. I don't know what I'll find. I might not even talk with him. I don't imagine it's easy to drop in on former presidents—even in Powhatan."

He removed the Bluetooth from his ear and put it in the passenger seat. Another sign read Arkansas State Line 8 miles.

His thoughts drifted back to the man outside Yankee Stadium. He assumed it had something to do with his mother, but her denial confused him. Whatever the identity of the man, how'd he get wind of the project? Ben suspected Dr. Epstein had intervened, but decided not. She'd be more aggressive with her involvement.

He reached for the iPhone, found the correct entry, and with the speaker on, he pressed dial. One ring, and after a moment, a voice. "Kenneth Simington speaking."

"Very impressive. An attorney answers his own phone."

The lawyer chuckled and said, "Well, don't be too impressed. I empty the trash cans and sweep the place out, too."

Ben laughed. "This is Ben Timmons. We spoke about some work my father contracted—Freedom of Information, an old case from over forty years ago."

"I thought I recognized your Midwestern tone. How are you?"

"Good, thanks. I'm a few miles out of Powhatan. Will you be in your office? I'd like to see the information."

"I…don't have the file." Simington continued, "I did, but someone broke into my office some months back. Several files were stolen, including your father's. After we spoke, I discovered the theft. Immediately, I requested a replacement, but Arkansas bureaucracy moves slowly. They're supposed to FedEx it to me on Monday."

"Several files stolen including my father's? Can you give me details?" The Middle Eastern gentleman resurfaced in Ben's thoughts.

"The other files were minor cases—simple divorce, land contracts. The file cabinet was overturned—very conspicuous. Now, I believe the target was your father's file from another drawer. That's why I didn't discover it missing right away. In my opinion, the other files were decoys."

"A forty-five year old case would warrant a break-in? Did you report it to the police?" Ben asked.

"The case involved a couple of Powhatan's prominent citizens. And, I did file a report. Powhatan's chief came out himself, but he seemed unconcerned."

The lack of interest by local police didn't surprise Timmons, "The police chief investigated some stolen legal papers? How many officers on the local force?"

"Actually, he's a sheriff, and I don't believe it was anything sinister. He was in the neighborhood—or so he said."

" How many?"

Ben could sense the attorney thinking about the implications. "Well, this is a small town, but the former president is in and out. He has the Secret Service looking after him. Police force, I would say—a dozen."

"Sheriff, huh?"

"He took the information, but no follow-up. Probably not high on his case list. And the other files were scanned in the computer, so I reproduced them, and forgot about it. Unfortunately, I hadn't scanned your father's."

Ben chuckled, "Damn! Why am I not surprised?"

Attorney Simington asked, "I've been assured I'll have the information on Monday. What's happened that concerns you? "

"Just a series of events—probably unrelated. Can we meet tomorrow? I'm not an attorney, so as I go through this investigation, I'll need knowledge of potential legal obstructions."

"Certainly, meet me at my office around nine. Where are you staying? Do you know anyone here?"

"Not a soul. I'll get a motel room, and see you tomorrow."

"There are several bed and breakfasts in the area. I'd be glad to direct you, and they're much nicer than a motel. Southern living at its finest."

Ben quickly considered and dismissed the offer. His father's business would undoubtedly attract attention, and a close living situation might be uncomfortable. "Thanks, but I might be just a day, or two. I'll get a motel."

"Suit yourself," Simington did not sound pleased with the decision. "Your father paid me a retainer, and I'm his attorney and yours. I feel a strong obligation to assist you. Your father told me enough for me to know you are going to need help."

"Thanks, Mr. Simington. I'll see you tomorrow morning." He ended the call.

He found the next number and dialed.

"Good afternoon, Powhatan Star Herald."

"Christina Turner, please." Ben struggled not to laugh. He could imagine the kidding the reporter had suffered through the years. Very few in his generation knew the music of the original Tina Turner. Reporter

Tina Turner, he wondered, was it a married name? If so, he thought she should have kept her maiden name, but then such things weren't done in the old South.

After a moment, "This is Christina. Can I help you?"

"It's Ben Timmons, Miss Turner. We spoke a few weeks ago about an old story. Remember? From 1967? Joshua Timmons died in the incident—justifiable homicide. You agreed to let me review the reporting on the case."

"I remember. I'm sorry, but those archives won't be available by order of the owner."

"Excuse me?" Ben's impression of Arkansas had taken a turn, and he'd just entered the state. "This is a very old case. Why would a review have any impact?"

Miss Turner hesitated, as if someone watched over her shoulder. "The information you requested isn't available. I'm sorry."

"No, before you hang up, who is the owner?" The phone went dead. "Ah, shit!"

Ben knew the information he'd accumulated about his uncle's case would upset certain citizens of Powhatan. His research on the major participants— some still living—found many of them were wealthy and influential. Why else would an old case cause such consternation? If the public records were accurate, he could raise some unpleasant memories, but no permanent damage. But the break-in at the attorney's office bothered him, and why would his uncle's case be the target? What or who was behind this? It crossed his mind that maybe his mother, Dean Epstein, and Janet Sharpton were right.

Even as New York City beckoned, he passed

another sign, Powhatan, population 3410. Proud Birthplace of President Andrew Pritchard Maxwell.

Chapter Four
Meeting the Locals

Timmons left his motel room and crossed the street for dinner at the Cider Barrel, a franchise restaurant known for its Southern cooking and culture. With few customers at the establishment, he took a seat, ordered, and a short time later his meal arrived. A little homesick, he thought of his sister, Susan. Cider Barrel was a favorite of hers.

As he looked at the walls of the dining area decorated with antiques, reminiscent of a simpler time in the nation's history, he smiled. Old photographs of complete strangers, hand tools for various tasks he couldn't identify, signs from obscure businesses, promotions of long-forgotten television shows, and—a requirement of every location in the chain—an animal head mounted above the fireplace. As he sipped his tea, he wondered whose job it was to procure all those old items.

He finished his meal, paid his tab, walked out the door of the restaurant, and scanned the area for points of interest. Northern Arkansas seemed short of tourist attractions, especially in this small town. A few hundred yards to the south he saw a flashing neon sign, Mosie's Pool Hall & Bowling. He deserved a drink after the long drive, and what better place. He headed for the blinking lights.

The unpaved parking lot, covered with loose gravel fill, held nothing but trucks. Most New Yorkers believed such vehicles belonged to ignorant rednecks. Being from Indiana where pickups were much more common, Ben had no such prejudices. Still, his senses were alert as he opened the door.

Inside, the cigarette smoke punched him in the face, and he missed New York's laws against public smoking. He looked to the right at five pool tables in the center of the space, a dozen worn leather chairs lining one wall, six wooden racks attached to the opposite wall holding ten cues each, and a dozen men playing or watching. They all turned to look as he entered. He nodded, and a few of them returned his gesture. Soft drink ads dominated the fluorescent light fixtures over the tables.

To his left were a wooden bar, barstools, and a dirty mirror on the wall full of advertisement logos and business cards. A flat screen TV above the mirror was tuned to the baseball game—St. Louis Cardinals in this area. At the far end, several shelves held rental bowling shoes. A stocky, crusty-looking man, balding, wrinkled shirt, untrimmed beard and moustache, stood behind the bar. He'd been watching the ballgame, but now, his attention fixed on Ben. Deeper into the building were the alleys, but only four people—two couples—bowled.

Ben walked to the bar and slid onto a stool. "No leagues tonight?"

The bartender grunted, "Summer leagues don't start for another week."

He couldn't think of anything to add, so, the two just stared at each other. "I'll have a Samuel Adams Lager with a slice of orange, if you have it."

The bartender stepped away from his position in front of the TV screen, squinted at Ben, leaned on the bar, and said, "This is a dry county, son."

"I beg your pardon?"

"Dry county! No alcoholic beverages served in these parts!"

"You're shittin' me?" popped out of his mouth before he could think.

Behind him from the pool table area, spoke a voice of authority, "Watch your profanity, boy!"

He spun around on the stool to look, and a rugged, white-haired man took a step forward.

"Excuse me, sir. Nothing intended. I thought the twenty-first amendment passed with FDR." As he turned back to the bartender, he asked, "Sweet iced tea with an extra slice of lemon?"

His new adversary hadn't finished with him "Where you from, son?"

He turned back to the man, and said, "Ben Timmons, sir," and extended his hand. The man took it with a look of disapproval. "I'm a student at NYU here on a project." The other pool players stopped to watch the exchange.

"Is that New York City?"

With images of the old movie *Deliverance* flashing, he said, "I'm sorry, sir. You are…?"

"Ralph Kinson's my name, and I'm pastor of the Shannon Baptist Church, right down the road a mile, or so. You're welcome to attend on Sunday." Pointing at his group, he said "They're members of my church. We enjoy a game every Friday with a little fellowship."

"Then, I apologize for my earlier transgression." Ben didn't think his attempts at charm had any influence on the pastor. "Yes, sir. NYU is in the heart of the city, but I'm born and raised in Indiana." In the pool hall less than two minutes, and he held the attention of everyone in the place. Ben thought it could be beneficial—news traveled fast in small towns.

"Are you old enough to drink in New York City?"

"I turned twenty-one in December. However, like most college students, I had a fake ID."

The minister rested the bumper of the pool cue on the floor with his hands around the shaft, as if strangling it. "So, they allow underage drinking?"

"No more than any other location." Ben looked around the room. "With the possible exception of this town." He realized the irony of discussing under-age drinking with a minister in a town that didn't allow over-age drinking.

The crusty bartender placed his iced tea in front of him. "That's a dollar, son." Pastor Kinson looked him over one last time and turned back to the pool tables.

Thankful for the diversion, Ben pulled two dollars from his pocket and laid them on the surface. The bartender took one and pushed the other back along the bar.

"It's a tip, sir."

Leaning forward, the man murmured, "Don't waste money, boy. And you ain't out of the woods, yet."

Ben nodded."I think you're right." Using his inside voice he said, "Really? There are no alcoholic beverages served here?"

"We have our share of moon shiners who keep us supplied." The bartender stood opposite him, but glanced at the ballgame. "During his time as governor, Andy Maxwell opened a gentleman's club on the west side of town close to his farm. They get around the dry laws somehow."

"Politicians usually get around the laws they pass."

"Yeah, that's the truth, `cept Andy didn't pass this one. He didn't do anything to change it—other than his club." The Cardinals had runners moving, and the bartender paused to watch. After the play concluded, he added, "You can get a drink out there, but there are rules. You have to be connected, and they charge membership. I've never been invited. Guess I don't qualify as a gentleman."

Ben chuckled. "An oversight on their part."

"They have dancin' girls, too. You know what I mean?" The bartender continued to watch the game and still used that soft voice.

Ben replied. "We have gentlemen's clubs in New York with similar services, too. Not local girls, I assume?"

"Nah, they bus them in from Jonesboro, Little Rock, and other places. They're mostly college girls working their way through school, or so the gentlemen believe. And some do more than dance, you know?" The inning ended, and crusty bartender turned to him. "What're you doin' here, if you don't mind my askin'?"

Ben thought he liked the man, but hesitated, "As I said, a project. Nothing more."

"What project could come out of New York University and involve Powhatan? Has to do with Maxwell, right?"

Ben avoided the question. "He delivered NYU's commencement address this week. Would you be Mosie, the name on the sign?"

"That's me! Mosell Hubbard." He extended his

hand. "Glad to know you, Ben. I heard you tell the pastor."

Mosie's grip was firm. An early lesson from his dad included detailed observations on a quality handshake. Ben thought Mosie must be aces. "Not to belabor a sore subject—"

"You're twenty-one," Mosie interrupted. "You're supposed to belabor 'til at least thirty."

His liking for the man increased. "I'm interested in the dry laws."

"You had it right. The twenty-first amendment never made it here. This is a religious community, and you met one of the major players."

Pointing toward the group behind, Ben said, "Pool, but no alcohol. I've read at various times in their history, Southern Baptists have been against movies, co-ed swimming, dancing, card playing. Tonight, they shoot pool with Christian fellowship. Seems like progress."

Mosie whispered, "They're Paul Newman fans."

"I don't—"

"You know, *The Hustler.*"

"Oh," Ben understood. "Didn't he get an Academy Award for that?"

"Nah," Mosie looked irritated. "They gave him the award for the sequel, but he was better in the first." Then he added, "We got a movie star livin' here, too."

Ben chuckled, "If you're talking about Miss Turner. I've spoken to her on the telephone."

"Her name's kinda the town joke," Ben didn't need the explanation. "She's good lookin', but too old for you." Another play in the ballgame caused the bartender to turn away.

Ben spoke to his back. "I study economics at school. Has the financial impact on local business been measured, or do people in this community really not drink?"

"The absence of temptation does reduce the numbers".

"Actually, statistics dispute the argument," Ben corrected.

"Gettin' a good education, are ya?" Mosie seemed to study him closely. "Oh, we have drinkers. They have to drive out of the county, and the closest saloons are across the Missouri state line."

"I saw that area on my drive here. A bar or liquor store on every corner just before crossing into Arkansas. It reminded me of casinos in Atlantic City along the Boardwalk."

"Never been to Atlantic City, but the state line is where you buy liquor in these parts—if you ain't a gentleman." While Ben laughed, Pastor Kinson approached from behind. Mosie grunted, "Told you he wasn't done," and turned back to the ballgame.

"We had a Timmons family in these parts some time ago. You related?" the pastor asked.

"Probably, sir," Ben replied. "My grandfather and grandmother moved from this area to Indiana in the late `60s."

"They'd be Lewis and Jenny Timmons?"

"Yes, sir." Ben studied the face of the cleric. He looked sixty, or so, old enough to know of the incident with his uncle. At a guess, Kinson would have been in high school in 1967.

"Your father Jack?"

"Yes, sir," Ben watched for his reaction.

"Jackson."

"Yeah," the pastor confirmed. "I went to school with him. I was a couple years older, and we played football. How's your father?"

Looking at his older face and girth, the NYU student had difficulty picturing the minister as a teenager on a football field. "He died in a car accident some eighteen months ago."

"I'm sorry to hear it." His regret seemed genuine. "I remember likin' your father. How're your grandparents—Lewis and Jenny?"

"My grandmother died shortly after my tenth birthday. Granddad's eighty-three and signs of dementia." He shrugged. "Thanks for asking."

"You're big enough, Ben. I guess six-two, two hundred pounds. Do you play football?"

"I'm on the lacrosse team at NYU, sir."

"Lacrosse? The Indian game with rackets?"

"Yes, that's it." Ben resisted a smile at the confused reference. "Historians believe the Ojibway played as early as the fifth century."

The minister seemed unimpressed. "Sorry about your grandmother and your father. I will remember them in Sunday service. Can I count on your attendance?"

Ben glanced at Mosie and saw a sly sneer on the bartender's face. "Yes, sir. I'll be glad to attend." He lied out of courtesy.

"Go to church often?"

A second lie served no purpose, "I'm not religious, sir. I respect you and your beliefs, but I have my own doubts."

"Many in your generation suffer so. Our members

discuss it often in Sunday school and Friday night fellowship. We don't just shoot pool. We talked about such things this evenin'." He pointed back to his companions, all standing and listening. Several nodded. "You should put down those text books and read *The Bible*."

Ben didn't want to pursue the topic, so he said, "Good advice, sir. I welcome your concern."

"That's a platitude, son." Ben sensed the man's agitation increasing. "I've heard them before from youngsters your age."

"I'm not ignorant of religious practices and teachings."

"NYU required you to read Marx's 'opiate of the masses' I bet."

"The reference was to the contradictions in the major religious works. I meant no disrespect, Reverend."

"You've read the Bible?" Kinson sounded unconvinced. "Yet, you don't believe Jesus died on the cross for your sins?"

Ben wanted to escape the situation, but his pride kept him involved. "I have difficulty with the concept, so I'm skeptical, yes, sir."

In a loud voice for the benefit of the church members, Kinson said, "The book tells how God sent his only Son to redeem mankind. That's the Christian word you should be reading.

"I struggle with the idea of human sacrifice."

You don't believe The New Testament?" Kinson asked.

Ben looked closely at the man's face. Somehow, this had become a test for the minister. Timmons didn't like the man, but he recognized the pastor's need to retain the confidence of the church members. As he looked past the reverend to the group in the pool area, they seemed genuinely interested, so he continued. "I believe it to be a purposeful work with an intended goal. I've read, sir, but I've not found faith. I need more convincing, but I do recognize your commitment."

The minister glanced over his shoulder to his group, smirked, and loudly said, "You must have only read the parts of the Bible that appealed to your point of view."

"Just as preachers teach only the commercially viable points?"

The smile disappeared from the pastor's face. "You were raised Catholic, right?"

The opportunity to allow the man to win had passed, "My mother is Catholic. As a child, I attended with my parents. And to answer your next questions, no, I've never been an altar boy, and I've never been abused by a priest."

"Good ballgame," Mosie interjected. "Can I get you another iced tea, son?"

Ben glanced at the owner, appreciative of his attempt to intervene. Then, he looked back at the pastor, not sure what to do, or say. He doubted the man's emotional control, and the pool cue, a potential weapon, kept him alert. "What's the score?" he asked Mosie, but did not take his eyes from the religious man with the flushed face.

Glancing at the television and seemingly, regaining his composure, Kinson said, "See you Sunday," before he walked back to his companions. He hesitated for one last word, "You'll find most in this community still remember the reason your grandparents moved."

"I welcome the opportunity to discuss it, sir."

"No need for discussion. The facts of the shootin' are widely known in this town."

Ben started to pass on responding, but couldn't. "I have a friend who's an intern at Cook County Hospital in Chicago. He's told me some interesting stories of cases through the emergency room." The minister did not respond. "In the winter the homeless sleep on the grates covering the ventilation shafts from the underground El. Warm air coming from the subway."

The reverend nodded, "I've been to Chicago."

"The facts were a man panhandled some cash from a well-meaning citizen. Instead of using it for food, he bought alcohol, which he drank. Intoxicated, he fell asleep on his grate in an alley. Another person came along in the night and swiped his shoes and socks. Warm and numb, he didn't know until the morning when he awoke screaming. In the night rats had eaten the flesh from his feet. My friend treated him when the paramedics brought him into the hospital."

Several church members reacted to the harshness of the story. "I can see you're no fool, boy, but faith in God doesn't relieve us of our responsibilities."

Ben looked closely at the man. "I'm more cause and effect, sir. I understand the problems of the homeless are often self-induced. Still, the man had a drink and fell asleep. Is it such a sin? Or do we blame the citizen who gave him the money, the clerk who sold him the liquor, the guy who hiked his shoes, or maybe, we can soothe our consciences by blaming the rats? I understand the facts, but I want to look deeper. Not to place blame, but to understand and change the next circumstance. I accept the fact we're all flawed."

"Recognizin' and treatin' those flaws is my job." He paused, but only a moment, "You trouble me, young man. I'm older than you, and I try to make allowances for your youthful naivety." His gaze moved from Ben to Mosie and back. "Foolishly, you preach tolerance to me, but expect all of us to be either black or white. With experience comes the understandin' that we all live various shades of gray. Yes, we'd all like endless days of sunshine, but mostly, the meanin' of life is discovered in the shadows. And over the years, I've learned the ones who live closest to the darkness are the most condescendin'." One last look and Pastor Kinson returned to his game table.

As the group's activities resumed, Mosie placed another iced tea in front of Ben, even though the first had not been touched. Back to his inside voice, he mumbled, "You have a way of makin' friends. What the hell was that?"

Ben shook his head, admitting confusion. "Usually, I'm known for charm and personality. Maybe I've lost my touch."

"For damn sure. Why the hell are you here?"

"I mean to investigate a family situation from '67. The pastor's familiar with the incident, anyway."

"Timmons—they're your family? Boy, that's forty-five years ago! Everyone here knows the story. Has nothin' to do with you."

The Shannon Baptist members had returned to playing pool, but several participants still glanced Ben's way. While watching the group, and especially, the minister, he answered, "I'm not sure. Probably should get my ass back in my rental car and point it toward

New York."

"Best idea you've had." Mosie leaned closer, and whispered, "There're people in this town you don't fuck with. That man's one."

"I gathered. They patronize your establishment. Are you a member, or the only pool hall in town?"

Mosie pointed, "There's another across town, but my tables are level. The fellowship bets on the games, and they like an even chance."

Ben laughed aloud. "I can't get a beer, but I can wager on pool? Right now, I could use a beer. Guess I don't qualify as a gentleman, either." They laughed together and cemented a new friendship.

Chapter Five
More Opposition

Ben rose early on an already warm morning. He hadn't slept well, partly because of thoughts on recent events, but mostly because of outside racket. Water Street in lower Manhattan had noise, but his seventeenth floor apartment kept him above most of it. A truck driver staying at the motel left his refrigerated unit running throughout the night. In the early hours Ben considered complaining to the front desk, but he figured the business catered to the trucking industry more than NYU students.

Up at six, he showered, shaved, brushed his teeth, and turned on the television to watch CNN. Punching on his computer around seven and checking email, he found four communications from Janet with detailed modifications to the economic model. As he reviewed her work, she amazed again with her ability to uncover and decipher pertinent information. A long explanation of possible ramifications accompanied the electronic transmission. She'd copied the rest of the team and Dr. Agbetheatha.

Several other members and the professor had responded to her comments, and Ben spent another hour studying those calculations. She'd asked for verification of the work, but he could not remember her last mistake.

In one personal email, she expressed excitement about starting Haulbarth on Monday. She called him a stubborn fool and thanked him in the same note for passing on the internship. She concluded with a promise to call later and begged him to be careful.

He chuckled, thinking how New Yorkers believed other parts of the country were like third world. Janet had traveled to many of the great locations on the globe—Paris, London, Singapore, Melbourne. Her experiences rotated around first class seats and five star hotels. He could not imagine his friend sitting in Mosie's, shooting pool, and drinking an iced tea.

He gave the model as much time as he could, saved the modifications to his hard drive, and went to breakfast at the Cider. While he enjoyed his bacon egg-white omelet and watched the comings and goings of the morning's patrons, he thought about Janet's latest submissions. After a year's work from some of the brightest students in the university, their calculations on money supply, currency movement, global investment, and economic impact after 9/11 showed interesting and disturbing trends.

The scientist in him demanded repetition of the conclusion and independent verification. The economist in him knew those goals might never be achieved. Dr. Agbetheatha had gotten involved in data collection, and maybe the professor could secure needed information from some Persian Gulf governments. His thoughts went to the mysterious Middle Eastern gentleman. Everyone in their group knew they were getting close to pointing fingers at some powerful entities.

Around 8 a.m., he got in the rental to drive to the attorney's office. He thought it might take time, because of his unfamiliarity with the city's layout, but ten minutes later, he sat in front of the building on Park Street.

Being Saturday, he didn't expect the lawyer to be in early, and his assumption was correct. While waiting, he reviewed the information in the file, and paid special attention to the hand-printed notes. Jackson Timmons's background as an accountant required detailed entries on his work papers, and the file contained many. He seldom wrote in cursive. His father's style embraced aggressive print, and as Ben read, he felt closer to his dad.

Ben inventoried the facts from the information, and then continued with the suppositions, filling in some gray areas. As a statistician, he recognized the flaws that depended upon unsubstantiated conclusions, but after a forty-five year gap, acknowledged the need to adapt. Many unproven assumptions had to be the basis and direction of continued investigation, or progress toward an accurate conclusion would be unachievable.

Eight-thirty, and still no Kenneth Simington. A large, uniformed man tapped on his driver's side window. He started to lower the glass, but decided to exit the car. The man stepped aside and allowed him out.

"Mornin', young man," he said with a voice of command. "I'm Sheriff Dan Rappart. I assume you're the Timmons kid?"

Ben had been correct about news traveling fast. "How are you, Officer?"

"Good, thanks for askin'." He answered Ben's unasked question. "You've been tagged by the town gossips and an old cop's hunch. Besides, I saw the plate on the car."

At six feet two inches himself, Ben looked up at the lawman. "Not many New York tags in this area?"

"We're not a popular destination for travelers, but we get an occasional Empire State plate. You're waitin' on Barrister Simington?" The mocking legal title practically spat out of the cop's mouth. "Swimmin' with the sharks?"

""I'm hoping to review some information he gathered for my father, but he said it was stolen. You investigated?"

"Stolen?" The officer looked confused. "News to me. What information, and when?"

"Perhaps, I misunderstood. Mr. Simington had a break-in a few months ago, and some files were taken. I thought he said you investigated?"

"Oh, yeah. Not much to go on. Kids and vandalism." The officer looked up the street at an old gentleman walking his Golden Retriever. Ben watched Rappart's eyes follow the man's approach, and saw the lawman's hands remove a cigarette from the uniform pocket. "Simington's biggest client was the shoe factory, but it closed some years back. All those jobs went to Asia. It's been hard on the local economy. I understand you think we should legalize and tax alcohol?" The sheriff flipped a lighter and lit the tobacco.

"Actually, I just ordered a beer," Timmons leaned against the rental. "I'm unfamiliar with dry counties."

The cop chuckled. "Ran afoul of the religious right, I understand." Ben said nothing. The officer puffed the cigarette and waited a moment before he continued, "Ken Simington does contract work, divorces, some public defendin' to make ends meet. He never caught on with the wealthier clients in this area—not that Powhatan has a ton of legal work. In this economy, evictions and foreclosures take most of his time. The wealthier citizens use the Little Rock firms, or some out of St. Louis. We get an occasional drunk, a few burglaries, had a bank robbery last year."

"And an occasional document theft," Ben interjected. "Police work must be pretty calm."

The old gentleman with the dog walked past, and the officer gestured toward him. "Nice mornin', Henry."

"Sure is, Dan." The man and dog on the sidewalk stopped abreast of the policeman and Ben. "That the young man everyone's talkin' 'bout?"

The lawman didn't respond. He gave the man a stern look, and turned back to Ben. "The department has local responsibility for escortin' our primary citizen, President Maxwell. His Secret Service detail directs us. Sometimes, I feel like a hired hand—not an elected official." Dissatisfaction with the arrangement clearly showed. "But, we all know who pays the bills." He took a deep drag on the cigarette, and the smoke punctuated his words. "I know somethin' of your business. You're lookin' into your uncle's case. Betty Pritchard shot him in 1967."

"My information has him killed by a Mrs. Staten. I don't know a Pritchard."

The policeman looked him over. "She married Staten, but after he died, she took back the Pritchard name. Her husband Ben, your name, died in 1994. He was older than her, and did very well. She's seventy-five, and lives out on the west side of town."

51

"Wealthy, huh?" Ben glanced toward Simington's office. "How did Mr. Staten make his money?"

The policeman leaned against the rear quarter panel of the car. "In this area, farmin's the only choice. We're the poorest area of one of the poorest states. Many years ago, Ben Staten invested in oil and natural gas exploration. Some Arizona investment group, and he and a few friends got rich. Seems everythin' he touched turned to gold. Lotta that money went to Andy Pritchard, too."

"Impressive wealth from farming and investing?" Leaning against the driver door, feigning a casual chat, Ben waited for the reaction to his question, but he didn't get one. "I've heard similar stories on Wall Street. Good to know fortunes are made in other places."

Rappart spat, apparently trying to remove a bit of tobacco from his yellow teeth. "Contrary to Yankee beliefs, there are some brains south of the Mason-Dixon Line." He took another drag on the butt. "Is that your goal? Wall Street?"

Ben hesitated, studying the face. A simple question, but the man's intention confused him. "I just finished my junior year, and I'm supposed to know. The only problem I have with Wall Street is I'm not sure creating wealth without creating value is a good thing."

"Interestin' perspective," Ben saw the officer's wrinkled brow and troubled look. "'Specially from an NYU student. Isn't that why you went to school there? Seems like Haulbarth would've done it. Oh, after the old man died, Ms. Pritchard put all her money in the market. She's done very well over the years. The past couple years in this economy, she probably lost the equivalent of the national debt. Still, I don't want her disturbed."

"I understand, Sheriff, but this incident centers on her actions."

"She's the victim," he corrected. "Your uncle triggered the incident and got himself killed. I've reviewed the case."

"Good to know." Ben inched closer to the man. "Since my file's missing, can I get a look at your information?" Ben saw the sheriff's irritation at being trapped. "And whatever the information, I believe I'll need to talk to Mrs. Staten at some point. I'll be discreet. I'm not looking for conflict."

The officer started toward his vehicle. "Boy, you're already past that, and you're causin' me a problem. I've a hunch you're headed for trouble. But, security's pretty good 'round here. Unless she wants, you won't get within a mile of her."

"The stolen files," Ben said, "they were the official records of the case. Mr. Simington exercised freedom of information to get them released for my dad."

"Stolen, huh? I'll look into it. And I'll run your request past the DA, but don't hold your breath."

"You reviewed the file," Ben persisted, "so can I ask you some questions? The theft delays my project and keeps me here."

"Glad to talk to the DA, but I don't do interviews. Ms. Pritchard's close to most of the officials in this area and has strong state connections." The officer had reached his car.

Ben tried to disguise his annoyance with a smile, "One more thing, sir?"

Rappart turned toward Ben. "Sure, son, what can I do?"

"Betty Pritchard, any connection to Andrew Pritchard Maxwell?"

"Well, most of the people in these parts are related—cousins, aunts, uncles, married relatives. Most can trace their lineage to the Civil War, and some to the Revolution. It's a matter of pride."

"Was that a 'Yes'?"

"It's a 'Yes', and be careful where you're goin' with this. You're pissin' off some rowdy rednecks. Some of them would love to kick some New York City ass. Can you fight?"

The question caught him off-guard, "I exercise at a gym near my apartment run by a former trainer of Emile Griffith. You've probably never heard of him, but my grandfather's a fight fan."

The big policeman said, "I've heard of him. He killed Benny Paret in the early '60s. A homo fighter, right? At the weigh-in Paret called him a faggot."

Ben knew the man baited him. His short time in Powhatan had exposed him to some interesting personalities. "I'm impressed by your knowledge of fight history, sir. Mr. Griffith stopped in once, a membership promotion, but his mind had clouded. A very nice man, but it saddened me to see the price he paid for his career."

"Yeah, right," the large man persisted. "Does the story mean you can fight?"

Some people were incapable of compassion, Ben thought. Then, he remembered discussions with his cousin, Jayson, about the toll police work took on empathy. He decided to give Powhatan the benefit of the doubt. "Can't I count on the protection of the local police?"

Ben watched the officer field strip the spent butt, military style, and put the filter in his pocket. He pointed to the office complex. "The fat bastard getting out of the SUV is Simington. Tell him I said that. And pray those rednecks don't know you work out at a homo gym."

Benefit of the doubt passed, and Timmons decided he'd had enough of the Powhatan policeman. "And how'd they find out, Sheriff?"

"You be careful, boy." He climbed behind the wheel and started the engine.

Ben waved to the policeman and turned toward the SUV, as a tall, white-haired, overweight man, sixty years old, or more, removed himself.

As he walked toward the vehicle, the passenger door opened and out climbed a beautiful six-foot tall, twenty-something blonde in a fabulously short white skirt. The sight of her tanned legs increased his interest. She watched his approach as she straightened her garment, covering only a few inches of long, perfect limbs. Rappart stopped his vehicle beside Ben, leaned out his window, and pointed, "That would be Tonya Pritchard, internin' for Simington. She's just finished second year at U of A law, and she's Ms. Pritchard's granddaughter. Small world, huh?"

"Why would she intern for a country lawyer?"

"Good question from the young man who just turned down Haulbarth." Ben wondered if her role had anything to do with the lost file, and decided not. She would've been at the University, and after the exchange with Rappart, Ben doubted the stolen file story had merit. The policeman looked him up and down, and said, "One more question, no gun—right?"

"I drove down from 'the Big Apple'. You can search while I talk to Tonya Pritchard."

"No, I trust you, but it's my job to know. Every good ole boy in the state packs a firearm. You remember that as you proceed." The point taken, Ben continued to look at the young woman. From the corner of his eye, he saw Rappart gesture toward beautiful Tonya. "Mosie's got a pool goin' on her. Cost you twenty to get in, but I hear the payoff's well over a grand."

The insult to the lovely woman left Ben cold. "I'm only here a couple days, officer."

"Well, good huntin', anyway. Every young man in town not like your fighter friend has tried her. A few old men, too." The police officer drove away, leaving Ben irritated and amused at the same time You had to admire a man who could insult the female and gay communities, all the time pretending righteous superiority.

Chapter Six
Legal Advice

Tonya Pritchard turned and said something to the large man. He looked over the top of the vehicle and asked, "Mr. Timmons?"

"Call me Ben." The closer he got, the better Tonya looked. She showed a practiced confidence in her blue eyes but said nothing.

"Let's sit down." The large attorney's face showed the strain of the heat and little drops of perspiration appeared on his forehead. "Like some coffee?" They walked toward the strip mall office with Kenneth Simington, PA on the door. Simington unlocked and held the door open. "My office is to the left, Ben."

As he turned, Ben glanced around the area—worn high-traffic carpeting, component office furniture, small seating area with uncomfortable looking chairs, and old magazines on the tables. Bookshelves along the back wall held legal texts, and Ben wondered about Simington's research capabilities.

Once inside the small, cluttered office, Tonya and Ben sat in identical chairs opposite the desk. Ben noticed Tonya's skirt length, barely mid-thigh while sitting. This young lady would be a distraction. Simington turned his attention to the coffee maker. "How do you like your java, Ben?"

"None for me, thanks."

"No coffee? What's with your generation? Tonya doesn't drink it, either." Ben looked toward Miss Pritchard while Simington continued, "I can't get started without my Jo."

"I tried coffee as a child, and didn't enjoy it." Her pleasant voice matched her appearance, "People told me no one likes their first cup of coffee, and you must acquire a taste for it—like beer. I've never understood drinking something unpleasant long enough to overcome the bad taste."

"I agree." Ben laughed. "About the coffee, that is, not the beer."

Simington interrupted. "I heard you offended the minister of our largest church. Not hard to do, and he takes tending his flock very seriously."

"He invited me to services tomorrow, so maybe, he's not too offended." Ben knew better. "I didn't mean to upset anyone," he added for Tonya's benefit. "Do they really bet on the games?"

"Oh, you got that from Mosie." Simington removed a large mug with both hands, added powdered creamer, mixed with a plastic stir stick, and sat down at the desk. "Mosie's an irritant to the pastor, and those pool and prayer meetings are divine retribution."

"I'm sure he appreciates the business," Tonya said.

"Now, what can I do for you, Mister—Ben?" The lawyer blew on his coffee.

Ben hesitated. "I guess I need some ground rules." The attorney looked puzzled. "Okay, I'll jump in. I'm concerned about the potential conflict of interest with Miss Pritchard." He looked toward her. "I'm sorry to question your professionalism, but I feel a need to be cautious."

"I just finished my second year. I'm interning in my home town and looking after my grandmother's affairs. I'm going to be involved, on one side or the other, so I'll have access to all information. I know the story and might be able to help."

"Why would you?"

"You know Tonya's family," Simington interjected. "She can get you an audience with her grandmother."

"And why would she intercede for me? I'd welcome the opportunity, but forgive me for being slow."

Before Simington could continue, Tonya took control, "If we're going to work together, let's cut the bullshit. Your goal's to restore your uncle's reputation, but to do it, you need to discredit a good many citizens in this town, including my grandmother. The implication being the original account of the shooting is untrue."

"My father began this quest. I only have his information and notes. I'd like to compare these to the independent public records." He saw his explanation didn't satisfy the young woman. "My father had questions. I'd like to answer them. I'm not looking for redemption at the expense of your grandmother."

Tonya Pritchard crossed her legs. "My grandmother is not a liar, and she's the injured party."

"We're here to help you, Ben." The old lawyer seemed oblivious to the purpose of his intern. "I'm embarrassed by the loss of your father's information."

"The sheriff seemed unclear about the theft of the file." Ben watched for a reaction. "You told me he investigated."

Simington looked toward Tonya, but she spoke to Ben. "Rappart has many topics on his mind, not all professional."

"Okay, no bullshit! I need the proper documentation for release of the file. I'm driving to Little Rock on Monday, not waiting on the file via FedEx. I assume you have the release I'll need?"

"I have it, and I can direct you to the correct department. Does that mean you don't trust us?"

"For god's sake, Ken!" Tonya uncrossed her legs and stomped her foot on the floor. "Just ask him how much?"

"I'm not doing this for money."

"You're a liar!"

"Tonya, we should—"

"Stay out of this, Ken." She glared at Ben "You passed on Haulbarth, because you think my grandmother's a better payday. So, I'll give you money to go away. How much?"

"Think what you want. When did you decide on this internship?" As she glared at him, he turned to Simington. "From what I've read, there are inconsistencies. The angle of fire seems wrong, and the story does not hold." He looked back to Tonya. "If your grandmother didn't lie, perhaps there were other reasons?" No reaction. "Stories from my family had your grandmother and my uncle involved."

"I've never asked," she muttered. "My grandfather died when I was a child."

"Well, laying our cards on the table, I'm troubled that a nephew of the victim oversaw the case as assistant district attorney. The investigation took only a few days to resolve and was not thorough in my opinion. I'm not trained in forensic investigation, so I'm confused over several points. Once I've reviewed the available information, a conversation with Mrs. Staten could end my project."

Under her breath, Tonya whispered, "She prefers Ms. Pritchard."

Simington laboriously got up from his chair and removed a manila folder from his credenza. "Here's the release for the records." He pushed it across the desk. Returning to his chair, he said, "I have a map in there and contact information. I told them to expect you."

Ben nodded in appreciation, "Sheriff Rappart seemed unconcerned about the break-in and the original file. Any guesses about that?"

Tonya spoke, "Rappart's a lecherous cop who stays in office by catering to the town's power brokers."

"Those elite include your grandmother, a former president, and from last night's experience, an intimidating Southern Baptist minister."

"From what I heard, you weren't too intimidated," she said. "The offer to settle remains open."

Ben turned back to Simington, "Can I ask, why Little Rock? Aren't there local records? And why were they sealed? The sheriff said he'd seen the information. How does that work?"

With a shrug, "I retrieved the local records," the lawyer answered. "They're in the folder. The original records remained sealed in consideration of the victim—Tonya's grandmother. The assault leading to the shooting, the details of the attack and subsequent events were never disclosed. Not in anything I've seen. Once the president won the election, virtually everything he touched in his life received classified status. His presidential library's in the capital."

"In that case what did the sheriff see?" Ben's gaze went from the attorney to his angry intern, and back. "Before my father died, he tried to find some answers. That's all I want to do."

"Before he died, he tried to extort money from my grandmother." Her words hit like a punch to Ben's face. "Why am I not convinced by your high-minded principles?"

Simington reacted. "Tonya!"

She glared at the attorney, and he bit his lip. "If I've misjudged you, Mr. Timmons, I apologize. However, I'm confident of my position."

The vindictive nature of her attack disturbed him. She'd bear watching and not because of her looks. Her eyes sparkled in ice cold defiance. She had many allies in the area—friends and employees. He remained alone. At the same time Ben knew his father had obsessed over the uncle's death for most of his life, and his obsession didn't involve money. She'd intended the accusation to be a weapon.

"I know where we stand on this issue, but I appreciate your honesty, if nothing else." Taking the folder, he rose from the chair. "I wish I had a better way to approach this. Let me review the case file and get back to you."

"Certainly," Simington said. "And Mr. Timmons, be careful," He extended his hand.

Ben shook the fat, sweaty fingers, "Thanks." Turning to Tonya Pritchard, he said, "I regret offending you and your family." She didn't take his hand and didn't respond. Remembering Sheriff Rappart and giving in to temptation, he added, "I hope to meet you in more pleasant circumstances. I'd be glad to buy you an iced tea."

She didn't turn her head or interrupt her stare. "You're going to get hurt in this." It sounded more like a promise than a threat.

Ben took one last look at her, nodded, and exited the office. As he crossed the street to his rental, he tried to organize his thoughts.

Simington would not be an asset. He wondered how his father found the lawyer, and why he'd used him. He doubted the legitimacy of the Little Rock information, but having nothing more, he'd have to use it. The sheriff had described the situation accurately. Actually, he felt he'd just gotten schooled by Miss Pritchard, and he had little doubt she'd find a way to make good on the threat.

Chapter Seven
Journalism

"Good afternoon, Christina." She looked up from her desk to see Dan Rappart. "The door's open."

Powhatan's newspaper published twice weekly—Thursdays and Sundays—and the day before each required dedicated effort to meet the deadline. Christina Turner had spent thirty-three years of Saturdays working on the Sunday edition, and everyone knew she edited, polished, and rushed to stay ahead of schedule. "Come in. Sit down. There's coffee," she gestured, but nothing more. Christina did not fetch coffee, even for prominent public servants.

"None for me." He slid his large frame into a chair. "You look good, Christina."

"And how is your wife, Sheriff?"

"Nice blouse. Silk, isn't it? You're a good-lookin' woman. Have I told you that before?"

She'd grown accustomed to his leer over the years. "Married men are not on my list, but I'm flattered by your compliments."

"We both know one married man got by that rule." She'd lived with her past for so long, she didn't even react. "Can't blame a man for tryin'."

"Yes, I can. What brings you here?" She knew, but her question honored the expected protocol.

"Ben Timmons," he answered. "A college student

64

in town to review his uncle's shootin'."

"I know the case." She set aside any pretense. "I've spoken with him."

"And can I ask the details of those conversations?"

In her professional life in Powhatan, she'd interacted with Rappart many times. He'd spent his life on the force, and in a small town, that required connections. His manner, his methods reminded her more of a used car salesman than a lawman. "Divulging such information contradicts the standards of my profession."

"Bullshit, Christina! That young man's askin' questions to embarrass prominent citizens and complicate my life. I'd expect your cooperation—for the town's sake and for Staten's memory, if nothin' else."

She'd disliked Rappart from their first meeting—an interview related to her job. Many times over those thirty years, she'd hated him. Fortunately, on this day she could at least tolerate him. "Don't try to use the old man's memory against me, Dan. You're over your head with such tactics."

Out of college she'd worked in Nashville, spending a couple years writing fluff pieces and obituaries. One evening, while accompanying the lead reporter for an interview, she'd met Benjamin Staten, a wealthy Arkansas farmer with political connections. Years after Staten's death, and even as Rappart sat before her with condescension on his face, she felt no shame. Staten continued to be honored, while she remained his whore. Over the years, the stoic presence of the wronged widow, the wagging tongues of the town's gossips, and the lecherous slurs from the local Casanovas had conditioned her—made her strong.

And the biggest slur sat in front of her desk, smiling. Not a friendly expression, only a tactic. "Why don't we both stop pretending to be virgins, darlin'? Did you help the kid?" Rappart's question brought her back to Benjamin Timmons. As she formulated her answer, he probed further. "Why would you help him, Christina? He's headed for trouble."

"He asked for my help, and I felt obliged."

"Bullshit!" Rappart spat out. "You've some motive, but you're goin' to get the kid hurt."

"That's not my intention," she said to Rappart. "I wanted to help young Timmons and get him back to New York."

"If that worked?" The sheriff paused, "Yeah, I can see your scheme."

"Some two years ago, I helped his father," she said. "The son's initial call surprised me, but yes, I didn't see why I shouldn't."

Rappart leaned forward to study her face. "Guilt? That's why you helped the kid?" She didn't respond. "My God, Christina! You're feelin' responsible for the father, so you're puttin' the son in jeopardy?"

"The father died in an auto accident." She wondered what he knew. "Why would I feel guilty over that?"

"That's a good point." He leaned back and linked his fingers behind his head. "Why are you still here, honey? I'm told Mr. Staten left you enough money. Why put up with this town's shit?" She didn't answer. A snarl crossed his face which he tried to pass as a smile. "He tied your money up same as mine, didn't he?"

"Go to hell, Dan!"

"Did you help Timmons?"

"Of course, I helped him with a forty year old case." She watched for a clue to his thoughts. "I thought his father deserved the truth, and I think the son does too."

"What'd you tell him?"

"He asked about the general content of the stories. I pulled the records and gave him the information I found."

"His questions? What were they?" He removed his hands from behind his head and gripped the arms of the chair..

"He had the location and rough dimensions of the site. I told him the building had been torn down years ago. He asked about body position, caliber of the weapon, entry wounds, exit wounds, points of investigation that should've been examined. The young man's intelligent—very intelligent. He asked about type of weapon. He'd calculated velocity, and he'd identified holes in the story."

"Shit—forgive my French!" He put his hands to his face and rubbed his forehead with his fingers. "Calculated velocity? How do you know?"

"He didn't trust me and avoided disclosing details, but I have a brain. In the confined space the caliber of weapon used would have created entry wounds, of course. However, the absence of exit wounds could have been caused by decreased velocity and indicated the greater distance of the weapon—well beyond the confines of the storage room. I'm drawing conclusions from the questions he asked. The reporter's notes included many details that never appeared in print."

"You have the original notes?" She nodded, and he continued. "You're not givin' them to the kid?"

"No, my boss instructed me not to."

He looked shocked. "You took this to old Ms. Pritchard? Why would you do that?"

"No," she answered. "Tonya told me to bury the records."

"That makes sense. Did Timmons say anythin' else?" His smug expression irritated her.

"No, I have not talked to him since he arrived, but I expect to hear from him. When he called yesterday, I couldn't talk with Tonya listening over my shoulder. She spent several hours here, reviewing the information."

The officer rested his right hand on his revolver, as if emphasizing his question. "Did she find anythin'?"

"I don't know. She took most of the old publications with her."

"Do you know what she took?"

"No." She felt her face flush with the lie, but she acted nonchalant. "I told the young man the file wouldn't be available to him, and I hung up. But I don't think he'll be deterred."

"I've a feelin' you're correct. Tonya has the information, huh?" He rose from his chair, "When you talk to young Timmons, keep me informed, Christina. Nice blouse, honey. Shows off your curves real good." She watched as he started to leave.

Then, he turned back. "Maybe you're not feelin' guilty. Maybe you're lookin' to hurt Ms. Pritchard over this, but you need to be careful." He paused, but she did not answer. "No matter how much money old man Staten left you, you don't want to get between Ms.

Pritchard and this case. I know she's treated you like shit over the years, but you were screwin' her husband."

She knew his words were meant to inflict pain, and she hid her reaction. "Is greed the only thing keeping you here, Dan?"

Her question stopped him. "Baby, you and I are joined at the hip. I'd like us to be joined differently, and I've a hunch that's soon. I'm gettin' to like Ben Timmons." He waved and walked out.

Any changes to tomorrow's edition had to be forwarded to the publisher within the hour. She had a few, but nothing major. For a second, or two, she relaxed and thought about Rappart's words. An old case buried in the shadowy history of this community, fodder for gossips never forgotten. They'd kept her sins alive all these years—a concession to Ms. Pritchard. Christina had felt powerless since Staten's death, but this situation gave her hope for a change. She had found a new hero in Ben Timmons.

The death of Joshua Timmons in 1967 could have happened exactly as recorded in the official file. The Star Herald reporter then covered the case throughout, but from the night of the shooting to a justifiable homicide verdict in court took less than a month, perhaps out of consideration for the victim, but she thought not. The story reported Mrs. Staten injured in the attack—bruising from the assault, a broken arm. However, no one in Powhatan believed the official account. Tall tales, speculation, sordid innuendo had fueled the scandal

Braxton Parker, the original reporter, died years ago. He and Christina worked together for a few years after her arrival, and then, he moved to Jonesboro to teach at the University. Before he left, they'd talked about the shooting, but he always remained guarded and his remarks were ambiguous at best. He knew the whole story, without a doubt. However, he'd come to some arrangement for his silence, too. She didn't have any evidence for her suspicion, but she understood the main players.

When young Timmons's father called, it gave her an opportunity to get involved. She'd lived with the widow's resentment toward her over the years. Maybe her ego or her anger interfered, but she saw a chance to repay some of the hurt and regain some power. She'd given the father all the information she could find, and only later realized the danger for herself. Now, Rappart knew. His awareness presented problems for her, and she needed time to consider options for dealing with him.

In her bottom desk drawer she'd retained a copy of all the information removed the day before by Tonya Pritchard. The old news stories retrieved from microfiche, Parker's original notes, unofficial interviews, even unsubstantiated rumors. Not a smoking gun, but they were too dangerous for the hands of an NYU student.

It might be human for her to resent the Pritchard family, but it would be more charitable to remove the young man from harm. She wished he'd return to New York City and get on with his life. She knew the death of his father, and the boy's inability to disconnect from that tragedy, prevented it. And for just one moment, she chastised herself for her excitement over the situation. She'd lost the father some time ago. The son offered many new possibilities.

Just as she put aside her thoughts and returned to her editing duties, she heard a noise in the front of the building. She looked up to see a good-looking young man walking toward her open office door. She wondered if he'd crossed paths with Rappart.

Chapter Eight
Intimidation

Saturday evening as darkness fell, Ben pulled open the door at Mosie's.

"Hi, kid," Mosie called, as he entered the alcohol-free bar. "I've got troubles with lane four. Back in a minute." He motioned toward Ben. "Pour yourself an iced tea."

Stepping inside and closing the door, he saw several couples in the bowling area talking and laughing. Apparently, the mechanical problem had delayed their match, and they cheered Mosie as he rushed past. A quick glance to the right confirmed the pool tables were unused, so he assumed little chance of trouble with the reverend this evening. One lone man sat in a chair against the wall involved in a newspaper. As the NYU student moved to the bar area, the man's gaze followed him.

Sitting himself on a stool, Ben saw the Cardinals' game on the television with the home team down, 3 to 2. He reached over the bar for a glass, filled it with ice, and placed it in front of him on the bar. As he poured the iced tea from a pitcher, the newspaper reader took the seat next to him. "Mind if I sit here?"

Ben enjoyed intrigue, but his short stay in Powhatan had increased his cynicism. The man didn't seem to be just friendly and looking for a chat. "Not at all, sir. My name—"

"Benjamin Timmons, yes, I know," the man interrupted. "I'm Ronald Phillips, the mayor. I'd like to talk with you. Call me Ron, son." Mayor Phillips tossed aside the paper, "I know why you're here, and I think I can help settle this issue." A noise from the rear of the building made them both turn. Mosie struggled with one of the pinsetters, unsuccessfully trying to free some obstruction. The bowlers had paired off, and each couple, seated and sharing quiet conversation, ignored the activity at the end of the lanes.

"Mosie's wanted to replace those mechanical beasts, but hasn't gotten 'round to it."

Ben turned back to Phillips. "What help might you give me, Mr. Mayor?"

Phillips leaned closer, making Ben uncomfortable. "Drink your tea, and I'll explain." He reached over the bar and retrieved his own glass and ice. As Ben passed the pitcher, he continued, "I know your mission, and I'd like you to reconsider. You're young and idealistic, and I admire that." He sipped his drink. "Your quest to resolve unanswered family questions is honorable, but in this case I'm askin' you to consider the broader picture."

"How so, Mr. Mayor?"

"Call me Ron." Ben hid his amusement at the man's insistence on use of the familiar. "I've read the file, and I know you feel there are unsettled issues." That statement made Timmons smile, and the mayor noticed. "What are you thinkin'?"

"It struck me funny that so many people have read the file, but I'm unable to get a look, Mayor."

"That's a fair observation. I can help with that, and

please call me Ron."

"Well, I'd be grateful to you, Ron. Do you have it with you?"

"No." The mayor tapped his fingers on the bar. "I can get it for you, but first, you have to be prepared to look at the big picture. One hand washin' the other, so to speak?"

"And whose hand would I be washing, Mr. Mayor?" Just then, the front door opened, and Tonya Pritchard entered, escorted by a young man the size of the University of Arkansas middle linebacker. Ben noticed the glance exchanged between Phillips and Tonya. Then he noticed the linebacker eyeing him, and his muscles tightened. "Never mind, Mr. Mayor. My question has been answered."

"Now, that's just unfortunate timin', Ben. Nothing more." He jerked his head toward the pool tables, and the two moved in that direction. "We were workin' on a compromise, Ben. Right?" Timmons watched as Tonya took a pool cue from a wall rack. She held it up, checking its straightness, and dissatisfied, put it back. Her escort finished racking the balls and moved toward Tonya to choose his own cue. "The city would be willin' to provide the official file to you, and in exchange for your agreement to drop this matter, it would compensate."

Tonya still wore the short white skirt from earlier, and as she leaned over to break the rack, the skirt hiked up, leaving little to the imagination. Ben caught his breath as he admired her body under the white garment, all the while apprehensive of her companion. He thought of Janet, another woman accustomed to getting her way. He'd never been at odds with Janet, and he wondered if she would ever utilize any of Tonya Pritchard's methods. He knew he should leave, but the woman at the tables intrigued him. "How much does Miss Pritchard think my investigation is worth, Mr. Mayor?"

"Well, I haven't gotten city council approval, but I can offer fifty thousand dollars to settle this matter. That is within my authority."

Ben watched as Tonya moved around the table and the linebacker followed. They seemed to be sharing an intimate conversation, but her eyes remained on the mayor and Ben. Her companion's hand, which had started in the small of her back, kept drifting lower on her body with each shot. His actions appeared to be for show, for he kept glancing in Ben's direction. The staged dance between the large man and Tonya didn't seem real.

"I would like to see the file, Mr. Mayor," he said.

"Does that mean we have a deal, Ben?" Timmons saw his excited glance toward Tonya. "If we have a deal, I can get you the file and the compensation in short order."

Apparently, Mosie had repaired the pinsetter, because a cheer from the bowlers accompanied his return to the front. "Hi, Ron. What're you doin'—?" He stopped as he saw the action by the pool tables, and glanced at Ben. "Maybe you should take in a movie this evenin', kid?"

"The thought crossed my mind."

"Do we have a deal, Ben?" Phillips sounded anxious.

Unsure of Tonya's intentions, he knew his heart couldn't live with the lie. A rejection would likely bring trouble, and he wanted to avoid stupid moves. Unfortunately, it seemed Tonya Pritchard had other plans. "No, I'm sorry, Mr. Mayor." As Mosie moved behind the bar, Ben's attention returned to the pool tables. "Show me the file. Don't show me the file. I'm not doing this for money. Tell the city council and the other interested parties."

"Is there any common ground here?" Tonya watched intently, and her large pawn's hand was now on her butt. "I hate to walk out empty handed." The mayor leaned close to whisper, "Give me somethin' here, young man."

"I wish I could, Ron. I can't give you what she wants. Sorry." Tonya's friend's eyes remained fixed in his direction—confused and pleading. Timmons almost felt sorry for his large adversary. Beside him, the mayor folded his paper and prepared to leave. "She's not really going to do this, is she?" Ben asked. The politician stood, threw a dollar on the bar, and walked out the door without looking back.

Mosie stood close enough to whisper as he pretended interest in the ballgame. "You might want to consider that movie, son."

"I'm not going to run, Mosie. That's what she wants, and I can't give her that, either."

"So, you'd rather stay and get the shit kicked out of you?"

"Is that guy in your Tonya pool?" Ben saw the surprised look on Mosie's face. "The sheriff told me about it."

His friend chuckled, and shook his head. "Naw, but I'd say he's the inside track."

"You might have to pay off." Ben said, but just

then, Tonya's thug walked in his direction. "Who is he?" Ben asked.

"Just one of the locals with a crush on her, I guess," Mosie whispered. "He's strong, but he's slow."

Ben glanced left and right for a weapon, but to the linebacker's credit, he dropped the pool cue on the table. "Hey, boy," he stopped in front of Ben's stool, "I don't like the way you've been lookin' at my woman."

Ben stared past the threat to Tonya, now sitting with her skirt hiked and no longer pretending to care. She was watching him with a smirk on her face. He returned his attention to the large man in front of him, not quite as tall, but heavier by thirty pounds. He'd played pool right-handed, and the watch on his wrist confirmed that. His jeans were too tight for a confrontation, so that could be an advantage. "We don't have to do this." he said, but he knew the desire to show off for Tonya would not subside with chat.

"Do what, boy?"

"Hank," Mosie interjected, "this young man is a visitor to our little town, and I don't want you givin' us a bad name."

"I know why he's here, Mosie." His attention never diverted from Ben.

Ben recounted the lessons from his father. "Never start a fight, but never back down from a bully. If you're in a fight, put your opponent down hard and fast. End the fight and keep him down. A serious fight is a quest for survival, not style points. Hurt, or be hurt."

Mosie tried again to distract Hank. "Tonya's playin' you, boy. You ain't goin' to win the pool this way."

"Shut up, old man, or I'll kick your ass after I'm

through with him."

Ben shook his head at Mosie, trying to defuse the situation. "Look, Hank, is it? I can't pay you what Miss Pritchard promised." He said this loud enough for Tonya to hear. "But I'll give you what I have." He pulled his money from his pocket. "I have twenty-eight dollars. How about dinner at the Cider Barrel? Hell, we can drive to the state line, and I'll buy you a beer."

"I'm not here to drink a beer with you, boy!" The man moved forward. Confident with his size advantage, he threw an off-balance right hand punch, which Ben expected. Ducking his head, he blocked the punch with his left forearm and stuck out his right foot. With his right hand, he grabbed the front of Hank's shirt and pulled. The man tripped, falling face first onto the floor, and Ben jumped on the man's back, one knee between his shoulders. Quickly, he grabbed the man's hair, pulled his neck back, and then dropped the other knee on the man's head. His face slammed into the floor, breaking his nose, splitting his lips, and chipping several teeth. Blood flowed from the linebacker's face onto the floor, and with it went the man's aggression.

Holding the man down, Ben shouted, "Enough! Enough!" He meant it as a question, but in the excitement of the moment, it came out as a demand. He kept one knee in the man's back and the other on his neck, his full weight holding the body on the floor. His hands gripped the hair, ready to hurt more, if necessary.

"I'm sorry I did that." He leaned closer, "Is it enough for you?" Hank grunted, and Ben got off his back. As he eased back on the stool, he remained alert as the man got to his feet. Blood continued to gush from his facial wounds, and looking at Mosie, Ben asked,

"Can he get some ice in a towel?"

Already, Mosie had grabbed a bar towel and filled it with ice. As he hurried toward Hank, the bloody man stumbled, and Ben grabbed his arm to steady him. Mosie took the other arm and put the towel gently against Hank's nose, mouth, and under his chin, trying to catch the blood. "The hospital's just down the street. I'm goin' to drive him. Watch the front, kid."

As his adrenalin decreased, Ben's anger grew, and he turned toward Tonya. She still sat in the pool area, relaxed, and seemingly, undisturbed. "Satisfied?" he asked.

"Not particularly." At least she was honest.

"Sorry to disappoint," he said. "That guy didn't have a clue, did he?" She remained silent. "Did you intend that performance for my benefit?"

"You flatter yourself, Mr. Timmons."

"Or were you prepared to pay him?"

"You'll find my word is gold," she said. He didn't doubt it.

"I'm a student of economics, Miss Pritchard. While I believe you could get me beaten up with your sexual favors as payment, tonight's events had money as motivation. How much did you promise Hank?"

"Less than you turned down from the mayor." Again, he believed her. "Why don't you view this as your fault, not mine?"

The bowlers had left their lanes and now stood at the end of the bar, watching and listening as Ben replied, "I'm not leaving without answers, Miss Pritchard. I won't be bought, and I won't be threatened."

"There are bigger and better fighters than Hank,"

she said. "A lot of men'd like to win Mosie's pool." That statement caused a stir among the onlookers.

"Well, maybe next time Mosie drives me to the hospital."

"That's what I'm counting on," she said as calmly as if discussing the weather. "I don't want you bothering my grandmother." She stood and straightened her skirt. "Return to New York before the blood on the floor is yours."

Just then, Sheriff Rappart walked in the front door. "Well, young Ben, I guess you did learn somethin' from Emile Griffith. I'm takin' you in, son."

. "Can you wait until Mosie returns? I'm supposed to be watching the front."

Tonya stepped forward to the sheriff, but her gaze remained on Ben. "No need to arrest him. Hank started the fight."

"That's not like Hank," Rappart said, and Ben watched him ogle Tonya. "Wonder what brought that on?" but Ben figured the sheriff knew the answer.

As she moved past the policeman, Tonya made a point of touching Ben's arm. "I hope you won't hold Hank's actions against us," she said and walked out the door.

After a moment, Rappart said, "I didn't know Hank was in the pool."

Ben shook his head. "Probably wasn't. Tell me about him."

The sheriff looked confused. "Just a local boy. His family has a farm outside of town."

"You described tonight's events as out of character for him?"

Rappart shook his head, "Big and strong, but a nice

kid. If I'd been here before it started, my money would've been on him. I don't know what you did."

"To be honest, I would've bet on him, too."

"Well, guess you're pretty good, son. You'd better consider the pool."

Ben chuckled. "What I know about women is a short conversation, but my knowledge of the Arkansas female is non-existent. And that woman's spooky."

"My guess is she'd be worth the education," said the sheriff.

"Hank might have a different opinion."

Chapter Nine
CSI

Corporal Jayson Craig, eight year veteran on the Elkton, Indiana force, drove his police cruiser into the downtown station garage at 11:50 p.m. Saturday night. Shift change and he had enough time to clean the vehicle, fill it with gas, and collect personals before the next pair of officers took the unit. Beside him sat his partner, Officer John Kase. Craig was not yet thirty. He and Kase had patrolled together for three years, but the corporal still treated his partner like a rookie. "Hey, Po-lice-man, make sure you clean lunch out of the vehicle."

"Corporal," Kase responded, "have I ever left the trash?"

Craig chuckled. "No, you haven't, because of your fear of God and me! I'll get the gas. Make sure you bring the arrest reports and the daily."

"You got it, Corporal! Anything else I can do for you?"

"No, Po-lice-man. You are an outstanding example of Elkton law enforcement, a credit to the department and the uniform."

"Thank you, Corporal. Now, get off my ass. Shift is over!"

"Yes, sir!" Craig laughed.

As he pumped the gas, Craig watched Kase inspect

the vehicle inside and out, discard the trash in a refuse container, and walk into the station. Kase was black, and to some, Craig's use of ghetto speak for policeman seemed racist. He didn't mean it to be, and Kase knew it. They both took it as a cultural joke between a white and black cop. Sign of the times, a bond built over their years, and each trusted the other to cover his back when needed.

Alone in the police garage while the last few gallons flowed, Craig felt the vibration of his cell phone. He removed it from his pocket and glanced at the screen. "Hey, Cousin!" he answered. "I hear you have successfully pissed off half the family—thankfully your half. Where are you?"

He heard a laugh and then the response, "I'm in Powhatan, Arkansas. Got here yesterday. Staying at a seedy discount motel. Sorry to call so late, but I knew you were on second this week."

"No problem, Ben. We're just changing shifts," Craig replied. "Living well and saving a few dollars, huh?"

"It keeps me under budget."

"There's that!" Craig laughed louder. "I should never have saved that wreck for you. You wouldn't be in this mess if I'd let them crush it."

"I intend to blame you."

"That would be my move. Glad you're safe," Craig said. "So, what's up?"

"I need some work done on the car. You still have the key to the storage unit?"

"Yeah. What work on the car?"

"I'm not sure," Ben replied. "Tell me if this is possible. Maybe I've watched too much television."

"I thought you were just a scholar. What do you need?"

"I'm guessing, Jay. Single car goes off a slippery road into a steep ravine—ruled an accident. Not much of an investigation. But, what's the procedure otherwise? What would you do if there's some suspicion?"

Craig hesitated, but only a moment. "The family is worried about you, and I understand why. Okay, if there's something unusual, a forensic team would gather evidence, inspect the car, collect fingerprints, fibers, whatever they could find. You got some reason to ask?"

"Not really," Ben sounded truthful. "Just playing a hunch, and it could be totally wrong."

"What hunch?" Craig asked.

"Nothing concrete, a series of unusual events, coincidences. People in Powhatan have been less than cordial."

Craig grunted, "Did you think opening a forty-five year-old wound would endear you? You think someone might have been involved in your dad's accident?"

"I talked to a local reporter today, Tina Turner."

"Not the singer, I presume. What did she tell you?" Craig asked.

"Actually, she goes by Christina Turner, and she told me nothing: nothing of value, nothing on background. And she didn't even offer me a glass of iced tea."

"So? What'd you get?" The officer's back stiffened.

"She gave me a direction—unintentionally. After I complete my task and return to New York, she still has to live and work with the main players here. Not much more than a point of a finger, but enough to play a hunch."

"Well, an expensive hunch. If I had something, the case could be reopened. A hunch gets you nothing from the Elkton police."

"Meaning, my dime?"

"You got it, cousin." Craig knew the price tag would be high. "I could pull a few strings, but most of it would be your bill."

"Can you get the force to do it, or do you know people?" Ben asked.

"I know people who do good work. What am I looking for?" Craig removed the fuel hose from the tank and turned off the pump.

"I don't know, but go ahead. I'll send some signed checks, and email my debit card information."

"No, I'll send my information to you. Just transfer funds to my account. I can cover the start. This isn't next semester's tuition, is it?"

He heard Ben's delighted laugh. "Mother threatened my tuition several times. And if she makes good on the promise, my grants, scholarships, and borrowing should get me through. Besides, my dad's insurance named me beneficiary. I should graduate without owing too much to NYU."

"That's good." Craig sighed. "This is deep shit without going bankrupt on top. He left nothing to your sister?"

"Half-sister, and not my dad's blood. Guess that decided the matter."

"Seems a minor technicality for life insurance. How'd Susan take it, and did he leave you a fortune?"

"Since you're doing me this favor, I will satisfy your insatiable appetite for gossip," his cousin said.

"I live such a boring life! Give me details."

"After the divorce Susan and Dad lost touch. I don't think she expected anything, not that he left much. Mentally unstable, according to my mom, and she convinced Susan."

Craig figured he owed his cousin the truth. "I kept in touch with your dad after the divorce. You were in school. There were times when I didn't think he had a full deck—sorry to speak poorly of the dead."

"I'm not offended," Ben said. "I know Dad's struggles before the accident. Hard to explain, but it has something to do with my inability to put his death behind me."

"An idiot on a mission," Craig said. "Your father's obsessions plagued him most of his life, but he was no fool. Detailed, exact, if he gave you information, you could bank it. I would not say this in front of your mom, but you get your smarts from your dad. I hope you find the answers to your quest."

"Thanks, Officer. How long?"

Jayson Craig fell silent, while he thought. Shortly after the accident, he'd secured the car at Ben's request. At the time he thought it the decent thing to do, storing it until the kid could gain some closure over his father's death. Had he known the subsequent events, had he known the kid's thoughts, he wouldn't have complied. At that moment, he wished the file had never existed.

Ben's mother, and even their old grandfather, had tremendous influence, and they were pissed. They had the ability and the tools to turn up the heat on everyone involved. He wondered about Arkansas. "It's your money, partner. I'll book some time, but a couple of weeks at best. You're implying something other than an accident, and if that is true, you have a target on your back."

"I don't mean to imply anything. Can you push the time?"

That troubled Craig even more. "You've got something?"

"No, just covering my bases."

"Yeah, right." The officer placated. "If I push the time, it costs more."

"Push it and thanks, Jay. I appreciate this, and I know the position I'm putting you in. You'll catch hell on my behalf"

"Glad to do it," he lied. "Tell me what's going on, when you get a chance."

"I'll call in a day or two. And I will transfer the money." The phone went silent.

"Hey, Corporal!" He looked up to see Kase standing in the garage doorway. "What gives? Shift's over! It can't take that long to gas a vehicle!"

"Just me and my old age, Officer Kase!"

As he approached his partner, he heard, "What's up, Jay?"

Police partners know everything about the other—family, friends, debts, affairs, everything. It has to be, or trust between officers couldn't be maintained. "A family matter—my cousin."

"Your cousin?" Kase asked. "The NYU student?"

"That's the one."

"Oh, shit!" said Kase. They turned and walked into the station.

Chapter Ten
Sunday School

After the call to his cousin, Ben secluded himself within the confines of the motel room, and worked into the early morning on the economic model. The events at Mosie's had shaken him too much for sleep. As he analyzed the massive amount of data accumulated within the structure, his nerves calmed.

Almost a year ago, ten students had come together with a competitive desire to achieve a grade in the university's toughest class and from its most revered business professor. NYU's best minds and all over-achievers, they excelled in economic study and analysis, had strong computer skills, and each was capable of using complex forecasting programs. The group felt secure inside Dr. Agbetheatha's classroom, using data mined from global information—some public, but more private, culled from more obscure and secure sources. Their skill rendered some government, financial, and corporate systems accessible to inquiry. Just ask the question, and many computer systems answer.

Some disturbing investment moves from wealthy Middle East families prior to the attacks caught his eye, and he wondered how Janet found the information. Narayan noted unscheduled troop movements along the Southern border of Russia, perhaps preparation to defend an American retaliation? He marveled at their work. At 2 a.m. he forwarded an email with the updated thoughts and his observations to classmates and his professor.

He decided to include Dr. Morris Preedlin, knowing the Nobel recipient would discuss any conclusions with Dr. Agbetheatha. Tired, he turned off the laptop and went to bed.

After a restless night, he rose early. A hot shower rejuvenated him and slowed the thoughts running through his brain. As he dressed, he turned his mind away from the previous night's work and back to Arkansas.

Church at 10 a.m. required his attendance. Afterward, he would drive to Little Rock, spend the evening, and arrive early Monday at the Department of Records. Pulling a few dollars from his pocket for the maid, he grabbed his bag, his computer, and headed for the door. A glance at his wristwatch confirmed enough time for breakfast before church.

He popped the latch on the trunk of his rental car. As he placed his belongings in the vehicle, he noticed two men across the street in the chain restaurant's parking lot. The franchise had morning activity, but even for Sunday, the suits they wore and their strained attempts to look nonchalant made them conspicuous. Maybe, the work of the sheriff, but he thought not. The small town budget wouldn't support such. Probably, more official, he concluded.

He decided against breakfast at the usual spot. He didn't want to make it too easy on his two companions, and a local diner a block to the north, Smokie's, beckoned him. The bright sunshine and the fresh air invited a walk.

He hadn't taken more than a few steps when Rappart's vehicle pulled into the motel followed by a black SUV. As the large man labored from the police car, a woman exited the other and walked toward Ben.

"Can we have a word?" the sheriff asked. His casual attire of short-sleeved shirt and tie hid his profession, and only the unit's markings disclosed the lawman's occupation. Ben knew police were always armed—his cousin on the Elkton force confirmed that—so he wondered where the officer concealed his weapon for church.

"Thought we'd have to get you up, but you're awake," the officer said. "Don't all college students sleep in on weekends?

"Guilty as charged. This is my exception. I'm going for breakfast. Care to join me? I'll even buy the coffee."

Rappart glanced at his companion, but she shook her head. "No," he said. "Not a social call. We only need a few minutes. Going to church?"

"I am, but how'd you know?"

Rappart laughed, "You keep forgetting about small towns. I know the pastor invited you." He pointed to the woman, "This is Special Agent Margaret Levitt."

Ben extended his hand. "My pleasure, Special Agent."

"Good morning, Mr. Timmons." Her formal nod irritated him. "The officer briefed me on last night's events."

Ben saw Rappart's displeasure at the devaluation of his position. Then Powhatan's top cop offered a manila envelope.

"What's this?"

"Local information on your uncle's case," the sheriff answered. "At the urging of President Maxwell, the DA released the file."

Ben took the envelope but did not open it. "The former president intervened?"

"An old matter with the potential to tarnish a great American's reputation," Agent Levitt took control of the conversation. "To facilitate your rapid conclusion, the president decided to be forthcoming with information, hoping for a speedy return to school."

Her dark hair was pulled into a neat bun at the back of her head. The tailored, black suit seemed to be the uniform of choice, and a strapped black bag over her shoulder probably contained her weapon and credentials. Low-heeled black shoes completed the ensemble. Good for running, Ben guessed. She had a pretty face, but the piercing, mistrusting eyes gave her a menacing appearance.

"Can I inquire about the potential tarnish of Maxwell?" he asked.

As the sheriff stood silent, she answered. "Your uncle attacked a prominent citizen, a relative of the president. In the course of defending herself, she fatally wounded the attacker. He died a short time later at the local hospital without regaining consciousness. The president, a young district attorney at the time, did what he could to ease the tragedy and protect his family. Most considered it understandable and completely accepted, under the circumstances. Anyone would have done the same." Timmons decided not to interrupt the lecture. "His handling of the situation received little notice, but now it contains the potential to damage his reputation. President Maxwell's management of the 9/11 aftermath elevated him to hero status, not just in this country, but around the world. The Secret Service is concerned about your motives."

"Why would the case have potential to damage anyone if it shakes out like you say?" Ben met her direct gaze. "Are you in charge of his security detail?"

"I'm lead agent on the president's protection."

Ben pointed across the street to the two suits, "Are those men part of your group?"

She threw an aggressive wave in the men's direction. "They were supposed to blend with their surroundings. In this area that's difficult. We've been watching since your arrival."

"And have I done anything worthy of watching?"

"This project—if that is your purpose—has some troubling potential. At the same time, we've received an inquiry from the FBI. Your name cropped up in some back-channel chatter about an econ class at NYU. Can you explain?"

Ben laughed, hoping it hid his concern about their data collection techniques.

"Did I say something funny, Mr. Timmons?"

"No, just..." Agent Levitt didn't seem open to witty anecdotes. "...our third-year group built a model to measure 9/11 economic impact. That's all."

Agent Levitt drummed her fingers against her bag, "Several enemies of America know your name. You're attracting some disturbing attention. Review the record and get back to us with questions. Hopefully, we can conclude this matter in a day, or two." Without waiting for his answer, she started back to her vehicle.

"Can I ask a question, or two?" She stopped, turned

back, but said nothing. Looking first at Sheriff Rappart, then at Special Agent Levitt and showing the envelope, Ben inquired, "The entire file?"

Rappart hesitated. "That's what we have."

Ben sensed his uncertainty and noticed the agent's annoyance with the local lawman. Looking at Agent Levitt, he asked "What is back-channel chatter, and why would my name come up? It's a third-year NYU assignment. Whose attention have we attracted?"

"You just completed your third year?" She glanced at her underlings across the street and appeared upset.

Ben followed her gaze, and saw the two watching. "Yes, term ended this past week. President Maxwell gave the commencement speech at Yankee Stadium."

"I accompanied him." Her attention returned to Ben. "So, your assignment concluded with end of the semester?"

"I attended graduation. Good speech." Her manner showed her lack of interest in small talk. "No, the project will go on. We've garnered some strong interest, but I didn't know of the government's involvement until a few minutes ago."

"Homeland Security monitors all types of communication, and when certain topics, specific subjects get mentioned, the scrutiny intensifies. I don't know what language triggered the reference." Her cold stare never left his face. "Can you give us details of the work?"

"Since 9/11, the Department of Homeland Security has taken on sinister form to many Americans." Ben waited for her reaction to his statement, but she did not flinch, convincing him she knew more than she revealed. "I've had the good fortune to work with some very talented students at NYU, constructing a model to identify economic anomalies related to 9/11. The information has been presented, and it's gained some interest—not just from NYU, but Columbia, Harvard, others."

"Why are you here, Mr. Timmons?"

He thought about the number of times he'd heard that question. He didn't trust her, but at the same time, he thought he might like her. "I'm working to finish a project begun by my father. He died in an auto accident before he completed it. Dad's favorite uncle was killed, and the circumstances surrounding that event troubled him most of his life."

"I'm not sure about you, Mr. Timmons. Are you carrying a weapon?"

Ben glanced at the sheriff. "Not the first time I've heard that question." Rappart shrugged.

"No weapon," Ben said. "I'm from New York City, and it takes an act of Congress to get a legal weapon."

"Can we look in your vehicle?"

He decided he might not like her. "I'm inclined to ask for a warrant or probable cause, but in the interest of goodwill..." He hit the key fob, and the trunk popped open.

"Good." She glanced in his rental, and then turned and walked to her SUV. She drove away without looking back.

Rappart said, "You have a way with the ladies, young man. First, you pissed off Tonya Pritchard, and now, Agent Levitt. Guess you won't be attending any community parties."

"If I do, it's obvious I won't have a date." The two men chuckled. "An interesting conversation..." Ben's gaze followed the SUV. "Why do you suppose she conducted herself like that?"

"She's got a poker up her ass, but that's not what she needs. I'll bet she's hot in bed."

Ben laughed aloud. Then, "How's Hank?" he said.

Without acknowledgment, the policeman walked to his car. "See you in church, son." As the sheriff exited onto the street, Ben felt the weight of the envelope. It was light. His father's file contained much more information without the official records.

He closed the trunk lid, unlocked the front door of the Ford, and threw the envelope in the passenger seat. Reading the file during the sermon might be disrespectful—certainly, his mother would die of embarrassment. It might be blasphemous, but he hoped God and the reverend wouldn't be offended. Right now, he wanted a relaxed breakfast, even with his two companions keeping tabs. Afterwards, church and the drive to Little Rock—a busy day ahead.

Chapter Eleven
Revelations

Shannon Baptist Church, a striking building of thirty thousand square feet, stood as a beacon on the south end of town. A long rectangular structure served as the column and two wings as arms completed the cross architecture. Red brick covered the entire complex and a tall bell tower captured attention at the front. An impressive portico adorned the entrance, courteously designed, allowing southern gentlemen to drop their ladies out of inclement weather. One wing of the cross appeared to be a gymnasium, and the other classrooms and staff offices. Ben guessed the paved parking area around the complex could hold several hundred vehicles. Stunning for a small community.

He parked, retrieved the envelope given to him by the sheriff, and walked toward the doorway. On a bright Sunday morning, families enjoyed the short walk, and several spoke to him as he grew closer. An unshaven, unkempt, gentleman wandered the parking lot, but the church members ignored him. He wore tattered coveralls with dirty work boots but didn't appear to be panhandling. A common sight in New York City, a homeless man in Powhatan surprised Ben.

In the Big Apple, he would've ignored the man, too. He knew the hazards of giving cash to some. The man looked directly at him as he walked to the

96

building, and without hesitation, Ben pulled five dollars from his pocket and handed it over. The man took the bill and tucked it in his pocket.

"Don't buy drugs." No subways in Powhatan, and unless the man knew a moonshiner, Ben knew alcohol would be difficult to find.

"I could use a beer, myself," the man grunted. Surprised by the comment, the boy watched the man stroll away. "Small towns," he thought. He shook his head and proceeded toward the entrance.

At the door, greeters welcomed and directed him to the auditorium. Inside the huge vestibule, a coffee shop sat to the right, busy with activity. Just beyond, a library summoned the passing crowd, exciting many bustling children with parents in tow. At an information center desk to the left of the large reception area, assistants passed out informational programs.

Deeper into the church beyond the foyer, couches, chairs, and tables were organized into several distinct seating areas. In various locations along the walls he noticed five large flat-screen televisions for broadcasting to the overflow crowds. Video streamed from the main hall and music played. As he walked to the sanctuary, he passed hallways on the left leading to the gymnasium and on the right to the offices, classrooms, nurseries, and play areas.

At the rear of the circle amphitheater, the Christian cross ran from the stage floor to ceiling and out to each side, surrounded by stained glass windows depicting popular Biblical themes.

On the left of the stage sat the band members—at least eight people with various instruments. Off-center to the right front, the pulpit waited for the minister. The congregation found their seats, and Ben moved to a secluded spot at the rear.

He placed his envelope on the seat and stood, looking around at the crowd activity. The choir wore red robes trimmed in white. He identified the sheriff at the rear, and Mosie sat over from the policeman. Surprised to see his friend, Ben made a mental note to ask about it next time he visited the pool hall.

In the front pews a commotion caught his eye, and he saw Tonya Pritchard escorting an attractive elderly woman toward the center—Tonya's grandmother, the woman in his uncle's story. They moved confidently, stopping to speak to well-wishers along the way. Behind them, several men in dark suits stood guard, and then came the former president and first lady.

Ben could not hear, but he watched Maxwell talking, waving, kissing the cheeks of the ladies and shaking the hands of the men. Out of office for forty months, he was still enormously popular throughout the country for his handling of post 9/11 events. The adulation seemed multiplied many times over in Powhatan's Baptist church. The former First Lady received equal attention as they moved into the front pew beside Tonya and her grandmother.

The music director started the service and the audience sat. As the choir sang, Ben opened the file to review it. Lost in study and his own thoughts, several minutes passed. The congregation standing and applauding brought him back to the present, as Maxwell rose and acknowledged the accolade. Tonya and her grandmother remained seated, and Ben thought that strange.

Going back to the information from the envelope,

Ben examined the official diagram of the crime site, a small storage room in the rear of the Staten office. He'd read in his father's information the building had been razed in 1996, but the dimensions of the space were included, and he assumed their accuracy.

In the sheriff's file, he discovered that in 1967, the former Mrs. Staten, the lady sitting in the front pew, held the position of bookkeeper at her husband's office. In the police interview and subsequent judicial review, she testified her work often required late hours, such as on the evening of the shooting.

Looking back to the documents, he read that Mrs. Staten purchased the .38 caliber revolver several weeks before the incident from a local man, Lee Roy Pittmann. A quick look through the papers failed to uncover any official interview with Mr. Pittmann. Not surprising. Ben knew weapons were bought and sold in a more open market some fifty years earlier, and the circumstances of the event did not depend upon the weapon.

Ben glanced toward the front row. The prime figure from the documentation on his lap seemed deeply involved in the words coming from the pulpit. The report said she'd suffered an injury in the attack, and that her attacker, Ben's uncle, accosted her in the small storage room at the rear of the building. Again, he thumbed ahead, looking for any explanation of how his uncle gained access to the office. He found nothing and presumed the front door was still unlocked, so he went back to the details of the attack.

Officially, the investigators listed it as unprovoked, but the margin penciled notes presumed a sexual motivation and revealed Ben's uncle as a known womanizer since his return from military service. Ben wondered about the author of the notes, the facts behind them, and the impetus for such conclusions.

Continuing to ignore the sermon, he turned the pages in his lap. The record indicated a snub-nosed weapon was used in the incident. With just a two inch barrel, it'd be convenient for a woman's handbag. Mrs. Staten's attacker grabbed her in the storage area while she put away some files. He tore at her clothes, justification for citing a sexual motivation as cause for the attack. He knocked her to the floor, breaking her left wrist. As he tried to get on top of her, she used her feet and threw him off to the rear of the small room. That's when she retrieved the weapon from her handbag, and fired twice. Ben read that section, again. Something seemed wrong in the description of the event, but he couldn't identify it. He made a mental note to return to the entry.

Autopsy records showed the first round entered his uncle's left side between the eighth and ninth ribs, traveling through several organs and lodging to the right of the spine between the ninth and tenth ribs. The doctor assumed the force of the first round turned the body to the right. The second round entered directly in the left side between the fourth and fifth ribs and lodged on the right at the tenth rib, a couple of inches from the first bullet.

Death had been ruled massive organ failure and internal bleeding from gunshot wounds. Using a pencil and writing on the report, Timmons calculated the trajectory angles, but he needed a calculator, a skeletal diagram, and his computer to be exact. He questioned the accuracy of the muzzle velocity figures. His father's calculations pointed toward the absence of exits wounds as a cause of concern in the original story. However, he allowed a short barrel would deliver less velocity. Ben looked for results of any firing tests from the investigation, but none were there.

Several interviews with citizens of Powhatan pointed to the uncle's obsession with Mrs. Staten. As he read, he tried to follow the progress of the relationship so many years before. In her seventies, she was still a handsome woman. Ben imagined her forty-five years younger. In his mid-twenties at the time of his death, Ben's uncle had just finished four years in the US Army, two in Vietnam. A handsome young man in his parent's photo albums, Joshua Timmons being a womanizer seemed possible to Ben. The family rumors had his relationship with Mrs. Staten starting early in 1967, soon after his discharge, but nothing in the official file substantiated that.

A single page, signed by the District Attorney at the time, not Maxwell, declared the shooting justifiable and absent any criminal intent. The DA declined to pursue the case, and the district judge agreed. Andrew Pritchard Maxwell wasn't the attorney of record, just a bit player, according to the official report. Ben wondered about the ex-president's role as he put the documents back in the envelope.

"Please recognize we are not alone with just our thoughts and reason." Kinson spoke as the closing music started. "With faith and trust, we are a community in God's image, graced with His mercy, and gifted with Christ's salvation. All that is required of us is acceptance and obedience. Please take God's gift offered to you and come forward to receive salvation, now."

The congregation rose, the music played and the choir and audience sang. At its conclusion, Reverend Kinson offered a final prayer and dismissed the crowd with well wishes and blessings.

As Ben waited for the crowd to thin, several people spoke pleasantly to him, while a few others eyed him, suspiciously. He made his way slowly toward the front, watching the friendly interaction of the congregation. He wondered how he could doubt the stories in the Bible and be envious of the believers at the same time. Many of his friends had varied religious backgrounds. During off-hours there had been discussions of beliefs and convictions, but Ben had never been capable of blind faith in anything. Janet Sharpton called it his Carl Sagan complex.

Just a few steps from the door, a young man not sixteen asked, "Mr. Timmons? Reverend Kinson asked you to wait in his office. He said he needs about a half-hour, but he wants to speak to you."

Ben thought about declining. He knew the subject of the conversation. "Sure, I can wait. Where's his office?"

"Straight down the hall in the right wing." The young man pointed.

"Thanks," he said, but he didn't mean it.

Ben considered going to his rental Ford to leave the envelope, but decided against it. As he walked toward the minister's office, he paused along the way to read various bulletin boards, admire activity photos on the walls, and watch parents retrieving their children from classrooms. The building emptied quickly, as the churchgoers hurried to other Sunday plans. With only half the thirty minutes lapsed, he sat down in one of the seating areas, picked up a religious pamphlet, and killed a little more time by pretending an interest in apologetics.

When he resumed his trip, he found Ralph Kinson, Senior Pastor, on a name plate halfway down the hallway beside a partially open door. As he entered, he saw Mrs. Staten sat in front of the pastor's desk. At the noise from the door bumping against the stop, she looked his way. "Excuse me," he said. "I'm supposed to meet the reverend here. I didn't mean to disturb you."

"Come in, young Timmons" Tonya's grandmother said, turning in her chair. "I asked Ralph to invite you. In your short time in Powhatan, I've heard some interesting comments, and I wanted to meet you for myself." She patted the arm of the chair beside her. "Do have a seat."

Ben hesitated but intrigued, he entered and walked to the chair beside her.

She smiled. "I'm Betty Prichard, but you know that. We're supposed to be adversaries, or so I'm told." He felt her stare. "I have plenty of enemies, but always room for one more. Many foes are my best friends. Maybe, I can add your name to that column?"

He hid any reaction. "This is an unexpected pleasure. I'd been told your security would keep me away, but I didn't see them outside."

"Do you think I need them?" she asked. "They're within earshot."

He thought he might like this lady. As he sat, she continued, "After your success dealing with Hank, they may need to use their weapons. Let's not call them." He recognized her attempt at humor, but he found nothing funny in the previous night's episode. Betty Pritchard noticed, "A crass attempt to stroke your ego, and you resisted. Very good, young man," She reminded him of his mother. Every utterance had an agenda. "Did you enjoy the service?" she asked.

"I wasn't listening, I'm embarrassed to admit," he said, careful to avoid another religious discussion with a prominent Powhatan citizen.

A pleased look appeared on the woman's face. "I don't struggle with the teachings, like you," she said. "Sometimes, that old windbag's better than a sleeping pill." Ben laughed. Ms Pritchard leaned slightly toward him. "He was rough on you the other night in the bowling alley." Ben shrugged. "Several members of the Friday prayer group regaled me with the details. Ralph likes to pretend his tired, angry messages still play to your generation." Her comments increased Ben's confusion. "Decades ago, intelligent members of my age group lost interest in Southern Baptist hellfire and brimstone. Traditional ministers try to exhort youngsters into accepting faith with threats of eternal torment and damnation. I see kids losing trust in their parents and grandparents, doubting the validity of older leadership. Why would anyone be surprised they'd doubt the God of those failed examples?"

"I didn't come here to judge," he answered. "And I don't know why some people see me as such a threat."

The years hadn't removed the youthful sparkle from her blue eyes. The passage of time had brought wrinkles to her appearance, but her confident manner accentuated her beauty and removed years from the face. "My granddaughter's impetuous," she answered. "I've spoken to Tonya about that."

"And how am I sure you weren't involved in Hank's actions?"

She spoke calmly, as if discussing the weather. "You can be assured for two reasons, young man. One, because I told you, and I don't lie in church."

Ben's doubts remained.

"Two, when I assign a chore to someone, it gets done."

Those words he believed. "Thanks, that's renewed my faith in humankind."

She must have been satisfied that he'd accepted her denial, because she continued, "Did you read the file?" and pointed to the folder.

"Yes ma'am."

"Not much of a read, if you ask me—no mention of the lives destroyed...lost. I've read more interesting inventory lists."

"I'm sorry to bring those memories back to you, but...." He didn't know what else to say and fell silent. She seemed satisfied with the awkward quiet, and just watched him. "I'm sorry," he repeated.

"I never got a chance to speak with your father, but my people believed he wanted money. Is that your purpose, too?" And just that quickly, her vulnerability disappeared.

He recognized the attempt to bait him and resisted an urge to react. "That wasn't my dad's purpose."

"Did you like your father?"

The question surprised him and he hesitated. "I...uh, I loved my father."

"That's not what I asked." Her stare bore through him. "A beaten dog remains devoted to its abuser, and we'd call that love. However, I asked if you liked your father—the type of man he was?"

His thoughts made him feel lightheaded. "Memories are a funny thing. Now, that he's gone, I remember only the good things. Yes, I liked my father."

"I had him investigated—one of the many benefits of money." Her statement sounded like an apology to him. "Financial troubles dominated your father's last years, much of it brought on by his self-destructive nature." He didn't respond and she persisted. "His career tanked when he got caught embezzling from an employer. He could have gone to jail, but instead, he gave the accusers his life's savings to avoid prosecution. Your father stole a few dollars from them, and they extorted everything from him. Pretty stupid of him." Timmons stayed calm and silent. After another moment, she said, "You already knew that."

He'd heard harsher assessments from his divorced mother, more than happy to inform him of his dad's shortcomings. When she'd disclosed the details to her son, Ben knew Connie Timmons's intended the information to damage the father/son relationship. He forgave her for that. He understood the pain she felt after the divorce, as she gathered herself to continue alone. She'd lost her husband's love and needed Ben's support. During other quiet moments, he'd provided the same assistance to his dad. "I knew my father's struggles, Ms. Pritchard. I'm not here to restore some lost family reputation, or complete a misguided attempt at retribution."

After another awkward silence, she said, "Let's start over, young man." She sounded sincere. "I never intended this direction for our conversation."

Timmons frowned. "The fault is mine."

"You're being gallant, and I thank you." Again, Ben didn't react, and the old woman leaned closer and patted his arm. "There are no secrets here, son. In faraway New York City, or Indiana, it might seem like some grand mystery, but here—not so much." As she reflected, he waited. "I'm serious, young man. Whatever your father's obsessions, they're not yours, and he wouldn't want you doing this."

"I don't know how to respond to that, ma'am."

She pointed toward the file in his hand. "I've done you a favor, and now, you can return to your college life." Her eyes narrowed, and she asked, "Or, are you self-destructive like your father?" He knew she didn't mean the question to be so hurtful, but he winced. "Of course, you want to believe your father had the best of intentions, young man." She stiffened in the chair. "I have money, influential friends, and political power."

"Yes, ma'am, I'm aware."

She shook her head. "I remember your grandparents and your father as a boy. He was just a few years younger than you when your family left this area for Indiana."

"Yes, ma'am."

"You say you don't want money." Her eyes narrowed, and he felt her stare. "What, then?"

He'd heard the question so many times over the past weeks, his answer was almost memorized. But as he looked into the face of the woman at the center of his quest, his words took on new meaning. "I lost my father some eighteen months ago, ma'am," he said. "I know my dad wanted the truth, and I'd like to give that to him. I didn't come here to pass judgment."

"Don't be so condescending, young man," she

snapped. "You arrived here with your mind made up."
She paused, "You think you're going to uncover some
long-buried mystery, but you're wrong. It's never been
hidden, and it's nobody's secret." He waited for her to
finish. "I've relived it every day for over forty years,
thanks to my family and neighbors in this town." And
in that moment her face showed all of her years. "The
record in your hand tells you I killed your uncle, but
you're sure I didn't. While relieving me of the guilt of
taking another's life, you're calling me a liar, and
naively believe that's better."

She was miles ahead of him in processing the
situation, and while he felt the need to respond, he
could only say, "Isn't that better?"

"So, you're here to give me absolution? Is that
your goal with this investigation? You've come to save
my soul?"

From behind him, he heard, "Absolution is not of
our faith, Betty," and the reverend walked past them
and around his desk. As he prepared to sit, he asked,
"Has the discussion been fruitful?"

Before Kinson could take his seat, Ms. Pritchard
said, "We need another minute, please."

Reverend Kinson looked confused and replied, "I
thought I might facilitate some solution."

"Get out, Ralph. Please." Her voice was calm, but
it demanded obedience. Without another word, the
minister hurried away. A moment later, she turned back
to Timmons, "Before your time, but you've studied the
Kennedy assassination?"

"Yes, ma'am."

"The official record came from the Warren
Commission, but a couple of generations have been

disputing it. Now, fifty years later, what does it matter?"

"The truth always matters," he said. "My father thought it did."

"Your father was wrong."

She turned away. Aware the conversation had ended, he rose to leave. Almost to the door, he paused and asked, "Did we solve anything?"

She turned in the chair and looked at him. "I knew your people, son. I felt I owed it to you," He turned to the door, but before he exited, she said, "Be careful, Ben Timmons. I'm a formidable enemy, and you don't want to add to my chores."

His pride wouldn't allow him to leave without saying, "I've been advised, counseled, and warned by members of this community, all pretending to know my mind better than me. It's very insulting, but I'll get beyond it."

"I hope you do," he heard her mumble.

He walked past the reverend without a word and left the church. As he continued across the almost empty parking lot with his Ford in the distance, he pretended calm and forced himself to stroll on the pavement.

Ahead, he saw a lone figure close to his vehicle, and recognized the homeless vagrant he'd given the money. Somewhat aggravated, he hoped the charity wasn't a mistake. The man moved closer to him as he removed his keys from his pants pockets.

Close enough for only Ben to hear, the gravelly voice said, "Boy, you'd better get your head out of your ass."

"I beg your pardon?"

The man glanced around to assure their privacy, and Ben saw a few other church members on the other side of the lot. "The five dollars seemed out of character with your story in the pool hall."

Events were coming too quickly for Ben. "Yeah, you surprised me, and I'm having trouble figuring out this town. Were you in the pool hall, or did it make the evening news?"

The man's brown eyes fixed on Ben's face. "Kid, you're in deep shit, and if you keep actin' like some naïve college boy, you're goin' to wind up dead. Do you hear me?"

"I g-got it," Ben stammered. "Who are you, sir?"

"Right now, I'm the only friend you've got in this town." Some people were leaving the front of the church. "Gotta go, son. If you're still alive, I'll see you in a day or two. My name's Pittmann."

"A warning, not a threat, right?" Ben asked softly. No response from the man, as he walked away from the church. "Pittmann? I've seen that name. Are you—?"

Pittmann turned back. "My daddy sold the gun, and my son knows you."

"Your son? Who's—?"

"His name's Hank."

Ben stood beside his vehicle, watching the man hurry away, and wondered about the exchange. He quelled his irritation with himself as thoughts of New York pulled at him. His nature to identify problems, plot solutions, and pursue them until achieved suited this situation. He believed he'd followed that approach on his trip.

Standing beside his car, feeling the warmth of the morning sunshine, he affirmed his commitment to his father's quest. Still, he'd be foolish to disregard threats to his life. The man advised him to stay alive, and he decided to put that on his list of things to do.

Chapter Twelve
Elkton Uncovered

Corporal Jayson Craig sat behind the wheel of the police cruiser, watching his partner assist a motorist with a disabled vehicle. Officer John Kase looked under the hood and gestured toward the malfunctioning engine, as the lady-owner appeared annoyed with her burden. Fortunately, only light traffic moved on Middlebury Street at midday Thursday, and the wrecker service Craig had called promised prompt service. Nothing more to do, but wait for their arrival. Among Kase's many talents, he dealt well with the public, and the Corporal watched his partner comforting and calming the lady's anxiety.

He pulled his cell phone from his pocket and called his cousin, as he'd been doing for several days. The previous day he'd contacted the Powhatan Police Department, and learned Benjamin Timmons left that area the previous Sunday. No one had heard from or talked to him, according to the desk sergeant in Arkansas. Without news for five days, Craig wondered where the hell Ben could be.

Ben's mother, Aunt Connie, had called Jayson that morning and blamed him for her son's absence. She, too, had called Timmons but hadn't received a response. Craig had been forced to update on his progress, and received an emotional explosion from her. In the course of their conversation she threatened his job three times. Unfortunately, she had the clout to carry through on the threat. The whole episode ran through his mind as he listened to the ring.

"Ben Timmons," said the voice on the other end.

"Where the hell have you been?" Craig all but shouted. "I've been calling for days!" He saw Kase looking his way.

"Hi, Jay," He heard the apology. "I've been out of pocket as they say. Laying low and working on a couple things."

Craig tried to calm himself. "Kid, this is not working. You've gotta keep in touch. I have the Powhatan police looking for you, and I thought about getting the FBI involved." As an afterthought, "What do you mean laying low?"

He heard the laughter on the other end. "Sorry, Jay. I'll get the money to you today. I had to disappear for a couple days, and my phone has been off. I turned it on to retrieve some email information as you called."

"I know it's been off. Your mother has been calling, going crazy in my opinion. What's happening?"

The wrecker had arrived, and while the driver conferred with the vehicle owner, Kase strolled back to the cruiser. "Your cousin?" he whispered, and Craig nodded.

"Just following some leads. I'm in Little Rock at the university, learning about forensics."

"Isn't forensic science fourth year at NYU?" Craig tried to lighten the tone.

"Must be, and what I've learned is these people are pretty smart. You said Mom's involved? So, you weren't being dramatic?" He heard the doubt in his cousin's voice.

"No, Ben, it's a little serious."

"I haven't been online, either. Did you send your bank information?"

"No, I didn't." Craig had dreaded this moment. "No need."

He waited for the long silence, "Why not? Didn't you get the car examined?"

"Listen, Ben, on Tuesday, I got an investigator from the South Bend department, and she looked at the vehicle. She spent a couple of hours going over the wreck. Looked like an accident, and we were just about to call it a day."

"Yeah, is that it, Jay?"

"Just before pulling the door down on the storage unit, we decided to look under the car. It took some effort. You remember, the damage to the front suspension had the whole thing lying on the concrete floor?" Craig gestured for Kase to keep an eye on the wrecker activity, and his partner nodded, but didn't move away.

"Yeah, the manager of the unit said when they unloaded it, they used the boom arm and chains to place the vehicle in the space."

"Well, we got the vehicle up using a forklift." While calling over several days without answer, Craig had dreaded this inevitable point in the conversation. "The technician looked at the suspension and found something. She took some scrapings and analyzed them." He paused, listening for some reaction, but his cousin remained silent, waiting. "She detected an explosive residue on the right front suspension."

"What?"

Craig searched for the words. Beside him, Kase leaned closer, as he observed the exchange. "It wasn't an accident, Ben." He paused, trying to think of something to say to relieve the strain. Words escaped him, and his cousin said nothing from the other end of the phone. Finally, "Ben?" he said.

"I heard you, Jay."

"I'm sorry to tell you this way. Tests confirmed the use of C4, but an old batch. And the way it was planted—a controlled explosion by an expert."

Another long silence from the other end followed. Kase gestured, questioning. Craig shook his head in silent communication. Then, he heard his young relative, "You said Mom knows?"

"Yeah," the officer answered. "Sorry, again. Your family knows and most have been calling around. You need to call your mom, Susan, just about everyone."

"How's granddad?" Typical of Ben to worry about the old man.

"With his mind, you're never sure," Craig knew Ben understood. "I visited him, but I don't know."

"Yeah," another long silence from the other end.

Officer Kase seemed impatient, but remained silent. The wrecker operator manipulated the controls and lifted the disabled vehicle. Once clear of the ground and towable, he attached safety chains. Just a few more minutes, and this event would be over. "Ben, I need to know where you are."

"You said I didn't need to send money?"

"No, this is now a murder investigation, and Elkton is paying the bill."

"Who's got the case?"

Craig knew the question offered the kid time to

recover. Benjamin Timmons didn't know any of the Elkton detectives. "Lieutenant Danielson. He's a good cop."

"Does he have anything?"

The voice sounded numb to Craig, but he continued. "Evidence of the explosion showed skill. The location couldn't have been more perfect, and whoever planned it knew what they were doing. Nothing unusual about a single-car accident, so they were counting on a hasty conclusion. Unfortunately, they got it, and if it hadn't been for your suspicions, they would've gotten away with it."

"Yeah, good for me," he heard from the other end. "Anything else?"

"The lieutenant wants me to pull you in," Craig expected the answer.

"No, not just now."

"Ben, he needs to see the information your father collected. It's evidence in this investigation."

"I'll scan and email it to you." The kid's matter-of-fact responses alarmed Craig. "Anything else?"

"We found a couple of cigarette butts in a stand of trees near the site. Very old and not sure we can get DNA, but it might be the trigger point. And it might be nothing, but we found an old cartridge."

"Maybe a hunter dropped it?"

"Well, if he did, we found it on the cigarette butts, and I'm past believing in coincidence."

"Yeah, me too."

"An unusual cartridge, Ben. Nine millimeter, but not normal. A little thicker. Looks like a Makarov round."

"What does that mean? A collector's weapon?"

"Probably," Craig affirmed. "We might never find it, but it's a start. Oh, and hundreds of fingerprints in the vehicle, and they're being eliminated one-by-one. However, one on the outside of the vehicle on the driver's side—a palm print—it's been identified."

"Yeah?" Craig could hear his young cousin's struggles with his emotions, but his voice sounded formal.

"It belonged to a deceased police officer from Powhatan."

"What?" Craig knew with that news he now had Ben's full attention. "Got a name?"

"Matthew Rappart. Danielson talked to the brother in Powhatan, the officer in charge. He said he knew you."

"Yeah, we've met. You said deceased?"

"Apparently, the palm print brother died in a hunting accident about a year ago. Accidentally shot himself." Kase's head hung through the window, listening.

"Rappart? Are you sure?" Now, a new strength to the voice on the other end of the phone.

"Yeah, deceased Rappart, the suspect, had been on the Powhatan force since his return from the military some forty plus years ago. The army wouldn't give us much, but what they released didn't indicate an accomplished soldier. No record of explosive training, and not much of a police officer, either." His cousin had fallen silent, again. "Looks like he's the guy, Ben. No reason his print would be on the vehicle unless…well."

"So, you think my father's file would be the motive?"

The owner of the disabled vehicle climbed into the

117

cab of the wrecker. The operator, now behind the wheel, waved to the policemen as he towed the car away. Still standing beside the police cruiser, Kase leaned closer to Corporal Craig. "It seems obvious it has something to do with your father's investigation." Craig waited, but his cousin said nothing. "Ben, you have a target on your back."

Another long silence, before he asked "How'd Sheriff Rappart take the questioning?"

Craig had questioned Danielson about that, "I don't know. It's an ongoing investigation, and I'm involved. They won't give me much more. I could gum up the works."

"Yeah, I understand." Ben sounded beaten and bruised.

Craig knew he had to get more from the kid. "Ben, why are you laying low?"

"Ah, just a hunch, another suspicion."

"Bullshit! We've played too much poker for me to believe that. What made you suspicious in the beginning, or better—who?"

Kase whispered, "Jay, you've got to get him in here."

He heard his cousin say, "It's a long story, and I'm whipped. At the same time, I need to turn off this phone."

A little desperate, Jayson Craig said, "Ben, you need to get back here for your own protection. You're not buying the hunting accident, are you?"

"No."

"The lieutenant doesn't believe Sheriff Rappart is buying it, either. Both would like to talk with you, and both want to see the information you have."

"There's a surprise. Rappart gave me the official local file. Why would he need my information?"

"Yeah, right," Craig said. "Ben, get back here, now!"

"I'm not leaving here without answers. You can help by getting some publicity on this. Remove some of the pressure. I hope they'll be less likely to kill me with a spotlight shining."

Damn, stubborn kid! "Danielson will bitch, but I can get your mom to do it. How do I get in touch with you?"

His cousin hesitated. "I'll use a public web service—maybe the library. Contact me via email. And I'll get a disposable cell and call. Will that do?"

"You need to come in."

"No." The voice sounded calm and quiet.

Craig knew his cousin, "Watch the use of your credit card. These are bad people, and they seem connected."

"Got it. Anything else?"

"Call your mother. I promised her. And Janet Sharpton back in New York. She's been looking for you—according to your mother."

"I'll call Janet and Susan. I can't talk to Mom. Will you call her, Jay? Sorry to ask."

"She'll give me hell, but yeah, I'll make the call. Sorry about all this, kid." Craig heard the cell go silent on the other end.

Officer Kase walked around the vehicle and entered from the passenger side. He looked at his partner and waited. "What's the kid going to do, Jay?"

Craig shook his head, "I don't know." As he reflected on the conversation, "Ben is one of the smartest kids I've ever known, the operative word in that sentence being kid. He could get himself killed, and I feel helpless here."

"Can you get Little Rock police to pull him in, for his own good if nothing else? Material witness?"

Craig shrugged, "How? I don't know where he is. Little Rock is not a small community."

"Why Little Rock?"

Craig shook his head, again, "He's got something, and too many people know it. He said he was at the university studying forensics. Let's get back to the station. Maybe, I can get the cops in Arkansas to pull him in? Let's switch," he told Kase. "You drive while I get on the radio." They both opened their car doors and started to exit, but Craig stopped, "Wait!"

Officer Kase looked back at his partner, "What? Why?"

Craig realized his head was pounding from the stress. As he massaged his brow, he said, "The kid doesn't want me or anyone else to stop him, and I owe him the chance to continue."

"Bad move, Jay! Danielson will give you hell!"

"Yeah, I know, but there's something about my cousin."

Kase's forehead furrowed, "He could become your late cousin very soon."

Craig stared ahead, "The thought's crossed my mind. Let's get back to work."

"And Danielson?" Kase asked.

Craig shook his head, "I'll fill him in at the end of shift." A cop—any cop—would be expected to demand, coerce, and intimidate a civilian into compliance. The lieutenant would be pissed, but Craig knew such tactics would not work on his cousin. First, he knew the kid too well, but mostly, Benjamin Timmons could never be described as your average school boy. The kid had a special quality, and Craig understood birds had to fly.

Lloyd R. Agee

Chapter Thirteen
Spring Time in New York

Friday evening in New York City, Janet Sharpton worked at her cubicle on the thirty-second floor of the Haulbarth Building in the financial district. A few people remained on the floor, and none seemed interested in her actions. Her first week as Haulbarth's summer intern, she had dined with the CEO, Howard Reezak, been interviewed by a Times reporter for a human interest piece in the upcoming Sunday edition, appeared on the local segment of *This Day*, and received an invitation from Dean Epstein to speak to incoming freshmen at future NYU orientations.

Throughout the week, as she basked in the limelight cast upon her achievement, she reflected on Benjamin Timmons's stupidity for passing on this opportunity. She savored her role as the Haulbarth recipient, but accepted her status as second choice. She'd enjoyed the week and looked forward to the summer curriculum.

The company utilized sophisticated software. It allowed management oversight of hundreds of diverse divisions in one location—one huge database. Janet received daily tutorials on various applications within the system, but her computer skills enabled her to go well beyond the basic instruction.

As time allowed, she browsed segments of the data

122

from investment activities within the conglomerate, familiarized herself with her internship duties, ever aware of the economic model and the much-needed information of governments, industries, and individuals. In her mind the end goal warranted the risk. Mindful of the history caused by a student's refusal of the Haulbarth internship, she wondered how NYU and the media would react if the new recipient got arrested for corporate espionage.

While examining 2001 data on money supply and Euro value fluctuations after 9/11, she felt her iPhone vibrate. She removed the cell from her pocket, but didn't recognize the number on the screen. Almost alone in the office, just studying a computer screen, she could multi-task. "Hello, this is Janet."

From the other end, "Hello, love-of-my-life,"

"Ben! Oh, my God! Where did you disappear? I've called over and over. Everyone in your family's called me. I spoke with your mother, and you know how that went! Damn it, why didn't you answer your phone? What's this number? Did you lose your cell?"

"It's a long story, and I'm working under some difficult circumstances."

"Yes, I know. Your cousin told me. Your father's death was not an accident. What's it mean?"

"Wish I knew." She heard him sigh. "Obviously, when I started, I never imagined these obstacles ahead of me. I might have stayed in New York."

"Bullshit, Timmons. You wouldn't have changed a thing. I know you had ideas about this mess, or you wouldn't have committed to it. My worry's for your safety."

"The thought's crossed my mind, too. I thought

only the good died young?"

"Not funny, Timmons," she snapped. "Are you coming back? Let me rephrase—you need to get back here."

"You have talked to Jay. That's all I heard from him. And, no, I'm not quitting." She admired and hated him sometimes.

"Ben, before we go on, I need to apologize for my description of your father. I know I hurt you." She paused. "What's the noise in the background?"

"I'm at the mall in Little Rock." He chuckled.

"I know you hate shopping, so you must need underwear."

"You're so clever."

"Well, are you at the food court for a nosh?"

"Nosh, very good, smart ass!" She so loved irritating him. "I'm using the public Wi-Fi. I've been reading the email updates with the various additions to the model. Couple of questions."

"Why are you in the mall on your computer?"

She noticed the distinct pause, "More of the long story."

"Got plenty of time, Timmons. Sitting here, relaxed, feet up, just watching TV. Tell me everything." Down the way the cleaning people were beginning their routine.

"Bullshit!" he said. "You're on Pine Street, probably the only one in the office. How's the intern doing in her first week?"

A vacuum cleaner began, the noise causing difficulty with the conversation. "The cleaning people are here. Let me move to the bathroom. Stay on, and tell me why you're at the mall."

"Just washing your hands, right?" She heard him laugh aloud.

"Go to hell, Ben!" She walked down the hallway and into the empty restroom. In the quiet, and more seriously, she said, "I'm glad to hear your voice. It must have been rough hearing the news about—Indiana. When I talked to your cousin, I cried."

His voice softened as he said, "Thanks, Janet. You're missed, and I need a hug. Wish you were here."

"Me, too." She leaned against the vanity, getting back to current matters, "Why the mall?"

"I've received several warnings in the process, and I've decided to take them seriously. And that was before I heard about my dad."

She did not like the sound of that. "What warnings?"

"Let's say some of the citizens of Arkansas are not fond of students asking questions."

"Have you met Maxwell?"

She heard him chuckle, again. "No, but we will."

"Why do you say that?"

"After my last warning, I disappeared from electronic surveillance. I'm pretty sure the Powhatan Secret Service tracked my cell, and possibly, the FBI."

"How could you know that? Wait. Did you say FBI?"

"According to Special Agent Levitt of Maxwell's Secret Service unit, our econ group garnered some attention. Back channel, whatever that means."

"Oh, God!" Her mind raced as she envisioned the various components involved in his last statement. "You're telling me the government is watching us? That's amazing!"

"Those of us who're not planning on reinventing the world are not so thrilled with scrutiny by the FBI."

"Ben, you realize this means we're close!" She could not hide her excitement.

"Janet, we don't even know what we're close to discovering, and if the feds are concerned, bad people could be involved, too."

"You consider the FBI to be good people? You and your Midwestern values."

"You can go to hell, too, my darling!" Now she realized how much she missed him. He continued, "You need to brief the group, Agbetheatha, Dean Epstein, and Preedlin. They all need to know, and it buys us some time—protection."

"What do you mean by that?" It had gone from funny to concerned excitement.

"Remember me telling you about the Middle Eastern guy at commencement?"

"Yeah," she remembered. "I thought you said—oh, right."

"No reason he would be involved with this mess in Arkansas. I should've seen it at the time, but I thought it must be related to my dad's stuff. No one knew about this project except my mom, a few family members, Dr. Epstein, and you. None of them would involve a wealthy Arab gentleman."

"You assumed wealthy. Still no idea about his identity?"

"None"—she heard him breathe into the phone—"and the cost of his suit would pay half my tuition next semester. That might be petty cash to you, but it qualified as wealthy to me." Then, he returned to her question, "I don't even know how he got wind of what we're doing. There are too many possibilities—Secret Service, FBI, police, journalists. It's hard to keep up, and my guesses trouble me."

"Give me a guess."

"Even before 9/11, the government monitored communication channels via technology we have little knowledge of. Thinking back to our phone and email exchanges on the event, the results, speculation on which countries might be involved, various terrorists groups, world leaders, this country's politicians, can't you guess how many alarms we set off? With the growth of Homeland Security and the paranoia rampant in our own government, yeah, I understand we've attracted attention."

"What the hell do you mean by that?" She appreciated his brilliance and ability to organize, and he had a way of working with diverse people. Still, she wanted this project more than he did, and it irritated her.

"We set out to shine a light on suspicious results after 9/11, but we wanted a grade in a college class. We've always thought we were right, mainly because our arrogance wouldn't allow us to think otherwise. Can't you see why so many groups feel threatened? And Janet, what if we're wrong? Over the past decade technology to monitor communications has gone from country to country. Hell, unemployed Russian scientists are said to be building the bomb for Iran."

"Ben, we're not wrong, or they wouldn't be so nervous."

"And that could be even worse." He sounded tired. "I have to go, Janet. Make sure you brief everyone, and be careful. Just do the internship and stay out of trouble.

127

You can email, but I'm going to be hard to get via phone. I'll call you, not the other way around. Okay."

"Wow, is it really that bad?"

She felt his closeness, "I don't want to find out. Bye."

"Ben, wait! The TV interview is next week. Can you fly back for that?"

"Nope, sorry."

Dammit, she hated him. "Have you called your mom?"

"Not yet, Janet." She waited. "It's complicated. I will when I can. Take care, my friend."

"You, too," she said into the silent phone. "I love you," but he was already gone. She put the cell in her pocket, walked out of the bathroom and back to her cubicle. The cleaning crew surrounded her workstation, so she closed down her terminal and grabbed her bag from the desk drawer. Her mind raced as she waited for an elevator and the ride from the thirty-second floor.

Exiting the lobby of the Haulbarth building into the evening gray and stale air of lower Manhattan, she saw only light traffic on Pine Street. As she turned west to make her way toward the subway station on Broadway for the ride to Long Island and home, she noticed a handsome, well-dressed, dark-skinned man walking toward her. He looked at her and asked, "Miss Sharpton?" A chill entered her body, but before she could react, someone grabbed her from behind. As she felt a pin prick in her neck, she mumbled, "Ben was right, nice suit," and then all went black.

Chapter Fourteen
Forensic Science

Ben sat in a public area of Little Rock's Park Plaza Mall, surrounded by multitudes of older shoppers, partying teenagers in their favorite gathering spot, and young children bored by the entire experience. In his lap his computer displayed the latest techniques in pathological and criminological examination. Earlier in the week, he'd been directed to several sites by staff members of the University Forensic Department, and now, while browsing, he thought about events from the past several days.

After Sunday's sermon in Powhatan and the warning from Mr. Pittmann, he exited the Shannon Baptist Church, and turned south on Highway 67 for the two hour drive to the state capital. A few miles away from the community, he passed a sign, Black Ridge 12 miles.

Every mindful of various warnings, he paid attention to his rearview mirror. No one seemed to be following, or if they were, they maintained a healthy distance. Then, a thought struck him. Just as he entered Black Ridge, a larger city than Powhatan, he turned off his iPhone, and pulled into the crowded parking lot of a strip mall. His vehicle stayed reasonably hidden and as he sat, he had a clear view of the highway.

After a few minutes, a black SUV, similar to the

one driven by Special Agent Levitt, sped by with three male occupants, trying to catch someone ahead. It confirmed his suspicion the Secret Service tracked his cell. He left the Ford rental, entered a Chinese restaurant, chose a window seat overlooking the parking area, and ordered a light lunch. After an hour and no activity in the lot, he felt certain the Secret Service had not bugged the leased vehicle. Highway 67 was the most direct route, but he had plenty of time. He got out a map and plotted a different course to Little Rock.

He enjoyed the thought of complicating Special Agent Levitt's task, and determined his cell would remain off. His efforts in Little Rock required privacy, and the indirect drive allowed him to formulate a plan. In Little Rock he'd used his debit card to withdraw cash from his account, knowing his transactions would be monitored. The New York plate on the car would be easily identified by local police, so after arrival, he'd park in a public garage. For the next several days, he'd travel by cab.

An older gentleman sat down beside him on the bench, momentarily bringing him back to the mall. The man looked at Ben, glanced at the computer with a look of disgust, and turned his attention to the overhead television. The man seemed uninterested and exhibited all the signs of a bored shopper. Timmons relaxed, going back to his internet browsing and allowing his thoughts to drift.

Upon arrival in the capital, Ben checked into a low-class motel, one that accepted cash and didn't require proper identification. He'd filled in a phony name and address on the registration card, signed the alias, paid two days rent with cash, and took the key. The motel clerk took little notice.

The room décor reminded him of a medieval dungeon, only darker—by far, the worst he'd ever seen, but the sheets were clean. Warm weather and no functioning air conditioning meant opening a window. Glad he hadn't saved the project for August, he stood in the middle of the room, looked at the surroundings, and wondered why the hell he didn't leave immediately for his Water Street apartment in Lower Manhattan.

On Monday, he'd arrived early at the Office of General Counsel in the capitol building. Lawyer Simington's directions were good, but the outdated documentation had several errors. Natalie, the young female clerk refused to honor Ben's request. She'd started her second week that morning, an underpaid clerk with the State of Arkansas, but said she enjoyed the job. After an exchange of phone numbers, the promise of a Wednesday evening dinner, followed by a fifteen minute wait, Natalie handed him the official file on his uncle's case, several inches thick and hopefully, more information than those provided by Rappart.

The other state employees paid him little attention, and without examination, he placed the documents in his bag and hurried out.

As he exited the building, he watched for any suspicious activity, but the downtown crowd made detection almost impossible. It comforted him to think any individuals trying to mark him would have the same problem. Then, another thought, and he went back into the building and hurried around a corner and into a bathroom. He stood with the door slightly ajar for a few moments—watching. In less than a minute two black suits ran past the door and down the hallway. He assumed Agent Levitt's subordinates were on the job.

"Excuse me, but I'd like to leave," said a voice behind him.

Ben turned to see a suited man of thirty with a look of curiosity more than annoyance. "Sorry." He stood aside.

The man started to leave, but didn't. "What's going on with you?"

Ben shrugged, a little embarrassed. "People following me, and I don't want to deal with them."

"Are you a criminal?" the man asked with a chuckle, and Ben shook his head. "I didn't think so. We get very little excitement in this building."

"Can you direct me to another exit?"

"Stairway door across the hall up to the second floor. Grab the elevator to the basement and follow the directions to employee underground parking. Through the garage, and you can get out a block from here on Rockefeller Avenue. Good luck."

Ben smiled in disbelief. Grateful to the man, he walked out the door and across the hall into the stairwell without detection.

Back in the flea-bag motel, Ben spent the rest of Monday and Tuesday morning reviewing the file and watching TV. He'd decided that more than two nights in any location increased the risk of discovery, so with an 11:00 a.m. checkout, he packed up and moved. The primary purpose of complicating the task of anyone searching for him, only slightly outweighed his hope for finding a better place. He cabbed across town to another rundown area and repeated the check-in routine at a business that seemed to rent rooms by the hour.

Thankfully, the air conditioning worked.

A southern fried chicken restaurant, within walking distance of the motel, provided the primary source of food—not a good thing, but manageable. The friendship between Ben and cheap greasy chicken ended freshman year, and after a couple of meals at the Little Rock location, he decided he hadn't missed it.

Taking advantage of Dr. Epstein's offer to help, on Wednesday, he'd contacted her at NYU. At his request, the dean telephoned University of Arkansas Little Rock Forensic Science Department and had been directed to Dr. Maureen Fitzpatrick, a medical doctor with a PhD. Apparently, the two women had struck a friendship, and afterwards, Dr. Epstein instructed Ben to contact Dr. Fitzpatrick at the university.

The old gentleman got up and walked away, apparently equally bored with mall television. Ben looked around the mall, enjoying the activity, and for a brief time, relieving his sense of loneliness. He glanced at his wristwatch, calculating how long he'd been online. Too long he decided, and time to move. Little Rock, the capital and the largest city in Arkansas provided plenty of places to hide, and he doubted the various agencies involved had brought all their resources to bear on him. Still, he knew more than half-an-hour online at one location made triangulation too easy.

Narayan Patel had emailed methodologies for him to use to avoid detection, but even the best efforts would eventually fail. The government—our government—had technology to spy on anyone. Timmons knew George Orwell was right when he'd written *1984*—he'd just gotten the date wrong.

On the way into the mall, Ben noticed a Starbucks across the way from the mall. Their Wi-Fi would allow his continued work, and if big brother searched for him, they'd have to start again. He closed down, bagged his computer, and strolled out of the shopping center, keeping a sharp eye out for any followers.

Immediately, he liked Dr. Fitzpatrick. She appeared impressed with his status at New York University, and after he'd explained his father's quest, her interest seemed to peak. Between semesters, she said she could offer some assistance. She balked at his insistence on anonymity of the various participants in the mystery. He'd present the facts of the case without identification, and she'd give her expert opinion on the merits and failures of the investigation. He explained his concern for safety if he involved her, but she looked unaffected. She and Ben were dependent upon the official reporting of facts, and according to Dr. Fitzpatrick, just as dependent upon unofficial notes and references—common in all case files.

They worked together for several hours on Wednesday, and started early on Thursday, going all day and into the early evening. During a break in their session, he received the call from Jay and the update about his father.

Early Friday, sitting in her office at the university, "Mr. Timmons," she said, "I recognize this case, so we can end the pretense."

"I'm reluctant to fully disclose, Dr. Maureen. There are some interesting people mixed up in this."

"Interesting, that's an apt description." In their time together, Timmons had observed Dr. Fitzpatrick's interaction with colleagues, staff, and students, and knew her as a harsh taskmaster. He recognized the coming reckoning before she delivered it. "My dear, Ben, I've taught at this university for twelve years. Prior to that, I worked for the Arkansas State Police on some of the most bizarre cases in this state's history. I received my medical degree years before you were born, and I've published seven text books on the science. I've seen things well beyond the violence of whatever video game occupies your limited youthful attention. My work has put people on death row, and I'm capable of filling in the holes of your little mystery. Let me commend your attempt to protect me by removing names, dates, most of the revealing information from the documents you're discussing." He remained quiet, as she glared at him. "More importantly, I know who we're discussing."

Sitting across from the desk in her office, he thought about the situation and his role with her involvement—potentially endangering her. "My father was murdered some eighteen months ago while investigating this event. I received that information yesterday."

A nurse stuck her head in the door, but before she could say anything, Fitzpatrick waved her away. The doctor did not seem surprised by his news. "You have my sympathy, and that information makes the work even more significant." She flipped open a file on her desk, "Ben, I've made the calls. I know just about everything of your background, and after examining the records, I believe I can direct you where you need to go with this project."

"Okay, I'm listening."

"Benjamin Staten, the husband of the shooter, a

self-made man, was a legend. Known as a businessman with great imagination, his involvements with various notorious figures in Northeastern Arkansas excited law enforcement, politicians, newspapers, and glory-seekers for years. It's popular to believe he made his money in farming and other investments, but the '60s in the South were tumultuous." She leaned back in her office chair.

"What are you trying not to tell me? I'm not forensically trained, but I've read the files. The official unedited record received from the state still had holes and my father's information plugged many of those. Where'd he get that?"

"I would speculate your father talked to the involved parties. My experience—the older the wrong-doers, the more they want to tell the story. Good for the soul. Redemption, or salvation, but I understand you struggle with that concept."

He shifted forward in his chair, "Who have you talked to about me?"

She ignored his attempt at levity. "I talked to Andy Maxwell. I know him well."

A frown creased his brow, "I wish you would've discussed that with me."

"I knew you'd say no, and getting him involved buys you some protection. You see, I agree you're at risk in this. I had a lengthy telephone conversation with Special Agent Levitt."

"I've only met her once, but she made an impression."

"So I understand. However, she's been close to the President for years, and she has his ear. Let's talk science and then practicality."

"I'm all yours."

"The scene of the shooting couldn't have been the storage room." She slid a diagram of the room across the desk.

"I suspected," Ben replied. "The measurements are wrong, and the angle of fire does not fit the confined space."

"Very good, Mr. Timmons!" She pushed another document to him, and he took it. "You should consider a career in forensic science. I can put in a word."

He chuckled. "I'll give it some consideration. In 1967, would a reasonably trained doctor or medical examiner reach these conclusions?"

"You're asking if professionals would've missed the holes in the evidence some forty years ago. Probably not."

"Again, just as I thought. Would a new district attorney—fresh out of law school—sign off on this investigation?"

"Given my professional standing at this university and the status of the individual, out of court, my answer is unofficial."

"I understand," he answered.

"Not without strong encouragement, and even then, his law career would be in jeopardy. We don't know the circumstances in Powhatan at that time."

"In your conversation with Maxwell, did you reference the inconsistency?" As an afterthought, "I realize the difficulty in that question."

The nurse returned, more insistent, and Fitzpatrick rose from her desk, "I'll return in a moment. Please look at those documents with my notes included. You can see where I contradict. We'll discuss when I return." She exited the office, leaving Ben to study.

The doctor's detailed calculations, diagrams, and velocity charts by caliber confirmed the small space could not be the shooting site. In her notes she referenced several other cases over her career with similar findings. Mrs Staten, or elderly Ms Pritchard, was left handed, and she broke the wrist on that arm in the scuffle. She testified she landed on the floor on the left side of the small room, and with a broken wrist, she must've delivered the fatal shots with her right hand.

More calculations confirmed the improper angles. According to the doctor, the direction of the shots would have Mrs. Staten on the other side of the wall, or would've required Ben's uncle to almost have his back to the shooter. In the space defined in the report, the caliber of the bullet and average muzzle velocity, the fatal shots would've produced exit wounds. There were none, and the physician had scribbled many notes about the contradiction.

She'd made some calls, gathered a deceased list of various Powhatan citizens involved. The list included the lead detective, the coroner, the reporter, the judge, the district attorney, the gentleman who sold the weapon to Mrs. Staten—all dead. Ben reread the column of names, and thought about the avenues open for discovery. His feeling of helplessness grew as he studied Dr. Fitzpatrick's unofficial investigation.

Just as he finished, she walked past him and resumed her position behind the desk. "I'm sure you have questions, but let me avoid them for a bit. Not much help for you, but I'm recommending an investigation through official channels. At some date in the future, I might be asked about my role in this, and that's why I talked to Andrew Maxwell."

"I appreciate your efforts, Doctor, but do you think that transcends the political power blocking the investigation?"

She paused and leaned forward in her chair, "A fair question and I don't know. Absent subpoena power, grand jury power, my suspicions will remain that unless I convince law enforcement. Without their consent, we may go nowhere."

"You believe someone murdered my uncle?"

"One thing I've learned over my years in criminology, people don't create shadows without diabolical reasons. The short answer, something happened other than the recorded information."

"Maxwell signed off on this."

"Yes, and that's your greatest problem, but it's his problem, too. By signing off, even as a young assistant, he's vulnerable. He's an American hero after 9/11, but you're threatening his legacy. You need to use that weakness against him. He's a formidable opponent, and his connections are deep. While he was in office as governor of Arkansas, many of his political enemies mysteriously disappeared. He's at a point in his life where he's more concerned about his place in history."

Ben rose to leave, "I take it you did not vote for him?"

"Actually, I voted for him every time." Confused, Ben could only smile. She noticed and said, "Politics and education make strange bedfellows."

"Thanks, Dr. Fitzpatrick. I hope this doesn't cause you any trouble."

"Don't worry about that." She waved the thought away. "Before you leave, there's one bit of information you missed, and it needs to be examined."

"What? I feel like I've missed a lot."

She tapped her finger on the desk."It's hard to describe Northeastern Arkansas during the '60s. You need to look closely." He watched her consider her next statement. "You said your uncle died about six months after his discharge from the military?"

"Yes, that's my understanding. He'd served four or five years in the military which included two tours in Vietnam."

She pushed one more document across her desk for him. "Your father's information indicates the army paid life insurance on the uncle."

He looked at the information. The paper indicated a payment to his uncle's beneficiary, Ben's grandmother, several months after the death. "Still in the army? What does that mean?"

"Old military records not in computers are held in Fort Leavenworth. And if this old case led to the event of your father's death, there are still some viable connections. Obviously, Maxwell and Mrs. Staten are worthy of investigation. Unfortunately, they have power and money."

He nodded understanding, "Connective tissue from 1967, should be easy."

"One more thing a young man would miss."

"Yes?"

"In the struggle, she retrieved the weapon from her purse." Ben remembered reading that and flipped the pages of the file. "She was putting documents away when accosted by your uncle. Why would she take her purse? It would have been in her desk drawer, not in a storage room."

"You're right, Doctor. A man would have missed

that."

"It's not evidence," she said. "Worth asking about, though." She rose behind her desk, "Ben, I'll do what I can from here. Keep me in the loop. And one more thing." He waited. "Find a journalist you can trust. Good resource."

"I will, Dr. Fitzpatrick," and then he thought. "Actually, I might already have one."

"Good. Be careful, young man."

He shook her hand, grateful for her guidance and her friendship. "Thank you, Doctor. I'll keep a sharp eye."

Putting aside those reflections, he entered the Starbucks and walked to the counter, "Can I have a Grande Latte?" He hated coffee, but in a Starbucks using their Wi-Fi, he thought his visit warranted a purchase.

The attendant said, "Would you like cinnamon, or a dollop of caramel?"

"No, thanks."

Ben dug in his pocket while the cashier rang the total.

He paid, tucked another dollar in the tip jar, and waited. After a minute, the attendant delivered a container of foamy latte. He walked to the auxiliary counter and tore open at least a dozen sugar packets, emptying them into his cup. Taking a seat at an out-of-the-way table, he took his computer out of the bag and connected to Starbucks service.

While he waited for the unit to boot, his thoughts returned to recent events. He'd changed motels, again, the latest one close to different low-quality restaurants, but he hated the food. On Saturday morning, Dr.

Fitzpatrick called his throw-away cell—he'd given her the number. She'd conducted a test firing in her lab as part of a class and confirmed exit wounds would've been present, so the description in the official file couldn't be accurate. Her findings didn't surprise him, and his appreciation of the doctor increased. She'd made the test results available to him on her site, and he thanked her.

As his computer sprang to life, his thoughts returned to Saturday afternoon and Starbucks. Before returning to the forensic websites, he decided to check his email. Five from his mother—whom he still hadn't called—two from Narayan, one from Dr. Epstein, one from Dr. Preedlin, several from other group members, but none from Janet. Then, he noticed one from Janet's mother. That confused him, and he clicked on it.

'*Janet did not come home last night. She is not answering her phone. Do you know where she is?*'

An arctic chill went through him. Quickly, he grabbed his iPhone, turned it on, and called Janet's number. He'd be disclosing his location to anyone searching, but he had to find her.

From the other end, a man replied.

"Hello, Mr. Timmons, so glad to hear from you. We need to talk."

Chapter Fifteen
Homeward Bound

After a restless night in the motel on the east side of Little Rock, Benjamin Timmons rose early for a shower and shave. Not yet 6:00 a.m., he left two dollars and the key in the room for the maid, grabbed his belongings, and headed for the rental, which he'd retrieved the evening before from public parking. Breakfast would be at the airport. He threw his bag and computer in the back, climbed into the driver's seat, started the engine, and sped off. The motel sat less than a half-mile from Interstate 440, and the Little Rock International Airport was on the Southeast side of the city.

Excited locals had told him of the airport's major upgrade since the Maxwell administration. As he entered Airport Drive from the interstate, he noticed the attractive buildings and neatly landscaped grounds, grayly lit in the early morning dawn. He parked on the second level of the long-term parking garage closest to the terminal, grabbed his luggage, and hurried toward the entrance. He stopped at a postal box to drop in a small package addressed to his sister, Susan. In it, he placed a thumb drive with all the information related to his father's project.

The evening before, the man on the phone told him a ticket would be left at the airline's counter. Ben hadn't stayed on the call long, but he did speak to Janet, who assured him she was all right. Before the call ended, the man told him not to contact the police and promised to allow Janet to call her mother. After it ended, he'd immediately exited Starbucks to avoid detection.

His flight departed just past nine, but included a stop in Atlanta. It would be past two before he arrived in New York. He showed his identification, retrieved the ticket, no baggage check—he'd put his toothbrush and razor in his computer bag—and headed for security. Through check-in without trouble, he had almost two hours until his flight.

His gate was not far down the passageway. On his way, he bought an egg sandwich, two chocolate milks, and a Sunday paper. Once he'd reached the waiting area for his flight, he sat down to eat and read. His nervousness caused a knot in his stomach, but he ate for sustenance, not taste. His thoughts blended into confusion, and he couldn't remember reading the newspaper. He glanced at his wristwatch, still an hour until his flight boarded. His mother's ominous ringtone sounded from his iPhone. "Good morning, Mom. Rather early, isn't it?"

"Damn it, Ben! Where are you? I've been calling, and you haven't picked up!" She used her no nonsense voice, effective since his childhood. It irritated him.

"I've attracted some attention, and I had to silence my phone. Bad guys were tracking me. Didn't have anything to do with any of your contacts, did it?" That'd upset her, but he needed to know.

"When your cousin called, and I could not find you, I talked to everyone I know. No idea where you were, if you were safe, nothing. You've heard about your father?"

"Yes. I talked to Jay a couple of days ago."

"I've been questioned by the Elkton police—a Detective Danielson. I'm probably a suspect. Ex-wives usually are." Self-centered, as usual, he thought. She continued, "And I've heard from the FBI. What does that have to do with your father's death?"

"Nothing. It's our economics project. A long story."

"Are you ending this mess? I demand you come home!"

"I'm returning to New York today, but just for a day or two—unfinished business." He couldn't tell her about Janet. He could hear muffled conversation in the background, probably one of her interns.

"You've been there a week, and I've heard from party members about you bothering Maxwell. Secret Service—"

"Let me guess. Special Agent Levitt."

"How'd you know?"

"Just a hunch," Ben ducked the full account. "She's been dogging me since arrival."

"I've talked to Tonya Pritchard several times. She's related to Maxwell, and she's asking questions about your business."

"Tonya's a Maxwell confidant and supporter. She's got the ex-president behind her, so that explains how she has access to all kinds of information."

"Just great, Ben! I hoped they'd help with my campaign. Instead, they threatened me with your mess. Will you stop this, now?"

Over the past several years, Ben had watched his

mother's ambition grow, and often, she made him proud. However, the political climate in Indiana, and ultimately the United States, left a distinct distaste in his mouth. Since the divorce, he'd felt the loss of both parents—his father to personal failure and his mother to professional success. Still, her request shocked him. "Mom, someone killed Dad, and no, I'm not stopping. I assume you're concerned about my safety, but quitting is not an option. I give you my word I'll be careful, but I'm going to see this through. For Dad's sake, if nothing else."

"What about my life? Have you considered the impact of this chaos upon me? I'm in the middle of a campaign, and questioning by the FBI will not help! I can see my opponent's ads already." He heard her slap the surface of her desk.

"Frankly I haven't considered you, or your political life."

"Great. Just what I wanted to hear!" She mumbled instructions to someone in the background. "Guess I shouldn't count on you for the campaign trail? You're still an Indiana resident. Can I at least count on your vote?"

"They're calling my flight, Mom," he lied. "I need to board."

"Wait, Ben, before you go—we've been fighting over this decision for months. I don't agree, I never will, but I'm sorry about your father. I wish things had gone differently. Any leads from your end?"

The question surprised him, and he was embarrassed. He mistrusted his mother enough to hedge. "Not much, but I'm going on with my search. I'll keep you posted."

"Why're you flying to New York? You drove down."

"I need to get back in a hurry on NYU business."

"Haulbarth, I hope. Oh, I've heard from Howard Reezak, too. He's pissed, and I don't expect to be receiving a campaign contribution."

"Trying to make me feel guilty, huh? Reezak's on the other side. I've talked to him."

"Son, sometimes, you act just like your father."

He laughed in spite of himself. "I'll take that as a compliment."

"I didn't mean it that way," she snapped.

"I know, Mother. You can still hope for Maxwell. I haven't talked to him, yet."

"For my sake, don't talk to him." He heard the noise, again, and realized it signaled someone in her office and was not meant to express frustration at him. He'd seen his mother in phone conversations directing her staff with gestures, foot stomps, facial expressions, all forms of non-verbal communication.

"I can't promise that, Mom, but he might not take my visit."

"What do you mean by that? You have something, don't you?"

"Bye, Mom, gotta go. I will try to call more often." He ended the call before she could respond.

As he put away his cell, he regretted keeping information from his mother. He'd thought about seeking her assistance with retrieval of Janet. The man on the phone hadn't threatened, but he'd implied. The man indicated he only wanted to talk, and Ben did not know why he believed him. But he did have Janet. Ben's gut said he had to let it play out as instructed.

The flight to Atlanta left on schedule and landed an hour later. The layover lasted almost two hours, so more time to kill. It'd only been ten days, but even under these circumstances, he looked forward to seeing Manhattan. Just being in the city would rejuvenate him, and he was doing something for Janet. Sitting at the gate in Atlanta's Hartsfield-Jackson airport waiting for his boarding call, he felt helpless, useless, inept, incompetent, what else? He'd always viewed himself as a problem-solver, logical and methodical, confident a resolution always existed. It just needed to be found.

As he thought about his conversations with the man in the Italian suit, Janet's kidnapper, he guessed at reasons for this meeting. He squashed any negative thoughts, any fears for Janet, He had to convince himself of her safety.

Almost a year ago, his class first discussed 9/11. History repeating itself, they'd talked of President Ronald Reagan's plan to bankrupt the Soviet Union with the bogus Star Wars technology arms race. The Soviet Politburo and several premiers tried to counter with their own investment in technology. Reagan had been out of office for several years when his plan succeeded and Gorbachev presided over the fall of the Cold War walls. A decade later, the class suspected Bin Laden of doing the same to the United States with the 9/11 attacks.

The man he'd met at commencement, Janet's kidnapper—Ben couldn't figure how he fit in the mix, but this trip justified his suspicions. In discussions over the year, many in the class pointed out the danger in their work. If—and they always started the discussions with an 'if'—their premise held validity, some governments and many powerful people would be threatened. Those threatened might respond with violence. Most acted like the project was nothing more than a playground game of cops and robbers. Ben never took it so lightly.

Touchdown at LaGuardia and Ben almost cheered. Off the plane and into the terminal, he hurried through the airport to the exit and into the warm afternoon sunshine. He looked up and down the arrival parking area. A man stood beside a black limousine holding the sign, Benjamin Timmons. He moved toward the vehicle—cautiously.

The man looked up and recognized him. Nodding, he threw the sign in the automobile front window, and motioned to someone in the back seat. The door opened, and Janet exited. The man pointed. She turned and seeing Ben, she jumped toward him. The kidnapper held her arm with his right hand and with the other conspicuously hidden in his coat pocket. Suddenly the man looked alarmed and pushed Janet back into the car. Confused, Ben turned to see a policeman walking in their direction. He spun back and shook his head. Stopping he pretended to be waiting for a ride. The cop passed Ben and the limousine without notice.

Ben continued to the limousine, and the man stood aside, allowing Ben to enter next to Janet. He placed his computer bag on the floor, and cradled his arms around her. "How are you?" he whispered.

"Okay," she answered, as their tormentor climbed in beside them, hand still in his pocket.

"As promised, Miss Sharpton is well, Mr. Timmons. Thanks for coming."

Ben looked at the man. "We've met. I remember

our conversation after NYU's commencement." He pointed to the man's hand in the pocket. "The suit doesn't befit a gentleman carrying a weapon—ruins the line."

"Very good, Mr. Timmons." He removed the pistol and placed it on his knee. "It's just for show. Product of too many American westerns."

"Nice," Ben said. "32 caliber Beretta Tomcat, right?" Janet looked at him in surprise. He shrugged. "My dad taught me."

The man opened the back storage box and put the gun away. "I apologize for this subterfuge, but with you halfway across the country, I needed leverage." He tapped on the privacy window, and the chauffer lowered it. "Just drive, Ari. We need time to talk, and Mr. Timmons and Miss Sharpton are more comfortable in the car."

"As you wish, sir." The driver spoke in a heavy Middle Eastern accent. The window went up, and the vehicle moved into the traffic leaving the airport.

"I know you worried about Miss Sharpton, and again, I apologize for my tactics. However, you seemed unconcerned, Mr. Timmons. Why is that?"

"A matter of logic, sir. I don't like anyone threatening my friends, but if you wanted me hurt, you could have left me in Arkansas. Several in that state are interested in doing just that." Janet frowned, and he shook his head to dispel her angst. "I didn't know who wanted a face-to-face, but I assumed it was to talk."

"Would you like something to drink after the long flight? Beer, wine, something stronger?"

"I thought Muslims opposed alcoholic beverages?" The irony of that statement and his first visit to Mosie's crossed his mind.

"How do you know my faith, Mr. Timmons?" He seemed amused rather than irritated.

"I'm guessing, Syrian, more the driver's accent. You were formally educated, England, I'd guess." Janet sat relaxed next to him, but he remained alert. For someone kidnapped by this man, she seemed very composed. "I don't mean to sound bigoted, but I'm trying to plot the lay of the land."

"I'm having a Scotch and Miss Sharpton's drinking a chardonnay," he gestured, opening the refreshment center.

"I'm fine." Ben hadn't expected his best friend and her kidnapper to be sharing a cocktail.

Their host closed the unit, and idly smoothed his wrinkled jacket as he replied, "A colorful euphemism—lay of the land. I've heard good things about you and Miss Sharpton. All warranted, I see."

Ben looked at Janet as he asked, "You allowed her to call her mother?"

"We complied with your request, and you reciprocated by joining us for this conversation. We are not enemies, Mr. Timmons."

"I've never had a friend compel me to travel under these circumstances. Care to fill me in on what the hell's happening?"

He showed perfect white teeth, accentuated by his darkened skin, "To the point, of course."

They passed New Yankee Stadium off to the right as they drove, and Ben's attention diverted momentarily. "Who are you, and what does this have to do with us?"

"My name is Aaban Hameed. Miss Sharpton has

been briefed. Obviously, her Jewish heritage prevents her from trusting an Arab—yes, I am Syrian and Muslim." His right hand went to his chest in a gesture of confirmation. "However, my mission is to assist you and your NYU economics group—if possible."

Now, it was Ben's turn to show amusement, and Janet squeezed his hand. "That sounds friendly, and thinking about our first meeting, your warning seemed like the opposite."

"Ah, you misinterpret, Mr. Timmons. My words were correct and to the point."

Ben's mind went back to that brief moment after Commencement. "You said my project had attracted some dangerous attention, and I should stand down. Weren't those your words, Mr. Hameed? I assumed you meant my Arkansas business." Ben glanced at Janet, but she remained calm, reserved. She sipped her wine and listened.

"I apologize for the obscurity of the message, but we hoped to dissuade you from the trip. We gained sketchy information from friends, classmates, and the rumor mill about your purpose for leaving New York. Turning down Haulbarth was extraordinary." Ben tried to put it together as the man continued. "We underestimated your determination. We hoped to gain your continued work on the economics project. And wasn't my warning correct? You have made some enemies in Arkansas."

"How do you know that?" Ben looked at Janet.

"Your country spends billions of dollars on secrecy, but in truth there are very few secrets members of your government won't divulge for a price."

"Why are you checking on me?" He froze, and

Janet squeezed his hand harder.

"Dr. Hameed believes we're close, Ben." She couldn't hide her excitement.

"Doctor?" Ben questioned. "And how would he know, Janet? This man hasn't seen any data. He's playing you." During their friendship, he'd been pissed at Janet so many times, but never more upset than now. "Damn it, don't you know this guy works for Al-Qaeda or Hamas, or some branch. No one in Syria has power or money unless they're members of those groups." Turning back to the man, "Who are you?" he asked.

"We're close, Ben." Janet insisted.

"Mr. Timmons, I don't believe we'll reach common ground without total honesty. I work for President Sadaam Abu Shakra and Damascus University. I have a doctorate from Cambridge."

"Dr. Aaban Hameed?" Ben had visited Cambridge during fall semester in London. "I read your article in *The Economist* about the Asian pipeline and economic growth related to the completion of the project. My compliments on your analysis. We used some of your data in our model."

"I am aware." He seemed pleased. "My associates and I gained knowledge of your group some months ago. We've watched you, Miss Sharpton, and others drive the model's growth, and it's been impressive. I'm reluctant to admit, our communications experts intercepted your submissions on a regular basis."

"Email, phone calls, what?" Ben asked, but Dr. Hameed remained silent. "In the fall with most of us overseas, that wouldn't be easy. Achievable, but not easy. Second semester, with all of us in New York City, it'd be easier if you were local." Ben waited, but still the man said nothing. "It's a class project, and nothing more."

"You're pretending naiveté, but it's not working. Miss Sharpton is more committed than you. That's troubling, or are you being protective? I apologized for my methods."

"Up until a few minutes ago, Miss Sharpton was my best friend." In response, she punched him in the arm. "I love her commitment, passion, and dedication to knowledge. However, I cannot condone tactics displayed by the governments and groups you support. Syria is in turmoil, and your boss is going down. Our project won't change his fall."

"I respect your mistrust, but I assure you I'm not a fanatic. I believe our world is on the verge of major restructuring, not based upon religious divides, but economic cooperation."

"We can't accept your assistance, Dr. Hameed." He wished he'd accepted the beer.

"Our offer includes keeping you alive, Mr. Timmons." He paused for emphasis. "Our President insisted upon that."

Timmons laughed, openly, "Oh, I have Syrian protection? Over the past ten days, I've been questioned by police, Secret Service, and maybe, the FBI. My mother's pulled my tuition. My life's been threatened. I've been searched for weapons, and all over a forty-five year old case. Earlier this week, I found out someone killed my father, and it's connected to the project in Powhatan. My third-year econ class pales. I'm committed to finding the truth."

He felt Janet's hand on his arm for comfort as the man said, "My point exactly, Mr. Timmons. Someone killed your father, because he ventured close to discovering something. Do you think they won't do the same to you?"

"They?" He didn't know the direction of the discussion, but it needed to play out. "I don't know who you are, and you're telling me about 'they'?"

"I'm a Muslim, Mr. Timmons. In your country that means I'm a terrorist. So be it, but your country has created extremists, too. Have you forgotten Oklahoma City?" Ben did not respond, so the man continued. "New world order has been around since the Carter administration. However, it hasn't happened for several reasons. Primarily, the United States has blocked it." He paused, but Timmons remained silent. "The population of this planet has surpassed seven billion without anything close to economic equality. The culprit—your country, again, Mr. Timmons."

"Yes, I've studied the Trilateralists. Their goal for economic globalism faded when Carter won just one term."

"Very impressive, Mr. Timmons." Ben saw the man studying his face. "We believe the current President has trilateralist vision, but his economic struggles make him look like an incompetent."

"Did I just hear a Muslim praise an American Jewish President for his open-mindedness? I don't believe any economy can spend its way to prosperity, especially with huge deficits. Japan failed miserably in the 90s, and the United States is failing now."

Hameed leaned forward for emphasis, "Yes, but is it economics, or the political divide that exists within your country and threatens to rip the very fabric of your republic?"

"I admit my country's troubles, and our history isn't without error," Timmons said. "But I haven't heard solutions from the Muslim world, sir."

"Ben," Janet implored, "let him go on!"

"Mr. Timmons, your country is five percent of the world's population consuming thirty percent of the world's known resources. It's been that way for a half-century, sustained by a strong dollar." Ben gazed out the window. "The past decade your country's economy survived by borrowing from others, but that avenue is coming to an end. What happens after that? I know you have questioned."

Ben looked back to the man, "Okay, you have my undivided attention."

"Aren't you watching the crisis in Europe? The United States is not immune from such disasters and has the most powerful military in the world. For years Washington, DC convinced the American people that freedom, prosperity, and charity created so many enemies, only a strong military could defend it. The US is good, and Muslims are bad. Both sides have extreme groups exerting influence and control, and under the guise of God's will, our cultures have divided. "

Barely audible, Ben said, "Have you forgotten the Jews? That hatred's gone on for thousands of years."

"No, I haven't forgotten, Mr. Timmons. Miss Sharpton and I shared this same discussion last night. She doesn't trust me, either, but she listened. That's all I'm asking of you. After that, I'll drop the two of you wherever you wish."

"You want me to help you blacken my country?"

"I'd like to help your group find the truth in your model. Let the world deal with that."

"How arrogant!" for that moment, Ben couldn't hide his anger. "You know the truth of our work, and we don't?" Ben looked to Janet as she continued to squeeze his hand. Barely visible, she nodded to him. "Okay, I'll listen," he said.

"My colleagues and I believe your group's project holds the potential to remove the cloak of pretense from many governments. Your premise, the economic benefit of the terror attacks, might garner awareness, not just in this country, but around the world. The disparity in wealth over the past century benefited the United States, but hurt other parts of the world. Most Americans believe God blessed the country." He paused, and Ben looked intently into his eyes. "Yes, Mr. Timmons, I know you don't believe that."

Hameed continued, "However, I believe in Allah's fairness. I don't believe He blesses one man, one country to the detriment of another man, another country."

"Your point?"

"The economic inequality of America against the world does not come from God, young man. It comes from the military."

"So much for capitalism, Dr. Hameed. Again, your point?"

"Many in my country, neighboring Middle Eastern countries, and others around the globe believe the United States is in economic decline. The political and economic path followed over the past several decades put the US at such a disadvantage, we don't believe the country can emerge. Little coming out of Washington indicates any change of direction."

"How does our economic model have anything to

do with that?"

"The size of your military worries so many. As the dollar devalues and the United States loses its ability to borrow and sustain the economy, political power in your country might be tempted to use the military for economic stability. Many around the world believe America may soon be Greece with the bomb."

Listening to the Syrian, Ben felt like he'd confronted his own dark side. "The purpose of the project is to reveal the problems and expose possible solutions. I won't relinquish control to foreign governments—especially yours."

Janet had remained silent, but now, she interjected, "Ben, he has a valid point. If what we suspect is close to being true, and a plan behind the transfer of wealth following 9/11 does exist, who knows what could happen if we threaten the architects of the mess?"

"I love my country. I don't believe that would happen."

"Hurt feelings aside, you're being shortsighted, Mr. Timmons. Your own Thomas Jefferson declared revolution a necessary tool for any government. We believe the US is ripe for such an event." Holding the glass, he shook it without drinking. "Your group raised the invisible cloak from the participants and threatens some powerful industries and individuals around the world, especially in your own country. In my opinion, your group must succeed, or your enemies will kill you all." Hameed paused, but Ben did not react. Then, he continued, "We hope the United States can recover from three decades of disastrous economic management. But, we cannot be sure, and we'd like to plan accordingly."

"Yes," Ben conceded. "The US spends too much on the military. However, economic decline involves the Middle East, too. As technology and new sources of energy emerge, fossil fuel's importance diminishes, and OPEC's influence in world economics disappears. Isn't that behind the fanatical desire to secure the bomb?"

"Mr. Timmons, can I asked you a question?" Ben nodded. "What happens to your country's economy if the world stops lending on the weak dollar? The government would monetize the debt. Your strength is economics. What happens?"

"Ben, we've talked about this in class," Janet interrupted. "We looked at various scenarios. We questioned what happens if some of the events were manipulated? Could citizens lose confidence in government and politicians? We've debated how that would alter the landscape."

"We were in the same class, Janet."

"Then pull the blinders off," she insisted.

"Why am I here?" Ben asked. "I appreciate the warnings, but if your goal is to scare me, my purpose has not changed."

The man pulled at the crease in his pants, straightening. "Your project in Arkansas has the potential to be a disaster for you. Your group project at New York University has the potential to be of great benefit to many around the world. We believe exposure of wrongdoings would deter the further use of military by your country's leaders. Without restraint in use of force, yes, Islam will continue to seek nuclear protection. Isn't it prophesied in your New Testament's Revelations?" That statement amused Ben.

"I'm sorry, did I miss the reference?" the man

asked.

"No," Ben twisted his mouth in a wry smirk, "Janet is Jewish, and I'm unconvinced. However, your citing of Revelations is correct."

"Under different circumstances, I would enjoy a discussion of Islam."

Ben nodded, "We can't be associated with your colleagues in any way. Whatever we might or might not have, it all becomes moot with involvement by any Muslim group. In this country so politically split, both Democrats and Republicans would condemn and dismiss our work. I'm not sure we'll get recognition, even if we're right, but I'm sure we'll get labeled traitors and ignored if we have any relationship to Islam."

"I agree, sir."

"Then, what are you asking?"

"Abandon your efforts in Arkansas and return to your work here. You'll still be in some difficulty—all of you. Your work has great potential, but carries great danger."

"Not until I find out who killed my father."

"I thought so." He glanced at his watch and tapped on the privacy window. Without acknowledgement, the driver turned. Ben recognized they were on Long Island, close to Janet's home. "My assignment includes protecting your life, if I can. Other than that, I'm offering nothing. I hope you will allow us to assist you." He opened the storage compartment and removed the Beretta. Ben prepared to lunge, but the man calmly removed the ammunition clip. In one hand he offered the pistol and the other the cartridges. "It's registered in your name, Mr. Timmons."

"I would prefer not," Ben said. "How'd you register a weapon in my name?"

"Does that matter?" Ben decided not. "Please accept as insurance," and the Syrian extended his hand farther.

Janet moved forward and took the objects from Hameed. "I'll change his mind." She put the Beretta and clip in her handbag.

The Syrian removed another bag from storage and handed it to Janet. "Additional clips and ammunition," he said. "I hope you won't need it," but Janet took the added items.

Annoyed, Ben continued, "Forgive me, but I do believe our project possesses the potential to change world economics. Your motives concern me, sir, and I'd like to avoid any further association. Our efforts will continue after my Arkansas task concludes. And even with constant work, the model might not yield results for years."

"Your quest to redeem your father and your uncle is that important?" Hameed asked. "I'm not overstating the threat, and Allah might not protect you. Under the circumstances, why refuse assistance from any venue?"

"Doesn't your religion call it ibadah—heavenly rewards? I feel compelled to find peace for my father by resolution. Ibadah—won't you grant me that, sir?"

The man sighed, "I feel in a different time, a different place, we would've found much common ground. Unfortunately, we are here."

Ben shifted slightly, "I'm not looking for martyrdom, Dr. Hameed. My goal is to find my father's truth, and afterwards, the truth behind our economic model. I don't intend to be a dupe for Washington, or a propaganda tool for Islam. I believe your help—any relationship—increases my danger and destroys my credibility. Thank you, sir, but we need to do this on our own."

"Can we put aside borders and nationalities? There are powerful elements across the globe opposed to your group's goals. Many will do whatever it takes to see you fail. Some you might view as friends would do you harm. Others you label as enemies would protect you. They're political and economic villains by American standards trying to help you. You need to know the difference."

"I appreciate the warning. I don't understand it, and I'll never accept your help, sir." Pointing toward Janet's bag, "Almost never. Considering the threat you used to get me here, I should have you arrested."

The man extended his hand toward Janet, "I apologized for my tactics, but I did not believe you'd accept any other invitation." Janet lightly grasped the hand. "Besides," Hameed continued, "I benefit from diplomatic immunity."

As Ben took Hameed's hand, "Makes perfect sense to me, sir. Can I at least count on your protection for Miss Sharpton?"

"Certainly." He paused and firmly clutched Ben's hand. "Friends in another life?"

"You can let us out here. We're close to Janet's home, and we'll grab a cab."

The car slowed but did not stop. "Before you leave, Mr. Timmons, are you familiar with the novel, *The Fountainhead*?"

Ben knew it. "Ayn Rand. My father read all her works, and he encouraged me to read that one. I complied out of obligation more than interest."

"You remind me of the main character, young man, uncompromising, unyielding, unforgiving." The gentleman tapped on the privacy window, again, and the vehicle pulled over. "In my youth I wanted to study architecture. I felt a calling to create, and what grander scale?" Ben watched him pause and reflect. "However, a different path took me." He opened the door, and Ben and Janet got out. "Be careful of the uncharted turns in life's travels, young Ben. Many of those changes in direction can never be reversed. Allah guide you, even if you are a non-believer." The man waved.

"Nothing we said required my attendance. Why did you bring me here?" Ben asked

"I needed this conversation to justify our investment, Mr. Timmons."

"Investment?"

"Miss Sharpton has the information." Ben looked at Janet, but she ignored him. "Goodbye, Mr. Timmons." The door closed and the car drove away. Neither said a word as they watched the vehicle disappear in traffic.

Janet turned to Ben, "*The Fountainhead*?"

Free on the street, his arms went around her for another hug, and he laughed. "You should read it," he said. "The lead character is like you—an asshole. I've heard you described as such, and it ran through my mind as the terrorist detailed his investment."

"You think he's a terrorist?" she asked.

"Don't be juvenile," he cautioned. "Nice guy, educated, connected, and high up in the Syrian regime. Of course, he's a terrorist. Who else does our government give diplomatic immunity to from the

Middle East? The scary thing, he's not a religious fanatic. His goals are different and involve us. I don't buy the reason he pulled me here."

"Maybe, he just wanted to give you the gift?" she was too smug.

"Tomorrow, we take that weapon to the police to make sure it's clean."

"It hasn't been fired," she emphasized.

"Yeah, right, maybe not in this country?"

"He did give me the information."

"Which we can't use," he interrupted. "Besides, I don't trust him."

She pulled back from him, "Did you miss the part where he said you could get killed?"

His shrug broadened, and he said, "Not the first time I've heard that in the past week." One more hug, "What did he give you?"

"We're close, and he filled in some holes. I looked at it briefly on his laptop, but it looks good. Much of what we suspected about Middle Eastern involvement in 9/11 looks right! We need to get it in the model!"

"You know we can't use it. I meant that," he said.

"Damn it, Ben, who's the asshole, now? We're on the verge of success, and I won't allow you or anyone to rob us of that! And who elected you god? It's a group decision."

He took her hand, "Let's grab a cab. I'm sure your mom will be relieved."

Chapter Sixteen
Executive Privilege

Monday, just before sunset at Bay Park on Panama City Beach, Florida, former President Andrew Pritchard Maxwell sat in a chaise lounge on the sand and watched the waves roll upon the shore. Secret service agents stood guard to the east and west along the coast to assure his safety and privacy. Earlier in the day, he and his staff had arrived at the new Northwest Florida Beaches International Airport, where he met with local mayors, the district's congressman, and Florida's governor. In a few hours, he'd give a speech at the Wounded Warriors fundraiser in the Executive Room of the resort, but at present, he dwelled on thoughts of recent events in Arkansas and New York City.

It'd been almost two years since he'd received his first briefing and heard the name, Jackson Timmons. The family moniker ignited an immediate memory from his early days as a district attorney in Powhatan. The update detailed how Jackson was the nephew of Joshua Timmons, the primary character in a case Maxwell believed long behind him. Jackson had requested release of files under freedom of information, and the Attorney General of Arkansas, Carol Millhouse, had called a member of his staff as a courtesy. She explained the law compelled compliance, and at the same time voiced doubt about the value of the release.

Such an old case, what could be the harm? His staff asked the Attorney General for a delay to allow research, and she'd agreed. Two months later, the father died in an auto accident, and Maxwell felt relieved to escape the inquiry and potential embarrassment.

In the two weeks since he'd delivered NYU's commencement address, the Timmons name reappeared to threaten again. After the speech, he attended the reception dinner at Bullard Hall, seated beside Helen Epstein. She bragged about the work of a Stern group of students and an economic model investigating 9/11, and she thought he'd be interested. He couldn't pull himself away from her description and without fully understanding the parameters and design of the structure, he remembered Timmons as one of the names in the group.

After returning to Arkansas, he instructed his staff to investigate the group's work, and specifically, any data pointing toward his administration. Two days later, Jack Timmons's son arrived in Powhatan to investigate the uncle's case. Incredible that one college kid was involved in a 9/11 investigation and a potentially embarrassing legal case from early in his professional career. Certain it was not coincidence, he ordered his staff to formulate plans for dealing with both situations without giving any clues to his vulnerability. An impossible task, his team howled from the beginning, but he needed them independent, and he wanted to know the extent of the risk presented by Benjamin Timmons.

As he gazed up the beach, he saw the Secret Service interrupt two female joggers exercising by the surf. He watched as the two got patted down, and decided he wouldn't mind searching the attractive taller one. After some pointing up and down the beach, the two went back the way they'd come. He resisted the temptation to allow them to jog by—he'd enjoy that—but Levitt would not allow it. His thoughts returned to the current problem.

One kid involved in two potential disasters, one youngster wielding power and exhibiting political skill—not likely. A college student couldn't do this, and certainly not an undergraduate. Some political enemies with a vendetta against him pulled the boy's strings. His eight years in office were gone, and he missed the power, the adulation, and being the focal point of the world. All past, and now, what to do? Write his memoirs? He didn't want retirement, but neither did he want to deal with a pesky college brat, offspring of the next Indiana governor. Maxwell couldn't understand the kid's purpose—get his mind around it.

The 9/11 events defined his administration and impacted every decision after. Those crumbling towers brought two wars, billions of dollars spent battling Al-Qaeda, and a trillion more on homeland security accompanied by exploding social spending, sky-rocketed oil prices, and budget deficits. No wonder the country stood on the brink of economic collapse. He set a sound strategy, but the current President had wavered. The Congressional Budget Office and economists explained the debt could be managed with a growing economy, and his did grow. Much had been driven by defense spending and consumer borrowing, but they found the revenue to keep him popular and prominent. Just three years after 9/11, he won reelection with little trouble.

He paused in his thoughts to watch the Coast Guard intercept a yacht about a half-mile offshore. A poor owner out to do some fishing had ventured too close to the resort. Turning his mind back, he recognized some mistakes. Dire circumstances required hard decisions and forced him to partner with bad people. Overall, he'd put his administration's record against any. He expected history to be generous to him. There'd always been some finger pointing, especially over the past five years as the country's economy collapsed. Still, when he left office, his popularity approached Reagan numbers. Why was this kid coming after him?

Willis Baker, his chief of staff, approached his position with a cell phone. "She's on, Mr. President."

Taking the phone from Baker, he said "Hello, darling, how are you? Sorry we can't chat, but I've an event this evening, and I need to change clothes. First, I need details of this mess."

He saw Levitt approaching, and gestured her away. Willis sat down in the next lounge to listen. "What does the Timmons kid have, my dear?"

"From what I understand, he's got you by the balls, Mr. President."

Maxwell noted the sarcasm. "Been there many times before, but always managed to stay on top. Still, what the hell does that mean? You're in this with me. What's the kid want?"

"I've tried to determine that. At this point I believe he's seeking redemption for his father, nothing more."

"Very noble of him, but we need to stop him. It'll take more than some kid to take me down. I've battled the biggest bastards of our generation. Get this little shit off my back." He knew that'd set her off.

"This mess belongs to both of us. We had a good plan, and I don't know how the Timmons bastard got a notion to dig deeper. If it blows up, we're both in jeopardy, so don't threaten me, you sonofabitch."

Maxwell saw his chief of staff shake his head as a sign of caution. He acknowledged with a shrug, "No threat, my dear. We're trying to deal with a situation, and we need information. And I didn't ignore your lead. A good plan, I thought, but who could've seen this kid coming." He didn't mean it, but the politician in him took control.

"Yeah, right, Andy."

"He's drawn some attention, so we need to go slow. We had him covered in Powhatan, but lost him after church. Apparently, he avoided detection by traveling to Little Rock. My sources said he picked up all the records on Monday. What do you have beyond that?"

"Right now, he's in New York City," she replied, and Willis confirmed. "The official records in his hands increase our exposure."

"Like I don't know that! How'd we lose him in Arkansas, and how the hell did he get to New York without detection?" Levitt kept her distance, but watched closely. Again, he gestured her away. "This kid can't be just a college student. He's been trained, or he's Houdini. This covert stuff is beyond a third year—even at NYU."

"I recommend you meet with him at the earliest. You're dealing with an analytical genius, and in my estimation, he'll put this together unless he's stopped. Has NYU given you any help? Come up with anything to get the kid off this quest? Or, how about Rappart?"

"I'm not sure about Rappart. He always has an agenda. Young Timmons is a pest trying to ruin my record. I assume he's returning to Powhatan? I'm here in Florida for the evening, but I'll be home tomorrow. What do you know about his plans?"

"I heard a rumor that Baker verified. Tomorrow morning, they're on *This Day*."

He looked at his chief of staff, and Willis nodded. "Shit! Why?"

"The dean arranged it, so I'm sure it's economic model related. Might not be much help, but that's it."

"What do they have to interest *This Day*?"

"I've looked, but complicated economic structures are not my background. I've had one or two confidants look at the information, and they've told me the work's solid."

"Goddammit! That's doubletalk. I don't know what the hell that means. Do you?"

"Are you vulnerable here? They're looking for 9/11 prior knowledge. Do you need to get on top of anything?"

He ignored the question. "Is that why he's back in the city?" he asked. "Damned kid!"

"That's all I have," he heard some activity in the background. "People are arriving, and I have to get off. Get Reezak to update the Haulbarth angle. And you need to get your econ people studying the work of the group. They wouldn't have Preedlin and Epstein so excited unless they had something solid."

"I hate those geeks. I did what the country needed, and all the armchair quarterbacks can go to hell! How'd you get their model?"

"It's a modern world, Andy. I paid for it, and one of those geeks intercepted it." He heard her greeting someone. "Don't do anything stupid. If we keep our cool, we can manage this. Reezak has connections to NYU, so ask him to get all the information from Epstein." The phone went silent.

He handed the phone to Baker. "Willis, I hate that bitch."

"She can be a chore, Mr. President." Even on a chaise lounge, Baker sat at attention. "I have some details, sir."

He stretched, and crossed his hands behind his head. "Tell me about Mr. Timmons?"

"It's confirmed by Elkton forensics, they found Matt Rappart's handprint on the father's vehicle."

"Points a finger directly at me, doesn't it?" He noticed a pause from Willis.

Willis stared into the Gulf without answering, but after a moment said, "Sorry, sir. This kid's smart enough to connect the dots. What do you want to do?"

Willis Baker had come onboard after he left office. He possessed the skills of a pencil pusher, competent but with no initiative to act without specific instructions. He kept all the paperwork in order and the schedules arranged. At this moment, Maxwell wished he had a fire-breathing chief of staff.

"Is the NYU group for real, too?"

Willis edged closer, "He traveled to LaGuardia yesterday. A car with diplomatic plates picked him up at the airport. Saudi, but we're pretty sure the contact was Dr. Aaban Hameed."

"Hameed! Great! How'd you get that?"

"NYPD tagged Hameed upon arrival. He went to

the Saudi embassy, and they lost him. On video, they identified him at the airport, and the Saudis confirmed he'd used one of their vehicles. Later, surveillance identified Timmons as the passenger."

"How'd Hameed get him back to New York?"

"We're not sure, but we've intercepted some phone calls and emails. We believe Hameed used one of Timmons's friends, Janet Sharpton."

"I've heard her name, too. She's one of the NYU group?"

Still at attention, Willis confirmed, "Yes, sir. She's the Haulbarth intern."

"Second choice, Willis," he put his hands on the arms of the chair. "Howard Reezak told me Timmons turned it down for this investigation."

"Are your political enemies using him?"

"Not that anyone can confirm, but it seems too incredible one kid could be involved in both avenues of this mess." He paused to reflect, and Willis remained silent. Then, "What about *This Day*? Do we have anyone in there to funnel information? Better, can we get the piece pulled?"

"I'll see what I can do, sir," Willis Baker rose from the lounge. "Don't count on it, though. Out of office, the media loves to sling mud—even at you, Mr. President. Can I get you anything?"

"Double bourbon." He needed a drink.

Willis hurried away.

He saw Agent Levitt gesture to her wristwatch, but he shook his head. It might be time to dress for the Wounded Warriors event, but he wanted his bourbon and needed the time for his thoughts. In his eight years in office, he'd battled Iranian fanatics, a crazy North

Korean dictator, Congressional sons of bitches from both sides of the aisle, opposition governors, industrial and financial pirates, and he'd felt more at ease during all those political crises than in this situation. Perplexed by his inability to handle a kid he had socks older than, it made him laugh. He considered Rappart, but put the thought out of his mind. The bitch on the phone had it correct—stupid.

Willis arrived with his drink, and sat back down beside him. Saying nothing as he gulped, he continued with unorganized thoughts. He couldn't believe the boy intended national and international turmoil. Some of his political opponents must be behind the kid, but why?

He decided against Epstein. She had loftier pursuits, but a move like this spelled political suicide. He considered Howard Reezak, but couldn't figure how Haulbarth benefited by any exposure. Actually, knowing what he did about the CEO of the Wall Street firm, they stood to lose with the revelations.

If this group was the real deal, could Preedlin and Agbetheatha have their own agenda? He knew the NYU professor, and he'd battled with the Nobel recipient over economics, but he couldn't see any gain for the universities, or the professors. Hameed's an ambassador for OPEC, nothing more. A well-educated Syrian, always bathed, combed, and fresh, but he smelled like oil to Maxwell. He claimed allegiance to Syria's Abu Shakra, but Saudi money backed him. In his eight years in office, he and Saudi Sheik Makmud clashed numerous times, and thinking back, he wondered about the Sheik.

The bourbon warmed and relaxed him, slowing his mind and relieving his stress. He left office a national hero and would have stayed at that level except for the failures of his successor. Cohen, had already been labeled the most incompetent president since time began, almost bankrupting the country with his attempt to turn the US into socialist Europe. And, he'd given the country the worst economy since The Great Depression. With so many targets in and around Washington, DC, why hadn't this Timmons gone after him?

"What are you thinking, sir?" He gazed on the surf as Willis studied him.

"Willis, when we get back to Powhatan, ask Mr. Timmons to dinner at the club."

"Guest list, sir?" Willis took a pad and pen from his pocket. "You can't meet without witnesses."

"Why not?"

"Sir, the finger of blame for his father points to you and old Ms. Pritchard. If something happens to him in the future, you need witnesses to any conversation."

"What finger of blame, goddammit?"

Willis looked uneasy. "We received some inquiries from Little Rock. While there, the young man got the University's forensic department involved. There are holes in the official record, but I assume you knew that, sir."

"Yeah, a few, but it was...necessary."

"One of the forensic people requested an inquiry into Joshua Timmons's death, Mr. President."

"Damn," he paused for another sip. "That would be Maureen Fitzpatrick. She called a few days ago."

"Guest list, Mr. President?" Willis insisted.

"Goddammit, I know you're right." Levitt had gotten more demonstrative, but he continued to ignore her. "I need top people on this kid. Get our economists looking at their project, and get the background on all involved. Find something on Timmons that puts an end to this. Maybe, it's as easy as money, but if it's not, I need leverage. Get it for me, Willis, before this gets any more out of hand."

"They're kids, Mr. President. I doubt a background check will turn up anything."

"I don't give a shit! Find something, goddammit! Put Levitt on it. She has contacts at the FBI and the CIA. Tell her to pull in some favors. I want details on all of them."

Willis looked uncomfortable. "She's going to see it as a conflict of interest—abuse of power and illegal."

"Shit, Willis, tell her to do it, or find another job!"

"Yes, sir." Willis looked at Agent Levitt as he struggled to get out of the seat. "I'm sorry, sir, but time to go."

"Yes, I know, Willis." He rose from his relaxed position in the chaise lounge. "One more thing, brief Murphy and O'Connell. Tell them to find answers." He turned to leave, but Willis stopped him.

"Sir?" He looked at his chief of staff. "I understand the rudimentary facts. But this Timmons shooting—is there any validity to the kid's suspicions?" Baker appeared shell shocked as he continued, "It will help with the investigation to know the extent of the exposure."

"Willis, 9/11 happened, and I dealt with it. I did whatever was necessary, as I have my whole life. This little shit wants to rewrite history, but he can go to hell. I'm not ashamed of what I did, but if you're asking whether I did everything by the book—go to hell." As

Levitt hurried to accompany him, he walked away from his chief of staff and toward the resort. Time to greet some other heroes.

Chapter Seventeen
Dress Rehearsal

Helen Epstein smiled at Abdelle Agbetheatha, as he held her chair at the Starbucks around the corner from Stern. Taking the seat, she glanced toward the counter where Morris Preedlin waited for their beverages. "I'm glad I caught you in the office, Abby. I wanted to discuss tomorrow's interview on *This Day*."

"Not at all, Helen," he responded, "I'm still cleaning last semester's clutter. Glad to get away for a few minutes."

"I've received some inquiries from members of the board." She waited for a reaction, but Agbetheatha seemed unconcerned. "They asked about the topic, and of course, I explained as best I could."

"How would the board members gain knowledge of a student project on economics?" Abby asked.

Just then, Morris arrived at the table. "Black coffee with two sugars—mine." He placed the container on the table by his chair. "A weakness of mine." He shrugged. "Two cups of chai tea." He placed them in front of Agbetheatha and Epstein. "I'm embarrassed to associate with you two."

As Preedlin took his seat, Epstein continued. "Our Columbia colleague possesses knowledge of that subject." To Morris, she said, "Abby asked about the board of trustees."

"I'm sure the members of NYU's board heard from some DC politicians."

The Dean watched Abby sip his tea, apparently, deep in thought. Finally, "So, the model's premise is no longer a secret?"

Preedlin laughed, "Well, you are going to broadcast it across the world tomorrow, if Helen doesn't pull the plug."

She watched Agbetheatha turn toward her. "You're not thinking of such, are you?"

"I'm weighing options." She tried to soothe him. "Morris has details, and then, we can discuss the best move." She knew asking Abby to be patient had to be difficult for him. With one hand she patted Agbetheatha's arm and with the other she signaled Preedlin to continue.

"When Helen received the first call from the chancellor last week, she asked me to make some inquiries." Epstein said nothing. "Besides increasing my fees on the lecture circuit, one of the benefits of my prize includes involvement in politics on a national scale. In addition to major think tanks and Congressional hearings, I've participated in dozens of Brookings discussions."

"Yes, Morris, we're both impressed and wish we had a Nobel." The Dean cut him off. "Get to your point." Beside her, Abby chuckled.

"I am humbled by your rebuke," Preedlin continued with amusement on his face, "I placed some calls to colleagues. Several received inquiries from the FBI, Homeland Security, Congressional Budget, and a couple of less ominous departments."

"How could they know anything?" A look of

surprise crossed Abby's face.

Morris sipped his coffee before answering, and Epstein knew he did if for effect. "Apparently, Mr. Timmons set a firestorm ablaze in Arkansas. My colleagues speculate the various agencies dug into his background at the behest of Maxwell. A short leap beyond basic investigation would be to access and scan his email. Your project got underway a year ago. Imagine the red flags such a scan turned up?"

Now, Epstein watched as Agbetheatha sipped his tea in silence. After a moment, she said, "The chancellor wanted to know why NYU students exchanged emails with China, Russia, Afghanistan, Iraq, Iran, Syria…you get the idea."

"And the subject matter set off alarms?" Abby shrugged.

"You must have discussed this?" Morris asked.

"Certainly," Agbetheatha said. "The class discussed avenues of discovery, but our plan to deal with such included contained explanation of an academic project. I don't believe anyone imagined FBI, or Homeland Security." The dean allowed Abby some time to digest. She noticed Morris did the same. After another moment, "If they read the emails, I'm sure there's nothing sinister in them."

"It doesn't work that way," Preedlin answered. "Since the towers, this country's spent billions monitoring communications of all kinds—trying to uncover the next attack. I'll bet not one email has been read and even less understood." The irritation showed on Morris's face. "Thousands of bureaucrats and underlings peeping through curtains, eavesdropping on conversations, conducting illegal searches under the guise of national security. They get evaluated and rewarded on potential threats. It's a numbers game."

"Morris, you make it sound like prevention's useless," Epstein said.

"Not at all, but spending billions of dollars searching for the boogie man won't be tolerated. Therefore, to maintain funding daily stories appear in the paper about the latest foiled terrorist threat. Who knows, your NYU class might be tomorrow's story."

"Don't say that!" Epstein tried to maintain calm.

In a quiet voice, Agbetheatha asked, "What did the chancellor and the trustees require?"

The dean turned to him, "With my explanation, they like the project. This university carries a certain expectation of controversy, and they appreciate the exposure. At the same time, they let me know if this blows up in our faces, you and I are at risk."

Preedlin grunted, "Figures. They call themselves academicians, but they're really just politicians."

"Regardless," said the dean "here we are. What should we do?"

"In all my years of teaching, I've never had a class like this one." Epstein saw the pride in Agbetheatha's eyes. "When this project started, I never imagined they possessed the ability to put it together. Over time, every teacher wonders why they do their job. Sure, there's a sense of accomplishment with each success, but too often, it's limited to one or two individuals. Maybe, a B student gets an A."

Beside her, Preedlin responded, "They all worship you, Abby."

The pleased look increased on Agbetheatha's face. "I've learned from them. Never has a group been so cohesive, imaginative, and driven."

"That would be Mr. Timmons and Miss Sharpton?" she asked.

"Ah, I'm honored to teach such a group. When I saw their combined abilities, I tried to help them as much as I could."

"I'll bet the Feds looked at you, too," Preedlin said.

"Since the attacks and with a name like mine, it wouldn't be the first time." A sadness appeared in Abby's eyes. "My work on behalf of the class might generate some tough questions for you, Helen."

"Morris prepared me for that, too. I know you tried to talk Timmons out of Arkansas," she said. "Now, he's drawn this unwanted attention to NYU via the FBI and others. Why do you think he did it?"

"A special young man," Agbetheatha's eyes never lost the glow. "Blood—especially in my culture—binds us to our past. However, it can be the building material of walls, barriers, insurmountable obstacles, too. That's young Ben's burden with his father."

"If that's true," the dean inquired, "why give up so much for this Arkansas goose chase?"

"Conviction. If you know it's right—even if everyone tells you it's wrong." He turned to look directly at her. "I've talked to him. He's in the city for a couple of days."

"Really?" the news excited Epstein. "Has he finished in Arkansas?"

"No," Abby answered, "but he will be at the interview."

And she knew the time to make a decision had arrived. "What about *This Day*?" She turned to Preedlin, "Morris, you put the interview together?"

The Nobel Laureate replied, "I'm not a fan of censorship—especially government strong arm."

"Abby?" she asked, but knew the answer.

"The students earned the recognition."

Now, she offered her own confirmation, "Okay, if we need to explain the project, once on national television is more efficient." Preedlin patted her arm, and Abby gave her thumbs up. "See you early tomorrow."

A wide grin crossed Abby's face. "You will never be so proud, Dean. The group is amazing."

"You'd describe them as such, even if they get me fired!" She pretended to scold Agbetheatha. "I'm too old to start teaching."

"And I'm too old to stop," he said.

She'd never known anyone as dedicated to teaching as her Arab friend. "Let's embrace this group. If Abby says they're worthy, that's good enough for me."

"Let's hope you don't regret it in the unemployment line," and Preedlin laughed aloud.

Chapter Eighteen
National Exposure

Timmons's alarm went off at five on Tuesday morning. Hurriedly, he showered, shaved, dressed in his best NYU prep, and walked out the door at six. He headed west to grab the 6 train, the most direct weekday ride uptown to Rockefeller Center. He swiped his Metro Card and entered the uptown side of the track. After a short wait, the subway arrived. A short time later, he got off at 51st and Lexington and walked the last two blocks. Dr. Epstein had given him the stage door number, and as he approached the broadcast studio, he saw Janet and Narayan waiting. He hugged Janet, shook Narayan's hand and asked, "Are we early?"

Patel shook his head. "Something's wrong. Dr. Epstein rushed past us and into the building. She didn't say anything, but she didn't look happy."

Ben looked at Janet. "Have you seen Dr. Agbetheatha?" he asked.

"No," she answered. "As you walked up, Narayan and I were wondering if he might be sick." Before he could ask, she snapped, "We're not dumb asses. We called, but he's not picking up."

Ben looked up and down the street. He'd been away less than two weeks, but as he stood not far from Time Square, he realized he missed The Big Apple. The area was constant with early activity. Citizens rushed past them without notice on their way to work. "I'm sure it's nothing," he said to his friends.

"You're an asshole, if you believe that." Janet had a way of keeping him on point.

He turned toward her and patted a shoulder. "I'm an optimist, my dear. Optimistish, isn't that the word?"

"Go to hell, Timmons!" She moved closer and motioned for Narayan to lean in. "I don't believe in coincidence and neither do you."

Ben had to admit she was right. Narayan asked them, "You think something's wrong with Dr. Agbetheatha?"

"I don't think he's sick." She answered Patel's question, but her eyes were on Ben. "Each unusual event increases my confidence in our work." He felt her grab his wrist to emphasize. "We're close!"

"What other unusual events?" Narayan showed fear in his eyes, and Timmons knew something troubled him.

Ben and Janet turned to their companion from New Delhi, and Janet asked, "What's happened to you?"

Taking a deep breath, he said, "My father works for Hindu Global. He's received some inquiries from his superiors." Ben recognized Narayan's situation as more tenuous.

Before Timmons could speak, "You're shittin' me!" Janet cursed too loudly, causing several people hurrying by to pause and look. "What does Hindu Global do?"

"It's a big company," Narayan looked embarrassed but couldn't avoid Janet's inquiry. "They're involved in the building of the pipeline."

"What did they say to your father?" Ben asked and watched Narayan's nervousness.

"They asked if he provided any information to me."

"Has he?" Janet asked, still too loud.

"No!" Narayan shook his head. "I've told my father about the project, but he's not involved."

"They threaten his position?" Ben asked, and Narayan nodded. "More?"

Narayan looked him straight in the eye. "They said what we're doing could be dangerous to the company and India's economy."

"And what the hell did that mean?" Before Patel could answer Janet's question, Dr. Epstein emerged from the backstage door. Narayan pointed, and the three classmates waited for the dean's approach.

She paused only a moment and looked at each of them. Ben felt her gaze. "The doorman at Dr. Agbetheatha's building said Homeland Security arrested him late last evening. Unfortunately, Homeland Security denies it. I don't know where he is, but I have the university's attorneys searching. We can assume he won't be here. The network's still interested in the story, and we're going on, provided you three agree?"

"Without Dr. Agbetheatha, wouldn't it be better to delay?" Narayan looked troubled.

"Dr. Preedlin," Ben answered, "he's been pushing for exposure of this project. I'll bet he pulled some strings to get us here?" He looked for confirmation from Dr. Epstein. "He's talked with you this morning?"

She ignored Ben's inference. "I'll need one of you to explain the work in Abdelle's absence." She looked at Ben. "Can you be informative, brief, and charismatic,

Mr. Timmons."

"It might be better with Janet. She's the Haulbarth recipient."

"You're full of shit, Ben!" He knew Janet hadn't been fooled. "We're not here for just an interview, and you know it. Just as you know what has to be done. I'm ready, and we've talked about this event. We didn't expect national television, but we've known."

"I'm confused by these events," Narayan stressed. "I'm not sure this is the right forum."

Dr. Epstein continued, "Miss Sharpton's correct. The game is afoot, so to speak. We have two choices. Either we quit, which is what they want, or we seize control in that television studio." She waited, "It's your choice, Mr. Timmons. Can you explain the project without putting morning America to sleep?"

"Wait," Narayan stressed. "Who is this unknown 'they'? Maybe, we should wait for Dr. Agbetheatha?"

"Dammit, Patel!" Janet straight-forward as always said, "What's the phrase in Hindi for man-up?"

"We have choices in this, don't we?" Narayan didn't even attempt to disguise his fear. "This is our decision."

"No, it's not." Ben looked up and down the street, again. To Dr. Epstein, "Does the show have any idea about this situation?"

She shrugged, "Morris Preedlin has pull in this town, young man." Ben stood silently and thought about the events. He knew his friends did the same. After perhaps a minute, Dean Epstein said, "The concern is real, and Abby might be the first prisoner. We need to consider this."

"What do you mean by that?" Narayan questioned.

"We'll find Dr. Agbetheatha," the Dean assured him. "Abby is okay. Whoever initiated Abby's arrest wanted to delay this interview. We need to decide if we're going to allow them to succeed."

Ben saw her studying his face. He looked at his two friends and said, "Who's on first?"

The four of them moved to the door, and the attendant opened it for them. Inside, Dr. Epstein walked them down the hall, through another doorway, across an empty studio and into a waiting room. None of the network people paid them any attention. The Dean impressed Ben with her ability to get around the television complex.

All the monitors in the studio were tuned to *This Day*, as Ann Markum interviewed a congressman about a Supreme Court nominee. The legislator sat across the aisle from the President's party and opposed the nomination for political reasons. Markum questioned the man very aggressively, but the politician held his own in the discussion.

"We'll be in here until they call us." Dr. Epstein glanced at her wristwatch. "Less than an hour, I would guess. I'm going to inquire about the time. Put those towels around your necks and wait for the makeup people." She hurried out before any of the friends could respond.

As Timmons tucked the towel around his collar, he mumbled, "Men and makeup make me nervous. Hope my homophobia doesn't dull my wits."

Narayan looked startled by the comment, but Janet just shook her head. "You're so full of it, Timmons." Then, more seriously, she added "Are you ready for this?"

Before Ben could respond, Narayan said, "I cannot do this. I'm withdrawing from this interview, and I'm done with this class." He threw the towel on the counter of the waiting room and turned to leave.

"Don't give up on us, Narayan!" Janet pleaded.

"No," Narayan insisted. "The class is done. I have my grade. I'm not comfortable with this direction, and I'm through. Tell the Dean I'm sorry, but I can't risk my family." He paused to look from Ben to Janet and back. "I'm not an American, and Homeland Security scares the hell out of me." He walked toward the door, but just before leaving he turned and said, "I am so sorry to do this," and went.

Janet turned to Ben. "Goddamned coward!"

"You're too hard on him, Janet." He sat down on the beige sofa, unable to find anything funny to say. "He's a child of privilege from a foreign country. His position in life could unravel if the United States or Homeland Security sent him home in disgrace. He felt threatened for his father. We're Americans. He's from India."

"Damn, Timmons! That country gave us Gandhi!"

He leaned back on the couch and stared at the door. "Yes, and they killed him, too."

They sat in silence for the next minute, and after a moment, she said, "We need his assistance to finish, Ben."

He shrugged and said, "I'll not condemn him for his priorities. I've suffered such for the past two weeks in Arkansas. Narayan deserves better, and he remains my friend—project be damned."

Janet looked puzzled, "If he'd had a pair, he could have gotten through the interview."

The smile returned to his face, "Cowards and heroes come in all shapes and sizes. In the end we're all trying to get along."

Four makeup attendants walked into the area, followed by the Dean. A quick glance around the room, and Dr. Epstein asked, "Mr. Patel?"

Ben looked at her, said nothing, and shook his head. The Dean, Janet, and Ben assumed their positions in the barber chairs in front of the mirrored counter. Three makeup specialists placed additional drop cloths and went to work. The fourth walked out of the waiting room without a word.

Several minutes passed with everyone lost in thought, or shocked at Narayan's sudden decision to withdraw. After ten minutes, or so, Timmons said to the woman at his side, "Can you take a few years off my appearance?" She giggled, but said nothing. "Who's the most famous person you've had in here?"

"Oh, I prepped President Maxwell about four years ago. He was here to address the UN. The interview was a big deal, and I did his makeup."

From the corner of his eye, Ben saw the dean and Janet turn in his direction. He asked, "And did you like him?"

"Oh, he was wonderful," the woman gushed. "Good looking, witty. He flirted with me."

"Yes," Ben replied. "I can see why."

From beside him, Janet grunted, "Shit, Timmons."

He glanced her way. "Dean Epstein knows him well," he said and the makeup girl looked at the Dean. "I hope to meet him one day," Ben continued. "If you got the President, you must be good at your job." He watched her in the mirror. "Can you give me a little more of a tan?" and everyone laughed aloud.

"Who's interviewing you?" she asked, as she highlighted his eyebrows with a makeup pencil.

Ben shrugged and looked to the Dean. "Tina Rodriguez," she informed them.

"Oh," the makeup specialist seemed less enthused.

"What?" Ben mused.

"She's a legend in this studio," the girl said. "Tina's very brainy, and her pieces are usually boring." The Dean, Janet, and Ben exchanged looks of concern. "Oh, I'm sure your session will be wonderful!"

"Be sure and watch, and I'll ask your opinion when we finish."

From beside him, Janet swore. "Damn, Timmons!" and then she added to the makeup specialist, "He thinks himself a lady's man."

Ben laughed, and it made him feel really good. And just as quickly, a thought hit him, and he wished his dad could see him do the interview.

Chapter Nineteen
The Audience

A half-hour later, Dean Epstein, Janet Sharpton, and Ben Timmons moved to the set across the studio from the main anchors' seating area. The lights pointed in their direction caused Timmons to squint, as the heat from the lamps and his nervousness caused him to perspire. Opposite them, Tina Rodriquez, the network's financial analyst, moved into the main chair and glanced at the notes in her lap. From beyond the camera, they heard Ann Markum, "Thanks for the update, Al. With us this morning, we have Dr. Helen Epstein, dean of New York University's Stern School of Business, and two of her students. NYU's third-year Global Economics class received national recognition for their just completed project examining financial benefits from the 9/11 attacks, and Tina Rodriguez has them with her. Take it away, Tina."

The lights intensified, the camera technician gestured to Miss Rodriguez, and she said, "I'm here with NYU's Dean Helen Epstein, and two of her students, Janet Sharpton and Benjamin Timmons. Welcome to all of you."

"Thank you, Tina," the Dean responded. "We're glad to be here this morning."

Ben glanced at the monitor beyond the set and saw a close up shot of Dr. Epstein. The interview continued,

"Dr. Abdelle Agbetheatha's Global Economics class is widely known and respected at NYU and around the country. Over his years at the University, he's turned out some of the finest econ minds in our nation and internationally. A reputation well-deserved, and we're sorry Dr. Agbetheatha could not attend."

"We'll do our best to represent NYU and make Abdelle proud," the Dean acknowledged without explanation.

Miss Rodriguez continued, "His class constructed an economic model which received recognition from numerous academic institutions—Columbia, Harvard, Duke, Stanford—to mention a few. Can you explain to our audience?"

"Yes, Mr. Timmons will elaborate," and Epstein turned in his direction.

Another glance at the monitor, and Ben saw his face filled the screen. He felt a trickle of sweat running down his chest, more from the lights than his nervousness. "Our class constructed a system to identify economic benefit from the 9/11 aftermath. The attacks devastated the country with the loss of human life and the adverse impact on the global financial community. However, we identified industries, countries, and economies with unusual benefit after 9/11. We accumulated data from various public sources and drew information from markets around the globe. Objectivity was our primary goal. We worked hard to eliminate any preconceived notions, accepted no conclusion without verification, and identified several anomalies worthy of further investigation."

Miss Rodriguez looked confused. "Certainly, the rebuilding which followed the attacks brought financial benefit to companies and industries involved. Nothing ominous about that."

"I agree," Ben continued, remembering the makeup specialist's warning to eliminate boring. "If I analyze a stock and recognize its potential for growth, I buy that stock, and it's perfectly legal for me to benefit when the value improves. But, if I have insider information, move on a stock when analysis won't support such conclusions, because I know something valuable outside public information, I've broken any number of SEC laws. I've benefited unfairly from prior knowledge."

His words seemed to capture the attention of the entire studio. "Are you saying your NYU class identified prior knowledge of the attacks—conspiracy participants?" Miss Rodriguez sounded incredulous. "Can you identify some suspects?"

Ben avoided the question for the moment. "We did not come here to blindly accuse. We've identified some anomalies worthy of investigation. We're college students without legal authority or investigative power. We can offer a direction, but nothing more. We've done that, and some academic authorities have given us recognition for our work."

Miss Rodriguez turned to the Dean, "Who're we talking about? Individuals? Countries?" but the Dean did not respond. "Such declarations are inflammatory without specific examples."

Never had Ben envisioned making the statement on national television. "The invasion of Afghanistan and Iraq propelled oil prices to historical highs. Each year for the past decade, the United States spent almost seven hundred billion dollars on foreign oil. We've

193

been dependent upon foreign oil for a half-century, but that amounted to three hundred billion more per year than before the tragedy. In the years since 9/11, we've had companies trading oil without owning one oil well, one tanker, one refinery. Some of them began such trading earlier than September 11th."

"You're telling me they had prior knowledge."

"I'm saying such unusual moves are worthy of question and investigation. Traders and brokers speculated with oil long before the Towers fell. We're more interested in the timing of such trades."

Ben looked at the monitor, and the close up went to Janet. Tina Rodriguez focused on her. "I need specifics."

Ben deferred to Janet, and she did not disappoint. "Prior to 9/11, the Taliban ruled Afghanistan and blocked plans for pipeline construction from the Middle East oil fields to the emerging economies of India and China. The United States invaded to combat international terrorism and search for Bin Laden. Billions pulled from this economy were invested in the war and now, the pipeline project. It's almost completed with Bin Ladin's capture just twelve months ago. The courage to make such investments without political stability defies the laws of speculation. Las Vegas gamblers wouldn't roll the dice on that. Curious turn of events."

"Are you accusing the United States and President Maxwell of invading Afghanistan for a pipeline?"

Ben watched Maggie Gobles and Ann Markum approach from behind Rodriguez. The network anchors stood in the offset darkness and observed. "Miss Sharpton's not accusing anyone," Ben interjected.

"She's stating facts gathered by NYU's Global Economics class. There are too many to cite here, but Janet has pointed to one example that has troubled all of us."

"So, you're saying the invasion of Afghanistan after 9/11 was an anomaly?"

Ben saw the show's star, Maggie Gobles, move closer. "We've identified patterns of questionable actions by individuals, companies, governments, and it's raised some questions."

"And that's why this forum is so important," Janet continued. Ben knew she could barely contain herself. "The menu of questionable decisions and activities is beyond normal comprehension. We wish to identify those accountable, but we cannot without access to decision-makers."

"We're interested in the menu you mentioned," the financial analyst emphasized. "Can you elaborate?"

Janet glanced at Ben who nodded, and she proceeded. "We believe Bin Laden planned to bankrupt the United States with his own version of Star Wars, the bogus weapon system from the Reagan administration. His ability to manipulate financial markets is verified by examining his own fortune. Prior to his death in Pakistan at the hands of the Navy Seals, he'd increased his wealth—indeed, it almost doubled in a decade. With all the money he'd spent on global violence, that's a remarkable investment accomplishment, unless you have prior knowledge of events. We analyzed his investment pattern and looked for similar activity in other groups, thinking collusion or prior knowledge."

"We do allow some savvy investors did their homework," Ben offered.

"These are wild accusations without substantiation. What do you have to justify any of this?"asked Tina.

"We have the interest of some of the best economists in the country," Ben answered. "What we do not have is participation by the decision-makers—past and present. With the exposure from this interview, we might gain access to additional data and improve the direction of our model."

"Have you received assistance from any government agencies, think-tanks, anything official?" Miss Gobles moved into the set.

The entire staff seemed enthralled, as Ben said, "We haven't presented our work to anyone in the government. We were moving in that direction, but Dr. Agbetheatha's absence delays it."

"His absence?" Gobles seemed confused. "Where is the professor?"

"Homeland Security arrested him!" Janet shouted, and Timmons gently touched her arm to calm her.

The show's anchor seemed unfazed. "NYU's instructor in charge of this economic model has been arrested?" She looked to Dean Epstein. "Has he been charged with a crime?"

"We learned of the arrest just this morning," the Dean answered. "NYU's attorneys are working on the matter, but when we started this interview, we had no additional information."

"And there's more," Janet said. "Ben's received inquiries from the FBI. President Maxwell's security people have questioned him about this project and other matters. If we're wrong, why are we attracting so much attention?"

"How have the president's people contacted you?"

Rodriguez attempted to regain the discussion.

Ben could not hide the smile. "It's a long story, but I've just returned from Arkansas. I've been in Powhatan, investigating a family matter from forty-five years ago which involved the President as an assistant district attorney."

"Fascinating topic, but still early in the process," Gobles looked to Dean Epstein. The people behind the cameras were waving frantically, but the anchor ignored them. "Dean, where do your students go from here?"

"Obviously, NYU has legal issues to solve for Dr. Agbetheatha. We've just concluded the school year, and most of the students are involved in summer internships which consume their time. We'll examine the project in the fall."

"And with that, we want to thank you for coming," Miss Rodriguez threw to another segment. "*This Day* will be back in a minute."

The intensity of the lights went down, and behind-the-scene technicians scrambled to other areas of the studio. Someone from across the area called, "Maggie, we need you here."

"No," she answered back. "I need a few more minutes. Can you go with Al's piece?" Ben, Janet, and the Dean remained seated and looked at her. A few feet away, Ann Markum stood and listened. "We didn't get to details," Maggie continued.

Ben waited, but Dr. Epstein and Janet seemed to defer. "We didn't intend to throw bombs, and we didn't want to inundate the audience with a lot of jargon."

Rodriguez remained seated, "Don't worry about offending me. Please go on"

"Economic models are widely used and frighteningly unreliable. Why has NYU's received attention?" All three television personalities looked at Timmons.

The model was the work of art, but the nuts and bolts of the structure were boring. They'd often joked about the need for explanation, and Dr. Agbetheatha compared it to the classic comedic routine by Abbott and Costello, *Who's on first?* The baseball comedy had become their rally call. It never failed to bring them back to the main point.

In a wide shot on just the monitor and as *This Day*'s cast and crew waited for the return from commercial, they saw Janet touch Ben's arm to assure him. He shrugged and began, "The 9/11 attacks stand as the greatest failure of intelligence agencies in the nation's history. Some in our group could not accept that failure, the likelihood of so many professionals overlooking so much was too great. We decided to investigate without politics, hoping to identify benefit from the attack, and eventually, linking that back to prior knowledge."

"I'm with you," Maggie Gobles leaned forward. "You're talking about a conspiracy. How can an economic model identify the conspirators?"

Janet corrected, "Realizing we were moving between personal politics, industries, national borders, and even religions, we resisted such labels."

"That's correct," Ben continued. "Economic benefit from 9/11 didn't necessarily mean prior knowledge. As I said earlier, a broker on Wall Street makes the correct move on a stock and receives benefit, that doesn't mean the broker had prior knowledge."

"So, some individuals, industries, and governments benefited from doing their homework, and some had prior knowledge," Maggie continued. "How do you identify the differences?"

Timmons looked at the faces behind the cameras. "Our theory, Osama Bin Laden realized he couldn't win a military conflict with the United States, and therefore, he devised and implemented a strategy of economic disruption. NYU's model measured the disruptions—both systemic and non-systemic. When we identified the non-systemic—meaning the economic movements outside the expected—we analyzed, searched for causes."

"What did your search uncover?"

Timmons continued, "Over the past decade plus, abnormal economic movement, triggered by 9/11, transferred trillions of dollars around the world. Our current decline into the worst economy since The Great Depression might not be happenstance," he nodded to confirm.

But, how about Maggie? "When all is said, what do you have?"

Now, Ben yielded to Janet. "We've identified companies, industries, and governments worthy of further investigation. A third year econ class, even at NYU, has limitations. We need help."

"From who?"

"Not knowing the end game, we can only speculate." As his classmate talked, Ben continued to watch the faces. "We might ask for assistance from the conspirators. However, those intelligence agencies which failed on 9/11 come to mind."

Ben looked at the network legend. "We have the

attacks triggering financial upheaval unseen in human history. A trillion dollars spent on Homeland Security. More than a trillion spent on waging wars." Ben paused for reaction, but *This Day's* members seemed intrigued and speechless. "We've witnessed the collapse of the American middle class. Eighty percent of the wealth in the United States has concentrated in the top ten percent of the population. Almost four in ten Americans are listed at the poverty line or below. Financial institutions, unwilling to invest in the American economy, are sending billions to the Middle East. We've seen non-oil industry companies speculating on oil, driving the price higher by manipulating the market. And the strangest circumstance, at a time when the US dollar is at its weakest, and the economy is the worst in eighty years, China invests at a record pace."

"And why do you think?" Markum questioned.

"Many politicians and economists have theories on that. I have an opinion, but nothing more."

Maggie Gobles turned to leave, hesitated, but then asked, "And you have connective tissue?"

"Absolute? No, of course not. However, we have enough proof to continue the work." The excitement of the event caused Janet's voice to be a little loud.

"An impressive group of students," Gobles emphasized. "I certainly hope this class is not full of lunatics." Gobles handed them each a card. "My private cell," she said. "Keep me informed." She shook Dr. Epstein's hand and started to turn. Then, one more question before she left. "Who's been doing most of the oil speculation?"

Ben and Janet both looked to Dr. Epstein. "Haulbarth," Ben said.

Now, the Dean broke training. "Oh, shit."

Ben spent a half-hour in the bathroom removing the makeup. As he emerged and made his way outside, crew members called, "Good luck." Janet waited for him as he exited the stage door into the bright New York morning. "I have to get to Haulbarth. Want to split a cab?" she asked.

"Sure," he said. "I'm leaving this afternoon."

"You're not going back to Arkansas with all this?" His ability to irritate her was one of the strengths of their relationship. "What about Agbetheatha?"

"Actually, I'm flying home for a day. As for the good professor, I assume the Dean and her team of attorneys will garner his freedom." Looking around, he said, "Where's the Dean?"

"Still inside," Janet answered. "Why are you going to Indiana?"

Just then, Dr. Epstein emerged from the studio and hurried to them—her face flushed and her eyes red. "I took a call from NYPD. They've found a body a few streets from Abby's apartment."

Ben stared at Janet's stunned expression. She asked, "You mean…? Oh, my God, no!" and she started to sob. As he held her, his own grief rose in his throat.

Lloyd R. Agee

Chapter Twenty
Interrogation

The second floor of the 19th Precinct resembled
the set of a *Law & Order* episode—drab olive walls,
dirty windows down one side overlooking 67th Street,
bulletin boards throughout covered in wanted posters,
metal desks in two columns across the squad room, and
New York's finest walking past without notice. Janet
Sharpton had never been in a police station, and as she
sat on an uncomfortable bench against the wall, she
watched the activities without involvement or
enthusiasm. She glanced at the clock in the hallway—
half past two. Guess Ben won't be flying out this
afternoon, she thought.

At the fifth desk on the left side of the room, a
detective questioned a black cab driver about a robbery.
From the accent, Janet guessed a Northern African
cabbie. The policeman struggled to understand the man,
and the exchange had gotten heated. Normally, she'd
listen to their conversation, but right now, her only
thoughts were of Dr. Agbetheatha's accent. He'd spent
most of his life on Manhattan Island, but it had not
eliminated his heritage—at least in his speech. Sitting
alone in the police station with just her mental shadows,
she imagined she could hear his voice.

A door to an interrogation room opened, and the
detective they'd met earlier, Calleran, exited with a

short, balding man of forty. "Officer, I'm not involved in this. I swear. I'm just the doorman."

"I believe you, Mr. Tollen, but you'll have to remain here while we confirm it." The detective motioned for a uniform to join him.

The doorman continued his plea. "Two cops showed up and flashed their credentials. I don't know Homeland Security shields from Boy Scout merit badges. They told me to let them in, and I did. What would you have done?" Janet thought the man sounded scared.

"We'll get you out of here as soon as we can." He turned to the uniform and said, "Make him comfortable. Just put him in one of the other rooms and no phone calls." The officer obeyed the detective, took Mr. Tollen's arm and guided him down the hallway.

"Do I need a lawyer?" he called over his shoulder.

"Hell no, man!" Calleran answered back. "The only thing you're guilty of is being stupid. If that was against the law, you'd get the death penalty." The uniform chuckled at the insult, but Janet winced. "You've got a chance of keeping your job by cooperating with us, so just sit your dumb ass down and shut up."

Detective Calleran looked toward Janet, showing no embarrassment, then turned and walked to the other end of the squad room. She thought the man crude, but he seemed capable. She hoped, anyway, and went back to aimlessly watching the office routine.

"How about corned beef or pastrami?" She looked up to see Benjamin Timmons with a brown paper bag in one hand and two crème sodas in the other. "It's Kosher."

"Not in the mood, Ben." The tightness in her chest made it difficult to breathe. "And I'm not hungry."

"I'm sorry," Ben sat down beside her. The bench creaked under the added weight. "I handle stress and grief with humor. It's a failing and a defense mechanism." He shrugged. "The redeeming part of the practice is it makes my mother crazy."

"I'm so surprised."

"You need to eat something." Again, he motioned to the bag, but she turned her head. He removed a sandwich as he looked around. "Where's Dr. Epstein?"

"Still in with the captain, I guess. That Calleran finished with the doorman some time ago. I don't think he learned anything." She watched him unwrap the corned beef and take a bite. "How can you eat?"

She hated the torture of this police station, but her emotional anchor sat across from her and munched on a sandwich. She cherished the twinkle from his bright blue eyes, loved his crooked grin, and hated him for going on with life instead of grieving with her. Finally, he said, "I'm eating because I'm hungry. It's important to do that, or so I've heard. Remember, I'm the logical one of the group."

"The group is one short," she mumbled, but he ignored it. Still, looking in his eyes, she wanted to cry.

"Any idea how long we might be? My flight goes out of La Guardia at seven." As he chewed, he dabbed his mouth with a paper napkin.

"You're still going?" She stiffened with shock and anger. "Our professor's in the morgue. Do you think you're immune?"

He shook his head. "No one is. You and the group can go on here. Dr. Preedlin will help. I've unfinished business in Arkansas."

As he took another bite, she insisted, "Ben, someone killed the professor. Who knows what they'll do next?" As an afterthought, she whispered, "Guess I owe Narayan an apology."

"Miss Sharpton. Mr. Timmons." They looked up to see Detective Calleran motioning them toward interrogation number 4.

"Mind if I bring my sandwich?" Timmons asked, and Janet suppressed a scream.

"No problem. Bring your lunch." As the detective waited, they rose and walked to the room. Calleran closed the door and motioned them to sit at a small rectangular table. A two-way mirror, Janet assumed, hung in one wall, and she wondered if anyone watched. The two classmates sat together on one side of the table with the policeman across from them.

Janet watched the detective watching Ben eat. Finally, the boy noticed and said, "I have another."

"Goddamn, son, thanks."

"How about a crème soda?"

"Great!" The policeman unwrapped the pastrami and took a bite. "I missed lunch. Happens often on this job, and I'm still fat. This a Mendy's?".

"You know your sandwiches, Detective."

"Every cop knows donuts and good deli food," he said, as he chewed. "You might not be as big a dumb ass as I thought, kid."

"What do you mean by that, officer?" Ben grinned.

"Just kiddin', son." The two chewed in silence for a minute.

Janet watched and pretended patience as they shared the meal and indulged in some macho challenge.

She'd never understand the male ego, and the need for gender superiority over total strangers. After a few more bites, she asked, "What can you tell us?"

Calleran looked at her but did not respond. "I watched your appearance on television, and I think you're both full of shit on 9/11. Excuse my French, young lady. Any idea who'd want to hurt Agbetheatha?"

Beside her and under his breath, Timmons said, "It's beyond hurt."

"What'd you say, smart ass?" Calleran glared at Ben.

"We're still in shock and a little numb. I didn't mean to condescend to your ignorance. I thought we were here to assist."

The officer took another bite of the sandwich. "That's okay, kid. I'm inundated with dumb asses, today." He swallowed, took a drink of crème soda, and put down the remainder of the sandwich. "Epstein's given the captain her version, and boy, what a work of fiction. Let me hear your story. How'd you get the professor killed?"

"Are you trying to piss us off, or are you naturally an asshole?" Ben never raised his voice.

"Dean Epstein."

The man turned toward Janet. "What?"

"It's Dr. Agbetheatha and Dean Epstein. They've earned the respect, and it's the least they should get from a New York public servant."

Beside her, she noticed Ben's pleased look. The detective sat without speaking. After a time, he smiled, too. "Okay, I'm impressed. You're both under stress, but you handled the grilling. I'm not bullshitting you, though. In spite of the TV's admiration of you, you're still full of shit, and so is Epstein. Dean Epstein," he corrected. "You're a class of wet-behind-the-ears kids, but you're pretending to be reshaping the world. No way, your professor got killed over this fairy tale."

Janet laughed, and felt better than she had all day. "Does that bad cop routine really work?" He glared at her as she continued, "And Detective Calleran's theory of the crime would be?"

"Not yet," the man grunted. "Some witnesses are helpful, even when they don't mean to be. Tell me your story before I show my hand."

Again, she laughed. "Psych 101? You might be over your head, Officer."

She knew the insult stung, but he did not react. "Let's get back to the reason you're here. Tell me about this shit."

Janet waited for Ben, but he remained silent. Then, she looked closer and realized he was sizing up the detective by watching and listening. "For the past year we've been working with Dr. Agbetheatha on our project. Recently, the work has garnered attention, and received praise from noted economists. However, after conferring with you, I'm sure they will rethink their positions."

He couldn't hide his reaction to that insult. "Please forgive my ignorance. Isn't that what the young man said? And I know ignorance is not a lack of intelligence, it's a lack of knowledge. There's a difference." She decided Calleran could hold up his end of a word fight. "I graduated from CCNY. You see, I didn't come into this world with a silver spoon up my ass." The policeman looked at Janet and paused. "Do you have anything solid, besides the writings of Nostradamus?"

"Oh, very good!" she complemented the officer on the reference. "So glad we're the good guys, or you'd be using the rubber hose by now." Ben and the policeman laughed aloud. "We're very close to proving our prime premise, but we don't have it, yet," she answered. "I agree with you. No reason for this."

Ben added, "I've been questioned about the project by President Maxwell's head of security. Janet's become acquainted with a Syrian, who's offered to help. I've heard the FBI and Homeland Security are interested, but I don't know for certain. It's possible we've attracted other attention." He sounded calm, but Janet could tell his mind raced.

"Wait!" The detective seemed irritated. "You're going to explain all that. Start at the beginning, and don't leave anything out."

"By the way, my background is rather modest by New York standards." Ben's need to correct the officer's misconception about wealth irritated her.

"Yeah, kid. And, your mom's about to be elected governor of Indiana."

"Well," Ben smirked, "I'm still undecided."

Calleran ignored him. "Every socialite in the city knows the young lady's family."

"Because our backgrounds are different from yours, you totally discount us and our work?" She despised the cop's investigative approach, but she recognized his intention.

"Just tell me the god damned story, so I can get you out of here."

Ben pointed in her direction and assumed a relaxed

posture in the chair. For the next ten minutes Janet told the entire story—every detail. As she explained, the officer continued to look totally confused. Occasionally, he'd ask a question, and one or two of them were relevant. Ben remained quiet beside her, watching and listening. "Last night, several of us were working and Facebooking with Dr. Agbetheatha. When I went to bed about midnight, he was still online. We were supposed to be at the studio very early. Obviously, he didn't make it."

"How did he die?" Ben looked at the detective. "Did he—? How?"

The officer put the last of his lunch in the used wrapper, crumbled them together, and threw them in the paper bag. "Guess I had enough. Thanks," he said. "Yeah, Mendy's makes a good sandwich." Janet looked at him without expression and waited.

"You might not be such a dumb ass." He sipped the crème soda while looking at each, as if trying to decide. Finally, "They tapped him twice—one in the chest and one in the head. Looked professional."

"Any idea about the caliber?" Ben asked.

Janet knew what Ben was thinking, but the detective asked, "Why?"

"Our Syrian diplomat gave me a weapon. Just a thought." Ben responded.

"You're not carrying a strange gun in New York City, are you?"

"It's new—unfired," Janet answered. "Dr. Hameed said it's registered to Ben. Is that possible?"

"I'll have to check." Janet recognized Calleran's distress. "This project and the other shit, you think someone killed the professor to stop you?"

Janet looked at Ben, but he seemed unwilling to elaborate. She turned back to the detective and said, "Ben is from Elkton, Indiana, but he's spent the past couple weeks in Arkansas, working on a family project. He's been away from the NYU model, and with Dr. Agbetheatha dead, we think someone wants the NYU project to end."

"Ah, that's bullshit. Someone's interested in your crap college class, so they kill the professor and scare the students? Bullshit!"

Janet had to admit the man had a point. "So, what's your theory, officer?"

"Wait a moment! He's right!" Ben almost jumped out of his chair. Janet watched him walk to the mirror and stare. She looked at his reflection in the mirror as he stood lost in thought. What's he thinking?

His back to her, she momentarily reflected on the 'what if' of Janet and Ben. Their first two years at New York University set the groundwork for their close friendship. Early in their junior year, working late one evening on the model, they'd talked about the possibility of a romance—jokingly, of course, because they both knew the reality of their existence.

Her family's money, social standing, and political connections obligated her to a particular future, and abandoning her Jewish heritage couldn't be considered. Ben felt unencumbered by family responsibilities—the benefit of Indiana nurturing and a solid belief in mind over heart. Her family required a Jew for a son-in-law, or at least a Jewish convert. Benjamin Timmons would never commit such an act of hypocrisy, not even for her. They hadn't talked about it since, but occasionally, her heart wanted what it could not have.

She and Calleran remained seated, watched and waited. Finally, and without emotion, he said, "The detective's right. No one would kill Dr. Agbetheatha to stop the project, especially after a national television interview. His death draws police, government, television, all kinds of publicity. His murder had nothing to do with NYU."

"What are you thinking?" she asked. "You believe someone from Arkansas did this?"

"This murder should drive the econ project even harder. A rational person, like me, would return to school and resume the work. Who'd want that to happen?"

He might be right, she thought. "Someone killed Dr. Agbetheata to stop you looking at Maxwell's history."

"What the hell are you two talking about?" Calleran seemed totally confused. "What's in Arkansas? Wait, you said something about Maxwell before."

As Ben continued to look into the wall mirror, Janet shared her knowledge of Northeastern Arkansas. As he listened, the cop's brow wrinkled, but he said nothing. He let out a guttural laugh as Janet concluded, "For the past two weeks, Ben's been trying to finish his father's work."

The man shook his head. "You can't make this shit up." He stretched and put both hands behind his head, and looked from Janet to Ben and back. "Someone's cleaning up a mess involving the ex-president? You two are working on an NYU project that could destroy the legacy of Maxwell's administration, and the kid's father gets killed over a 1967 case, also involving the man?"

He moved his chair away from the table, turned slightly so he could see both, and asked, "Any proof? Anything close to evidence?"

Ben turned away from the mirror and looked at the detective. "Not a bit. Can I get out of here? I've a plane to catch."

"You're shittin' me, kid." Janet watched as the two males exchanged stares. Finally, Calleran said, "You've either got balls of steel, or you're the dumbest bastard who's ever walked in here." Ben did not answer. "You could be wrong, kid."

"Yeah, it's occurred to me," Ben said. "Why don't I believe I am?"

"It makes more sense than a killing linked to 9/11." Janet waited for one of them to respond.

"Again, can I get out of here?" Ben insisted.

The detective opened the drawer on his side of the table, removed a note pad and pen, and slid them across the table. "I have to investigate both sides of this," he said. "Write down the names of the students and anyone else involved in the NYU class. Also, I'll need the lead detectives in Indiana and Arkansas."

"I can do that," Janet answered. "Let him leave."

"Write down the kid's contact information, too." He looked at Ben. "I'll check the gun registration and get back to you." Seemingly, as an afterthought, he said, "Off the record, take that god damned gun with you—and plenty of ammunition."

She saw Ben react, but he said nothing. "Can I walk him out?" she asked.

"I should place you under arrest for your own protection." He rubbed his chin. "You're crazy in my opinion." Janet and Ben waited. "Yeah, get the hell out of here!"

Janet moved with Ben out the door and toward the stairs. As they hurried, he talked. "The officer might be right, Janet. If I'm wrong, you're in danger going on with the project. Get Dr. Preedlin's help. He and Dean Epstein will need to assist, and if you can, use the media to keep the spotlight on it. It's up to you to hold the others together. Tell them Dr. Agbetheatha's death was my fault and had nothing to do with them." They moved across the station and out the front door of the 67th Precinct.

"What if you're wrong?" she asked.

"Yeah, you're right. Tell them the truth, and if they want out…well."

In the street bright with afternoon sunshine, she said, "And if you're right, whoever killed the professor will not hesitate to do the same to you when you show up in Arkansas."

"That's occurred to me," he answered. "I'll need some insurance before I get back to Powhatan."

"Where do you get that?" she demanded.

On the sidewalk, the pedestrians bumped them as they hurried past. Ben looked around at the activity and took a deep breath. "I do love this city." He hugged her and said, "Right now, I'm on my way to Indiana, Kansas, and Little Rock. It will take a few days to get back to Powhatan." Then, he kissed her for the first time.

"Why'd you do that?"

"I might never see you, again," he said. "So, I broke the rule."

"Then, break it, again," she said, and he did.

One more hug, "Take care."

"Why Kansas?" she asked.

"No time," he started to move down the sidewalk, looking to hail a cab. "I'll call with details, but it'll be a burn phone. They can track my cell."

As a Yellow Cab pulled over to collect him, she called, "Be careful, and take that damned gun with you!" Some of the New Yorkers hurrying past paused to stare at her. "Stay alive!"

As the cab pulled away, he leaned out the window and yelled, "You, too!"

She waved and wondered when she'd see him, again. She watched the cab turn left at the corner, heading east toward the FDR Drive, the fastest route to his apartment, and he needed his bag. She stood on the busy street, staring at nothing. Calleran had it right. You couldn't make this shit up!

Chapter Twenty-One
Back Home Again in Indiana

The afternoon cab ride from 67th Street to Ben's Water Street apartment took an hour. Even after the cabbie hit the FDR, traffic remained slow and steady to Battery Park. Alone, in his seventeenth floor abode, Timmons grabbed his bag and headed for the door. Then, Janet's words stopped him. He looked at his wristwatch, and roughly, calculated time for the trip to the airport. He went back into his bedroom, opened the bottom drawer to his wardrobe, and removed the Beretta. Ben threw the weapon, holster, extra clips and ammunition into a box and stuffed it with old newspapers. He taped and addressed the package to himself, care of general delivery at the main post office in Little Rock. He placed all the stamps he had on the small parcel and hurried out.

The bundle fit in the postal drop box on the corner of Water and Wall Street. It'd arrive in a few days, he guessed. Some post offices required pre-registration online for general delivery, but he didn't have time. He'd do it on the plane, or in Elkton. He had little time to waste, and his father always told him better to act now and apologize later. Besides, he knew he could legally mail a gun to himself, but also, it required full disclosure to the carrier—in this case, the Post Office. Still, ownership of the weapon didn't transfer, so how much trouble could it be?

US Airways flight 6769 left from La Guardia at exactly 7:00 p.m. As it turned out, his flight had internet access, and he easily registered for postal general delivery. His package would be at Little Rock's main post office when he arrived.

Another internet search confirmed the absence of carry reciprocity between Arkansas and New York. Dr. Hameed's permit would do him no good in Powhatan. He knew he had a few days, and maybe he wouldn't need the Beretta. For whatever reason, his brain told him to keep the weapon.

A direct flight, his plane touched down at O'Hare just before 8:00 p.m., Chicago time, and with just his carry-on, he exited the airport in no time. He knew he'd missed the last South Shore train to South Bend, so a rental car was his only option. Luckily, Quality Car Rentals allowed a twenty-one year old to leave with one of their cars, but not without maxing out one of his credit cards.

With O'Hare behind him, he remembered his other rental parked at the Little Rock airport. He figured Agent Levitt's people had found it by this time, and he assumed they'd planted an electronic locator. He chuckled, thinking she wouldn't fall prey again to the Black Ridge stunt which had allowed him to escape surveillance from Powhatan.

As he traveled the Kennedy Expressway toward downtown Chicago, he hoped his clothes and other personal belongings were still in the Ford Taurus. He had his computer, the most important item, with the NYU project data and his Arkansas information. The thumb drive backup he'd mailed before leaving

Arkansas's capital should be in his sister's hands by this time.

Just north of the Loop, he picked up the Dan Ryan Expressway and continued south to the Skyway.

As he sat in a line of vehicles, waiting to pay his three-fifty toll, he looked to the restaurant beyond the booths. It brought back the memory of his first visit to the Windy City and his first meal at that spot. He and his father were on their way to a Cubs game in early September when he was seven years old, and the Cubs were twenty games out of first place. Sitting in traffic, he thought of his dad, that wonderful day at Wrigley, and even the fast food on the Skyway.

Ten minutes later, he cleared the congested traffic, and after another few miles, entered the Hoosier state. Fourteen days prior, he'd driven completely across central Indiana on his way to Arkansas. On this night as he drove, he thought about the events of the past two weeks leading up to his hasty departure from New York. He ran the details through his mind, hoping he'd miscalculated. Each time, it brought him to the same conclusion and Dr. Agbetheatha's death.

His thoughts went to his first class session with his econ professor. What were the man's words? "A narrow mind benefits only the narrow-minded. Our understanding of economics is limited only by our inability to think beyond ourselves. While you construct your model, you must think past its constraints. Doing that while constructing and following the discipline of the science will allow you to grow it, improve it, and ultimately, succeed."

The stop in Elkton seemed unnecessary, but he welcomed the opportunity to see his sister, his grandfather, and his cousin. Still, with so much to do elsewhere, he needed a short visit and was anxious to continue with his plan. He knew he needed to give time to the lead investigator on his father's case, but—in mid-thought he froze, as his professor's words hit home. The day's events had given him an assumption, but he had leaped to the conclusion. If he rushed, he'd escalate the risk of overlooking important data. As an afterthought, it'd increase the danger to his life and others involved. Thank you, Dr. Agbetheatha, he thought.

Light traffic on the Indiana Toll Road allowed him to make good time. As he drove, he thought about his return to Arkansas. He needed a plan to further irritate Agent Levitt, and render useless any planted tracking device. They'd find him soon enough when he arrived in Powhatan, and he didn't want to assist.

Two hours later, he turned into the driveway of his childhood home on Wedgefield Court. His mom's job kept her in Indianapolis, so the house remained dark and empty most of the time. As he let himself in, the house smelled stale from inactivity, and he wondered when his mother had last been home. Almost midnight, Elkton time, so he climbed the stairs to his bedroom, threw his clothes on the floor, and fell into bed. Exhausted, he slept soundly in spite of the turmoil of the previous twenty-four hours.

Up at eight-thirty and out the door by nine, he grabbed breakfast on the fly. The drive thru window at a fast food yielded an orange juice, chocolate milk, and a breakfast sandwich. He ate as he drove, and just as he finished, he turned off Waterfall Drive and into the downtown Elkton station parking lot. Quickly into a space, he exited the car and hurried to the entrance. Ben stopped a passing officer, "Excuse me, sir." The uniform turned toward him. "I'm looking for Detective Danielson."

The policeman looked him up and down and said, "Second floor, rear of the building."

"Are all detectives on the second floor of police stations?"

"What?"

"Nothing, officer," Not the time to be funny, he thought. "Thanks for your help."

He started to walk toward the stairs, but the man stopped him, "You're the kid from that TV show?"

Ben did not want to get into a discussion, but he did not want to lie, either. "Yes, I'm Ben Timmons, and I was on the show."

"Yeah, thought I recognized you." The policeman looked at Ben but did not go on. Ben felt he should say something, but damned if he could think of anything. Finally, the cop said, "The lieutenant will be glad to see you. He'll be the guy with the red hair."

"Thanks," and again, he started to walk away.

"Your cousin's on patrol, but I'll have dispatch contact his unit."

Ben waved and went up the stairs. Déjà vu from twenty-four hours earlier, but the furniture, bulletin boards, and postings appeared newer, cleaner, less used. Elkton benefited from a lower crime rate and fewer budget cuts, he guessed. Toward the rear of the squad room, he saw the man described by the officer. "Excuse me, Detective." The man turned to him. "I'm—"

"Benjamin Timmons," the man interrupted. "Glad you're here, son." He pointed to a chair beside his desk.

"Sit down. Can I get you something to drink?"

"No, thanks," as Ben looked around, he noticed other detectives looking his way.

"Are you sure?" the man insisted. "How about a Sam Adams?"

Ben smiled at the detective. "Talked to Sheriff Rappart, have you? I can't believe that story made it home."

"The best story I've heard in a long while." He laughed, and his companions joined in. "Boys, this is the Timmons kid—Jay's cousin." Several stepped forward and shook his hand. A few more patted him on the shoulder. "And we saw you on television, too." Ben remained silent. "How the hell did you get into this mess?"

"I was hoping you could tell me," Ben answered.

"Kid, in just a few days you've become the biggest celebrity from Elkton—bigger than that basketball player. What's it been, twenty years?"

"I have his autograph. He visited when I was in high school," Ben remembered. "He had a pretty good NBA career."

"Yeah," the detective allowed, "but, if your mother gets elected governor, he slips to third on the list." Timmons watched him open his desk drawer and remove a folder. "I read your father's file, thanks for sending it. And I've added your contributions over the past days. Pretty good mystery."

"Why does it feel like a 'but' is coming?"

The detective looked at Ben, and lowered his voice. "What's your opinion of Rappart?"

Ben knew where the question led. Jayson had filled in some of the information. "I've talked with him a few times, and he's been pleasant enough. A bigot and misogynist, but other than that."

Danielson continued, "Your dad was murdered, and we're prepared to name the perpetrator. It seems the killer was the brother of the sheriff, Matthew Rappart. We found his palm print on your dad's vehicle, and no other reason for it to be there. Unfortunately, he died in a hunting accident last year. For Elkton, neat, clean, and case closed."

He thought he hadn't heard correctly. "No offense, Detective, but you're shittin' me?" He waited for a response, but the detective resisted. "You're satisfied with that scenario?"

As his companions listened, the Elkton detective looked uncomfortable, "Wish I was, son. I don't have the people, resources, or legal authorization to go beyond the conclusion I've just given you. My hands are tied."

"By whom?" but Danielson didn't reply. "You don't believe the man from Arkansas acted alone and killed my father." Ben waited, but nothing. "We're talking about a conspiracy behind my father's murder related to that folder. Somehow, it involves ex-president Maxwell and a few prominent citizens in Powhatan. I'm not getting much assistance from them, but that's understandable. I'm pissing in their pool." He paused, but the detective's expression didn't change. "With or without Maxwell's knowledge or consent, others acted because of that file. Isn't Elkton interested in the other conspirators? I'm hoping for some help." Again, he waited, but more silence. "Who do I need to convince?"

Danielson turned and looked at the other

detectives, "Don't you guys have work to do?" Several looked irritated by the request, a few went to their desks and pretended to work, while others walked to the opposite end of the squad room. After all had gone, he leaned closer to Ben. "You're pushing a pebble up Mount Everest, boy. It can't be done. Powerful people have lined up against you—in this town, this state, Arkansas."

"Care to name names?" The detective just shrugged. "My mother's running for governor. Have you discussed this with her?" Danielson nodded. "Look, Officer, I'm not interested in the politics of this, and I know the implications of pursuing this matter."

The policeman cleared his throat. "I'm three years away from my thirty. I'll be fifty-five when I hang it up." Ben thought he looked older. "I know in my heart I'm meant to be a cop, and I'm a good one. However, I'm not throwing my career away on this." The detective appeared uncomfortable—boxed in. "I'm sorry, kid. I truly am."

"Someone killed my professor yesterday. I know you're aware of that." Again, Danielson nodded. "New York police are searching for a link to our model. However, I believe it's related to this."

The policeman looked around the squad room and lowered his voice even more. "I agree with you." His admission surprised Ben. "Without a confirmed link, I'm prohibited from pursuing it."

"I've run into several roadblocks over the past days." He looked at the detective, hoping to relieve some of the man's distress. "What help can you give me?"

With a hint of excitement at the prospect of real

police work, Danielson said, "Let's go over the information, and I'll give you my take. Maybe, that will help you and not get me fired. I hope it doesn't get anyone killed."

"I appreciate that, and you wouldn't believe how many times I heard that over the past few days."

"Yes, I would, kid. I believe you've heard it often, and if you keep on, you'll hear it more." Ben did not reply. "You need to get out of this—somehow."

"If it was your father, would you?" Now, the detective shook his head. "My cousin talked to you?"

Danielson leaned forward and whispered, "I've given him all I have. He'll fill in some more of the holes." Leaning back in his chair and speaking loud enough for others to hear, "Let's go over the details."

For the next hour Ben and the detective went over the facts of his father's death. Danielson described the military background of the suspect. He explained the type of explosive device and its location on the vehicle. With the aid of a diagram, he identified the suspected trigger point in the stand of trees. He told Ben they'd found two cigarette butts, both the same brand, indicating the killer's position at the moment of detonation. "Our forensic people say substantive DNA from the butt's a long shot. Been on the ground too long."

"What brand of cigarette?" Ben asked.

"Camel filters, why?"

"Just curious." He knew the detective didn't believe him. "You got a positive ID on the palm print?"

"Ten point perfect match."

Ben saw his hesitation. "It seems you're holding back."

The detective leaned closer and spoke softer. "As I said, my thoughts could get you in trouble, kid." Ben waited. "The plan was good and almost succeeded. Jay told me you asked him to look, again. What about your work in Powhatan started the question?"

"Too many roadblocks and the power of the press," Ben replied. "A Powhatan history lesson and a hunch." Several of the other officers were drifting back toward the desk where Ben and Danielson sat. Ben didn't mind. He realized they'd been listening, anyway. "You think the print was planted?" The detective sighed. "How could anyone do that?"

Another shrug, and Danielson ignored the others and explained. "Son, you're dealing with real professionals. Not like the stuff you see on TV, but the real thing. If you get too close to these people, being smart won't help you." The warning sent a cold chill down Ben's back. After a moment, the officer continued. "It could be the dead guy's print—probably is. But, it was sloppy and inconsistent with the rest of the plan. I've been in this business too long to believe in coincidence."

"No chance to confirm?"

The officer tapped the folder on his desk. "Two problems with that," he said. "If I could get a court order to exhume—

"Don't tell me," Ben interrupted. "Cremation?" The detective confirmed, and Ben shook his head. "My next meeting with Sheriff Rappart should be interesting. That brings me back to co-conspirators. How do we search? How about phone calls?"

A look of stress tightened the detective's face. "To get that, I need probable cause and more than ashes. No judge is going to give me a warrant to search every call over an indefinite period of time. That's our legal system, son."

Ben sighed in exasperation, "Any chance to identify the source of the explosive?"

The detective looked at him, "Did you take a criminology class at NYU?"

Ben laughed, "I've got a Little Rock friend in the business."

Danielson tapped the folder, "Well, good guess. The explosive was old stuff, according to the lab. Identifiers were added some twenty years ago, but the C4 used on your dad's car didn't have any. Older stuff probably stolen from some National Guard armory."

Most of the other detectives had returned to the desk, listening. Ben asked, "There should be information on thefts from military installations?"

"Unfortunately, not that unusual."

"You're kidding?" Ben glanced up at the faces of the other officers. A few nodded, confirming the officer's last statement. After a moment, he asked, "Could someone plant a palm print?"

The detective's brow furrowed. "Not likely." Ben expected that response, but said nothing. The detective added, "A good spy could plant fingerprints and forensics might miss it. A faked palm print would leave telltale evidence, and the techs would find it. Nothing to indicate a plant."

"So, it was Rappart?"

With another shrug, the officer said, "I'm not the smartest guy in the world, but I can't get my mind around it. Professionals put this plan together, everything but the palm print." The detective paused, as

Ben remained silent. After a moment, Danielson said, "See if you follow. The plan of a single car accident was sound. They almost got away with it, but something got you curious. I think the palm print was the fallback. If we did find it, we were supposed to be pointed toward Rappart, and he's dead. If I'm right, Rappart's hunting accident was part of the plan. If I'm wrong, well…"

"Detective, I'm trying to be understanding, but with so much doubt in your mind, how are you signing off on this bullshit?"

He leaned closer, again, "Officially, I'm doing what I'm told. Unofficially, I'll do what I can." He hesitated to look at the other officers around his desk. Then, he continued, "Understand, my hunch about the palm print lacks any evidence. I think we're being played. I can't prove it, and I don't know how they'd do it."

Ben asked, "Anything else I can help with while here?" as he stood and prepared to leave.

"What do you have in mind? I don't get the feeling you're satisfied."

Ben mused, "Just considering my next move."

With a shake of his head, the officer said, "Son, I know you and your friends are geniuses, super nerds, whatever. However, what you're thinking isn't legal." Ben did not respond. "That didn't scare you, did it?" Still, Ben said nothing. "Okay, think about the fact your TV appearance will draw attention. Not just to you, but your entire group."

Those words hit home with the intended implication. As he pushed the chair back toward the desk, he tried to hide his reaction. "Thanks for the advice, Detective," and he extended his hand.

But, before the policeman could take his hand, the other detectives separated, and an attractive woman approached. "Is this the young man in question?" She frowned at Ben.

Danielson did not move from his seat. "Yes, Chief. This is the Timmons boy." He looked at Ben for the introduction, "Chief of Detectives Hanna Karver."

Ben started to extend his hand, but before he could, she snapped, "I saw you on *This Day*. Have you seen the market this morning?"

"No." But he could guess. "I've been here all morning."

Her stern gaze traveled to the other detectives, and without prompting, they dispersed. "The market's taken a dump, and the analysts attributed it to you and your girlfriend's interview." She looked at Danielson. "Have you briefed him?"

"Yes, we just finished."

She looked at Ben but spoke to the officer, "Back to work on your open cases." She turned and exited the squad room.

"Nice lady," Ben said.

"Actually, she is." The detective agreed. "You might want to give her the benefit of the doubt. I don't know what kind of pressure she's under."

"Because of me?" Ben asked, and the detective grunted. "I'll take your word." Ben extended his hand. "If you get the chance, tell her I'm sorry. I'm just searching for the truth."

Gripping his hand firmly, Danielson said, "She knows that, and in spite of the obstacles, you've got friends in this. I want to do more, so keep in touch.

And, son, I'll do what I can from this end."

"Thank you, Detective." Ben waved to the others and moved away from the desk. "I'll check in from time to time."

"Don't hesitate, son. And if I need to talk to you, I'll contact you through Jay." Ben started to turn, but Danielson stopped him. "One more thing, kid."

"Yes, sir."

"The cartridge we found. Jay told you, right?"

Ben had forgotten about the cartridge. "Anything significant?"

"An old cop's hunch, but I think that was the mistake."

"Jay said it was an unusual nine millimeter."

"Right," Danielson said. "Thicker, full metal jacket, Makarov." He waited for a reaction, but Ben did not understand. "A Makarov is a Soviet pistol."

"What," Ben started. "I don't…Vietnam?"

"You got it, kid. A collector, and probably, over sixty years old, if that helps."

Ben laughed, "Unfortunately, most of the main players in this production are over sixty."

"Well, whoever hid in that stand of trees stepped in shit by dropping the cartridge. If you can, follow the bullet."

"Thanks, Lieutenant. I'll keep you posted." Ben walked down the stairs. Outside the Elkton Police Station, he removed his cell and dialed. After a couple rings, Narayan answered.

"How are you, my friend?"

Narayan's voice broke. "I'm so sorry about the interview, Ben. You know if I had any other choice—"

"Forget it," Ben interrupted. "You did what you

had to do."

"Thank you for that," The stress in Narayan's voice increased. "Dr. Agbetheatha…?"

"I think his death's on my shoulders, but I'm not sure," Ben knew his words would soothe his Indian classmate.

"I talked to Janet," Narayan answered. "She told me your theory. It makes sense, but you could be wrong."

"And that brings me to the purpose of the call. I need a favor."

"Whatever I can do, I will help."

Ben appreciated Narayan's commitment without knowing the extent of involvement. "My father's death, the prime suspect is dead, but there had to be others involved. Elkton's police can't do a telephone search without a judge's okay. It doesn't look like I'm going to get much help."

"What am I looking for?" Ben knew Narayan was calculating the work involved.

"November and December two years ago would be a start. I'm looking for calls from Indiana to Arkansas and back. You should begin with the Elkton and Powhatan area codes. Burn phones, whatever you can find. Any kind of pattern."

Patel stayed silent, and Ben knew he was planning. "That's a big order. It's complicated to write such a program and hack the carriers."

"And I know it's risky."

"Forget that," Patel said. "I owe you."

"You're a prince among men, my friend. But don't get caught." As an afterthought, Ben said, "Blame me, if you do."

"It will take me a few days."

Ben saw his cousin, Jay, and Officer Kase approaching, so he waved. To Narayan, he said, "That's okay. Work on it as you have time. I know you're internship at Goldburg is complicated, and I've other leads, too. There might not be anything to find, so I appreciate your efforts."

"Ben,"—he heard the sincerity in his friend's voice—"be careful."

"Got it, Narayan. Talk soon." He ended the call just as Jay and Kase arrived. "Hello, officers."

Kase shook his hand. Then, Jay asked, "Are you finished inside? How'd it go?"

"Just fine," Ben lied. "The case is practically solved."

"Yeah, bullshit!" He could never fool his cousin. "Over coffee you can tell us the story."

"Lead the way," Ben replied, and the three walked away from the police station toward a downtown Starbucks.

"How are the Cubs doing?" Ben asked.

"Kid," Jay used the word for emphasis, "early in the season, but they suck!" Ben laughed aloud. It felt good to be home, even under these circumstances.

Chapter Twenty-Two
Kansas Over The Rainbow

The waiting room of the Official Military
Personnel File Archive at Fort Leavenworth, Kansas
had air conditioning, but Ben guessed the room
temperature still approached 80°F. Friday, 3:45 p.m.,
and he hoped military workers were like those in every
other office he'd visited in his twenty-one years. Want
something done quickly and without too much
scrutiny? Ask for it late Friday afternoon, and threaten
to delay someone's weekend start. Fifteen minutes
earlier, a Staff Sergeant looked at his request form,
asked a couple of questions about his relationship to the
service member, grunted once for Ben to wait, and
disappeared into the back of the building.

The lack of activity, in and out, confirmed the
OMPFA was not a popular area of the post.
Occasionally, a uniform walked by and glanced his
way, but no one paid much attention. On his lap a
twenty month old *Time* magazine showed a cover story
titled The United States of Amerijuana. His surprise at
the age of the publication was surpassed only by his
amazement the Army allowed the magazine on the post
in the first place.

The lack of timely information did not prevent him
browsing the article. He remembered his father's stories
of marijuana abuse in Nam, and NYU had its share of

users. Many times on late evening walks through Washington Square Park, he'd been solicited by the night people, "Hey, dude, wanna buy some weed?" As he browsed the article, his thoughts turned to Elkton.

After his unsatisfactory interview with Detective Danielson, he had lunch with Jayson and Officer Kase. Later, he visited his grandfather at the nursing home. He hadn't seen Grandpa Lewis for almost a year, and the change in appearance and the progression of the dementia startled Ben. His granddad called him by his father's name, Jack, and kept asking about his grandmother. Ben did not correct him, but that only angered Lewis Timmons, causing him to shout and ramble on about various events in his life. At one point he screamed, "God dammit, Jack, leave Betty alone! She did what was necessary! We all did! What would you have her do under the circumstances?"

The statement dumbfounded Ben, and he tried to press his granddad, but the old man's mind went elsewhere. "I lost my money in the stock market crash. Bunch of thieves! Be smart and don't give them a dime." Ben guessed he referenced the stock market correction of 1987. "This goddamned place took the rest! I've tried to get out, but they lock us in our rooms!" The plea bothered Ben. "Connie put me here, that bitch. She helped these bastards take the rest of my money. Can you get me out of here? Where's Jenny?"

"Granddad…Dad, tell me about Betty!"

His screaming brought a nurse and two attendants in their direction. They monitored, close enough to intervene, if necessary. "Powhatan's a shithole! We got outta there at the right time. Betty did that. I'd have stayed, but Jenny made me leave. She couldn't get over

Joshua."

"How, Granddad?" But the old man broke into tears and begged to be taken out of the facility. The staff members tried to soothe him, and Ben watched as they gathered up his grandfather and escorted him back to his room.

The nurse, RN Donna Gomez on her badge, remained behind, and Ben asked her, "Is this normal?"

Ever diligent in her duties, she watched closely as the two attendants assisted Lewis Timmons down the hall. Ben guessed Gomez was his mother's age, but taller. Her dark brown hair held no hint of gray. She wore a royal blue uniform, neatly pressed, and a stethoscope hung around her neck. "He's had better days, but they're getting fewer." She turned to look at him. "I see your sister often, but not you?"

He didn't think she meant it as an insult, just an inquiry. "I'm going to school in New York. I don't get home as often as I'd like. Susan's a frequent visitor?" He knew his sister had an amazing capacity for kindness, but visits here were beyond the call of duty, especially since she was related to Lewis Timmons only by her mother's marriage.

"Oh, yes, couple times a week at least. She's wonderful with your grandfather. On his good days, they'd talk for hours."

She wrote something on the clipboard she carried, but Ben could not read it. "I hate to impose, but I'm putting together some family history. Any idea what they talk about?"

She shrugged, "You saw him. He rambles on about Arkansas." Another look down the hallway satisfied her. "When your father was alive, he'd visit your grandfather, but they argued all the time."

"Again, any particular subject?"

She looked at him, as if trying to decide. "I'm sorry, young man. His mind is mostly gone. I wouldn't put stock in anything he said." Just then, she received a page to another wing of the facility. "I have to run. Good luck to you, young man," He thought she was leaving, but then, she turned back. "I saw you and the young lady on television." He waited for follow up, but instead, she hurried away.

Thinking of Elkton, he did not notice the Sergeant's approach until he sat down beside him. "Young man, your uncle's file is being copied, but it'll take a few minutes, and I have an appointment on the other side of the post. Can you come back on Monday to retrieve it?"

That sounded like trouble. "I'm only here for one day, and my uncle's military record is very important. I'm on a mission." A true statement for the most part, and he hoped his plea would sway the regular.

The non-commissioned officer looked at him, and then, glanced at the wall clock. "I'll ask the corporal to stay and complete the copying."

"I'm very grateful, Sergeant." The soldier stood, hurried out the door, and Ben assumed it was to address the lower rank. A minute later, he returned and rushed out of the building. He didn't have the file in his hand, yet, but he hoped the corporal, somewhere in the back, was just as anxious to start his weekend. As he thumbed the old magazine, he decided the Friday afternoon tactic might work, and remembered Dr. Fitzpatrick's assistance. How she knew so much about Fort Leavenworth, he could only guess.

The *Time* article said medical marijuana use in California generated over fourteen billion dollars in annual sales, and some municipalities were attempting to tax it. He chuckled to himself as he realized only an economist would find that interesting. Going back to his father's stories of drug use in Nam, he'd read statistics on the percentage of addicted vets from that war. His dad told him the North Vietnamese financed much of the war on American drug sales. He thought that would have been a great third-year project, and maybe, it wouldn't have gotten Dr. Agbetheatha killed.

Wednesday evening over dinner at the Cider Barrel, he'd questioned Susan about her visits with his granddad, but she evaded his pointed questions. She claimed her visits were aimed at comforting Grandpa Lewis in his final days. Ben had to admit Susan's character allowed such acts of charity, but visiting a non-blood relative with dementia defied Mother Theresa's heart. It confused him, "Did Mom ask you to look after him?"

"Can't I do a kindness without an ulterior motive?" He saw her irritation. "You think every action has an economic purpose and reaction. He's an old man, and I feel sorry for him."

"Okay, sorry for the implication." He decided to move on, "Maybe I'm feeling guilty your heart is better than mine, and should just thank you." That brought delight to her face. "The nurse said he'd talk about Powhatan. Anything I might use?"

"Use? What? I'm supposed to give you a smoking gun?" He'd upset her, again. "He rambles about lost fame and fortune. I wish you'd drop this and go back to school."

"I'm sorry, Susie, but I can't."

She pressed him. "I miss him, too. Not like you, I know, but he wouldn't want you killed." She paused for effect. "How about Janet? She can't be happy about this?"

"No, she's not, but she tries to understand."

"Are you two ever going to get together?" she asked. "You should."

He shook his head, "Two ships passing in the night—forgive the cliché. She's Jewish, and her family requires a husband of their faith. I'd have to repudiate everything I believe." His explanation didn't satisfy him, but he knew his sister would understand. "I can't do that to myself, or anyone else. Janet and I are friends."

Susan reacted to his hesitation. "Bullshit." She seldom used profanity. "This is the twenty-first century, not Old Testament." She pointed. "Eat your dinner. After all, I'm buying, and this is probably a treat for you."

A grin crossed his face, "Always good cooking at the Cider."

Thursday morning, he rose early and drove to Susan's house. They said goodbye as she went off to school, and he took one last stop by the police station on his way out of town. Detective Danielson had nothing more than the previous day's information, clapped him on the back, and told him to be careful. A few minutes later on the Indiana Toll Road, his rearview mirror reflected Elkton.

He parked the rental car at the Grant Park underground, and checked into the Inter-Continental, his dad's favorite hotel in downtown Chicago. He spent the afternoon strolling around the Miracle Mile, and later, took the Blue Line to the Cubs game at Wrigley Field, a night game. In the fifth inning, his cell sounded the ominous theme, and he saw Mother on the screen, so he ignored the call. He assumed she'd talked to Susan, and he wasn't in the mood. In the top of the eighth with the Cubs down seven runs, he made his way back downtown to his hotel.

Friday morning and up early, again, he had breakfast in the hotel's restaurant, retrieved his car from the parking garage, and headed for O'Hare. An hour later, he'd returned the rental and shuttled to the terminal for the 11:15 a.m. flight to Kansas.

A noise in the hallway brought him back to the personnel file office. A captain looked him over, and moved into the storage area, maybe to speak to the corporal copying his uncle's file. As he listened, he heard muffled voices, but could not understand. For a second he thought about investigating, but decided against it. Pretending to be oblivious might work in his favor, so he returned to the magazine.

Mid-afternoon when his flight landed in Kansas City, and quickly, he visited every rental car counter at the airport. In spite of offering any number of credit cards for security, none were willing to rent a vehicle to a twenty-one year old with an out-of-state driver's license. He understood Kansas business was more conservative than New York City and Chicago. Just as he'd decided to cab the forty miles to Fort Leavenworth, one attendant mentioned a shuttle bus to the military base. He found the stop and waited with the other passengers, all soldiers of various ranks. Three women and four men, most returning from leave and one from a family funeral, huddled in the shade and watched for the vehicle. As he sat, he listened to their conversations with talk of deployment. He felt ill-suited to converse with these people, even though they were his own age.

The bus ride cost him a dollar, but he tipped the uniformed driver a five and received a strange look. "No tips, son." He took back the bill. "You on the right bus?"

"Yes, sir, I'm going to Fort Leavenworth."

"Don't call me 'sir', I work for a living." His words caused Ben to hesitate. "You need to enlist first, boy."

"I'm on a personal matter at the office of records." Ben waited for the response to his statement, looking for an indication of procedure.

The driver seemed to understand, "They'll stop and search you at the gate. Any issues?"

"No, sir. Sorry, just the way I was raised."

"Nothing wrong with that, son." As he drove, he looked at the extended rearview mirror over his head. Recognizing one of the other soldiers, he said, "Simon?"

From the rear of the bus, "Yes, Sergeant."

"Get this boy through gate security."

"Yes, Sergeant." A young soldier waved at Ben.

"Sit down, son, and when we get to the gate, go with Specialist Simon."

"Thank you, Sergeant."

"No problem, son."

****

"Mr. Timmons?"

He looked up to see the officer standing in front of

him with two hands wrapped tightly around a manila envelope. The file, Ben assumed, "Yes, sir."

"I'm Captain Marins, and I have your uncle's information." He gave the folder to Ben. "I hope you don't mind, but I reviewed the data—briefly. Looks like a good soldier, but mind if I ask why you're interested in this old record."

The officer took a seat beside Ben. "Joshua Timmons was my father's favorite uncle. Uncle Josh's death in 1967 troubled my dad the rest of his life. When my father died some eighteen months ago, I found his information on the case, and I hoped to complete his project. That brought me to you."

The officer frowned. "Your uncle died long before you were born."

"I'm just trying to finish some family history. Answer a few questions."

"You don't find kids your age interested in history of any kind."

Ben shrugged, "Call it a hobby."

Marins pointed to the information, "You'll see he worked for CID when he died." Ben assumed that was supposed to mean something to him, but it didn't. Apparently, the officer recognized his confusion. "Criminal Investigation Department, CID, the army's equivalent to NCIS."

"Got it." But, as the thought ran through his mind, confusion mounted. "Why? He'd arrived home some months before, and my family thought he'd been discharged."

"You can read it." The captain said. "CID recruited your uncle after his re-enlistment." Pointing down the hallway, "I'll walk you out."

Ben's plan to push the army on Friday afternoon had worked, but now, the captain's anxiety to get him out the door had backfired. "Sorry," Ben apologized. "He'd re-enlisted. That's the first I'd heard, and I don't think anyone in my family knew. How could he have still been in the army at the time of his death?"

"Well, if you're a student of history, Vietnam and the years after saw an explosion of drugs moving from Southeast Asia to this country. During the war, much of that drug revenue went to support North Vietnam, but the CIA indulged in drug-running to support their operations." The officer paused for effect. "Various branches of the Fed tried to stem the flow, but they were too easily spotted by the bad guys. The army was the first branch to use soldiers planted in their local communities to gather information and evidence, and from the dates in his file, your uncle had to be one of the early recruits."

Ben's mind raced, but as they neared the front entrance, his steps slowed. "I know economics drove the United States to act on both sides of various conflicts in our history. Israel and the Arab states come to mind. The Iranian crisis in the '70s. Afghanistan in the '80s."

"Very good, young man," the officer glanced at the wall clock. "Vietnam wasn't the first conflict that had the government and business on opposite sides. You wouldn't believe how many servicemen returned from Southeast Asia with addiction problems. Supplying was big business in this country, and much of the revenue benefited the enemy. CID recruited trusted individuals, and in turn, those soldiers went undercover to gather intel on drug movement. Your uncle was still in the army, tracking drugs."

"Powhatan was prominent in drug traffic?"

The captain nodded, "You'd be surprised how many apple pie communities flourished from drug traffic after Nam. It's in the file, son. The suspected reasons your relative went back to his hometown as a spy."

They were at the entrance. "The army sent my uncle undercover, and a few months later, he's dead. Why wouldn't they question that?"

Marins seemed troubled by his question, "Probably did, but the army went by the account presented by local authorities. Your uncle attacked a woman." Ben's mind raced, and the captain did not miss it. "What do you know, son? I can see the wheels turning."

Ben stood several inches taller than Marins, but the captain was an impressive figure in his uniform. "I know everyone's in a hurry to start the weekend. At some point I'd like to talk to the officers involved with my uncle's case?"

Marins seemed genuinely interested in Ben's project. "After forty years, son, they're probably all dead. However, after you review the file, shoot me an email with questions, and I'll do what I can."

"Thanks, sir." Ben extended his hand.

Gripping it, Marins said, "You're uncle didn't die as the record indicates, did he?"

"No, sir."

"Any proof?" the captain asked.

"The location is wrong, the angle of fire is suspect, the math doesn't corroborate the official version," Ben answered. "I have a forensic expert who agrees."

"Dammit! I figured as much after reading the file."

He thought for a moment. "Can I get a look at your information?"

"Yes, sir. What will you do with it?"

The captain sighed. "I might be able to get CID to reopen the case. The problem is most of the involved parties are probably dead, too."

"Not all, sir," and Ben saw the unasked question in his eyes. "There are several rather prominent individuals who want this matter to remain closed."

"How prominent?"

Timmons watched closely for the officer's reaction, "One of the wealthiest families in Arkansas and maybe, an ex-president."

"Shit!" an obvious sign of stress on the man's face. "Arkansas, so it's Maxwell? You're saying Maxwell is mixed up in this?" Ben did not respond. After a moment, the captain asked, "How'd you get onto this?"

Ben decided to trust the officer. "My information comes from my father's efforts. After my dad's death, I decided to continue the investigation. His murder was supposed to look like a single-car traffic accident."

"Goddammit!" and then he seemed to realize the significance of Ben's last statement, "I'm sorry for your loss, kid," and Timmons appreciated the gesture. "Someone involved with Maxwell killed your father to keep this buried?" Again, Ben said nothing. "Can I see the information?"

"I have the file with me, if you'd like to copy?"

"Give it to me," and Ben dug in his bag for the file. "I'll copy it and be back in a few minutes."

"That would be great, sir," Ben watched him disappear into the back area.

Fifteen minutes later, he returned and handed the

file back to Ben. "Looks like good work, son. Ever thought about the military as a career?"

"No, sir."

"From what I've seen, CID'll want to get involved," the captain said. "Right now, I need to get you out of here. You can take that magazine."

Ben shook his head, "No, thanks," he said. "California's dealing with the problem differently these days."

"I'm from Santa Cruz."

"Ah, so maybe you know." They shared a laugh. Then, Ben asked, "Can you tell me something about Army fingerprints?"

"From the 1960s?" Marins pointed at the file in Ben's hand. "All manual and maintained in the soldier's 201 file." He must have seen the question in Ben's eyes "The 201 contained an individual's complete record. When a soldier changed posts, he received his orders and instructions for handling and delivery of his 201 file to his next command."

"Fingerprints were manual in the '60s, but has it been automated?"

"Sure, we use computers, but if you're asking me about a fingerprint from forty years ago." The officer shook his head. "Good luck with that."

"I was afraid of that," Ben said.

"You've got a print?" Marins asked.

"Maybe."

"If you want me to find a fingerprint from Nam, you're going to have to provide a name,"

As they exited the building, Ben noticed two gentlemen in dark suits. "These two agents want to speak to you," the captain said.

The taller man stepped forward and presented a credential, "Mr. Timmons, I'm Special Agent Sullivan. I need you to come with Agent Holmes and me."

Ben thought about Dr. Agbetheatha and considered running. "Am I under arrest?" he asked.

"No, you're not, but we need you to come with us." Both Agents stepped forward, prepared for his reaction. "We're aware of your circumstance, and we want to assure you, we are agents. However, if you want the captain to confirm, we will wait?"

"Wait," the officer piped in. "I recognize you. You're the kid from television. I saw you earlier this week. What the hell are you doing in Kansas?" He looked at the two agents, and said, "Guess your uncle can wait." Then, he added, "Their credentials were checked at the gate. They wouldn't have gotten on the post with phony ID."

Ben thought that, but the Army's assurance comforted him. "Thanks for your help, sir." He turned to the two special agents and said, "I was just trying to get an A in my econ class. Where're we going?"

Chapter Twenty-Three
A Gentleman's Drink

As Sheriff Rappart drove his late model Cadillac down winding County Road 14 toward President Maxwell's club, the Star Herald's managing editor and chief reporter, Christina Turner, sat beside him, wondering how a public servant could afford such a vehicle. The prime subject of local blabbermouths, law enforcement benefited some and punished others around Powhatan based upon bankbook more than justice. In whispers, mostly behind closed doors, gossips said Rappart benefited from Lady Justice's blindness more than the common man.

"I wish they'd widen this road," he grunted, as the pavement narrowed around a left hand curve.

"I don't have any trouble getting my compact through here," she answered. "Maybe, I should've driven?"

"Come out here often, Christina?" She saw him glance at her legs. "You've got the build of a dancer." She ignored his remark, so he continued. "No, I'm tonight's designated driver." A small deer ran across the road about one hundred feet in front of them. "He should be good size by huntin' season."

"I'm not drinking at this function," she said. "I'm supposed to be working." Rappart accelerated along a straight stretch of road, and the chitchat ceased.

She knew dinner with the ex-president wouldn't be a social event. She'd been summoned, along with the sheriff, to disclose everything she knew about Benjamin Timmons.

In the three days since the *This Day* interview, Timmons's instructor had been murdered, and national attention had shifted to Maxwell and his administration. Conspiracy theorists claimed a link between Dr. Agbetheata's murder and the former president. Over the past two days, she'd fielded over a hundred media inquiries, seeking comments on the ex-president's reaction to the new scrutiny. It had gotten so bothersome, she'd turned off the telephone, but the fax machine and emails filled the void.

Yesterday, the networks broke a national story on Benjamin Timmons's recent stay in Powhatan, investigating his uncle's death and his father's murder, apparently linked. International media picked up that story and flashed it around the world. Seemingly, the architect of 9/11's recovery had been connected to two, maybe three, murders—no evidence, but that hadn't stopped the fanatics, or television's talking heads. The pending scandal turned out of control so quickly, it pushed the current President and his terrible economy from the headlines.

The job required her to question Powhatan's most distinguished citizen. She'd filed her request through official channels, meaning the President's chief clerk, Willis Baker. Tonight's dinner had been arranged at Maxwell's club.

"How many phone calls you received?" Rappart asked.

"Too many." She looked at him as he drove. "I've

ignored them, but you can't do that at the station, can you?"

"Mildred on the switchboard threatened to quit." He added more seriously, "I'm afraid we're just gettin' started. God damned kid!" He glanced her way.

"On the record, how do you stand on your brother's involvement?"

She saw signs of his irritation at the question, but he controlled his temper. "I'm not gonna answer that on the record."

"Okay," she conceded, "off the record." The situation strained relationships in the small community, and she feared she'd need his cooperation in the future.

He glanced in her direction, but the road required his attention, so he drove and remained silent. She knew he was trying to decide whether to trust her, and in her profession she'd seen the same look many times from people she questioned. "Off the record, I know my brother could've done it. I talked to Elkton's Detective Danielson, and he has a strong case. Looks like Matt killed the kid's dad, but I don't know why. I assumed he did the task for hire."

Christina knew that information, for she'd talked to the detective several times, too. She'd wanted to see Rappart's reaction to the question and hear the answer. "It's not a leap to guess who hired him. I mean, Matthew had been a handful for many years. Actually, since he'd returned from the war, so I understand."

"Don't fake compassion for my sake, Christina. We both know what you thought of Matt, and I know what you think of me."

"Have it your way," she said. "Your brother's been involved in past crimes, suspected but never caught.

This is the first one he's screwed up." Rappart didn't answer. "Seems he's always been connected and had good friends in high places."

"Go to hell, Christina." He turned into the club entrance and stopped at the gate. "Tellin' the press my brother did it won't get Maxwell and his group out of the spotlight. And in spite of our pendin' dinner briefin', I won't throw Matt to the wolves until I know for sure."

The Secret Service agent approached, and he lowered his window. The agent looked inside, showed recognition, and waved for his companions to come near and inspect the vehicle. While the agents went about their work, Christina and the sheriff waited. "Nam messed Matthew up. Maxwell and Staten took him under their wings and got him a job on the force. Maybe, they shouldn't have."

The journalist looked at the policeman, trying to interpret his last statement. "Why'd they do it?" She knew the answer, but Rappart's honest reply surprised her.

"Matt could be used by those with power. He'd compromise his principles—what few he had—for money. Ain't it funny how powerful people need that kind of personality, while the rest of us could do without it. If Matt did it, he went to Indiana on an errand, and I'm sure he got paid. I haven't looked at his financial records, but I will." He turned to look at her, and as always, his eyes went to her breasts before her face. He'd done it so often, he didn't even try to hide it anymore. "And how 'bout you, Miss Turner? You talk of Matt's connections, but the gossips know you've got dirt on everyone in this county. You're our version of J.

Edgar. If not, you'da been fired and run out of town long ago. And everyone knows 'bout your relationship with Staten. Everyone!" he emphasized.

His gaze went back to her blouse, and continued down to her legs. Earlier, while dressing for the evening, she'd decided slacks were too informal for dinner. Now, she realized there were other advantages to nice legs, even ones with a few years on them. She took a deeper breath to torment him. "So, why are we really here?" she asked.

The gate opened, and his attention went back to the agent waving them ahead. "You know why we're here. Maybe not like Matt, but we're all on the payroll, just waitin' for them to tell us how high to jump." After another moment, Rappart proceeded slowly up the drive to the posh Gentleman's Club. The evening's small attendance allowed Rappart to park in front.

The two exited the vehicle, but before proceeding toward the club, she asked, "You still believe in a hunting accident?"

Rappart walked up two steps to the entrance, and she followed. A headwaiter greeted them at the door, and two female staff members stood at the ready. "Good evenin', Sheriff and Miss Turner. The President and the Pritchards will be here, shortly." He pointed across the huge foyer toward the left. "Mr. Baker is in the study. I can bring drinks. What will you have?"

"Mrs. Baker not joinin' us?" Rappart asked.

"She's not feelin' well, sir."

"That's too bad." Turner felt his eyes on her. "She's a nice piece after a few drinks."

The head servant glanced at Christina and asked, "What are you drinkin', Miss Turner?"

She looked at him, took another deep breath, and said, "I'll have a Diet Coke with a slice of lemon."

Turner recognized her deep breathing did not go unnoticed by the policeman, or the maître d. "I'll have a sweet iced tea, thanks," Rappart said.

The waiter looked flustered by the drink requests, but he gestured, and one of the staff members went to fetch. He stepped aside, and Christina preceeded Rappart toward the formal study.

As she walked, she looked at the elegant surroundings of the main hall. A coat room off to the right remained unused because of the warm Arkansas evening. White marble floors sparkled under the huge chandelier hanging from the center of the twenty foot ceiling. Cherry wainscoting enclosed all the walls accented by tasteful wallpaper. Maxwell had the club built while governor of the state, about fifteen years ago. Wallpaper had been passé for some time, and the lack of updating surprised her. Several paintings hung on the walls, and she recognized reproductions of Picasso, Renoir, and Degas. She understood the originals hung in Maxwell's house in Palm Beach.

As she entered the study, followed by the sheriff, Willis Baker rose from the sofa to greet them. He approached, extended his hand, and as Christina complied, he squeezed it lightly. She watched as Rappart's handshake startled Baker—the sheriff demonstrating his macho persona. Regaining his composure, Willis said, "Come in. Sit down. Let's chat before this evening's dinner."

"Your job's to prepare us, Willis?" The journalist in her asked the question, but it surprised Baker and made her driver laugh.

Maxwell's head clerk appeared irritated, but Rappart rescued him. "Cut the man some slack, Christina. Let him fulfill his duties." He moved into the study and plopped onto a huge easy chair in front of the inactive fireplace. He looked around the room. "This is my first visit inside, you know. Nice study, Willis."

A study, Christina thought. The dimensions of the room were the size of her house. The interior design complemented the scheme of the foyer with bookcases, a large stone fireplace, and glass doors in one wall leading to a patio by the swimming pool. She walked to a sofa across from Rappart and sat.

Baker moved to the fireplace, placed his arm on the mantel, and leaned. The position gave him the ability to view them both while he spoke, but he looked awkward. "I'm grateful you accepted the invitation."

"Didn't really feel like an invite," the officer replied.

Baker continued, "So many things coming together at once. We've developed a strategy to deal with every contingency. Your assistance with managing this situation will be appreciated and remembered by the President and Ms. Pritchard." A knock at the door interrupted. The headwaiter entered with a tray and two drinks—a Diet Coke and an iced tea. He placed one on the coffee table in front of Christina and the other on the end table beside the sheriff. After Baker nodded, the man hurried out and closed the door.

The reporter lifted her drink and sipped before she asked, "How are you managing?"

Willis chose to obfuscate. "Well, obviously the events in New York City are disquieting. Our assumption is the university and the New York police will require Mr. Timmons' full attention for some time. We've formulated a plan if he returns to Powhatan."

"When," Christina corrected.

Baker appeared confused by the statement. "I beg your pardon?"

"She said 'when'," the sheriff responded. "I believe Miss Turner has given her opinion on the quality of the young man's investigation."

Baker turned to look at her, and as he did, she crossed her legs. Baker took little notice, but she knew Rappart enjoyed the view. "Yes, that's exactly what I meant. I talked to Elkton, the Timmons family's hometown. He's already visited and gone. I don't have details of his next movements, but I'd expect him back in Powhatan over the weekend."

"You think he'll return and continue looking into this old case?" Baker looked pale.

"I don't understand the specifics of their economic model," she said. "However, Mr. Timmons performed extraordinarily well in the television interview. His explanation reached millions, and I've heard the Brookings Institute has requested to view their work."

"You're sure of this?" Now, Baker seemed to suppress panic.

"No, I've just talked with the media participants here in town and around the country. We've got more journalists here than the Middle East peace summit in 2007. You can't get a motel room for fifty miles."

"I know," Baker mumbled. "Sheriff Rappart, what's your opinion?"

She studied the officer sitting across from her and realized he paused to think about his response. Over the years Dan had protected his older brother numerous times, gotten him away from official misconduct inquiries, shielded him from brutality charges, and turned a blind eye to questionable business acquaintances and practices. But now, with the brother dead, she knew Powhatan's top policeman didn't believe the story of a hunting accident. Also, she knew throwing away his career didn't enter his plan, and the people involved in this could take his job. They'd take his life without much more effort. "I agree with Christina." While he spoke, his eyes never moved from her legs.

Multi-tasking, she thought. He acted a buffoon, but she knew his abilities. How he'd use them, she didn't know. "What's the plan for that contingency?" she asked Baker.

"You mean, if—when he returns?"

She ignored his correction. "The President and Ms. Pritchard have great wealth and connections. He can write his own ticket, provided he ceases this investigation into the shooting of his uncle. You can imagine Ms. Pritchard's very upset."

"Yes, I can see how she would be." Rappart turned to Baker. "How is Tonya handlin' this mess, and what does she know?"

"Wait!" Christina interrupted. "This young man is a top student at one of the most prestigious universities in the country, a youngster who just turned down the Haulbarth internship to investigate these deaths, and your plan is to bribe him to go away?"

"No good, huh?"

Now, Rappart chuckled at the explanation. "Willis, only a person totally driven by money believes everyone else so afflicted. The people in this study might be consumed, but I don't believe Ben Timmons suffers the sickness."

"Well, damn! It's my idea, and no one liked it. Actually, Tonya had approached him about money, and been turned down. I recommended increasing to a more substantial sum."

"How much?" Rappart asked, but Baker did not respond.

"And what plan did they like?" she asked.

"Well," Baker moved to the sofa and sat down beside Christina, "they'll tell you over dinner." He pushed a button on the table to summon staff. "I need a drink."

"The iced tea isn't workin' for me, either." Rappart looked at Christina. "Baby, you might be drivin' us home." His eyes moved down her legs, and as he watched, she uncrossed them for him. "Willis, I'll have a scotch rocks, and make it a double," he declared mid-smirk.

A knock on the door and the headwaiter entered. "Yes, sir?"

"Miss Turner?" Baker asked.

"I'm fine with my Coke, thank-you."

He turned to the waiter, "One appletini and one double scotch rocks."

With the servant gone, the sheriff asked, "I'm sure your plan will work, Willis, but what's the other contingency?"

"The project involving 9/11 is so complex, well beyond the comprehension of the average citizen. We're going to discredit them. Make them out to be lunatics. With every assertion they make, we'll bring a dozen of our experts to refute it."

Christina sighed, and she saw Rappart slump with realization. "You're goin' to implement a war of attrition on a college class at NYU?" he asked.

"It's become a media war, and we have deeper pockets. It's worked before, so we'll run them out of money. When these kids start talking conspiracy, we'll make them sound like Lenin and Trotsky before the revolution." As the room fell silent, Willis looked at each, as if allowing his words to sink in.

Their plan didn't surprise Christina. She'd seen the Powhatan power brokers at work many times in her years on the newspaper. Finally, she mumbled, "Pre-revolution, Lenin and Trotsky had a lot of followers, and I believe the revolution succeeded."

Baker said, "You know what I mean. We'll discredit them on 9/11, and no one will listen to young Timmons about his uncle's case."

A knock on the door, and the waiter returned. The drinks were placed beside Baker and Rappart, and the servant made his exit. A few more moments of silence, no one seemed to know what to say. Certainly, Christina didn't.

Then, Rappart said, "Christina, you have some beautiful legs. I'd like to explore every inch of them, and red panties. Nice touch." He winked at her as he rose from his easy chair and stretched. "Willis, I'm not drinkin' with you, you sonofabitch! You'd better come up with a better plan. These are just kids—untarnished by life's corruption and independent in mind and heart. They still have faith in their leaders and believe in the inhabitants of this small planet. Slingin' mud is beneath the man's standin'." He turned to leave but at the door, he paused. "How about some god damned truth? Seems the kid deserves somethin'!" Then, he was gone.

Christina sat with Baker, wondering if she should follow. They hadn't had dinner, and she knew after he calmed, Rappart would return. Beside her, Baker seemed stunned by his words and actions. "I can't believe he did that," he said, and took a long drink of his appletini.

Christina looked closely at the man, and noted a hint of perspiration on his upper lip. "I didn't think he had it in him," she said.

Baker clinched his fist. "Late in his career to get morality, don't you think? I'm not sure how to explain the conversation to the President." Christina watched at Baker took a handkerchief and patted his brow.

"An investigative reporter, certainly, one with my experience, would conclude these kids are close with their theory."

Willis said nothing and continued to sip his drink.

"And, how close is Mr. Timmons with his investigation?" She waited, but he remained silent, looking out the patio doors. "I'm not sure Maxwell's plan works, but it sounds like the counsel of the reverend? You're working for fools, Willis."

"And what would you have us do, Miss Turner?" His anger flared. "We're open to suggestions. These are college students conducting a political attack."

"Willis, the queen bitch and her lackey ex-president have a big problem." Christina drank her Diet Coke, and suppressed a look of satisfaction while they waited for dinner.

Chapter Twenty-Four
A Night in DC

Janet Sharpton wandered the corridor outside the Oval Office, looking at the paintings, pictures, and framed documents on the walls. Each held a particular significance in the nation's legacy, and as she browsed, she tried to recall each historic event. One photograph showed President Teddy Roosevelt at the digging of the Panama Canal. Another had President Ronald Reagan walking the White House grounds during his recovery from the failed assassination attempt. Farther down one wall, a family gathering of the Kennedys displayed the happiness of Camelot. Before she could get a close inspection, the attendant moved in her direction, restricting her movement away from the waiting area. Silently, she complied with the unspoken restraint and moved back toward the secretary's desk.

She paused in front of the wall clock, a Howard Miller, she guessed. Just past midnight, the start of a new day before the previous one had ended. Dr. Preedlin and Dean Epstein relaxed in chairs along one wall opposite the desk. Neither seemed to mind the cramped seating area. They shared a moment of quiet conversation, and Janet did not want to interrupt them.

Down the corridor in the opposite direction, another attendant stood guard, obstructing her movement in that direction, so she ventured over to the lady sitting at the desk. Janet figured nothing was normal about this meeting. In the late hour, adrenaline and curiosity were keeping her going.

She looked at the impeccably dressed woman, well-practiced at ignoring her surroundings while she worked over what appeared to be an activity schedule.

"I enjoyed *The West Wing*." The secretary glanced up but said nothing. Janet persisted. "Lily Tomlin played you, right?"

The secretary threw another glance in Janet's direction, maybe with a touch of disapproval, but still did not respond. From the seating area, Janet heard Dr. Preedlin chuckle, so she tried one more time, "President Bartlett—Martin Sheen," but elicited nothing from the lady protecting the oval office entrance.

Haulbarth had terminated her internship at the end of the day. Reezak sent an underling to inform her, not unusual for him. Still, she thought he should've handled the situation himself. She would have, had their roles been reversed. The news upset her, but she wasn't totally surprised. She and Ben had discussed the possibility as fallout from the television interview and speculated on various reactions as scrutiny intensified on Wall Street. Reezak's charge escorted her back to the work station and stood guard while she gathered her belongings. Outside the building with hardly a chance to breathe, she'd been collected by Secret Service, driven across town to JFK International, deposited at a remote gate, and asked to wait. An hour later, Dean Epstein and Dr. Preedlin arrived at the same gate with stories of being plucked from Long Island by other servants of the government.

The head of Stern expressed dismay at Janet's

dismissal by Haulbarth and promised to speak with Reezak. Janet thanked her, sincere in her gratitude of the dean's support, but also, confident Reezak would not back away from his decision. While they waited, they discussed the events of the past few days. The three New Yorkers assumed Benjamin Timmons was en route, but no one knew from where, and the government employees wouldn't comment.

Janet tried the secretary once again. "When is Benjamin Timmons arriving? I assume that's the delay?" The President's secretary remained quiet. "Why'd we use Dulles? I understood government flights went through Reagan, but we flew from JFK to Dulles on a private jet?" Still nothing from the desk, but Janet continued, "Security?" She caught a telltale look from the secretary. "This is an unscheduled visit?"

"Can I get you a beverage? Maybe, something to eat?" the lady asked, and Janet took that as a sign of acknowledgment to her last question.

"No, thank you." Janet replied. "We were served on the flight down." Just then, she saw a White House page escorting her classmate. "Ben!" she called, causing Dr. Preedlin and Dr. Epstein to rise from their seats and turn in the direction Janet looked.

He hurried to her, took her in his arms, and squeezed her in a crushing hug. "It's good to see you."

She resisted returning the hug, but with the closeness, she breathed in his fragrance in spite of herself. She hoped he didn't notice. "Where'd they apprehend you?" she asked.

"Kansas," he said. "They grabbed me before I found Oz." Before she could question, the dean and Dr. Preedlin approached.

"Very exciting stuff," Dr. Preedlin said. "Think we're here for a campaign poster?"

"My first national election," Ben replied. "I admire the President's attempts at social restructuring, but he's no economist. His opponent's a party retread, so from now until November, it should be interesting."

"I'm not sure he wants our endorsement." Preedlin laughed. "With this late night gathering, I'd guess the opposite."

Then, Chief of Staff Willard Boyle emerged from another office and headed their way. "I believe you're right," Janet said, and pointed.

As all turned in the direction of her gesture, Boyle said, "Thanks for coming. Dean, it's good to see you, again." He took Epstein's hand in his, and with the other, patted her arm. "Dr. Preedlin, I apologize for the late hour."

"It's good to see you, Bill." The two shook hands. "The last Congressional budget briefing, wasn't it?"

"Yes," and as he spoke, Boyle looked at Timmons and Janet. "We were on opposite sides in that debate. I'm hoping we find common ground this evening. Ms. Sharpton, congratulations on your Haulbarth selection."

As he took her hand, Janet replied, "Thank you." She resisted giving an explanation, and wondered if he knew about the termination of her internship. She didn't know how he could, and assumed, she was being paranoid.

He continued, "I know your parents. They've been staunch supporters of the President, and I trust that'll continue through November."

She knew political solicitations were illegal in the White House, but declined calling him on it. "My parents continue to admire President Cohen."

Now, he patted her hand, "We look forward to working with them in the coming months." Then, he turned to Ben. "Mr. Timmons, I'm grateful for your attendance. I know something of your summer quest, and I appreciate your participation in this discussion."

"It's a privilege to meet you, sir." Timmons sounded sincere, and that surprised Janet. For a second, she wondered about Ben's politics. Considering his Midwestern roots, she'd always assumed he leaned to the right. "I have a guess, but can you tell us why we're here?"

"Certainly," Boyle gestured to the three chairs in the small seating area, "Please." Dr. Preedlin and Dean Epstein took their seats. "Ms. Sharpton?" He motioned to Janet, but she shook her head, so he sat down. Ben stood beside her. Boyle signaled to the page, and the young man moved forward. "Tim would be glad to bring drinks?" Individually and collectively, they declined and the page moved away. At the desk, the secretary continued to ignore them.

After a moment, Boyle said, "First, let me apologize for the subterfuge. With Dr. Agbetheatha's murder, I'm sure the actions of the Secret Service in collecting you were unsettling."

Janet looked at the dean and Dr. Preedlin. They seemed content with Boyle's apology and allowed him to continue. "The President wanted to speak to the NYU group about the economic model. Dr. Preedlin's participation is a welcomed addition." With that, the polite formalities concluded. Looking directly at Dean Epstein, the chief of staff said, "Your appearance on *This Day* had some negative impact on the national and international markets. We've recognized the downside of such actions, and we wanted to understand the motivation of the group. Two days ago, we assigned several experts to review the model."

"I didn't authorize that," Dean Epstein interrupted. "How'd you get access?"

Boyle seemed amused by her question, but did not respond. "Conspiracy theories have been around since 9/11. Bloggers have speculated about prior knowledge by President Maxwell, the military, the CIA, the FBI, even some New York cab drivers. It took years for the furor to die down, but finally, the morons found a new topic. Then, the television interview revived their demons and gave rise to a new crop of idiots. Nice work for NYU's Stern, Dr. Epstein. Forgive my bluntness." Janet could see the dean's struggle to remain calm. "Our experts have said the model, and the thousand directions it points, seems without merit and unworthy of notice without the professor's murder."

Dr. Preedlin asked, "What experts?" Janet felt Ben grip her hand, and she quelled her reaction, while the Nobel recipient continued, "Are you saying, Abby's death gives credibility to a flawed model?"

"That's exactly what I'm saying," Boyle's smugness irritated Janet, but Ben's grip remained firm and kept her silent. Let Dean Epstein and Dr. Preedlin handle these baseless accusations.

"Does that mean we're suspects?" the dean asked. "Why are we here, Bill? You brought us here for something other than this pointless indictment."

"I'm not in a position to discuss the murder investigation," the chief replied. "It's only been a couple of days, but my last briefing indicated few leads." Now, Janet felt his eyes on her and Ben. "The President wanted to speak to Mr. Timmons and Ms. Sharpton."

As Boyle looked at each of them, some activity and muffled conversation came from the desk behind them. Then, Lily Tomlin said, "Mr. Boyle, the President will see you."

Boyle rose and gestured toward the Oval Office. "Please keep an open mind during the meeting." The secretary opened the door and waited at the entrance.

Chapter Twenty-Five
Politics and Economics

The chief of staff walked ahead, followed by Dean Epstein and Dr. Preedlin. Ben extended a hand for Janet, allowing her to walk ahead. "No profanity in the Oval Office, my dear," he said as she passed.

"Go to hell, Ben," she whispered. "Preedlin's right, though. Very exciting stuff, don't you think." They hurried to catch the rest of the group.

The Oval Office seemed smaller than she'd imagined. Her childhood bedroom had been larger, and certainly, better decorated. The office's focal point rested in the center of the room, a seating area with the famous presidential seal rug. Sacred tradition, she knew, but gaudy beyond description. Still, she felt a sense of power and prestige in the room. Then, she looked at the desk in front of the windows leading to the West Colonnade, and there sat President Jeremiah Cohen. Early Saturday morning, and he wore a kippot of the Jewish faith. The President looked up, rose from his chair, and walked from behind the desk to greet them. "Welcome, good citizens!" and he took the dean's hand. "Good to see you, Helen."

"Thank you for the invitation, Mr. President."

"I do apologize for the late hours and the tactics necessary to collect the group." Cohen turned to Dr. Preedlin, "Morris, I always feel inferior in the presence of a Nobel laureate."

As they shook hands, Dr. Preedlin said, "You're being too modest, Mr. President. It doesn't become you."

"Touché, Professor. You've uncovered my secret. Ever the politician." He looked at Janet and took her hand. "It's nice to see you, Ms. Sharpton. I trust your parents are well?"

"Yes, thank you, Mr. President."

"Give them my warmest regards." She watched as Cohen's eyes moved to Benjamin Timmons, and as Ben extended his hand, the President paused before taking it. He seemed to be sizing him up. "I know your mother, young man. How's her run for the governor's seat?"

Janet assumed the question carried a hidden intent, but Ben did not react. "It goes very well, Mr. President. The polls have her ahead. Still early, though."

"We're across the aisle, but I respect her as a worthy opponent." He released Ben's hand, and said to the group, "Please sit down."

Two comfortable sofas were on opposite sides of the rug, presidential seal in between. Timmons and Janet sat on one side, Boyle, the dean, and Dr. Preedlin on the other. An executive chair completed the seating circle, and the President sat in it. "You wouldn't believe how many Sabbaths I've spent in this office." He crossed his legs and placed his hands on the arms of the chair. Looking at Janet and Ben, he continued, "As I'm sure Mr. Boyle explained, NYU's television appearance created quite a sensation. Your individual celebrity shot through the roof, but the cost on our economy and my administration has been pretty steep. I assume you've seen the reaction of the markets?"

A chorus of acknowledgements came from his audience.

"Mr. Boyle might have impugned the NYU model, but I recognize your work contains some merit." Janet glanced toward the chief of staff, but he did not react. The President continued, "I'm not an economist, but earlier today, I received a briefing from a crowd of them. Several from DC think tanks and two from the Brookings Institute. You can imagine, the group had unlimited opinions and suggestions."

As the President paused, again, Janet glanced to Chief of Staff Boyle, the dean, and Dr. Preedlin. All seemed composed, devoid of any emotion. Beside her, Ben's breathing never changed, and he remained relaxed. She could sense where the conversation was going, and she knew Ben did too.

The President continued, "Ben and Janet, I need your assistance to suppress this investigation—for the good of the country."

A sharp rush of joy engulfed her, and just as suddenly, a sense of fear replaced it. While she tried to formulate a response, Dean Epstein said, "Mr. President, it's unfair to put such pressure on two college students." Janet looked at the dean, "I've talked to Morris—Dr. Preedlin about the reaction from the street, and I'm confident the market will settle in a day, or two."

"Do you believe that, Morris?" The President waited.

"I'm not sure Mr. Timmons and Ms. Sharpton can alter the investigation going forward, Mr. President. Their appearance on *This Day* was meant to bring some protection to the group. Unfortunately, those efforts were a little late for Dr. Agbetheatha. What's on your mind?"

The President gestured to Boyle, and he took up the explanation. "NYU's economic model and the explanation on the TV disturbed major investors in this country and around the world. Such disturbance adversely impacted the markets and carries the potential to disrupt the entire economy. On top, it's creating international uncertainty about the US's political intentions. We're too close to the last financial meltdown to risk this."

"That seems terribly dramatic, Bill." Dean Epstein sounded doubtful. "It's a school project."

"Really, Dean," Boyle chided. Janet watched him prepare for battle. "Over the past three days, the media printed dozens of stories about NYU's model. Have any of you been interviewed?" He paused, but no one answered. "I thought not, so where do you suppose they're getting the information?" With the President's apparent silent approval, Boyle continued, "Speculations about American firms tied to the conspiracy are endless. Major players in the defense industry, Homeland Security, many of our allies have been implicated as conspirators profiting from the fall of the Towers. Every blogger with a keyboard chimed in and fueled the rampant conjecture. Major players on Wall Street watched their stock fall by billions of dollars on blind speculation. That's three days, Dr. Epstein."

As her mind raced, Janet listened, but said nothing. Beside her, Ben also seemed content to wait and listen. Dr. Preedlin asked, "How are Ben and Janet supposed to aid in defusing the situation?"

Janet saw President Cohen take up the argument, "I'm a Jew sitting in the Oval Office. Since my election almost four years ago, the Muslim world's waited for me to embrace Israel and attack every Arab state. It seems the Middle East remains prepared for the next world war, or Armageddon, if you're a believer in Revelations. " Janet felt his gaze upon her. "Ridiculous, I know, but that's the reality I face."

"Forgive me, Mr. President," Janet said, "we considered various scenarios regarding our work. Proving or disproving our model doesn't change unrest in the Middle East."

President Cohen uncrossed his legs, placed both feet firmly on the floor, and leaned forward, "The fall of the Towers killed three thousand citizens and upended the political and economic systems in the United States and around the world. That September morn will always be remembered as the day terrorists attacked this country. The previous President used those ashes as justification for two wars in the Middle East, and the country embraced those actions." The President's stare rested firmly upon Ben. "Now, a decade later a group of NYU students wants to undo all those deeds by proving US industries, investors, politicians, indeed residents of the White House not only knew, but participated in the plan and completion of the attack." Janet glanced at Ben, but he remained calm, looking directly at Cohen.

Seemingly, the President realized his intensity and attempted to relax by leaning back in the chair. "The implication upon America's cornerstones is enough to disrupt the markets. Can you imagine the results of proving such?" He paused, but no one ventured, so he continued. "A national panic led to Homeland Security and The Patriot Act. Our fears of new 9/11s allowed us to forsake many of our most sacred freedoms. How much of it was necessary, and how much was overkill?"

Beside her, Ben remained motionless and silent, so Janet tried to prod his participation. "Sir, some weeks back, this discussion took place in Dr. Agbetheatha's classroom. As the model gave shape to some of our worst suspicions and pointed fingers at some of America's trusted friends, we talked about the global fallout from proving our premise. At the time, it seemed like fantasy. It still does, but our goal remained to find the truth of the attacks. I'm troubled by any political situation where fact is a problem."

"We don't have truth, Ms. Sharpton," the President said. "We have wild speculations by Dr. Agbetheatha's class. Any proof is years away, don't you agree?" He did not wait for her to reply. "Meantime, those wild speculations have thrown a shadow on us all."

"Mr. President," Dean Epstein interrupted, "I'm confused about what you seek from this meeting. What do you expect from us?"

Cohen continued, "According to all the pundits, I owe my election to the popularity of President Maxwell. I'm the coattails president, able to overcome being Jewish, even among the religious right in the South." Now, he looked at Dr. Preedlin. "But, Maxwell left me with many problems, too. I inherited a collapsing economy, an unfunded social security system, exploding defense spending, financial ruin triggered by high-risk debt from several decades of—what's the popular term used by the talking heads?" He looked at Boyle. "Kicking the can down the road," and his chief of staff nodded.

Dr. Preedlin leaned forward on the sofa. "Excuse me, Mr. President, but isn't that a reason to bring these issues into the light?"

"I long for the sterile environment of academia, Morris. Unfortunately, every morning I'm briefed on the real world of troop movements, weapons developments, border incursions, speculations on the next 9/11. With accurate data and full access, it could still take years to prove the premise of the model. I can't give you that time, and I won't allow wild speculations to undermine a very fragile peace. I can't see the benefit for proving any of it."

"Again, what are you asking of us, Mr. President?" Ben's voice startled Janet.

President Cohen looked at Ben, but Boyle explained. "Starting tomorrow, we're prepared to disavow the accuracy of your model. We have experts ready to undermine the project, and they'll sell the argument. We'll have one of them on every news show until the message gets out, and we'd like NYU and the students to cooperate. Assist us by sitting out. In a few days, the bloggers will find another windmill, and the model will go the way of other conspiracy theories."

Dean Epstein interrupted, "Mr. President, these students put thousands of hours into this project. Abdelle Agbetheatha's death is somehow related. You can't expect Ben and Janet to walk away. If they allowed your experts to undermine without challenge, it effectively kills any chance to resurrect the project in the future." Janet watched her turn to Dr. Preedlin, looking for support, "Morris, can you help me out with this?" but the Nobel laureate remained silent, as if in deep thought.

The President spoke, his voice very quiet, but his words echoed. "The events leading to the current economic malaise began long before that fateful day. Many were the unnoticed and unreported votes in Congress. Over the years, we moved the world's largest economy from the farms, factories, and offices of middle America to the high rises of Wall Street with dollars chasing nickels in derivatives, buybacks, and hedges." He paused a moment. "I read one of the investment groups offered a global derivative. Morris, what the hell is a derivative, and how the hell do you hedge on the world's economy? Maybe, you could explain the math behind that calculation? A young computer geek writes a program, utilizing several sophisticated algorithms and the farmer in Iowa sells short and makes more money than planting a crop of corn. How is that good for the country?"

"Mr. President," Dr. Preedlin glanced at the dean while he spoke, "Abby paid me a great compliment when he involved me in the project, but with all that has happened, I'm reluctant to interject myself in NYU's business."

"We're beyond that, Morris," Boyle sounded irritated. "Give us your thoughts."

Dr. Preedlin's displeasure toward the chief of staff showed, but he addressed the President. "NYU attempted to identify potential architects of our economic malaise. I've dedicated my life to the science, and when I started, economics was the pursuit of efficiencies in markets. We studied the phenomena of unlimited demand with limited supply and the ultimate goal of finding equilibrium in the system. The whole world's benefited from fairness in distribution."

"Your point, Morris?" the President asked.

Janet watched Preedlin deliver his argument. "At some point in our past, the United States changed the goal from fairness to return on investment. In my opinion Washington and Wall Street have cooperated on this for decades to the world's detriment. The system's been corrupted, and these kids believe they can identify the mother of all atrocities."

The President adjusted his tie and smoothed his jacket. "I read your file, Ben," dismissing Preedlin's plea.

Beside her, Ben shifted on the sofa. "I didn't know I had a file," he said.

"You're a musician, and a fan of The Beatles?"

"Yes, sir."

"Unusual for someone so young. After all, The Beatles broke up twenty years before you were born."

"The influence of my father, Mr. President." Janet glanced at Dr. Preedlin, but he seemed to accept the change in direction.

"I knew that," Cohen admitted. "My favorite Beatles's song is *Revolution*. Do you know that one?"

Janet looked at Ben and saw him smile. "I know it well."

"John Lennon sang about his desire to change the world, but he emphasized that destruction wasn't part of the plan." Cohen turned to Dr. Preedlin. "I've had just forty-one months, Morris. Yes, I agree with you. Management of the system by our elected officials has been terrible—borderline moronic. And since that September day, it's been criminal. I know our education system has been in decline, but to overlook this, we'd have to be the dumbest nation in history. However, I don't think destruction holds the answer. I need more time, and NYU's model jeopardizes that." The President turned away from Dr. Preedlin and addressed Ben and Janet. "That's what I need from you two. Much of what you and your group have done is historic, but it carries great risk. I need to manage that risk in the near term before I can hope to correct any of it in the future. Will you help me?"

Janet sat in silence beside Ben while the others waited. While she thought, her heart continued to pound in her ears, and suddenly, the eagle on the rug didn't seem so gaudy. Her parents had told her stories of President Cohen, his dedication, his drive to succeed. Even though he sat in silence beside her, she knew Ben had already decided. And with that, she made up her mind.

"Well, Mr. President," she said, "as a child, I envisioned this scenario—sitting in the Oval Office, some issue of national importance before us, and the President asking for my assistance. However, this is not the game of children, now." She looked to the other sofa with the chief, Dr. Preedlin, and Dean Epstein waiting. "I don't know what Ben will decide," she continued, "but, with all due respect, I have to decline, sir."

"Are you sure?" Dean Epstein asked.

"Yes, Dean." She felt Ben's hand touch her arm in silent assurance. "I heard the words—matter of national importance, avoiding destruction of the system, and global economics. If we are correct, manipulation of the system has brought us to the brink of ruin. Allowing those architects of destruction to remain in the shadows does not seem patriotic to me. It seems criminal."

"Young lady," Boyle interrupted, "you might disagree with the man, but you need to be aware of the office."

"I respect the man and the office, Mr. Boyle." Janet paused to look at the faces in the group. "But I can't go along with this request."

"Didn't buy any of it, Ms. Sharpton?" Cohen questioned her with a look of subdued determination on his face.

"Forgive me, Mr. President, but I've heard bullshit before." Again, Ben touched her arm, but she pulled away. "Dr. Agbetheatha had a favorite line from an old movie. I can't do it with his accent, so it loses something, but he would tell us not to piss down his neck and try to convince him it was raining." A look of shock appeared on the dean's face, but Dr. Preedlin laughed.

The President looked to Ben. "Mr. Timmons, can we entreat you to convince Ms. Sharpton?"

Janet turned to look at Ben. His gaze met hers, and she detected a sadness. "I don't know the results of our model. I'd hoped for continued work in our senior year, but without Dr. Agbetheatha." His words were a painful reminder to her. "Going forward will be Dean Epstein's decision, along with the powers at NYU. I assume you've already had discussions, and this meeting seems to convey they've agreed to cooperate?" Cohen confirmed without words. Ben looked at Janet, and she felt his closeness. "Thanks for the consideration, sir, but you don't need us to agree, do you?"

"You and Ms. Sharpton have bright futures, Mr.

Timmons. I'd do a disservice to my position, if I allowed this to be a real negotiation."

Janet looked at Dean Epstein, but she sat in stunned silence. Ben continued, "Sir, over the past few weeks, I've been pushed, pulled, prodded in various directions. Each interested party tried to guide me away from the direction I wanted to go. This meeting seems very familiar."

"I'm sincere in my request, young man." Cohen leaned ever so slightly toward Ben. "At today's press conference, I fielded questions about possible Saudi royal family involvement in 9/11. Your recklessness forced me to repress accusations directed at Syria, Egypt, Libya, Iran, and Pakistan. After that press conference, the stock market fell six percent in afternoon trading."

"I love my country, sir," Ben's voice stayed soft and the room quiet. "I don't want to harm it in any way. You're asking me to hide—indeed—destroy the truth. I've always believed Al Qaeda's goal was the economic destruction of the United States, and on that basis, I've been amazed over the past ten years, as I watched our leaders blindly stumble toward that end. Our model might dispel the notion of a blind stumble, and it might uncover an involved plan by many participants. Please don't ask me to destroy that, sir. Dr. Agbetheatha deserves better from us. And forgive my impertinence, but the country deserves better from you, too."

Janet watched Cohen's eyes move from her face to Ben's and back. "Bill, will you explain to Dean Epstein, Dr. Preedlin, and the students?" Cohen leaned back in the chair, and for the moment, closed his eyes.

"Our team of analysts identified data in the model

of dubious origin." Boyle waited for the effect from his statement to sink in.

"What do you mean?" As Dean Epstein asked, her eyes went to Janet and Ben.

"Our analysts identified information that could only have been provided by America's enemies." The dean's gaze remained on Ben and Janet. "We assumed Dr. Agbetheatha's contacts provided the data. However, in the end it will be NYU using propoganda provided by Al Qaeda, the Taliban, Hamas, Syria, Iran. Is that the legacy you desire, Dean?"

"I'm sorry to use this against you," President Cohen looked at Ben and Janet. "I'd hate to see your futures undermined. By the end of next year, you will have spent two hundred thousand dollars on an NYU education. Misplay this, and that investment could be worthless."

"Mr. President, that threat is beneath—" the dean reacted.

"Helen, you should consider the impact on endowments." Cohen's statement quieted her.

"I'm working on a project in Arkansas, Mr. President." Ben looked at Janet, and now, she touched his arm. He winked at her. "It's a family matter, and I don't know how long it will take."

"I know of your summer, Mr. Timmons."

"Yes, sir, I'm sure you do." He paused probably to gather his thoughts. Janet admired his practical side, but wished he'd hide it in this situation. After a moment, he said, "Sir, whether I agree or disagree with your handling of the national economy, I do recognize the problems you assumed when you took office. And I do understand many of the nation's problems originated with bad decisions from decades before. You've tried to monetize the situation with deficit spending, and I disagree with that approach. Eventually, payment of the national debt will come due, and my generation will suffer that burden. I think we have a right to know how we got into this mess."

"I agree with you, young Ben." The President had a look of resignation on his face. "I entered this office with the hope of uniting a divided country. We're not just economically divided, but culturally, morally, religiously, and educationally—all joined by a universal state of confusion, ignorance, if you will." He looked at Dr. Preedlin. "Morris, I've studied and admired your work for years. Surely, you understand the precarious nature of a global economy."

Preedlin answered, "I do, Mr. President."

"Then, please help me persuade Ms. Sharpton and Mr. Timmons. We can't tear it down and start over. We have to tweak it, slowly."

"Sir," Ben said, "in my opinion we suffer from a political system that has rendered ninety percent of the population irrelevant. The right moves further to the right, and the left moves further to the left. Elections are being decided by the ten percent in the chasm, and the election process invests billions of dollars, trying to convince six percent. Don't you think such a process sells the average American short?"

"Such statements play into our plan, young man." Boyle couldn't hide his pleasure. "Americans get the type of government they deserve."

Janet watched Ben ignore him and look at the President. "The politicians strike fear into the poor, the affirmed, the elderly, the uneducated, and the minorities. Both parties pretend to be concerned, all the while ignoring the real needs. Over the past decade the United States has seen an erosion of the middle class. This economy has more college-educated fry cooks than at any time in history. Regressive practices abound like alcohol and cigarette taxes, state lotteries, public-funded casinos, bingo parlors, payday loans, a long list of vices and scams designed to take back as much as possible. Why do it?" Just as she thought he'd concluded, he continued, "I'd hoped we could regain the educated participation of the ninety percent without the use of fear and prejudice. Is that too much to expect?"

Cohen sighed and stood, "Well, it's been a long day. Thank you for coming." The group rose from their seats in respect to the office. Janet saw that the President's eyes never left Ben. "I'm sorry we couldn't come to an agreement." He did not extend his hand, and Ben did not reply. After a moment, Cohen said, "You're going to lose on this matter." He turned and walked across the office to the glass doors leading to the colonnade. Before he exited, he paused, "I inherited this. I can't fix it in forty-one months. Good Sabbath." Everyone watched him leave.

Boyle said to Dr. Preedlin and Dean Epstein, "We have a flight ready to return you to New York." They looked at each other, but said nothing. "Mr. Timmons, a flight to Little Rock will not be available until morning. We'll put you in a hotel for a few hours."

"That's not necessary," Ben shook his head. "I'll wait at the airport."

"Suit yourself," Boyle said. "Thank you for coming."

"I'm not going to New York," Janet heard herself say. "I'm going to Little Rock, too."

"What?" Dean Epstein asked. "Are you sure, Janet?"

Ben said nothing. She continued, "Yes, I'm sure. I've always wanted to visit Arkansas. Seems like a good opportunity."

Ben chuckled, "You'll fit right in. I have a possible love-interest, and I can't wait to introduce you. The two of you can compare silver spoons." She punched his shoulder and laughed. "Seriously," he continued, "you need to go home. It's still dangerous."

"I'm going with you," she said.

Boyle left them at the secretary's desk, and two attendants escorted them through the West Wing to the back exit. On the walk, Dr. Preedlin asked, "Any idea how they got the information? Even for the federal government, that was pretty complete."

"My guess," Ben said, "the President made a deal with a Syrian educator."

"And who would that be?" Dean Epstein asked.

"Dr. Hameed." And immediately, Janet knew he was right. "I wonder what kind of deal Hameed brokered with the President. Can you imagine a Syrian negotiating with a Jew in the Oval Office?" Then, before they all climbed into the black SUV, Ben said to Dr. Epstein, "I assume you'll pull the plug on our project?"

The dean looked at him, said nothing, patted his arm, and climbed into the vehicle.

Dr. Preedlin leaned close to Janet and Ben, "She'll have little choice on the project. It sounds like the powers at NYU made a decision. Finish your business in Arkansas, and come see me when you get back to the city."

In silence, Janet and Ben entered the other SUV for the short ride to Reagan International. At the terminal a Secret Service agent held the door and handed them two tickets for an 8:00 a.m. flight to Little Rock. "Be careful," was all he said.

As they stood on the sidewalk, watching the vehicle drive away, Janet said, "We should've accepted the offer for the hotel."

Ben shook his head, "No rest for the weary and I can't sleep. Too much has happened over the past few days. My mind is racing, and this latest episode changes the whole ballgame. I wish you'd go back to New York, Janet. I sense trouble ahead."

"Me, too," she said. "That's why I'm going with you."

Chapter Twenty-Six
What's Love Got To Do With It?

Dan Rappart sat in a corner chair and watched the moon beams streaming through the skylight over Christina's bed, casting a faint ambient glimmer over her naked body. He, too, was naked, trying to decide whether to wake her, or get dressed and leave. As he sat admiring her curves and listening to her breathing, he felt overwhelmed by the pure pleasure of looking at a woman who had just given herself to him. Fifty and still beautiful, he wanted her, again, and felt an immense satisfaction in gaining her charms.

The pounding in his chest and the throb in his abdomen reaffirmed his desire, and all thoughts of leaving disappeared. He'd been trying to bed Christina since old man Staten's death, so tonight had to be savored. He knew she played him for a fool, and he didn't mind letting her think it. A buffoon seldom received such rewards. He'd let her think whatever she wanted, as long as she made payment in her bedroom. So, he sat quietly in the darkness with a look of satisfaction on his face.

He knew he'd surprised Willis and Christina by storming out of the study, interrupting the meeting. Mostly pretend on his part, but he'd kept them guessing. At this stage in his life, dignity and honor had been sacrificed long ago, but he liked Ben Timmons.

Rappart recognized the eventual end of the kid's journey. Nothing he could do about it, he didn't have to relish it, and he didn't enjoy pencil pushers like Baker plotting to destroy the kid. Rappart knew it meant nothing to Willis, or Maxwell. They'd never been in trenches, never depended upon the sacrifice of others, and never witnessed real courage like Ben's.

Too many years ago, he'd cast his lot with old man Staten and after his death, Ms. Pritchard. He'd turned a blind eye to their arrangements, allowing business to be conducted with only a minimum of legal scrutiny. They'd appreciated his cooperation, and he'd been well compensated. Over the years, he'd learned to ignore the faceless victims pummeled under the wheels of greed. Ignoring the meek had become second nature. Why the change of heart over this issue—this kid?

Maybe, defending Ben Timmons had something to do with Matt. Even as boys, the brothers had never been close—always going different directions. Protecting Matt, helping him keep a job and covering sins, had more to do with family name than affection. Now, allowing the kid's destruction by Maxwell and Boyle also destroyed Matt. In the darkness of Christina's bedroom, he wondered how much he'd care, if Rappart wasn't the last name.

After the episode of storming from the club study, he'd smoked a cigarette and hurried to the dining room, arriving with the rest of the guests. He earned a knowing glance from Christina, a scowl from the President's chief of staff, but Maxwell and the Pritchard ladies didn't seem to notice his tardiness. He took a chair in the middle of the table, and even though Reverend Kinson sat beside him, he ordered a scotch on the rocks. "Been a long day," he said to the reverend, and the minister nodded. Ken Simington took a chair on the other side of the minister and ordered coffee. Christina and Baker sat across from Rappart.

Maxwell sat at the head of the table, Tonya on his right and Ms. Pritchard on the left. "Ladies and gentlemen, thank you for coming." The President's words brought a sense of order to the proceedings. "While you're getting your drinks, I'd like to introduce you to a special guest." All eyes turned to the other end of the table and the mystery lady sitting beside Special Agent Levitt. "Dr. Maureen Fitzpatrick is a forensic pathologist from Little Rock. She teaches at the university and works with LRPD. Welcome, Maureen."

"Thank you for inviting me, Mr. President." The sheriff looked at the lady for several seconds, trying to guess her role in this evening's actions. She noticed his gaze, so he turned away. The scene would play out soon enough.

"I'd like to go ahead with the discussion before dinner," the President continued. "We're here to discuss this Timmons situation, and I want each of you to be candid. Our goal this evening is to formulate a plan to repress this young man's investigation into a very old, painful tragedy in our community's history. We've got nothing to hide, so feel free to speak your mind." He paused for a glance at Ms. Pritchard. "While I admire the courage of youth, reliving the event does nothing for Powhatan, or the citizens." Rappart noticed a few nods of approval from the group, but no one spoke. "To begin, Levitt will brief the group on the young man's movements, as we know them. After she finishes, I'll ask Dr. Fitzpatrick to give us her take. Agent Levitt, please."

Rappart's eyes turned to Levitt as she rose to her feet. "First, I'd like to remove the staff and the other agents." She motioned to her underlings, and they hurriedly cleared all non-participants to the discussion. As the doors closed, she continued, "When Mr. Timmons left Powhatan twelve days ago, he traveled to Little Rock and retrieved the official record of the 1967 incident. After reviewing the documents and with the help of NYU's dean, he contacted Dr. Fitzpatrick. She'll detail those meetings."

The pathologist acknowledged this with a slight gesture, but nothing else. "Mr. Timmons returned to New York last Saturday for unknown reasons, and, of course, on Tuesday the NYU group made the appearance on *This Day*. I've spoken to Detective Calleran with the NYPD about the murder of the students' professor, Dr. Agbetheatha, a Muslim from Lebanon."

"With a name like that, I didn't think he was from Ireland," the reverend uttered, causing Maxwell to laugh and Levitt to glare.

"I hope I pronounced his name correctly," the agent paused, but no one felt compelled to correct her. "That murder seems related to the NYU project, although Detective Calleran told me Mr. Timmons believes it has something to do with Powhatan."

"Why the hell would he think that?" the President interrupted. "How would anyone here even know of an obscure NYU economics professor, much less want him dead? God dammit, Levitt! Excuse me, Reverend."

"He's not that obscure." Tonya seemed bored by the President's brief tirade.

"What?" He turned to Tonya, but hid some of his edge. "Did you say something, dear?"

She looked more irritated. "I said Dr. Agbetheatha's contributions are well known in the field of national and global economics. He's won numerous awards and held one of the most respected positions in academia."

Now, it was the President's turn to look annoyed. "They're witch doctors! All they do is calculate, using equations no one understands. They make wild-ass guesses, and when they're wrong, they give you another algorithm that explains the error caused by government manipulation. It's all bullshit!"

Maxwell's statement brought an end to the brief discussion, and after a few seconds of silence, Levitt continued, "There doesn't seem to be any connection to the professor's murder and this local situation, sir. However, it's too early in the investigation to eliminate the possibility."

She hesitated, and looked at Rappart. From that telltale glance, the sheriff guessed what was coming. "Young Benjamin found something from his few days in Powhatan. He has a relative on the Elkton police force, and Timmons got them to re-open the investigation of his father's death."

"What'd he find?" Maxwell interrupted.

"Excuse me, sir?" Levitt looked confused.

"You said he found something that started Indiana looking. What'd he find?"

"I don't know, Mr. President," she looked at Rappart, again. "Detective Danielson told me the young man triggered the investigation, and they found evidence of murder and Matthew Rappart's palm print on the vehicle." Now, the sheriff saw several pairs of eyes turn in his direction.

"Know anything about that, Dan?" and he had to calm himself over the question.

"No sir, Mr. President." He started to end with that, but decided not. "I talked to Danielson, and he suspects the print to be a plant."

"What the hell does that mean?" Rappart watched the ex-president's anger rise to the surface. "Is that even possible? Maureen?"

Now, all eyes turned to the pathologist. "A palm print would be impossible. I would look for other evidence. I haven't spoken to the Elkton detective, so I don't know his thinking."

"Impossible! There!" Maxwell looked indignantly at Levitt. "So, Matthew Rappart did it, and he's dead. Damn good thing, too. Indiana would be looking to put a needle in his arm." The ex-president's gaze landed on the sheriff. "You cremated the sonofabitch, so we can't confirm?" Rappart only stared back at Maxwell. "God dammit! Go on, Levitt."

"Mr. Timmons left New York on Tuesday evening for his home in Indiana. He spent one day in Elkton, one day in Chicago, and today, he visited Fort Leavenworth, Kansas."

"Why Kansas?"

"Military records, Mr. President," Dr. Fitzpatrick cut in.

"That's correct, sir," Levitt confirmed. "He picked up his uncle's military file."

Maxwell looked at Ms. Pritchard, as she spoke for the first time. "Did Fort Leavenworth give him the complete file?"

Levitt hesitated, "I don't have a confirmation on that, ma'am, but it's a forty-five year old case. I doubt they withheld anything."

Ms. Pritchard turned to the President, "We didn't get anyone in there ahead of the boy?"

Maxwell looked embarrassed, "No, we missed it." Then, he looked up and asked, "Maureen, how'd you know about Fort Leavenworth?"

"Ben and I discussed it last week." Dr. Fitzpatrick looked embarrassed.

"God dammit, Maureen!" The President's voice was overly loud, and Rappart wondered if it was for Ms. Pritchard's benefit.

"Anything else, Special Agent Levitt?" Tonya asked, ignoring Maxwell's theatrics.

"He had a flight scheduled for this evening, returning to Little Rock. We've tagged his car at the airport." The agent glanced at the notes in her hand. "At the request of President Cohen, Secret Service agents intercepted Mr. Timmons, and he's on his way to DC. Tomorrow via commercial airline, he's supposed to return to Little Rock."

"Wait, the Secret Service took the boy to Washington. The kid's going to see Cohen?" Maxwell asked. "Why?"

Again, referring to her notes, "My sources tell me the President is pulling the plug on the NYU project."

"And how the hell is he doing that?"

"He's using articles of the Patriot Act. The NYU project has been linked to terrorist countries."

"That's great!" Maxwell's mood changed noticeably. "Willis, we can use that!" and the chief of staff jotted notes. Excited by this new information, the ex-president chatted in subdued tones with the Pritchards. Levitt stood for a second longer, and then, took her seat.

Across the table, Christina and Dr. Fitzpatrick were in deep conversation. The good doctor detailed the kind of information in an old military file, and the journalist paid close attention. Rappart turned to the reverend, "Where do you suppose this is going?" The sheriff's glass was empty, and he wanted a refill. He looked around the room, but there were no servants. "Guess the rest of the discussion will be in a dry county."

The reverend didn't appear to appreciate his humor. "His words about your brother were harsh. I'm sorry for that, Dan."

"I appreciate your kindness, Preacher, but the shit's hit the fan. That kid's back tomorrow, or Sunday, and he's coming with proof in his hand."

"I put my faith in God, Dan."

"Preacher, I think God might be on the kid's side in this matter." With that, Reverend Kinson turned away, so Rappart silently looked around the table. The conversation between the pathologist and the reporter continued, monitored by the special agent and the president's chief of staff. At the end of the table, Maxwell conferred with the Pritchards, and the reverend listened. Rappart looked at Simington, sitting beside him. The attorney said nothing, shrugged, and sipped his coffee.

After a few more minutes, Maxwell banged on his water glass with his bread knife. "Listen up, people. We're going to get on Cohen's bandwagon and tie Timmons to Islam. If it can kill the NYU project, it should help us. Everyone know their roles?" He paused, looking at each participant. "My legacy's tied to this, so no slip ups." He waited for a moment. "Let's have dinner." Maxwell motioned to Levitt, and she keyed a transmitter and spoke. A moment later, the servants returned to bring the meal, and activity around the dining room increased. With alcohol flowing, Rappart ordered another drink, and with encouragement, even the reverend had a beer.

During the main course, Maxwell took up the conversation, again. "Dr. Fitzpatrick, when Timmons gets back in town, what's he going to have?"

All eyes turned to the good doctor. "First, Mr. President, I want to disavow any participation in tonight's strategy. I'm here to offer my expertise, and hopefully, as this matter plays out, preserve the reputation of the state."

"Goddammit, Maureen! I know that!" He slammed his fork on the table, and one of the servants hurried to replace it with a clean one. "Stop being so politically correct and answer my god damned question."

Rappart, as well as everyone else, saw the frustration on the face of the doctor. "Mr. Timmons has information accumulated by his father, a very complete file. I don't know the origin of the information, but it was a first-rate job." She paused a moment, and Rappart thought it a tactic to control her anger at Maxwell's antics. "Benjamin Timmons has a keen mind, and he'd calculated the angles of fire, velocity of the weapon, location of wounds, and from that, he concluded the storage room couldn't have been the site of the shooting." Rappart turned to look at Ms. Pritchard. She noticed his gaze, but she didn't react. Tonya, on the other hand, showed a great amount of stress. Dr. Fitzpatrick continued, "A notation in the file indicated Joshua Timmons had not separated from the military at the time of his death, meaning he was working undercover." Again, she paused, and the hesitation went on for several seconds. "My experience tells me his mission in Powhatan at that time was to track drug shipments from Southeast Asia. Benjamin Timmons went to Fort Leavenworth to confirm that."

"He's gonna have all that?" Maxwell didn't ask it like a question. "Shit!"

Tonya said, "Let's finish dinner and dismiss everyone. The three of us can confer afterwards."

Maxwell nodded, "Yes, yes, everyone enjoy the dinner, so we can adjourn."

A half-hour later, as they exited the club, Christina excused herself and moved out of earshot to take a phone call. As he stood chatting with the reverend and Simington, Rappart kept an eye on her and wondered about the topic of the conversation. Another five minutes, she returned, said good-bye to everyone, and got in the vehicle.

Maybe it was the scotch or that tight skirt she wore, but when they arrived at her door, he made a clumsy move on her, and she didn't resist. While his hands explored her body and his tongue in her mouth, she practically pulled him into the house. He couldn't get her clothes off fast enough, almost tearing them away. Only seconds in her house, they fell into her bed.

In the twilight she shifted just a bit and let out a faint snore, bringing his thoughts back to the present. In the night calm, he listened to her, continuing to admire her naked form. All the time she'd resisted his advances, he'd convinced himself her role as old man

Staten's mistress prevented it. But after the old bastard died, Rappart had still been denied her bed. Tonight, he'd taken all of her, and in his mind, it'd been worth the wait.

At the same time, he realized she hadn't suddenly succumbed to his charms. Something had changed in their relationship, and he knew she'd given him sex to divert, confuse, or make him susceptible to her directions. He wondered if she thought he'd kill Timmons for her. Was she that deeply involved? Whatever Staten had on her, he still dictated to her from the grave.

Early Saturday morning, and he'd be on call in a few hours. He knew he should get dressed and go home to his wife. Still, the beautiful body in front of him held him captive, and if Christina was willing to pay the price, it'd be an insult for him not to accept. He rubbed her naked butt, rousing her. "Hey, baby." As she rolled onto her back, his mouth moved to her breasts, and he positioned himself over her. "I need you, again," he whispered. She didn't refuse. That should have worried him, but he had other things on his mind. "I've got time for one more go. Why don't you pretend to love me?"

Chapter Twenty-Seven
Into the Fire

He left Powhatan in the morning darkness, and on the drive to Little Rock, had watched the sun come up. A much nicer day than the last time he'd tracked a Timmons, and the memory of Indiana's cold sent a chill through him. Eighteen months later, and still that night wouldn't leave him. Another goddamned rice farmer.

As the sun moved higher, the freshness of the air blowing into the open car window lifted his spirits and diverted his thoughts from the task ahead. Entering the capital, light mid-morning traffic greeted him, and he had little trouble getting across the city to the airport. He parked his vehicle across Airport Road in a hotel parking lot, not wanting to attract attention, and walked over to Arrival.

Inside the terminal, cameras monitored the entire area, standard airport practice since 9/11. Airport security personnel on foot reinforced the electronic surveillance, and he knew it'd be problematic for his task, so he'd prepared. Large dark sunglasses disguised his facial features and a large cowboy hat, pulled down, hid his hair. The rest of his wardrobe consisted of nondescript articles selected for just this situation. He'd even changed his wrist watch, wedding ring, anything that could identify him. A small carry-on bag provided two advantages—it helped him blend into the surroundings and held the tools of his task ahead.

All the cameras were high, so he kept his head down, and after only a few minutes, he'd identified the security personnel and timed their patrol routine. Casually, he exited the terminal and headed for the parking areas. He had to find Timmons's rental car.

The only cameras visible in parking were at the entrance and exit toll booth, reducing his anxiety as he searched. No hurry, plenty of time, just had to find the vehicle with a New York plate. If the kid was lucky and had parked in a busy location, the job couldn't be completed, and the plan would have to be scrapped. He could be back in Powhatan for lunch.

But, the kid's luck had run out, and he'd parked the Ford on the second floor of the adjoining garage—one of only a handful of cars on the parking level. Security patrolled the garages, too, so he stood out of site and watched, timing their route. He waited for more than an hour, but after that time, he was confident of the routine. Twenty-two minutes between patrols—not a lot of time, but good enough. Some C4 with a remote detonator should do the trick. He surveyed the parking area for a strategic location, obscure enough for him to remain unnoticed, but with a view of the Timmons's parked car. At the far end of the area next to the exit stairway sat a trash dumpster that could hide his presence.

Sure of his timing, he waited for the patrolling officer to clear the area before he approached the vehicle. Opening his bag, he took out plastic gloves and pulled them on his hands. Next, he removed a police issue Slim Jim and worked on unlocking the car door. It took him a few minutes to work the magic on the

Taurus, but finally, he got it open, reached inside the driver's compartment, and popped the hood latch.

He checked the area before removing the C4 from the bag. Quickly, he pressed the plastic explosive against the engine firewall, positioning it just ahead of the steering wheel. The resulting explosion would go directly at the kid. No chance of surviving, especially when the fuel in the gas tank ignited, too. Next, he readied and placed the detonator. The trigger with fresh batteries remained in the bag. He surveyed his work one final time, and it met his approval. Everything perfect, he was just about to close the hood.

"Are you having car trouble, sir?"

Leaning back from the engine compartment, he looked toward the voice. At the rear of the vehicle stood a traveler with a suitcase, the owner of one of the other parked cars. His mind raced, trying to decide a course of action. Hiding his hands from sight, realizing they'd be difficult to explain, he removed the plastic gloves and stuffed them behind one of the engine hoses. "Dead battery," he told the guy, casually lowering the hood a bit to hide his real intent. "I guess, it's been parked here too long."

"Yeah, I travel a lot, too," Good Samaritan said. "I just got in from Dallas. Do you have jumper cables?"

He'd brought the Makarov with silencer attached, all in the bag at his feet. A quick glance around the parking level confirmed no other passersby to bother them. "No, I don't." The guy looked hard at his face, so no other decision could be made. "Can you give me an assist? I'd really appreciate it."

"I'm just up the corridor," the guy said. "Let me pull my car over here." As Good Samaritan turned to walk away, he bent down to his bag and retrieved the pistol. The man hadn't taken more than a few steps when the loud whoosh of the weapon caused him to lurch forward onto his face. Blood stained the back of his shirt, and his suitcase slid along the concrete.

Another rice farmer, he thought. He grabbed the abandoned suitcase and threw it behind one of the other parked cars. Hastily, he took the dead man by the arms and dragged him toward the dumpster. He moved quickly, because the Samaritan wasn't a large man, but the stress of the situation still winded him as he stuffed the body into the container.

Rushing back to the Taurus, he took electrical wire from the carry-on bag. The remote detonator was out, now. He could no longer afford to wait for Timmons's arrival, not with a corpse in the dumpster. He'd have to direct wire the explosive to the starter. Crude, and no fail safe, but the do-gooder had forced a change of plan. It took only a minute to complete the bomb. He closed the hood, and even though the explosion would destroy any prints, he used a rag and wiped—just in case. Quickly, he put everything back in the bag and hurried past the dumpster to the stairway. Just before he rushed out, he surveyed the area one last time. Damn bad luck for me, he thought.

Five minutes later, he eased back into his vehicle in the parking lot. The June day in Arkansas grew warm, especially as the sun rose higher in the sky. He'd thought about stopping in the heart of the city and using a cab to the airport, but he'd rejected the idea. Guessing he might have to spend time waiting before the job's completion and needing to leave immediately afterwards, he'd decided to use his own vehicle. Now, with windows down and the radio tuned to a local country music station, he relaxed and settled in for the wait.

He checked his wristwatch. The kid's flight was not due to arrive for almost two hours, leaving him enough time for a relaxing breakfast. He closed up his car and headed to the hotel restaurant.

Afterwards, as he sipped his coffee and read the Saturday *Arkansas Democrat*, he thought about Ben Timmons. He had difficulty cataloging all the kid's movements and accomplishments over the past two weeks. The NYU student's actions had most of Powhatan's prominent citizens in an uproar, and everyone knew how close the boy was to putting the whole story together. The investigation had created a perilous situation for several prominent Powhatan citizens, making it much too dangerous for the kid to survive. He regretted that thought, knowing C4 waited for the turn of an ignition key.

Like everyone who'd lived for any amount of time in Northeastern Arkansas, he knew much about the area's history. The accepted story of old man Staten's fortune coming from farming played well with the tax people and the bankers who laundered the money, but citizens in the community suspected other revenue streams built the old man's fortune.

Soon after, Staten had politicians and police on his payroll, and his power connections kept his group in control and out of trouble. Joshua Timmons's arrival on the scene in 1967 had shaken the foundation of the organization, and his death a few months later forced the whole operation to move from Powhatan. Even though the setup moved, the brain trust remained in the small rural community where police and courts came with a firm price, and most other residents were disenfranchised enough to overlook the bending of laws and rules. Before his discharge from the army, he'd been recruited by Staten cohorts who needed his particular skill set. He shared a disregard for laws and rules, and his anarchist willingness proved a strong selling point for his new career.

He glanced at the clock on the wall of the restaurant, and realized the time had come to get back to his car. Timmons should be arriving soon, and that thought sent a pang of guilt through him. He genuinely liked the kid, and he wanted this job to be over. He knew the long drive back to Powhatan wasn't going to be good for his conscience. Still, at his age and after so many years in the shadows exacting vengeance or inflicting punishment for other people, he realized morality hadn't completely abandoned him.

An hour passed as he waited, but Timmons hadn't arrived. The stupidity in which this half-assed move had come together was matched only by the absurdity of no escape plan. If Timmons didn't show up, how'd he get the explosive out of the vehicle? The body in the dumpster would be discovered, probably later today. What then?

As he waited, he thought about one of their last conversations before the kid left town. "Tell me something, Ben." He'd looked closely at the boy's face, "What do you really hope to accomplish from nosin' 'round in ancient history? And don't give me redemption of your father, closure, or that other psychological bullshit. What's the real reason?"

The youngster grinned at him, "You've taken away

my platitudes, forcing me to really examine my motives. You should've been a therapist." They both laughed, and then he explained, "My father's idealism brought me here."

"I thought he was an accountant?"

"Runs against the teachings of the profession, doesn't it." Then, his face grew serious, "He always wanted to make a difference. He didn't want money, power, or celebrity. He would tell me to make a difference, and if I did, I would truly touch immortality."

"Wow, that's deep," he'd responded. "I don't know what the hell it means, but it's heavy."

"Thank you for the generational clichés," Ben replied. "I didn't know what it meant until after he'd died. Standing at his grave site, looking at the stone, and it hit me. The sum of my dad's life written on that rock—his name, birthdate, and the day he died. Not much to show."

"Isn't that how we all end up?"

"I guess, but as I stood there at his graveside, for the first time in my life, I understood the significance of making a difference."

"Was he a religious man?" he'd asked.

And then the kid said something he still couldn't work out. "I think he was a hopeful man, and don't we all hope our life's journey to death brings more than just an end.".

His thoughts of past conversations were jarred away by the sound of an explosion. He looked to the parking garage and telltale flames, smoke, and debris flew from the second floor. Other travelers ran from the area, men, women, children, some crying. Security and maintenance personnel emerged from all directions, pointing, shouting, waving the travelers away from the building. A few grabbed fire extinguishers and rushed up the stairways, or ran up the entrance ramp.

He watched for just a minute more, and then, time to go. Powhatan called to him, and he had more work to do. He started the engine, backed from the parking space, and headed away from the airport. "So long, Ben."

Chapter Twenty-Eight
Press Conference

Andrew Maxwell stood on the top landing of Powhatan's courthouse and looked at the gathered reporters on the steps below. Mayor Phillips, at the outside podium, extended the obligatory welcome to the visitors of the press, and prepared to start the news conference by introducing the ex-president.

Standing beside Maxwell, Willis Baker looked nervous as he whispered bits of advice, pointing out obvious topics to avoid. Special Agent Levitt stood at her usual position to the rear of the President, alert and ready to react to any situation. Several of her colleagues positioned themselves at strategic locations, and others circulated through the crowd of twenty members of the fourth estate and several hundred of the town's citizens. A few of Sheriff Rappart's men were positioned at each end of the street, rerouting traffic.

As he waited, the ex-president studied some of the faces looking his way. The people of Powhatan stared blankly and waited for his words of wisdom, as if he delivered manna from heaven. He'd long despised press conferences. He considered most reporters morons, whose only talent was constructing a coherent sentence. Nothing about that allowed them to ask questions and pass judgment on society's achievers. With all the asses he'd kissed over his political life, he'd never enjoyed the performances required to appease a lesser-talented group of press critics.

Phillips jolted him from his thoughts and back to the present situation. "Please welcome our finest citizen, President Andrew Maxwell."

He moved forward to boisterous applause from the locals and nothing from the reporters. The press considered it unprofessional to acknowledge any political figure, but their lack of recognition still irritated him as he took his position at the microphone. "Good afternoon and thanks for coming." He recognized several kindly faces in the journalists' cluster and made a mental note to depend upon those folks for most of the questions. "Before I open the forum to questions, I'd like to address the appearance of the NYU students on *This Day*."

In the middle of the town square, he could almost hear a pin drop. "Immediately after that tragic September morning, conspiracy fanatics ran wild with stories of complicity by the government, financial institutions, businesses of all sizes and types. According to some, everyone in our economy, short of panhandlers, made a buck off 9/11. I admit, the construction of an economic model is a novel approach, but the truth remains the same. The United States suffered an attack by terrorists and responded accordingly, as was its right under international law and the basic common sense of any moral individual."

He looked closely at the faces and recognized the effects of his words were positive and well received. "The enemies of America intended to destroy this country. Those enemies would stop at nothing short of their goal—including the use of impressionable college students. I urge the administration of New York University to review the class's study and recognize it for what it is—a flawed mechanism. President Cohen said as much this morning, and I concur." Traditionally, he opted for the local connection. "I'll throw it open to questions. Christina, go ahead."

He waited while a wireless microphone passed to Ms. Turner—more for the benefit of the crowd than for Maxwell.

Turner started. "What's your thoughts of Benjamin Timmons participating in the NYU project and showing up here in Powhatan, also?"

His staff had planted the first question with the local reporter. "I understand young Timmons has a promising future, but the criticism he's received goes to the heart of his judgment. I don't know his motivation, but there's nothing to these stories. Nothing at all."

Maxwell looked for other friendly faces in the group. "Tom, all the way from Little Rock, do you have a question?"

The mic passed, again. "Yes, sir. I'm told Timmons has several police departments interested in the information he's collected about an old case of yours. It goes back some forty plus years, when you started your career. Will you elaborate?"

Tom Wilkins had been a friend for twenty years, but the tone of his question sounded anything but friendly. "I suspect political motivation behind these baseless accusations. Like this great country, I, too, have enemies, Tom."

He realized the platitude didn't play when Wilkins didn't pass the microphone. "What would be Timmons's motivation, sir? We know his background as one of NYU's top students. What would be his interest in defaming you? And if totally baseless, why are several police departments interested in the information?"

Sonofabitch! Maxwell thought. "Tom, we live in a world where suicide bombers strap explosives to themselves and climb on school buses. I'm sure in their warped minds, they justify their actions. I believe Timmons is of the same mind." He regretted that statement as soon as it left his mouth.

"Are you equating the kid with a suicide bomber?" The mic had been passed, but Wilkins called out loudly enough, and everyone waited for an answer.

"No, I'm not calling him a suicide bomber, Tom." Maxwell thought about ending the session, but realized that would not play well. "Zealots justify their actions, regardless of cost. I'm not aware of Timmons's motives, but they seem to have gone beyond reason."

"Have you met with him?" someone from the back shouted.

"I haven't." Maxwell glanced at Baker, but he seemed helpless to assist. "As I said, I've heard these kinds of wild accusations for years. This one has garnered some attention, primarily due to the student's appearance on television. Because of that, I've decided to address it and put it behind us. My character, indeed my moral fiber, drives me to face situations head on. I've never hidden, and I'm too old to start now. I'm telling you there's nothing to this witch hunt into an old case."

Another voice said, "I've seen the information, Mr. President. The kid has raised some legitimate questions about the handling of the 1960s case. Can you confirm the accuracy of the Powhatan information and brief us on the entirety of your role?"

"Who asked that?" A man in the back raised his hand. Maxwell did not recognize him. "How'd you get the information, son? I haven't seen it."

The mic moved back to the journalist. "We got it from NYPD, sir. It seemed unrelated to their investigation of the NYU professor's murder, and they allowed us to review the information."

"Mighty nice of 'em." Maxwell saw Baker inch toward the podium. He knew Willis felt helpless with the new direction of the press conference. "Hell, yes, I'll attest to the accuracy of the information on that case. Was everything perfect—I'm not a pathologist, so I'm sure some details might have been missed. However, in the '60s, we weren't so politically correct, and we focused on protecting the victim." A cheer went up from the local citizens at that. After the noise subsided, he continued, "In my role, I represented the citizens of Powhatan and protected a dear friend. I've never been concerned about the feelings of the bastard who perpetrated the crime, and the hell with Benjamin Timmons diggin' up the hurt from that event."

As the applause ceased, Margaret Buxton with the *Jonesboro Tribune* asked, "Mr. President, it's difficult to refute some of the points made by the students about the financial movements prior to the September tragedy. Is it possible a group of companies or individuals did have some earlier knowledge and received cooperation around 9/11 without your knowledge?"

Willis Baker almost leaped to the podium, but before he could interrupt, Maxwell answered, "No, not possible. You're asking me to justify the whimsy of crazy people. It can't be done." As he spoke, he noticed several journalists were answering their cell phones. "Al Qaeda attacked the United States without provocation, and such speculations demean the memories of those lost on that day. To imply that any American had prior knowledge and did nothing to prevent those events is an insult to all Americans."

A hectic discussion continued among the reporters. Maxwell looked on, confused, as several of them hurried away from the press conference. "Are there any other questions?" The remaining press moved down the steps of the courthouse, seemingly oblivious. "Any other questions?"

As Mayor Phillips took the microphone back, Baker moved beside the ex-president. "A goddamned disaster, Willis," and Baker nodded. "What happened there at the end?"

"I'm not sure, Mr. President."

"Regardless, it got me out of a tight fix. I thought the questions were supposed to be softballs."

Just then, Christina Turner hurried up the steps. "What just happened, Miss Turner?" Baker asked.

She glanced at the chief of staff, but addressed Maxwell, "News from Little Rock, sir."

"Well?" His impatience rose. "What?"

She pointed to her fellow journalists, "They're all in a hurry, because someone tried to kill Ben Timmons at the airport."

"What?" His chief sounded incredulous. "Is he dead?"

"Nothing's confirmed," Turner said. "A vehicle exploded at the airport, and in the middle of the fire trucks trying to put out the fire, someone identified it as the boy's rental car. Apparently, the police are being very tight lipped."

"Goddammit!" Maxwell uttered under his breath. "Get on top of this, Turner. I want details by this evening, and I don't care who gets in your way."

She hurried away. "Willis, what dumb shit did this? It's good for us, if the boy's dead, but if someone's going to kill him, why the hell didn't they do it before all this got started."

"I agree, Mr. President." The concern showed all over Baker's face. "While we're denying everything, it makes us look guilty. However, if Timmons is dead, we can manage it."

"Now that's confidence, Chief of Staff Baker, but what if the kid's not dead?" Maxwell needed a plan in place.

"If he's not dead, he just became more of a national story, and that will give him more credibility."

Maxwell frowned, "Get our people on the phones and find out." Then, "Let's hope the sonofabitch is dead. If you can find out who killed Timmons, tell the beautiful bastard I want to buy him a drink before he's arrested."

Chapter Twenty-Nine
Southern Comfort

Not wanting to ask directions from anyone in Powhatan, Timmons Googled the Staten address and received instructions—west of town down Ozark Plantation Road. He'd expected Old South architecture, but as he pulled into the cobblestone driveway, the modern design of the home surprised him. Large, as expected, but the house was of red brick with clapboard accents made from modern composite and vinyl. The architect had given the owners a taste of the past with a large columned portico on three sides of the house. As he stepped onto the porch, he noticed it had been made from preformed concrete, detailed to look like sculpted marble.

Janet characterized his reluctance to seek directional assistance as male ego, but really, he wished to stay hidden as long as possible. Some Powhatan citizen intended to kill him, and he thought Ms. Pritchard might be involved. He'd been determined to talk with the lady again, but his ability to pull unencumbered into her driveway surprised him. Being safe and staying hidden seemed important, but he knew its value disappeared as soon as he pushed the doorbell beside the huge entrance.

A black lady in a tailored, formal maid's uniform opened the door. "Can I help you, young man?" she asked, her diction clear and precise, almost British.

"Yes, ma'am," he replied. "I'm hoping to have a word with the lady of the house."

"And your name, sir?" she asked, but he could tell from her expression, she recognized him.

"I'm Ben Timmons."

"Wait here. I'll announce you, but I'm not sure Ms. Pritchard can see you." She closed the door before he could utter a thank you, leaving him on the porch. He stood for a moment, admiring his surrounds, and then decided to walk to the south side of the house. The enormous porch showed little signs of use, and even with all the entertaining the Pritchards must do, the outside of the house was pristine—ready for display. The lawn was manicured well enough to make golf course managers envious—not Kentucky bluegrass, the preferred choice in Northern Indiana. Too hot in Arkansas, he guessed. It looked like ryegrass and fescue, better suited for the temperatures. At various locations around the huge yard, several groundskeepers carried out their maintenance routines, while keeping eyes focused upon him.

His decision to exchange vehicles had nothing to do with perceived threats and was only meant to complicate Agent Levitt's task. Ben and Janet had moved his belonging to the new rental and driven only a few feet toward the parking garage exit when the employee sent to fetch the Ford triggered the explosion.

After the fire department extinguished the fire, police investigators found another body in a nearby dumpster. What followed was another long session in the police station, endless questions, and one solemn visit to the morgue to view the remains of his latest victims—according to LRPD.

Detective Heuter promised to delay release of any information about the explosion until Ben and Janet returned to New York. When Timmons refused the offer, and Janet rejected Ben's pleas for her to leave, the policeman threatened to arrest them. Finally, exiting LRPD mid-afternoon, Ben's first chore was to retrieve Hameed's gift from the post office.

The NYU students spent the night in a Little Rock motel, guarded by local police. On Sunday, after another emphatic refusal from Janet to leave him, they'd resumed their trip to Powhatan, where this latest scheme was devised.

The large oak trees on that side of the Staten house had been strategically placed to provide shade for the entire structure. One huge garage stood apart from the main house. Behind it, neatly mown pastures led to a stable more than a quarter of a mile away. Several horses—they looked like thoroughbreds—grazed in the field.

He strolled to the front of the house, but the maid hadn't returned, so he decided to explore the north side of the structure. As he rounded the corner, he noticed a handsome elderly woman some forty feet down the porch, sitting on a wicker chaise lounge. The maid stood beside her. "Miranda will be happy to fetch you a mornin' beverage, Mr. Timmons?"

The cordial tone of her question surprised him, "No, ma'am, I'm just fine."

"Then, do join me for this conversation, young man. It's nice to see you, again. I've been expectin' you." She motioned to a matching wicker upright chair across from her

Even though she reclined in her chair, she seemed taller than he remembered from their meeting in the minister's office—certainly tall for her generation. Her eyes revealed a distinctive confidence, and in this setting she possessed the manners of a matriarch. "I hope you'll forgive my unscheduled visit, Mrs. Sta— excuse me, Ms. Pritchard." He thought he'd offended her, but then, a faint smirk crossed her face. "I apologize, ma'am."

"I don't know what you've heard, young man, but I'm not a frail old woman. Don't treat me as such." Now, she openly smiled at him, revealing straight white teeth. "You're wonderin' about use of my maiden name?"

Lacking a response, he remained silent.

"You've been busy since our last meetin'. My people have struggled to keep up with your travels." She paused to sip coffee. "I'm sorry about your professor," she said, and he wondered about her possible involvement. "Even at my age, I remember the teachers who influenced me."

Timmons didn't want to discuss Dr. Agbetheatha. "I haven't enjoyed this project, ma'am. I wanted you to know, and I'm sorry for intruding."

She took another sip, eyes peering directly at him. "Oh, you pretend to be an honorable man. You've passed judgment on me, and now, you want to proclaim your condescension."

"Ma'am, I haven't judged anyone, and if I'm causing aggravation, I'll leave."

"You give yourself too much credit, young man. More ruthless, dangerous men than you have attempted to cross me over my years, and none have caused me the least anxiety." Her statement was meant to dismiss him, he thought. "I told you when you arrived here several weeks ago with your mind made up. Your travels have been nothin' more than a justification for your judgment of us—me." Calmly, she turned the cup in her hands. "How's your mother? I'm sure this project has taken time away from her campaign."

He recognized the lady's obfuscation. "Ma'am, I'd like to ask a couple of questions?"

"You don't expect me to answer, do you?"

"I have no control over you, ma'am. I am grateful you've given me the time, and as I said, if I'm disturbing you, I'll leave. It's your prerogative, but I'm not the only one on this porch who's passed judgment."

She stared at him. "Why don't you tell me your story, and I'll decide if I can add anythin'. Please, don't deprive me of your efforts to unravel a forty-five year secret. I've been briefed daily on your movements."

"Ms. Pritchard, I wasn't sure I'd even see you, again. I've been told your security's better than Maxwell's." She didn't respond, nor remove her gaze from his face, and then he realized she had consented to his visit. "I'm unprepared for a dissertation."

"I'm givin' you an opportunity, young man. It's your decision to accept it. Otherwise, leave me, and I'll continue to enjoy the day."

For the past weeks, he'd been peeling this onion one layer at a time. Just when he thought he'd reached the center, he discovered another onion underneath. In the middle of a deadly chess match, he suddenly found his opponent three moves ahead. "My uncle was Army CID. He'd been posted undercover to Powhatan and discovered the real source of Mr. Staten's growing fortune. Before he could report the details to his superiors, you killed him—supposedly. I'm told by the Army under the circumstances, his death would still have been investigated but not the sexual assault charge. On that basis, the Army accepted local accounts of the shooting."

Her expression gave nothing away. As stoic as a statue, she held her coffee and listened.

"I've found members of Army CID willing to assist. They've speculated about involvement by the CIA with the drug trafficking, and also assumed your group was told how to cover the death of my uncle." He never removed his eyes from her, but still nothing. "It'll take CID some time, but the release of the CIA files should verify the connection."

"I'd like more coffee," she said, putting the container on the wicker table beside her. "Are you sure I can't get you somethin'?" She gestured, and a moment later, the maid appeared. "Mr. Timmons?"

"No, ma'am."

"Miranda, more coffee, please." The maid hurried back into the house. "You were sayin', young man?"

"My father struggled with his uncle's death. It changed his life. Can you shed some light?" Ben knew she wouldn't answer, but he felt he owed it to his father.

The patio door opened, and the maid hurried forth with a coffee pot. She filled Ms. Pritchard's cup and asked, "Can I bring you anything else, ma'am?"

"Will you ask Tonya to join us?"

"She left right after breakfast, ma'am," the servant replied. "She's spending the day in town." The maid went back inside.

"Young man, as I told you, I had your father investigated. His struggles had nothin' to do with his uncle. He seemed obsessed with failure, and if he couldn't achieve it, he'd create it. I'm wonderin' if you possess the same qualities." He identified her attempt to bait him. "I'm seventy-five years old, and I can barely remember the events. What do you suppose those files will reveal? There weren't any computers. After all these years, do you think the CIA can even find it? Many of the main players are buried. And those still alive—well, my generation's not holdin' up very well." He recognized a worthy adversary. "How's Lewis?" she asked.

Her motive in asking about his grandfather confused him. "It's been a struggle over the past couple of years," Ben confessed. "He's not the grandfather I remember."

"I know him as a good man," and she stared past him, seemingly reflecting. After a moment's silence, she continued, "Your story's pure speculation, while I have the official records on my side, and it's hard to overturn the statements of the dead. I can admire your efforts and at the same time recognize a waste of time."

"I'm not looking for a confession, Ms. Pritchard." He knew the truth, even without her agreement. "I'm doing this for my father and my family."

"Are you tryin' to give honor to the dead that you never gave them while livin'? And what price are you prepared to pay?" For the first time, he saw some emotion on her face. "Isn't that the purpose of our lives? We do so much for the benefit of family and friends, tryin' to protect and sustain them." She must have seen his confusion. "You think it's for the money?

Sure, that's what you tell yourself, but really, it's so you can shield your loved ones. You want to give them opportunities you never had." After a moment of reflection, her voice grew soft, "Prevent them from experiencin' your failures. And after that sacrifice, they judge and condemn your decisions."

"Ma'am, the Army's investigating the death of my uncle, NYPD the death of Dr. Agbetheatha, Elkton's probing the death of my dad, and after Saturday's events, the Little Rock PD's involved, too."

"You imply I was involved in that act?" she shrugged. "I told you before, my assignments get completed."

"Uh—it's still being sorted out, ma'am. Sorry." Now, she really had Ben rattled. "My point is all those events have one thing in common."

"I'm sorry you had to go through this, young man." She took the coffee cup, but it seemed more to occupy her hands than to drink. "I'm sorry for your loss, but I'm too old to apologize for my life." She stared across the yard, and he wasn't sure what she saw. "When I was a child—" After a moment, she looked directly at him. "But, I put away childish things a long time ago."

As they sat in silence, a light breeze blew across the porch, increasing his awareness of the pleasant Arkansas morning. The conversation struck him as surreal and serene—a startling contrast. After a bit, she added, "You have powerful people opposed to you. I've never met a saint, young Ben. I don't believe in them. As a confessed sinner, I've lived with my decisions for many years."

"Yes, ma'am. I'm not the police."

"You're more dangerous than the police. Cops are

realists, young man." He didn't understand her comment. "Do you know why I took my maiden name after my husband died?" Ben shook his head. "Oh, you can speculate. Appease an old woman's vanity."

Timmons thought about giving her a platitude, but knew her keen mind would see through any attempt to evade her question. He saw the defiance in her eyes, and knowing a little of her background and with first-hand knowledge of her granddaughter's approach to life, he decided to be honest. "You wanted to shove it down their throats."

A slight look of amusement touched the corners of her mouth. "I agree with Tonya that you're very handsome, Mr. Timmons. I'm told you're a scholar of some achievement, and we've seen your abilities to avoid trouble." The confrontation with Hank still bothered him, and he wasn't interested in her false praise. "One so young, and you know a little of women, too."

"No, ma'am. Just basic psychology."

"The Pritchards and the Statens have done a lot to build this part of Arkansas." She made a grand gesture with one hand. "Oh, it might not look like much by New York City standards, but this is the heart of America—not Wall Street. In the '60s, we lived in the poorest region of one of the poorest states. A hundred years after the Civil War, and Arkansas hadn't forgotten and certainly, hadn't recovered. This area had nothing but God-fearing, poor people with only their pride and a healthy mistrust of Washington. An opportunity presented itself, but not for greed and profit. We were told we'd do a service for the country, and it offered us a chance to survive."

"I'm sure your neighbors appreciate you, ma'am."

"You think we were just drug dealers, right?" She placed the cup on the table. "Like the World War One flyin' aces, Mr. Timmons, I fear you'll soon be in flames and spinnin' out of control. And when you've impacted earth, your enemies will salute you from the clouds and drink a toast in your honor. You deserve more."

Ben rose from his chair, "I've taken enough of your time, ma'am. Thanks for seeing me." He turned toward his rental car, but then, he paused. "They're not all dead, Ms. Pritchard. And they don't all have dementia. I'm betting a few still possess a conscience and listen to the moral voice of their god. Good day, ma'am."

"What's your hurry, Ben? Let's have breakfast, and I'll bore you with more old stories."

She sounded sincere. "I'd enjoy that very much, ma'am."

Chapter Thirty
Catching Up

Following the same Monday routine for almost thirty years, Christina Turner arrived early at the newspaper office to review the weekend events from national and international sources. At the beginning of her career, she read faxes and followed up with telephone calls to clarify facts and points of interest. In her youth, journalism involved relationships with other reporters, and not only did she ask questions about the news, but also, she learned about life, family, and friends.

The computer and the internet changed all that, almost overnight. Today, she surfed the web for stories of interest, and if she had a question about one, she'd email and wait for a response. For most twenty-first century journalists, a phone call wasted time and money. Voicemail screened all calls, and only a special few were ever returned. The age of technology put an end to many of those human relationships. It made her feel old, and she missed the free exchange of ideas without the buffer. In her opinion, technology had destroyed her world.

Usually, she started with international news, but today, she went directly to the latest postings on Saturday's explosion in Little Rock. Two bodies had been recovered from the site in an airport garage, but the police refused to identify the dead. On Sunday, the lead detective had promised the names as soon as the victims' families had been advised, but by the end of the day, still nothing from LRPD.

After browsing only a few of the latest stories, she realized the names weren't released. Maxwell had never taken delay well. Her credibility with the former president diminished throughout the weekend, as she failed to provide the identity of the victims. She knew the ex-president's people suffered the same results, so their failure relieved some of her stress.

Tonya Pritchard, already in the office when Christina arrived, seldom visited the newspaper, even though she owned the business. However, since Ben Timmons arrived in town, Tonya's appearances increased, and her work always had something to do with the kid's project. As Christina looked out from her glassed office, Tonya studied a computer screen, reading and scribbling notes.

In other parts of the office, various staff worked. At the front, Harvey Mohr, who managed operations and logistics, busied himself by updating an equipment maintenance chart. Across from him, Molly Baltz talked on the telephone, purchasing supplies, or checking shipment schedules.

While Christina watched, the front door opened and in walked a young lady with sandy brown hair, dark eyes, and a milk-white complexion. Her hair was pulled back and tied, and her blue blouse, khaki slacks, and brown shoes were off-the-rack. She carried a cheap purse, a notebook and a mini-recorder. On her very pretty face, she wore the worst pair of black, horned-rim glasses the profession had ever seen.

She asked Harvey something, and he pointed back toward Christina's office. As the young woman approached the open door, Turner saw Tonya took notice of the visitor, too. The young lady leaned her head in and asked, "Miss Turner?"

She waved the young journalist in and pointed to the chair across from the desk. "What's your paper, honey?"

As she sat down, she answered, "I'm Sarah Greenburg with the *Daily* out of Elkton, Indiana." The young woman pointed to the plaque on the wall behind her desk. "You're a Winchell recipient. Congratulations."

"Thanks. If you can hang in the trade long enough, they give you one as a consolation." Turner accepted a business card offered from the young reporter, and read the details, as the young lady's eyes studied her award. Tonya must have heard the exchange, and she moved back toward the office. "What brings you to Powhatan, Miss Greenburg?"

Tonya moved into the doorway, and the young woman rested her gaze upon the paper's owner while she responded. "One of Elkton's citizens was murdered some eighteen months ago, Jackson Timmons. A Powhatan resident, Matthew Rappart, was identified as the likely suspect, but I understand he's dead?"

"He died in a hunting accident more than a year ago," Tonya answered. She moved forward and extended a hand to the young reporter. "Forgive my intrusion, I'm Tonya Pritchard, owner of this publication." The two barely touched hands, and Tonya took the other chair.

"It's my pleasure, Miss Pritchard. I have your

name on my list, so this meeting is fortuitous."

"Where'd you go to school, Sarah? You can't be more than a year, or two out of college?" Christina purposely delayed the coming exchange.

"Indiana University," the young woman answered.

"Pretty young to be traveling on assignment. You must be pretty good? Have I read any of your stories?"

"I doubt it," the reporter replied. "I'm learning the business."

"Well, Indiana's a good program. Pyle School of Journalism, isn't it?"

"They named a journalism school after Gomer?" Tonya asked. Christina watched for a reaction.

"Ernie Pyle was a World War Two journalist," Sarah replied, still calm over the insult. "He's an Indiana legend."

"Why do you have my name on your list, Miss Greenburg?"

Christina saw the young reporter throw a glance of apology in her direction before replying. "Most of my information comes from police and citizens in Elkton. Ben Timmons's relative on the police force was very helpful." She turned a few pages of her notebook to some detailed notes. "I understand you tried to force Ben Timmons out of town with the use of physical violence?"

Christina's heart pounded at the thought of a pending eruption. "I never laid a hand on Mr. Timmons," Tonya answered as her voice remained calm and her manner relaxed. "He got into an altercation with one of the locals."

"This local have a name?" She might be young, Christina thought, but the woman had style.

"I don't recall," Tonya's voice remained subdued. "We can make inquiries. I believe the police took a statement."

"Thanks, but I'll get it from the sheriff," Greenburg answered. "He's on my list, too. So, you're saying, you didn't hire a local to intimidate Mr. Timmons?"

"Intimidate?" Tonya shook her head. "I didn't hire anyone." Her meaning was clear, as the two young women stared at each other.

"With the news out of Little Rock about an apparent attempt on Mr. Timmons's life, you can see why I'd ask the question."

Now, it was obvious Tonya struggled with control, "We are all awaiting details of the Little Rock story."

"What can I tell you, Miss Greenburg?" Christina tried to redirect the conversation.

With one hand, she started the recorder and placed it on the edge of the desk, while retrieving a pen from her purse with the other. Then, she opened the notebook. "As I said, my information is from the Elkton PD. I'm interested in Matthew Rappart."

Christina shrugged, "His brother's the sheriff, and he'd been an officer on the force."

"I'd like some additional background on his brother before I talk to the policeman."

"Wait," Tonya said. "He killed the Timmons man and now, he's dead. It seems neat and clean to me, so why the interest?"

The reporter paused, as if considering her words. "The Elkton investigation is being handled by a detective Danielson. He's been communicating with your sheriff, but hasn't been satisfied with the level of cooperation. It's understandable the officer might be interested in protecting his family name."

"If you knew Dan Rappart, you'd know his level of cooperation is the same regardless of the names involved." Christina realized it sounded petty, but she didn't care.

"Well, my job is to stay ahead of the investigation."

"What investigation?" Tonya asked. "Why haven't they moved on to other cases? I'm in my final year at U of A law, and this sounds like a waste of resources."

"I don't manage Elkton PD's budget, but they're confused by the sequence of events leading to the car crash." That sounded ominous to Turner. "Danielson's looking for a Makarov. It's a Soviet pistol, and a popular collector's item from the Vietnam War. From what my boss told me this morning, Little Rock PD is interested, too. Probably, the same weapon."

Turner saw the color draining from Tonya's face. She hoped Miss Greenburg missed it. "What's so special about a Makarov?"

"Apparently, this particular one is central to the investigation of the Timmons murder. I don't know the Little Rock connection. It's probably a prize from that war. Do you have a list of Vietnam vets in this area?" Greenburg paused, and Christina suspected it was for effect. "I'd like to talk to them." Her gaze remained fixed on Tonya.

"I don't know," Tonya replied. "You just missed the Memorial Day parade. You could have counted them."

The young reporter had moved beyond being courteous. Staring at Tonya, she said, "There's a dead Timmons from the 1960s, a murdered Elkton citizen with the same name, and someone tried to run Ben Timmons out of this town with violence. The common thread is your family, Miss Pritchard." The young reporter paused, but Tonya said nothing. "It casts a shadow of suspicion in your direction."

"You should be careful" Tonya's voice stayed soft, but didn't disguise her anger. "You don't know how quickly I can get you fired."

Greenburg showed a strange smile. "I'll take that as a confirmation, Miss Pritchard." The young woman closed her notebook, leaned forward and turned off the recorder. "Well, thanks for the assistance. I'll get the rest of the background from the brother." She put her pen in her purse and stood up. "I understand several investigative groups are arriving today—Army CID, Elkton and Little Rock police. I'd appreciate an update on any press conferences scheduled in the coming days. My number's on the card."

She turned and walked out of the door and across the office. She paused to thank Harvey, and then was gone.

Christina watched until the front door closed. "How's a Makarov involved in an explosion at the Little Rock airport? They're passing it off as a mechanical malfunction." The color still hadn't returned to Tonya's face. "Obviously, faulty wiring wasn't a cause."

"What are you implying?" Tonya snapped. "You think I'm involved in murder?" She paused for thought. "Yeah, the fools involved in this are pointing to me."

"You said Dan Rappart was the weak link in this plan. I'm supposed to divert him from investigating his brother's death. Why am I letting him ride me morning, noon, and night if you're working another angle? Hell, Tonya, someone died in that explosion!"

Tonya Pritchard leaned back and closed the glass door to the office. Lowering her voice, she said, "I didn't have anything to do with the explosion, and don't get righteous with me, Tina. Did you think you'd earn this kind of money delivering papers? I told you Rappart would follow his urges. It's Ben Timmons who's been more of a problem than we figured. How'd he put all this together?"

"Did you try to kill him?" She couldn't believe she asked the question. "Maxwell's had me calling all over the state for information about the explosion. Should I have asked you?"

"I was here all weekend with hundreds of witnesses." Tonya sounded indignant. "I don't know who's involved in this mess. I'm trying to protect my grandmother, and it's to your benefit to help. That's why you're letting Rappart ride you."

Christina watched for a reaction. "What do you know about Matthew Rappart? He didn't kill the boy's father, did he?"

"How should I know? Do what you're told, Tina, or I'll hand the blame for this mess to you. You know I can do it."

"My payment depended upon protecting your grandmother, keeping this investigation from implicating her. That's all I signed on to do. These additional chores demand more money. And I never expected murder."

"I didn't agree to murder, either. Plans change, Tina. We've all got to adjust. I'll try to get you more money, but I don't know all the names involved in this."

Turner's mind raced, as she tried to figure a way out. Her stressed, shallow breathing had given her a headache and her heart pounded in her ears. "And if that young reporter is right? We're about to be invaded by investigators from all over the country. If the young woman's a good poker player, and I'll bet she is, we didn't hide our cards very well."

"The question about the pistol surprised me. The Timmons father died in an automobile. How'd the Elkton police get wind of an old Soviet gun?"

"Do you know anything about the gun, Tonya?"

"No, I'm as confused as you about all this. The clues are all over the map, and I can't imagine anyone will ever put it together. Certainly not in court."

Christina didn't feel assured. "Ben Timmons is not worried about a court date." She regretted ever getting involved. All these years spent trying to protect Staten's legacy and she'd succumbed to greed. "What now?" she asked.

"It's still a forty-five-year-old case. That's in our favor. And Maxwell will do whatever necessary to keep it buried. Besides, if the investigators are men, you might just have to increase the activity in your bedroom to keep them all confused." Tina reacted to the insult like a slap in the face. "One thing's sure," Tonya continued, "Sarah Greenburg will be difficult." Turner watched Tonya in deep thought. "Did you see the clothes?" she asked.

"I dressed the same way, just out of college."

"Yeah," Tonya confirmed, "but the manicure on her finger nails cost more than the rest of her outfit combined. You didn't do that out of college." Christina knew Tonya was correct. "Check her out, and remain calm," Tonya said. "This will still work."

Chapter Thirty-One
The Value of a Life

Betty Pritchard sat at her breakfast table and watched Ben Timmons move the Eggs Florentine around the plate. "Miranda is widely known for her recipe, young man. You risk offendin' her by not eatin' it."

Across the kitchen, the servant folded towels at the counter, and Timmons turned to address her. "I'm sorry, ma'am. It's very good. I'm just having difficulty finding an appetite this morning." The maid nodded.

Betty Pritchard continued, "I've admired the way you've handled yourself, Mr. Timmons," She meant the words as a compliment, but recognized he wasn't receptive. "You've been on national television explainin' a complex project to the illiterate masses— and very well, I might add. You've matched wits with the Jew boy in the White House while he shut down that very project. Several police departments around the country dance to your words, and you've survived an attempt on your life. I find it hard to believe the stress of this meetin' has you undone." His eyes remained on her, but he did not respond to her comment. "Weren't you expectin' somethin' like this when we talked a couple weeks ago?"

He placed the fork on his plate. "I accepted your invitation to breakfast, Ms. Pritchard."

She knew her attorneys would want Miranda out of the room—no witnesses. However, her servant had been in the Pritchard household long enough to know most of the story and had, undoubtedly, filled the rest in her mind. She trusted Miranda, even if her lawyers didn't. Her legal team wouldn't want her to even engage this young man. The risks were too great, they'd tell her. "Shall we put our cards on the table, young man?" A pleased look crossed her face, "I love those old metaphors. Or would that be an idiom?"

"Yes, ma'am," he said, but she didn't know which reference he confirmed. "Who killed my uncle?"

"Oh, let's not dispute forty-five years of history. I shot him. Can we leave it there?"

"I guess this isn't church," he replied.

At this time, truth didn't matter, she decided. "So, you've discovered my sins. What penance shall I perform?" She saw him smile.

"Pastor Kinson would be upset with the Catholic term."

She laughed, too. Across the kitchen, even Miranda showed amusement. "I like you, Ben," she said. "I wish you'd never gotten involved in this."

"I could say the same to you, ma'am."

"You had more choice than I." She paused to reflect, and the room fell silent while she remembered, the only movement being her finger tapping on the coffee cup. In time she asked, "How's your history knowledge, Mr. Timmons?"

"Ma'am?"

"Ever hear of Kuomintang?" She watched for his reaction.

His brow furrowed, and he answered, "Yes, a

group out of China that stood against Mao after he and the Communists took control." She watched his face, knowing his mind raced as he processed her question. "Air America?" he asked.

Betty Pritchard glanced at her maid. She, too, couldn't hide her interest and had given up pretending to be busy. "The agency used drug profits to combat communism for years before Vietnam. When they decided to expand that business model to finance their actions in Southeast Asia, they needed a location in this country which fit their needs."

"How'd Mr. Staten get involved?"

She knew he could burst with questions, but she admired his restraint. Even if he asked, most of his inquiries would need to go unanswered. "As a young girl in this county, there was only one difference between a rich man and a poor one," she said. "Neither one had five dollars in a bank account. The rich man owned the land, and they both worked it in the hot sun 'til their backs broke."

She gestured to her servant to refill her coffee cup. "Oh, the farmer could borrow against the land, and that's how he planted his crops. If the weather was good and the markets held, he'd make enough to pay back the bank, and maybe, add a new plow or a couple head of cattle to his herd. Rich and poor." She fell silent.

After a moment, Timmons asked, "How did you get into business with the CIA?"

She put down the cup, leaned back in the chair, and pretended to be relaxed. "You're an economics major? Have you studied the post-Civil War South?"

"Yes, ma'am."

"Well, you studied it, but the people around here lived it. My parents and grandparents could teach you first hand."

"You're talking about the economic retribution extracted from the South after the war?"

"It might have been a hundred years, but the South hadn't recovered. Most Southerners in general, but this area of Arkansas in particular, could sing 'God Bless America' with unequaled enthusiasm and not trust the federal government five cents worth." She shook her head. "It was strange times, Ben Timmons. It's hard to explain to someone from Indiana."

"Forgive me, ma'am, but you're not trying to convince me your husband got into drug trafficking because of a misguided sense of patriotism?"

"Young man, I admire your efforts, but we're on opposite sides. In the privacy of my home, I'm goin' to be honest with you. I feel I owe you that much, and I'm too old for the pretense." She knew Miranda could hear, but she leaned forward and lowered her voice. "After this conversation, we're enemies, again, and I have money and political connections. All you have is right, and that don't mean a hot damn in these times. You're goin' to get my best efforts, and it's nothin' like you've ever seen."

"I'd expect nothing less, ma'am."

She continued, "My husband did it for the money. Oh, it took some convincin', because no one in this part of the country liked the Kennedy boys. Even after Dallas and the assassination, things grew worse. The civil rights movement with assistance from the North tried to destroy our way of life in the South. It might have been the right thin' to do, but the South wasn't ready for Washington to shove it down our throats. So, when opportunities came for us to take back some control, well…"

"How long was your husband involved?"

She didn't answer. "Initially, we were provided protection, but eventually, we had to build our own layer of connections. By that time, we had enough money and plenty of people with a like mind and a hand out. For a time, it was too easy, and we really did believe we were fightin' communism."

"Until the CID placed a local boy into the mix?"

Again, she didn't answer. "You'll never piece it together for the courts, young man. Not after all these years." Her eyes went to the patio doors, and she looked at the beauty of her estate. "My husband's name was Ben, too. We married young, a common affliction at that time in this part of the country." Outside, a squirrel ventured onto the porch to search for leftovers.

One of God's creatures, she thought, living its simple life and oblivious to the evil just a few feet away. The sin was hers, but she felt compelled to block this young man's investigation. She didn't know why. He carried no threat, and most of her past associates had died years before. Why hurt a squirrel? God couldn't want such a thing.

She heard Timmons ask, "Ma'am, are you okay?"

She turned to the boy, "We managed distribution for a good part of the South and Midwest. At first, we called ourselves patriots and believed we served the country, but after a few years, we got accustomed to the money."

"You processed?" he asked. "I ask, because the stuff transports at a lighter, easier-to-conceal pure weight. It gets cut to street quality just prior to distribution." Nobody's fool, she decided. "You said you had distribution, so did you cut it?"

"We did well for a decade, or more," she said. "By then, the political climate changed, and the South American cartels took much of the business. My husband struggled to stay involved, but I'd lost interest."

"Is that when you lost your oldest child?" His words knifed into her heart.

She looked into his face and saw compassion in his eyes. "On a high school trip to Memphis, they found my dead son in an alley with a needle in his arm." His expression didn't change, and she struggled to hide her pain. "So, my God decided to punish me in the Biblical sense, and ever since that day, I've wondered why my sins destroyed those I loved. One child dead and the rest left me, one by one. They hated their mother and father, but they loved the money. Today, I only have my granddaughter."

"Did you like your husband, ma'am?" His question struck home as she knew he intended, but she tried to conceal it. The young man was human, after all, and he wanted his pound of flesh.

"I've tired of this conversation, young man." She gestured to Miranda. "Please escort Mr. Timmons to the door."

He rose from the chair but just before he exited, he turned back. "I appreciate your seeing me, Ms. Pritchard. I never intended to put your life on trial."

As she watched him turn and walk away, she thought how much she liked that young man, and found herself hoping for his safety.

Chapter Thirty-Two
One Step Closer

As Ben left the Pritchard estate, he Googled the Pittmann farm's location and found it a few miles up Rural Route 6. He drove slowly, irritating the few other drivers on the remote narrow road. When one did speed past, a gesture usually accompanied it.

After a couple of miles, the pavement ended, and he drove the final miles on clay and gravel. The numbers on a rusty mailbox indicated his destination, and he pulled from the gravel onto a rutted dirt road leading to the farmstead. The small house, in need a coat of paint, strategically rested under a group of large oak trees, much like the Pritchard estate. He noticed all the windows open, so he assumed the trees provided the only air conditioning for the house.

A hundred feet north stood a large barn, constructed from rough sawn lumber with a tin roof and a large silo attached. Two farm hands shoveled manure from the confined grounds of the barn's feed lot onto a flat-bed wagon—a cheap source of fertilizer for the crops.

Exiting the vehicle, Ben recognized Hank, his adversary in Mosie's, as one of the workers. A sense of foreboding touched him. If a confrontation ensued, he doubted he'd be able to sucker Hank again, and now, the large man had help. The other farm hand was equally big, but without the menacing look. Ben took a chance and waved a friendly greeting. He considered pretending he didn't recognize Hank, and quickly, decided not. "I'm glad I got to see you, again. I wanted to apologize."

"Is this the boy that whopped your ass, Hank?" the other man asked.

"That's him," Hank answered, throwing his shovel down and moving toward Ben. The other farm hand followed. "I'm glad to see you, too."

His pride wouldn't allow him to get back in the car, and he repressed the thought. "I'd like to talk with your father."

"How do you know our ole man?" the other hand asked, confirming he was Hank's brother.

Now, the two were only five feet away, and Timmons remained on guard. "I met him a couple weeks ago. He offered help, and I'd like to accept." His gaze never left their faces, but they didn't look threatening. Under different circumstances, this could pass as a friendly chat. "You know why I'm here?"

"Yeah, we know," Hank answered. He must have noticed Ben's nervousness. "Don't worry, we're not going to kick your ass. Two on one wouldn't be fair."

Ben stood close enough to Hank to see his broken tooth had been repaired. "I'm sorry about our first meeting, and I'm glad to see you've recovered."

"Tonya paid for his repairs," the brother answered.

Ben looked at Hank, and he nodded. "She gave me the money she promised and paid my medical bills."

"I guess that's good?"

"Nah," Hank replied, "I wanted a piece of her ass, so I missed that."

"I don't think she'd give it up for that." The locker room discussion about Tonya Pritchard made Ben uncomfortable.

"That's what I told him," his brother interjected. "She's a wealthy bitch, and she played him. Hank wanted to lay her, and he wanted that money in Mosie's pool. I hear it's near two thousand."

"What'd she tell you?" Ben asked Hank. "I mean, why'd you agree to do it, really?"

"She told me to kick your ass, and she'd see I won the pool." Hank shrugged, "I didn't know your story until later."

"You didn't really believe her?"

Hank pulled out a pack of cigarettes from his pocket. "You're from NYU, right?"

"Yeah," Ben answered.

"You probably don't understand, but 'round here, nailin' the rich bitch is every poor boy's goal."

"She's the prettiest girl in three states and got more money than God," the brother said. "If it wuz me, I'd make a video to sell on the net."

Ben laughed in spite of himself. "And you believed her?" he asked Hank again. He looked into the large man's eyes, and something troubled him.

"Sure did," Hank acknowledged. "I'm just a dumb farm boy, but you're from New York City. How's she playin' you, Timmons?"

"Isn't it strange how beautiful women can manipulate gullible men anywhere in the world?"

"Bullshit!" the brother spit the words. "I've heard the stories 'round town. You're causin' trouble for all of 'em."

"How do you mean?" Ben asked. "I've been led to

believe the whole town's against me."

"We might be poor farmers," Hank said, "but we're not stupid. We know the source of ole man Staten's money. That's what pisses me off about Tonya pretendin' to be better than us. She's got more filth on her than I'll ever have."

"Hank!" The three turned to see Mr. Pittmann standing in the barn doorway. "That manure ain't goin' to spread itself on the field.". The two boys went back to work, as their father approached. "Glad to see you're still alive, son. I heard 'bout Little Rock."

"Thank you, sir." Then, Ben asked, "How'd you know about that?"

"How 'bout a seat in the shade," the man said, pointing toward a couple of Adirondack chairs under a tree. "Hank's right, son. We ain't stupid."

They moved out of the sun and sat down. "I didn't mean to imply you were, sir. It's just, Little Rock is supposed to be under wraps for a couple days."

"Call me LJ," he said. "I'm Lee Roy Junior. As a child, everyone called me Junior, and since my daddy died, it's been LJ. As far as knowin' about the airport, the agency leaked your name on the rental car." He stared at Ben's face. "Ask your questions, and I'll do the best I can."

Ben appreciated the straight-forward approach. "First, I'm confused by Hank's reaction."

"Oh, he'd like to kick your ass, son, and with a little less cockiness, prob'ly would." The man removed rolling papers and a container of tobacco from the pocket of his overalls. "Hank hadn't been on the floor since fifth grade. He said you tricked him, but he still went down. Call it respect. Close as you're goin' to get 'round here."

"Thanks for that," Ben said. "I wanted to ask about the weapon your father sold to Mrs. Staten."

"Figured as much." LJ lit his cigarette with a disposable lighter. "I'm not gettin' in the middle of this—'specially with all the stuff you've been doin'. Thought you should know the truth, but I'm not repeatin' it to anyone. Got that? It's a small town, boy, and I've got to scratch out a livin'."

"Yes, sir."

"My daddy didn't sell the gun to Mrs. Staten. He sold it to Andy Maxwell."

"You're shittin' me!" Again, out before he realized it. "Sorry, sir—LJ."

Pittmann smiled. "My boys don't know that. I've never told 'em. My daddy told me before he died. He took money from Staten for keepin' his mouth shut. Don't know how much, but we'd never been land owners until then."

Ben's mind was in a fog. "I hadn't considered such a thing."

"Can't use it. I'm not repeatin' it after this and it's hearsay, anyway. Won't hold up in court, but it could ruin me in these parts."

"Guns were bought and sold very freely then. No bill of sale, I assume?"

Ben noticed Pittmann's hesitation. "Well, I'm not sayin anythin' else."

"You have something with Maxwell's signature, don't you?"

"Son, I can't afford life insurance, but I wanted you to know." LJ rose from the chair and walked toward the barn. "Safe drive back to town, boy."

"One more question, sir?" Pittmann stopped. "I'm looking for a Makarov. You seem to know weapons."

He scratched his chin and took another drag on his cigarette. "I thought I'd seen most of the gun collections in these parts, but I haven't seen one of those."

Ben saw he was thinking. "How might I go about finding it??"

"What's a Makarov doin' in your mess, son?" Ben didn't answer. "Try the gun range." He pointed north. "A mile or so, and you might find a spent cartridge. It'll look like a 9mm, but very old. A casing that old will be almost black. It's a long shot, but even collectors like to shoot. Course, some ole spent brass don't get you an owner, but it's a start." With a wave, Pittmann continued into the barn.

As he returned to his vehicle, Timmons motioned for a word with Hank. His opponent said something to his brother, and then, walked over. "What do you need, Timmons?"

Out of earshot of his brother, Ben said, "I know I didn't win a fair fight."

"What do you mean?" Hank glanced back to confirm his brother and father could not hear.

"You didn't want to win that fight?" The look on Hank's face confirmed Ben's suspicions. "You didn't want Tonya to make good on the promise, or win Mosie's pool. I'm sorry I got you into this mess." Hank looked nervous, but said nothing

Ben returned to the Toyota. Almost noon, and he had an afternoon appointment in Powhatan. The gun range would have to wait.

Chapter Thirty-Three
Rook to King Four, Check

Driving away from the farm, Ben pondered the
revelation that Maxwell had purchased a weapon from
LJ's father—the gun which had killed Joshua Timmons.
This was a powerful piece of information, but he'd
honor Mr. Pittmann's request to keep the information
confidential. If Ben's plans worked out, a meeting with
Maxwell loomed in his future but he couldn't use the
knowledge of the gun purchase to gain full disclosure
from the ex-president without outing LJ. He realized
the danger in such a move, not only for himself, but
also, the Pittmanns.

A sign indicated Poplar Springs just three miles to
the west and he decided on lunch before returning to
Powhatan to give him time to organize his thinking. He
hoped Janet had stayed away from trouble. Knowing
her, he doubted it, and that worried him. He should
have insisted she return to New York. If anything
happened to her—he put the thought out of his head.
His iPhone playing the theme from *Gandhi* brought him
back to the present. "Hello, Narayan," he answered.

"Greetings, my friend," Narayan's formal speech
pattern reminded him of the Pritchard's maid. "I've
forwarded the results of the telephone search to your
email."

"Great! Any trouble? Meaning, you weren't

arrested, or anything?"

"No, I got in and out of several databases without notice. It's disquieting how easy it was. A great business opportunity exists in IT security."

"That's more your line, because you're a genius."

"I noticed some patterns to the calls around the time of your father's death. I tried to trace the numbers, but most were burn phones. I sent locations where the calls originated based upon tower triangulation. And the one number I could identify was a retirement home in Elkton. Is that your grandfather?"

The question stunned him like a punch to the stomach. "A pattern of calls with granddad's number in the mix? I'll look."

"Yes, and if I can do anything else, let me know."

As Ben ended his call, he tried to imagine how his grandfather fit in the situation. He wanted to pull over and retrieve Narayan's email, but the plan for the day was in motion. Investigating the pattern of phone calls to Elkton would have to wait.

As he drove, he decided to make one call. Jay's voicemail answered. "This is Ben. I'm sending you a package—Express Mail. Can you run the prints for me? I'll explain later. Thanks, Jay." He had confidence Janet would be able to collect the necessary items.

After lunch in Poplar Springs and just past two, Ben pulled the rental into a parking space in front of Powhatan's courthouse. He spied Janet across the street on a bench, talking to two men. She saw him, but neither acknowledged the other. They had agreed it was too risky. Before leaving the car, he pulled up his pants leg and removed the Beretta and holster from his ankle. He didn't want to set off any metal detectors as he entered the building. Casually, he pushed the weapon under the driver's seat out of sight.

Pedestrian traffic in town was light. His goal to remain inconspicuous as long as possible disappeared as soon as he exited the vehicle. He took a copy of his father's file, and walked into the building. The policeman tending the metal detector watched him remove his belongings from his pocket, and place everything with the folder in the plastic container. He stepped through without incident, and collected his things. "I'm looking for the district attorney."

The officer pointed, "Three doors down on the right."

"Thanks." He walked down the hall and opened the door.

Inside, Sheriff Rappart waited. "Hello, son. I've been worried about you. I heard about Little Rock, and there're all kinds of rumors flyin' 'round here."

Ben shook the man's hand. "Did the DA tell you I was coming?"

"After you called him this mornin', he called me. Asked me to sit in on the conversation. You don't mind, do you?"

"I'll be honest, Sheriff," Ben said, "your brother's palm print makes it difficult for me to trust you."

Rappart looked intently at Ben. Finally, he said "Son, remind me never to play poker with you. I can't read a thing from your face. My brother had issues, as the psychologists would say. 'Round here, people thought him fuckin' nuts." Timmons laughed. "Sure, kid, my brother could've killed your father—not hard to believe."

"If your brother was the murderer, and now, he's

dead, that's the end of the story."

"Yeah, that's how it shakes out. What's on your mind?" the sheriff asked.

"I don't know," Timmons answered. "Meantime, the DA hopes you can talk me out of this plan?"

"I wouldn't presume to do that. Hell, I don't know you that well. He figured your next move and wanted me to hear it from you."

"Glad I'm so predictable."

"Not predictable, son. Ballsy is more like it. Are you sure you want to do this?"

The inner office door opened and a man of thirty appeared. "Won't you come in?" he asked. Ben and Rappart walked in and sat down across from the man's desk. "I'm Bob Satula." He did not offer his hand. "Is that the information?" The DA took the file from Ben, opened it, and began reading. After a couple of minutes, he looked up. "You're asking me to convene a grand jury dependent upon this?"

"That's correct," Ben replied. "My understanding of Arkansas jurisprudence allows me to make such a request based upon the evidence I've just given you."

He continued to read, "Mr. Timmons, this is a forty-five-year-old case. Much of your evidence is supposition. I don't have the resources to commit to your vendetta." He glared at Rappart.

Beside him, Rappart shook his head. "He's right, son. What do you hope to get from this?"

"Mr. Satula, I've given you my information. I've presented the same documents to Elkton, Army CID, NYPD, and Little Rock. They're all investigating various crimes related to my supposition. If you're going to stand aside, that's your prerogative. But they'll all be arriving shortly, and I believe a grand jury will be convened." Ben stood up.

"Wait," Satula said. "Give me an hour to review the information, and I'll make some calls. Will you talk to President Maxwell's chief of staff? I'll get him down here."

"I'll come back in an hour." Timmons and Rappart walked out of the door.

As they exited the building, the sheriff said, "Boy, you've got brass ones."

"I didn't mean to be rude, but I'm aware the local sentiment favors Maxwell. The information I've gathered has been uphill, especially from this community. I had to force his hand."

"You did that!" Rappart looked around the town square. "You're beginnin' to attract some attention."

"Can I ask you a question?"

"Sure, son. Anything."

Ben saw several citizens pointing his way, and a few who looked like reporters were hurrying toward him. "Do you think your brother killed my father, or do you even care?"

"No, I don't think Matt killed your dad!" He sounded angry. "Hell, yes, I care!"

"Then, why haven't you done anything about it?"

"And what the hell am I supposed to do?"

"The palm print's strong evidence," Ben allowed. "Your brother probably did kill my dad. But, let's assume he didn't. Why do you suppose the real killers set him up?"

Ben could see Rappart thinking about his question, "Well, I guess—"

"They'd already decided to kill him, too—thus the

hunting accident. And they had a strong hunch you weren't going to be a problem. Do you think that's it?"

"But the hand print on the car—I can't figure it."

"Yeah," Ben agreed. "But strong enough evidence to deter the half-hearted. My point exactly. If not your brother, how about those two at the airport? Don't they deserve your best efforts?"

Chapter Thirty-Four
Negotiation

Timmons sat on a bar stool at Mosie's, reviewing Narayan's data he'd downloaded to his iPhone. Mosie stood behind the bar, watching a ballgame on television. "What's the score?" Ben asked.

"Two to one, Cardinals."

"Unusual for an afternoon game this time of year?"

"It's a makeup for yesterday's rainout." Mosie answered. "Supposed to be an off day for both teams." Mosie went back to the game, and Ben continued to study the call patterns.

"I heard about the explosion in Little Rock," his friend said. "You were lucky."

Ben shrugged, "I'm a lucky guy." He thought about the two bodies in the morgue while Mosie gave him a funny look.

"Why'd you switch the Ford?" Mosie asked.

"I intended to irritate Special Agent Levitt. I figured she'd marked the car at the airport."

"Have you talked to her?" the old man asked. "Maybe her people saw something?"

"LRPD is handling that," Ben answered. "I don't have much standing with the Secret Service."

Three bowling lanes were being used by a handful of teenagers. Other than that, the place was quiet. "The reporters will eventually find you in here."

"I know," Ben said. "I'm supposed to be back at the courthouse in a bit."

"Kid," his friend asked, "are you sure it's not time to head for the tall cotton?"

"Again, my compliments on the colorful euphemism considering we're in farm country."

"I didn't intend to be articulate," Mosie said. "I'm serious."

"I know," Timmons said. "I'll be leaving by the end of the week."

"Are you at th' motel down th' street?"

"Uh, yeah." He regretted the lie, but didn't want to divulge too much, even to Mosie

"My place's been full until most of the reporters tore out of here on Saturday. Pretty good business with the out-of-towners. Not much to do in Powhatan." Something happened in the game, and it caught his attention. "Course, they bitch more than you about no beer. A bootlegger could've made a fortune the past few days."

Ben laughed, "It's been so long, I've probably lost my taste for it."

"I doubt that. You look like you practice a bit." Just then, the front door opened. "Afternoon, Reverend," Mosie said. "Can I get you an iced tea?"

"I'll take a soda pop, if you don't mind." The reverend took the stool beside Ben. "How are you, son?"

"I'm good, sir." He wasn't in the mood to deal with Reverend Kinson.

Mosie placed a glass in front of Kinson and pretended to turn his full attention to the ballgame. "I brought you a gift," the reverend said and laid a

Contemporary English Bible on the bar.

As the reverend drank, the awkward moment caused Ben to hesitate. "Thank you," He didn't know what else to say.

"I know you've read it," the reverend allowed. "I'm hopin' to convince you to read it again with more of an open mind. Maybe God can reveal the words to you that I couldn't express." Ben looked at the gift without responding. "So, you're goin' to see this through?" Kinson moved the glass aside and rested his elbow on the bar.

"Yes, sir."

"You're thinkin' the blood of those two in Little Rock is on your hands?"

The question surprised Ben. "Something like that."

"A lot of people around here think the same thin'."

"And how about you, Reverend?"

"I believe we're livin' in a world where evil is winnin'. I believe the good people have to work twice as hard." The minister sipped his coke. "And because I'm a Christian, I believe we'll eventually face our own destruction and God's judgment. I know you don't believe that, son. That troubles me, but I'm convinced your motives are sincere."

"Forgive me, sir, but you've changed your mind in the past couple of weeks."

"No," Kinson said. "I believed then and I believe now your course is perilous, not only for you, but for several of my charges. That's the basis of my opposition to what you're doin'."

"How can discovering the truth be such an act against your God's will?"

"My God?" Kinson's voice remained calm, and

that surprised Ben. "There's only one God, son."

Ben saw Mosie take a step back from the television, obviously listening to the discussion. "I'm sorry, sir. It's difficult for me to compromise these days."

"I'm a forgivin' man, Ben. It's a major part of the profession."

"And the blood on my hands?"

"It's not blood you shed, son." He got off the stool, laid a dollar on the bar. "If you need to talk."

As the door closed, Mosie continued pretending to be involved in the ballgame, leaving Ben to his thoughts. As the inning ended, Ben checked his watch. "Mosie, do you have a plastic bag?"

Mosie reached under the bar. He gave the crumpled item to Ben who carefully, picked up the Bible and placed it in the bag. "I've got to be at the courthouse," he said and hurried out.

He opened the driver's door, placed the bag on the passenger seat, and a voice behind him asked, "Timmons?"

He turned as Hank Pittmann approached. A little confused, Ben pretended to be relaxed. Only a few feet away, Hank extended his hand holding an envelope. Ben started to take it, but then, paused. "What's this?"

"You know what it is," Hank said. "My dad told you what he had."

Ben shook his head, "I can't accept it." He held up his hands, indicating refusal. "And even if I did, I promised your father I wouldn't use it."

"Look, I know what it is, and I'll square it with my dad. We have an offer on the farm, and we're sellin' out at the end of the season. You can keep it under wraps 'til I let you know."

Ben shook his head, "No, I won't take it." Hank turned to leave.

"Wait," Ben said, and Pittmann looked back. "Why are you doing this? I mean, this is not the act of someone who…" He hesitated.

"Someone who was willin' to beat the shit outa you for Tonya Pritchard?"

"Ben smiled. "I'm not sure I would've expressed it quite like that, but yeah."

"I guess, I thought I owed it to you."

Now, Timmons was totally confused, "I don't know how to respond to that."

"You're the only one around here who knows, and I didn't see judgment in your eyes. When Tonya told me the deal—" Hank shook his head. "Kid, you know what I'm offerin' you, and you're not takin' it. You're either the dumbest sonofabitch I've ever met, or—" The large man turned and walked away.

Activity in the small town square had increased from earlier, and Ben assumed word had gotten around about his pending meeting. He pulled into a vacant parking space in front of the courthouse, and delayed a moment to finish listening to a song on the radio. His real purpose was to remove the Beretta from his ankle and shove it under the seat. That accomplished, he left the car.

The reporters remaining in Powhatan had taken residence on the courthouse lawn under several trees, trying to combat Arkansas's afternoon heat. He saw Janet among them, but didn't acknowledge her. As he approached the building steps, several of the journalists moved forward, but he stopped them with a gesture. "I can't talk, now," he called. "I'm running late." It felt arrogant of him ducking the press as he hurried up the steps.

He followed the same routine through the metal detector, but this time he didn't need directions. As he retrieved his belongings, the officer said, "They're waitin' on you."

"Thanks," Ben said. "I'll apologize for my tardiness."

"Do you think any of them will apologize to you? Good luck, son." And the officer went back to his business.

The reception area of the District Attorney's office was still empty, but his door was open. Inside, Ben saw Satula, Rappart, and a third man he did not recognize, certainly the ex-president's chief of staff.

Satula motioned him in without comment. The third man spoke, "I'm Willis Baker." He extended his hand, and Ben shook it before sitting in an empty chair next to him. "Mr. Satula told me about your request, and I appreciate the opportunity to discuss the situation." Baker glanced at Satula, and the DA gestured for the chief of staff to proceed. "I looked at the file."

"My file?" Ben interrupted with a frown for Satula. "Are you the president's attorney?"

"Uh…no, I'm not."

"Look, son," the DA said and leaned forward in his chair. "I'm trying to avert a battle. I'm not worried about protocol."

"We're not enemies in this, Mr. Timmons." Baker's words sounded more plea than statement. "We'd like to avoid a grand jury, and I'm here to ask if there's room to negotiate?"

"I'm not in control of the proceedings from this point. I've been assured investigators with other agencies will be arriving in Powhatan to take up this cause."

"That's right, Willis," Rappart said. "There's one from Elkton in my office as we speak. I've received calls from Army CID. They're arriving this evening, and Little Rock will be here tomorrow."

"God damn!" the utterance seemed out of character. "The president's interested in going forward with justice, and welcomes the opportunity to address any issue from the other investigators. However, he'd like to avoid the embarrassment of a local procedure. His enemies in the press would convict him with the indictment."

"I don't presume to know the law," Ben said. "I've just finished my junior year of college. However, it sounds like you believe you can manage the other investigations?"

He waited for Satula's reaction, and the DA didn't disappoint. "You're implyin' we'll turn our backs on wrongdoing. That's a damned insult."

"I've brought you evidence worthy of an investigation," Ben said, "and I'm wondering what you're going to do about it."

"Wait, Mr. Timmons," Baker said. "We're prepared to do battle in the public eye, if necessary. You're attacking America's 9/11 hero. The president deserves better."

"There's strong evidence my family and I are the victims in this. I lost my father as part of this conspiracy." He looked to see if his words made any impression. "We live in a country of rules and laws, but sometimes, they don't apply to the highest bidder." He could tell he wasted his time. "Gentlemen, I'm through with this inquisition."

"I can get you an audience with the president," Baker said.

"I had an audience with the president in DC a few days ago, Mr. Baker. As a matter of fact, this meeting reminds me a great deal of that one."

"No," Baker grunted frustration. "President Maxwell."

"I don't know what the purpose would be for such a meeting, Mr. Baker."

"I'll guarantee you can discuss these issues with the president—openly and honestly."

"I doubt the president will be forthcoming in the conversation. His attorneys wouldn't allow it."

"He'll be perfectly candid, I guarantee," Baker answered.

"And what am I supposed to give the president in exchange for this audience?"

"Back off the push for a grand jury," Baker said. "The other investigations will run their course. We don't need this embarrassment in the president's backyard."

"I can't commit until I hear the president's answers to my question, sir."

"Then, it's a deal?" Baker asked.

"I'll need to bring one other individual with me," Ben said. "A member of the NYU group is in the area."

"I think that will be fine," Baker extended his hand, and Ben took it in agreement. "Let's meet tomorrow afternoon at the club? Say, five o'clock? I'll ask the

Secret Service to escort you."

Rappart and Satula got up from their chairs. "Thank you for your time, gentlemen," Ben said, and he and Rappart started to leave.

"Oh, Mr. Timmons, one more thing," Baker stopped them. "I'd like to keep this discussion out of the press."

"The one protection I've had is the press, Mr. Baker."

"I understand that, but if we avoid any incendiary statements over the next twenty-four hours, perhaps there will be a joint statement after tomorrow's meeting."

It sounded like a politician's agreement. "Yes, sir."

"Good," Baker's face beamed. "If you gentlemen will excuse us, I need to speak with Mr. Satula."

The sheriff walked with Ben to the front exit without speaking. Outside, the policeman said, "I hope ya' know what you're doin'."

"Just playing it by ear," Ben said. This deep into the game, he still didn't know how the players shook out—Rappart included.

Chapter Thirty-Five
Additional Questions

Janet Sharpton stayed with the group of reporters for most of the afternoon. It helped facilitate her cover as a journalist from Indiana and gave her an opportunity to ask questions in an open forum.

At half past two a gentleman hurried into the courthouse. "Who's that?" one of the reporters asked.

"That's Willis Baker, the ex-president's errand boy," came the reply.

"What's going on?" another asked.

"Timmons must be pushing for an official investigation. I believe Maxwell wants to avoid that. It seems Baker and the DA're running interference."

"Why would Timmons want a local investigation? The good citizens of Powhatan are not going to abandon Maxwell. What's the purpose?"

"It's a grandstand play, but it's publicly embarrassing to Maxwell."

"Baker looked like he was in a hurry."

"Yeah, I assume he's preparing for the next meeting, later today."

"Where's the kid? We should talk to him."

"He's not talking to us. Whatever the plan, you've got to admire the kid's guts."

Fifteen minutes later, Janet saw Sheriff Rappart heading toward the courthouse, and she ventured forward. "Officer, can I ask a question?" Their earlier meeting had revealed Rappart's mysognist side, and she didn't relish another conversation.

"Sarah, isn't it? Lookin' good, darlin'!"

"Is Timmons getting his grand jury?"

The sheriff stopped."How'd you know 'bout that?"

She pointed to the crowd of reporters behind her. "Speculation has been flying all day. The consensus is the locals are trying to still the crisis."

"Pretty good guessin', young lady." Rappart shook his head, "Ben's due back at three. We should have a good idea 'round three-thirty. Maxwell, Baker, and the DA are not going to roll over for the kid."

"Any chance he gets what he wants?"

Rappart stopped and looked at Janet, "I wish I believed it, but I'm not sure what the kid wants. He's tryin' to paint Maxwell into a corner, but beats the hell outa me why'd he do it this way. I've gotta get in there, honey." He rushed up the steps.

As she drifted back to the bench in the shade provided by two large oak trees, someone asked, "What'd he say?"

"Only that Timmons is due back by three." Janet answered.

Just past three, Ben parked in front of the courthouse. As he walked to the building, several reporters moved to intercept him, but he motioned them away, saying he did not have time to talk. While she watched Ben disappear into the courthouse, she asked Leonard Simms, "What's this mean?"

"I don't know, girlie," he answered. "I came down here to look for an angle on the 9/11 story. I didn't know anything about the local connections until I arrived. It shocked the hell outa me when I found Timmons in Powhatan. It's got the makings of one great tale."

Janet noticed Christina Turner at the back of the group, alone and, seemingly, in deep thought. As Janet approached, a welcoming expression crossed the reporter's face. "Hello, Sarah."

"Miss Turner, I'd like to talk with you?"

"Call me Tina, honey. I see you got a chance to meet Rappart."

"Yes," Janet replied, "over lunch. He didn't give me much on his brother."

"I'm not surprised," Turner answered. "He's spent most of his life protecting Matt, and to do that, he's had to avoid most questions."

"Was the brother that bad?"

Turner cocked her head to the right, "He came back from the war with a chip on his shoulder. He acted like the world owed him something for what he'd done. I don't know, maybe we did, but it got old very quickly."

"Was he capable of killing?" Janet's thoughts went to the palm print.

"Yeah," Turner said matter-of-factly. "A small-town bully who wanted to move up in the world, he could do almost anything."

"Obviously, Ben Timmons doesn't believe Rappart's brother killed his father, and neither does the lead investigator in Elkton. How about you? The palm print is pretty damning evidence."

Turner shook her head. "I don't know how anyone could fix that. But no, I don't believe Matt killed Jack Timmons. I wish I did."

"That sounds like you know something. Care to share?"

Turner looked at Janet and said, "Your approach this morning upset Tonya. She's very vindictive. Don't underestimate her. She has money and powerful friends, and they're not all boy scouts."

"Thanks for the warning." But Janet didn't understand the local reporter. "Why are you here, Tina? Your colleagues believe you've ruined a promising career by staying in this town."

"My colleagues?"

Janet tried not to react to the mistake she'd made. Turner moved closer and whispered, "Who are you? You're not an Elkton reporter?" Turner stared at Janet, as if trying to decide. "I talked to your editor," she said.

Janet tried to remain calm.

"He spoke very highly of you."

"I'll remember that when I ask for a raise. Did you check on all reporters in town?"

"Just the ones with special talents," Turner answered. "You intrigue me, Miss Greenburg, or whatever your name is. Tell Ben, it's a pretty good plan."

At that moment, Timmons and Sheriff Rappart emerged from the courthouse. All the reporters, including Tina, moved across the lawn. The officer went in the opposite direction, but Ben moved down the steps toward them. "I'm sorry, but I've agreed not to talk to reporters."

A storm of protest erupted from the group. Questions flew from all directions, but Ben held up his hands and shook his head.

"Mr. Timmons, I'm Sarah Greenburg from Elkton.

Can I have a word?" Janet shouted.

"Miss Greenburg, I'll tell you what I can, if you agree to share it with the others." Ignoring a howl of protest from the group, Ben extended his hand for her to come forward. "It's the best I can do," he said.

As Ben and Janet moved away, Janet asked under her breath, "Is your plan working?"

"I don't know. We're meeting with Maxwell tomorrow at five."

"We?" she asked.

"Yeah, hold your cover until then. I told him I'd bring a member of the group, but I didn't identify anyone."

"Won't the Secret Service have to vet us?"

"He's out of office, and hopefully, it won't be like the White House. I'd like to get this meeting behind us, and then, you and I are on our way back to New York."

"You think that will do it?" she asked.

"I don't know my father's killer, but I have an idea." He didn't go on with his thought. "Yes, the investigation will have to go on without us. If they can't make a case with what they have, well—did you get the finger prints?"

"Yes," she answered. "I had lunch with Rappart, along with Mosie and Simington, too. But nothing on the Makarov."

"The Makarov's a long shot," he said. "No one's seen one since Nam." Then, "You got good prints?"

"How do I know?" she asked. "The waitress thought I'd lost my mind buying their drink glasses for souvenirs."

Ben laughed, "Yeah, she'll tell them, and someone will figure it out. Our window is closing."

"There's only a handful of living Vietnam vets in the area. It shouldn't be hard to get search warrants." She touched his arm, "One more thing. Miss Turner isn't fooled by my act."

Ben didn't seemed surprised, "She's too smart. I can't figure her connection to all this." Then, he changed directions. "We'd need probable cause for search warrants, and even that might not be enough. I've an idea," he said. "We'll save it until we're ready to leave town." He leaned closer to her. "I'm going to unlock my car and then, go back and talk with Miss Turner. That should hold most people's attention. In the front seat is a plastic bag with a Bible. Take it, and the items you have to the post office and Express Mail them to Jay."

"A Bible?" she asked.

"Got it from the reverend."

"You think—" She had difficulty hiding her shock. "You're a bastard, Ben Timmons." He didn't argue and headed back toward Christina Turner. The reporters gathered around him, and the attention of the locals focused his way, leaving Janet to the dirty business.

Chapter Thirty-Six
Passion's Reward

With the events at the courthouse concluded, Christina Turner considered returning to the newspaper office. All the reporters who'd abandoned Powhatan on Saturday were now on their way back, and many who'd never been to the area planned a visit. She decided to avoid the issue—at least for the afternoon—and drove home.

As her house came into view, she saw the police cruiser parked conspicuously in front. She turned into her driveway and got out. As she did, Dan Rappart pulled his large frame from the Powhatan vehicle. "Hello, Dan. Nice of you to wait for me," she said sarcastically.

"I need to talk to you, Tina."

"Talk?" she asked. "That'll be a new one for you, won't it? Park in front of my home, please."

"It's a small town, girl. People know."

"It they know anything, Dan, it's because you've been bragging all over town."

"You flatter yourself, woman," he said. "You're not that good."

"Go to hell, Dan!" She turned toward her door.

He grabbed her arm, "We're goin' to talk. I don't care if we do it on the street."

She pulled from his grip, "Come inside." They

moved onto her porch, and she unlocked and opened the door, "Forgive me, if I don't offer you a drink. Sit down, Dan."

"I'll stand," he said. "I'm not going to be here long. The Timmons kid is back. I just left him at the courthouse."

"I know," she replied and sat on a stool at the kitchen counter

"Yeah, I assumed. He's got it figured out," Rappart said.

The words sent a cold chill through her, "What do you mean? What did he say?"

"Nothin'. He doesn't trust me any more than I trust you. But his play at the DA's office took guts. He wouldn't have made that move without havin' all the pieces to the puzzle."

She felt light headed, "How? I mean, he must have said something."

"He's tryin' to flush his father's killer, and if he's successful, it might get him killed." He moved a step closer, "I want to know what you know."

"I don't know anything." She knew he wouldn't believe her. "You're guessing."

"Baby, you think me a buffoon, and maybe, I've earned it. I'm tellin' you the kid has it figured out." He dropped down on the sofa. "Listen, Tina. I'm not dumb enough to believe you suddenly fell in love with me. I enjoyed sharin' your bed, and it was okay even if you just laid there." She remained silent. "I couldn't imagine why you'd do it for anythin' other than money, but I figured ole man Staten left you plenty."

She said nothing, as he turned his head, looked out of the window, and stroked his chin with his hand.

Finally, she said, "Dan, you need to go. The neighbors will be talking."

He didn't acknowledge her comment. "If Staten left you money, why'd you stay here and put up with the gossips, finger pointin' from busy bodies, and back bitin' from the Pritchards?"

"I'm tired," Turner said. "You'll have to go."

He didn't move. "If Staten didn't leave you money, you'd have blown this place long ago. The only reason you'd stay is to protect your interests." Her breath caught in her throat. "Ms. Pritchard has your money tied up somehow, doesn't she?"

"Please leave," she said. "I need you to leave."

Still, he didn't move. "Ms. Pritchard's opinion hasn't changed about you, so whatever you're mixed up in involves Tonya." He watched her , and she tried not to react. "God damn, Tina. You're one dumb bitch. Tonya's not goin' to give you any money."

She jumped up and walked to the door. "I need you to leave."

He followed behind, then stopped. "Are you mixed up in murder?" He stared at her. "Yeah, that'd explain why you helped the kid. You weren't feelin' guilty. It was to control him somehow. You intended to spite Tonya, but she had the power. She's holdin' your money, too." Turner didn't know what to say to change his thinking. "That Pritchard bitch meant to play the kid, but he got away from her."

"Got it figured out, do you?" This late in the game, and Rappart was doing the honorable thing. "Better late than never."

"My brother's been labeled a killer, and I don't think he did that one. I'm goin' to look after my family's name."

"That's very decent of you, Dan." She struggled with her light-headedness. "Worry about him after he's dead, because you didn't give a damn about him while he lived."

She didn't see his hand, but the blow across her face drove her backwards. "And you?" the calm in his voice didn't mask his anger. "You judge me. You're willin' to be the Pritchard's whore, but you're goin' to pass judgment on me?"

She tasted blood inside her mouth. "Get out."

"I've been under the Pritchards' thumb my whole life. Years of practice have made me good at it, and I'm tellin' you, not this time." Before he walked down the steps, he said. "You remember I told you, there'll be no money. You're bein' played like the rest of us." She held her composure until she'd closed the door, and then, out of sight of Rappart, her emotions won.

Chapter Thirty-Seven
Approaching the Finish Line

Timmons and Janet had logged a late night examining the telephone data sent by Narayan. She'd gone to bed around midnight, but Ben put in an extra couple hours replaying his conclusions. He kept looking for any miscalculations in his construction of events leading to his father's death. Around two, he went to bed.

Before she left him the night before, Janet told him she planned an early return to Powhatan. Her cover as an Elkton reporter held up reasonably well the previous day, so she wanted to ask more questions around town. She promised to stay away from Christina Turner and Tonya Pritchard. When he roused himself around noon, he discovered she'd already gone. Ben knew she'd be inquiring about the Makarov pistol, but he didn't expect her to be successful. Whoever possessed the weapon had kept it deep in the shadows for over forty years.

Ben bought a couple of newspapers and enjoyed a leisurely lunch at a local cafe. Wire service stories about the investigation surrounding the airport explosion dominated each paper. A little past three o'clock, he got the rental and headed for Powhatan. He arrived just before four.

The pool hall wasn't busy, so Timmons decided to hide there until time to meet Maxwell. As he walked in,

Mosie said, "Son, the town's full of reporters, and they're lookin' for you. A dozen have been in and out of here all day. They said they'd checked the motel, but you weren't there."

Ben hesitated. "Sorry about the lie. I meant to stay out of sight."

Mosie grinned. "If I wuz in deep shit, I wouldn't trust anyone, either."

"Mind if I hang out here for a bit? I'll leave if any reporters show up."

Mosie motioned for him to take a seat at the bar. "How about a beer? I've got some in the fridge. I can't sell you one, but I can give it to you."

"Is that true?" Ben asked.

"Nah, if you're a business and a non-gentleman, you can't even have an open container. But, what the hell. With all goin' on around here, I don't think the beer police are about."

Ben chuckled. "I'm supposed to meet Maxwell at his club in about an hour."

"I know," Mosie said, as he put two beers on the bar. Ben wondered how the old man heard about the meeting with Maxwell, but he explained. "I think Maxwell's people leaked it to throw off the reporters. They've got the courthouse staked out."

Ben took a sip. "I hope the ex-president won't think unkindly of me if he smells beer on my breath."

"I don't think you could do much to change his opinion of you."

Again, Ben laughed. "I think you're right."

"Kid," the old man said, "I don't know all you've been through, but I've a pretty good idea. Has it been worth it? I mean, knowin' what you know, would you still do all this?"

"There are some things I would've done differently."

"Then, why're you doin' it?" Mosie looked completely dumbfounded. "Is there money in this I'm missin'? Tonya Pritchard offered to pay you off, didn't she? Hell, I understand they were goin' to pay your father. If they had, none of this would've happened."

"Several of the key players in this mess have tried to use that lie against me. I don't believe my father was interested in their money."

"Believe, but you don't know for sure?"

Timmons shook his head. "My father had so many unresolved issues in his life. It's an easy lie to attach to him."

"You're the goddamnest kid I've ever met." The old man looked disgusted. "You don't know why your father was doin' it, but you're plowin' ahead."

"The lie about paying my father allows them to justify their actions." Ben didn't want the beer, but holding the bottle kept his hands busy. "My dad didn't want money, and that's not my purpose, either. Not everything has a price tag."

"You sure it's a lie?" Mosie asked. Ben did not respond, so the man continued, "You're speakin' a foreign language to me. I'd take the money and forget all this." Mosie laughed. "Boy, I hope you and your high ideals stay alive. Anyway, hide out here from the reporters." Just then, the door opened and in walked Janet. "Oh, I spoke too soon, son. One of them found you. Miss Greenburg, isn't it? You've lost your glasses."

"No," Ben realized it was time to explain. "I asked

her to meet me here. This is my friend, Janet."

Timmons saw the confusion on Mosie's face. "Your friend? Is this the Janet you told me about?"

Janet seemed pleased at the revelation, and Ben pretended embarrassment. "No, another Janet."

She extended her hand, "It's nice to finally meet you, Mosie."

"We were—" Ben started to explain.

"No, I've got it figured out," Mosie said. "Pretty slick. Care for a beer?" Janet glanced at her wristwatch.

"Always time for a beer," the old man continued. "Did you find your Makarov?"

"No, I didn't," she answered. "No one seems to know of it. I'm not sure it exists."

"Tell that to the guy in Little Rock." Ben answered.

"What?" Mosie asked. "Somethin' at the airport?"

Ben took one last gulp of beer, "We'll meet again, Mosie." He shook the man's hand. "I'll talk to you before I leave."

Outside the pool hall, the Secret Service waited and fell in behind their white car, as they embarked on the short drive out of town. "How do you want to play this?" Janet asked.

Ben shook his head, "I don't think Maxwell is going to reveal anything."

"Then, why are we doing this?" she asked.

"At the time it seemed the only concession I was going to get." Ben recalled the awkwardness of the meeting in Satula's office. "The DA refused to convene a grand jury. When Baker offered this talk as a compromise, I took it."

"So, when we ask the questions, and he doesn't answer?"

"Try to hold your New York temper," Ben glanced her way. "Remember, he's a former President of the United States."

"Bullshit," Janet sounded annoyed. "If he's done what we think…"

Just before five o'clock, Ben and Janet arrived at the Gentleman's Club. More Secret Service agents spent several minutes examining the vehicle before the two NYU students were allowed through. At the front of the club another agent pointed where to park. As they got out of the rental car, the man said, "The President and Mr. Baker are already here. You'll be searched inside."

"You know who we are?" Ben said.

"Yes," the agent answered, "I know your story."

"Then, I need to give you something without causing a major crisis." The agent moved closer. "For protection, I have a weapon around my ankle. Can I give it to you to hold?"

The agent's hand went to his firearm at his side. Ben bent down, pulled up his pant leg, removed the Beretta, and handed it to the agent

"I've heard the news, and I understand," the agent said. "I'll have it for you when you leave."

Ben and Janet continued into the club, and just inside the door, they were searched. Then, the agents directed them to the study where President Maxwell, his chief of staff, and several staff members were waiting. As they entered, Maxwell and Baker were seated in large easy chairs directly across from a sofa. A table between them held a bottle of Irish Whiskey and two glasses. Neither man made an effort to stand and greet them. "Please come in and sit down," Baker said. He motioned to the people behind him. Several exited the room, but two men in suits remained. At the door leading to what looked like a patio, Special Agent Levitt stood guard. "Have a seat," Baker reiterated. As they walked to the sofa, President Maxwell watched them, but said nothing.

Chapter Thirty-Eight
Fireside Chat

For half an hour, Andrew Pritchard Maxwell sat quietly in the club study, listening to the exchange between Willis Baker and several staff lawyers. The last ten minutes of the discussion turned to an argument as many of the lawyers demanded the pending meeting be cancelled. "Dammit, these kids aren't stupid!" Willis argued. "They're expecting full disclosure. I promised it, and that's why Timmons delayed his grand jury demand."

A chorus of voices took up the response, most directed at Baker, but a few tried to persuade Maxwell. He sipped his drink, but hardly listened

"Mr. President?" he looked to the open door where a Secret Service agent stood. "Your two visitors are here. We'll have them available in a minute, or two."

"Show them in when ready," he said, and then turned to the gathering behind him. "Two of you can stay to listen—nothing more." He motioned the rest toward the door. "Levitt?"

"Yes, sir," her voice came from behind him.

"You stay, too, but detail of this meeting never leaves the room."

Baker took the seat at his side.

"Try the whiskey, Willis. It's very good, and I've a feeling you could use a drink."

"I'm not much of a—" Maxwell threw him a glance.

Baker took a drink of the whiskey and as he swallowed, his face winced from the shock. Maxwell shook his head, amused by Willis's polite lifestyle. "Before the kids get in, let me say to all of you, I'm in control of this meeting." He glanced at the two lawyers seated behind him. "I've got a goddamned law degree, too." He turned in his chair and waited.

The door opened again and several agents escorted the two college kids into the room. Maxwell didn't move from his chair, and Baker followed his lead. "Mr. President," he said, "this is Ben Timmons and Janet Sharpton, the two students from NYU." Maxwell watched as the boy and girl took a seat.

The chief of staff's need for formality irritated him. "I know who the hell they are!" Maxwell looked into the eyes of the two students, and he didn't like what he saw. Over the years he'd grown accustomed to one of two different expressions on the faces of youngsters. One amused him—the look of awe that accompanied the first meeting with a President of the United States. The other irritated him—the look of defiance or rebellion the weak minded adopt without basis or reason. Maybe it remained from the '60s, and those kids had inherited it from their parents.

But as he looked at Timmons and Sharpton, he saw confidence. They weren't intimidated. They weren't defiant, and he didn't like it. "Janet Sharpton," he said. "I know your parents."

"Yes, sir," the girl answered. "My father's a big admirer of yours."

"Thanks for that." Maxwell retrieved his glass.

"Your family's help after 9/11 was invaluable." After a sip, he turned to the boy. "I know your mother, but she's on the other side. How's her campaign going in Indiana?"

"Very well, sir," the boy answered. "In spite of my actions, or so she tells me."

Maxwell knew it to be true. "I saw your performance on TV. I've never been so impressed by college students—even from NYU. Both of you sounded like you knew your stuff. I understand you have some questions for me."

"Should we lay out some guidelines?" Baker asked.

"We agreed to an open forum," Sharpton said. "That's our only guideline."

"In exchange for this meeting, Mr. Timmons will withdraw his request for a local grand jury. That's agreed?" Baker continued.

"Mr. President," Ben said, "the information is in the hands of the authorities. I don't believe you'll avoid other grand jury involvement. I'm not sure this meeting gains you anything." Maxwell saw the boy look past him to the two suits sitting in the rear.

"You don't want to feel like you're extorting this meeting from me? Very honorable of you, young man." He returned his glass to the table. "Perhaps, you've heard of me? I've a bit of a reputation for handling crisis situations."

"I didn't mean to be impertinent."

"My public image and my real personality are very different." Maxwell continued to watch their eyes. "I'm not the buffoon the press portrays. Good-natured, benevolent father-figure plays well among the common people on the campaign trail, but doesn't play well in the offices and hallways of Washington. I have enemies, and I've earned every one of them."

He picked up the bottle and refilled his glass. "I'm told you both have bright futures, if you don't screw everything up with this episode." Neither college student acknowledged his remarks. "What do you want here? I mean, your attempt to embarrass me and tarnish my legacy is dangerous for both of you, and I don't see any payout."

"I didn't have an agenda when I started, sir." A faint look of concern crossed Timmons' face.

"And now, son?"

"I've had several people trying to kill me, because of this investigation. My resolve has increased a bit."

"Do you know why I took this meeting?" Maxwell's question seemed to confuse them. "I don't give a goddamn about your little project, son. You think you've uncovered some long-buried secret, but I don't give a shit. I wanted to meet and have a conversation with these two great minds who think they've unraveled conspiracy secrets about 9/11 and exposed my damaged history. I wanted both of you to understand, I'm the smartest sonofabitch in this room and in my eyes, you're fools." Still watching for their reactions, he retrieved his glass.

Beside him, he thought Baker almost fainted. "We should begin, Mr. President." Baker motioned to the youngsters on the sofa.

Timmons took up the challenge. "Sir, in the few days prior to 9/11, short selling of stocks in the companies directly impacted by the tragedy— specifically, the airlines and many of the financial institutions housed in the World Trade Center—went up two thousand percent above normal. To a marginal statistician, such activity would indicate prior knowledge. There's no way anyone could randomly pick such a scenario and profit by millions, potentially billions. However, investigations into these unusual transactions were specifically tabled by members of your administration. Why'd they do that, sir?"

Maxwell rolled his eyes toward the ceiling and sighed very dramatically. "Son, those are unfounded speculations made popular by political enemies. I'm surprised your group fell for such lies."

"Sir," Janet said, "we have detailed statements from employees of several stock exchanges who recorded the trades. All official records of the transactions were removed by the Maxwell administration. However, we have many hand-written notes from those employees."

Maxwell studied the two students for clues to their motives. "In my opinion the explosion of social media has adversely impacted our society. Huge numbers of our population say or do anything to get their fifteen minutes of fame. There's very little shame in our culture, which means a total loss of pride and respect. Damn little in this room, too."

He saw Timmons glance at Sharpton, but she didn't react. "Sir, a series of denials wasn't what Ben and I expected."

"Child, when you ask me about things that never happened, the only thing I can offer is denial."

"Wait," Baker interrupted. "Let's try this, again."

"Shut up, Willis," Maxwell shouted. Turning back to the NYU students, he said, "In spite of what you might think, I don't enjoy reliving 9/11. It stained my administration and damaged my legacy. But, it's a part of my history, and I don't think my name will ever be mentioned in the history books without that reference."

Janet persisted. "In our model we've identified unusual transactions in our own economy and around the world that seemed related to the events. Too dependent to be coincidence and the likelihood they were random is beyond measure—one chance in ten billion."

"You and Timmons have thrown out so many wild guesses, and you want me to give credibility to your foolishness by confirming or denying? I can't do that."

"Mr. President," she said, "we've uncovered financial transactions that merit investigation. With the power of the US government, we could confirm our suspicions, or lay such matters to rest. Instead, the government's blocking us, when it seems they'd be interested in the answers. It looks like the government has something to hide. Some of these unusual transactions involve several agencies of the federal government."

"Goddamned fools!" Maxwell didn't hide his defiance, "You want some honesty?" Baker moved forward in his chair, but the ex-president motioned for him to be still. "You and Timmons are idealistic children, unfamiliar with the real world in which we live. John and Jane Doe don't understand what you're talking about—much less care. Economic models, put options, monetary movements prior to the attacks, it's all bullshit to the average American." He gulped down several swallows from his glass.

"Do you know what it takes to win the White

House?" He waited, but neither responded. "I had to convince the wealthy people in this country to give a billion dollars for my campaign. Do you think they do that because they have the best interests of the poor and uneducated in mind? Hell, no! To get a billion dollars, I made deals with many of those honorable elites like Sharpton's parents. It takes financial promises to the wealthy donors that when you're in office, you'll make them even wealthier. If my deal is good enough—better than my opponent's—I get the money. It's that simple, and I played the game very well."

"Mr. President," Baker cut in.

"No, Willis, they have a right to know," Maxwell said between gulps. "I got the money, but the key to winning elections is getting enough votes from the poor. The rich can buy the campaign, but the poor fill the ballot boxes." He took another drink. "And do you know how you get the votes of the poor? You promise them pie-in-the-sky—free health care, a chicken in every pot, or a car in every garage—more entitlements. Hell, calling it entitlements is bullshit. It's Robin Hood. You spend your political career calculating how much you can rob from the rich to bribe the poor and maintain order. Bullshit! And you expect to scare me with exposure for playing the game better than most. Good luck to you."

"Are you saying you were complicit in the economic redirection that's taken place over the past decade?"

The ex-president looked at the boy's sad eyes. "Do you think I wanted to destroy the country? Believe me, there are plenty of politicians in Washington who do. You're given a complex mess of budgets filled with foreign aid which isn't anything more than a bribe. You're paying some despot in some oil-producing country to maintain control and continue the oil flow. Across that border, you're paying his enemy for the same thing, and they're working against each other.

"Here in this country, it's deals and trade-offs. I can't get funding for education in Michigan unless I let some idiot in Texas have a howitzer on his front lawn. You try to do more good than harm, and sometimes, the margin's damn slim."

Timmons's voice sounded calm. "And the determination of more good than harm is subjective? Your own values come into play?"

He sat his glass on the table. "You can go to hell, young man! Your pretended naiveté won't play with me. I was trying to save the god damned country, whether you believe it, or not." He ran his finger around the rim of the glass while staring at the girl. "Miss Sharpton, your family has more money than God. If they wanted, they could cure homelessness in the greater New York area. But, that's not how it's done, is it?" Janet shook her head, but remained silent. "No," the ex-president confirmed. "What's my benefit from donating? How do I pay less in taxes? Let's rig the system to make more money tomorrow?" Now, he looked at Ben. "You know economics, Timmons. Am I right? Tell me how you think we got to this point."

"Sir, we started this project because we needed to understand the situation."

"No," Maxwell didn't let him off the hook, "I'd like to hear the opinions of you two children." The ex-president hadn't expected this direction of discussion, but he enjoyed the sound of his own voice. "Why don't you two scholars dazzle me with your knowledge of how we arrived at this mess?" He waited with a faint smirk on his face.

Ben spoke. "There'd been budget deficits before, but this hole originated with the Reagan administration."

"Reagan floated the idea of Star Wars." Janet took over. "That triggered massive government spending in defense. Social programs couldn't be cut and the defense industrial complex exploded with growth, financed by budget deficits,"

"Okay," Maxwell allowed, "you know the basics. How'd we go from there? Go on, Timmons. Show me how brilliant you are."

"The country's economic decay has been disguised over the past few decades," Ben said, "fueled by consumer borrowing pushing an unstable economy and massive government growth financed by deficits."

"I'm enjoying this," Maxwell said. "Do you two want a drink?" Both shook their heads while he poured more whiskey into his glass. "No?" He picked up the glass. "Where were we?" Maxwell looked at Baker, but his chief of staff had only a confused stare. "Oh, budget deficits. Hell, you know it couldn't be maintained. Not the path we were on." He sipped his whiskey while the room remained quiet.

Janet said, "So, you did try to alter the course of the country?"

"Not alter," he said. "We tried a complete pivot. A slight course alteration might delay our trip, but we'd still arrive at the same destination. I wanted to write history—not just live out the mistakes of my predecessors. We were in a war, and I made battlefield decisions. That's how I want to be remembered."

"We've been involved in Middle East politics for a century with no end in sight. As long as we needed oil, we were at their mercy. When I entered office, we were a minor oil producer. Today, we're the largest in the world. How's that for a pivot?"

Maxwell wanted another drink, but thought he'd had enough. He looked at the faces of the students, but couldn't detect anything from their expressions. He saw the stunned look on the face of his chief of staff. "What the hell's wrong with you, Willis?" The two suits behind Baker looked as stunned as he did. He must have divulged too much. "Go on with your questions, children."

Maxwell watched Sharpton shrug toward Timmons.

"Sir," the boy said, "do you stand behind the original findings in my uncle's shooting?"

He really wanted another drink, but again, he resisted. It struck him that his ears felt warm. He put his hand to his forehead and mopped the perspiration. "Levitt, can you check the thermostat? It's hot as hell in here. There's not a court in the country that'll reopen your uncle's case. I have the official records, and too many of the participants are dead. Your calculations make good reading, but in a court of law, they're unsubstantiated speculations. You're fucked, kid." He decided on one more drink. "Like you two, when I was young, I saw the world as black and white. I had high ideals, and I expected the world to function accordingly. However, I recognized the error of my thinking very early on, and I recommend the same for you." Some of the whiskey had splashed from his glass onto his shirt, and he wiped it with his hand. "There's no black and white, kids."

The two students rose from the sofa, but he remained seated. Baker rose and escorted them to the door. "The Secret Service will see you back to town."

Maxwell fired his parting shot. "You're wasting your time. President Cohen and the industrial might of the US won't allow you to win the big battle, and I will win this small one. You two need to concentrate on your studies, and let us manage the country."

Without comment, the students walked out of the door.

Chapter Thirty-Nine
Assessment

As they exited the club and headed for their car, the agent said to Ben, "I put the weapon under the driver's seat."

And as the two students walked past him, the man whispered, "How'd it go in there?" Janet and Ben stopped and looked at him. "Most of us know what you're trying to do."

Ben looked at Janet and shook his head. "Would you say we struck out?" he asked her.

She said, "Pretty near a perfect game for Maxwell."

"That's too bad, kids." The agent returned to the front of the building.

As they stopped at the gate, another agent asked, "Do you need an escort back to town?"

"No, thanks," Timmons said. "We're okay from here," and he accelerated onto the county road. As he drove, he thought about the meeting, and Janet must have been doing the same.

After a couple of miles, she said, "You don't really think we struck out, do you?"

"Of course not," Ben answered. "I didn't want to divulge too much to the agent."

"Do you think Maxwell has a drinking problem?"

"He can drink, but I don't think he was out of

control."

"Then, why'd he do it?" she asked. "That was more than I'd hoped to get in my wildest dreams."

"Ms. Pritchard surprised me the same way yesterday," he replied. "I can't figure the main players in this. It's like they think themselves invincible, or something."

"Basically, he admitted to most of our suspicions, but also, said we'd never be able to prove it. His arrogance offended me."

"I don't think he meant we'd never be able to prove it," Ben said. "I think he meant we'd never be allowed to prove it." He brought the vehicle to a stop at an intersection and looked for any cross traffic. No other vehicles in sight, but he did not proceed. Instead he looked at Janet, "I believe we were just threatened by an ex-president of the United States."

"Very exciting stuff, don't you think?" Janet appeared pleased. "However, I don't believe the current president kissed us on the cheek the other night. Must be a world record? Maybe, we should contact those people who monitor such things?"

"Why do so many Jewish people seem to relish adversity?" Ben laughed. "There's something to be said about getting along."

"Bullshit!" she replied. "You have a lot of nerve to lecture me about getting along. How many friends have you made in the past two weeks?"

"Not many." He thought. "Maybe, one or two?" He made the turn and continued.

"My family—definitely, my father—believes the quality of one's life is enhanced by friends and relationships, but the true worth of one's life is measured by the ardent opposition of enemies."

"I believe your standing in the faith just went up, my dear." He recognized her pleasure with that thought.

"What now?" Janet asked. "What more can we do?"

Ben shook his head, "I think we're done, or at least, we need to be."

"What about the palm print? Shouldn't we hang around until we hear from your cousin?"

"How about dinner? Our last evening in Powhatan deserves a good meal." He saw the skepticism on her face. "Come on," he continued. "After we eat, I've got one last errand, and then, we'll head for Little Rock. With any luck, we can be back in the Big Apple by noon tomorrow."

"What's the errand?"

"It's a long shot," he shrugged. "Still looking for the Makarov. I'm hoping for something solid on the finger prints, but just in case, there's a firing range outside town." He pointed to the north. "Probably, won't find anything, but we can look before we leave."

"A firing range? God help us!" she said.

"Relax," he replied. "It won't take long, but my mind won't allow me to leave without looking. Besides, I'd like a chance to shoot the Beretta before returning it to Dr. Hameed."

"Blood-thirsty savage," she said, and they both laughed.

Chapter Forty
Only the Good

The man watched the twilight gray turn to darkness and enjoyed the unusual coolness of the evening. He hoped he'd miscalculated the conclusion of the day's events. After leaving Maxwell's club, Timmons and the girl returned to town for supper. They'd spent a couple hours in the restaurant, going over the conversation with the ex-president, he assumed. All that time, he waited across the street, out of sight and trying to decipher their next move. As the evening sky turned darker, they got in their car and headed north.

With the inquiries about the Makarov, he suspected they were headed for the old target range. He followed them from a safe distance until they'd turned left onto Rural Route 6, and he thought he guessed wrong about their destination. If they were bound for the firing range, they should have turned right. He hoped they were going elsewhere, but most likely, they'd mixed up the directions. Still, he had to be sure, so instead of continuing to follow them, he decided to wait at the complex.

Their questions about the man's Vietnam souvenir puzzled him. How had they gotten onto that information? It had been his mistake to use it in the airport garage on the Good Samaritan, but the kids were looking for it before. He didn't think anyone in the world knew about the weapon, but if evidence existed, it would be found in those catch boxes on the firing line. He doubted any spent cartridge remained in those old troughs, but he knew, if anyone could find proof of the weapon, it'd be Timmons.

He'd parked well down the road away from detection and hiked back. Now, as he stood in the shadows by the spotter's station, the Makarov with silencer rested on the scorer's table beside him. The man had intentionally brought the weapon out of respect for the kid and his efforts to reconcile his father's death. He knew tonight's plan, if it played out, wouldn't resolve his problems. The NYU student had stirred trouble from Powhatan to Little Rock and all the way back to the kid's home town in Indiana. Likely, if he killed the boy tonight, the whole scheme would still unravel, and he'd still go down with it. However, he couldn't see any other course of action, and they could only put the needle in his arm once.

He wanted a smoke, needed a smoke, a craving he'd never been capable of handling when on a stakeout. The warmth of the smoke soothed his shortness of breath. The routine kept his hands busy, and it calmed him. His aim was more accurate with that bit of nicotine coursing through his lungs and arteries. In the still of Arkansas's night, he wished he'd brought those precious weeds with him.

Below, he heard a vehicle enter the parking area, and he saw the headlights in the distance. After a moment, the lights went out, and car doors slammed—two. He heard voices and recognized Timmons's and the girl's. Dammit, he felt bad for the boy, but the girl had nothing to do with any of this. She'd chosen to be friends with the wrong nosy kid, and didn't deserve tonight's wrath. He shook his head, trying to dispel the troubled thoughts, and then reached over and picked up the pistol.

A flashlight moved along the walkway and turned toward the firing line. Hidden by darkness, he listened to their voices. In the dim light, he could tell they spotted the cartridge trough and moved to it. Both kneeling, the girl held the flashlight while Ben started sifting with his hands. He heard the girl asked, "How will you recognize one cartridge out of all these?"

"It's a thicker nine millimeter, and I suspect it'll show some age," Timmons replied. "Makarov ammunition is difficult to find in the United States, unless you're a serious gun collector."

Damned kid! How did he know that? And the man wondered what he'd done to give away the presence of the weapon.

He moved away from his hiding spot behind the spotter's station, squared his feet toward the target and breathed deeply, letting the cool air fill his lungs. Slowly, he brought the Makarov up and aimed. He heard Timmons say, "All firing ranges recycle the brass to offset expenses. Most serious gun owners retrieve their own, so finding anything is unlikely."

He heard Janet ask, "Elkton was only guessing about the weapon. What if they're wrong, and someone else dropped the bullet at the scene?"

The man silently cursed himself in the darkness, realizing he'd made a mistake in Indiana. Apparently, he'd been careless when he removed his hands from his jacket pockets. In the darkness, he heard Timmons say, "If I'm wrong, we waste some time and get a little dirty. No big deal."

Hearing that last statement, the man hesitated, but only for a moment. He took careful aim and pulled the trigger. The pistol bucked in his hands, and even with the Poseidon suppressor, the report was loud.

"Ben!" he heard Janet scream, and he watched as Timmons sprawled in the dirt, and then, the two scrambled behind the storage lockers along the firing line. "You're bleeding." Her voice held concern and fear.

"No shit," he heard the pain in the kid's voice. "It must have been a Kryptonite bullet," and the man smiled at the kid's joke. "I'm bleeding."

Obviously, Janet had no medical training. As he listened to the two students, he lowered the weapon to his side. No hurry. He had plenty of time. "I need something to stop the blood." He heard the girl's fear.

"First aid kit's in the trunk of the car." The kid sounded cool under stress, and the regret swelled in the man's chest. How had everything gone so wrong to lead him to this place and this time? "I'll press with my good hand while you tear my shirt." He heard what must have been the ripping of the kid's clothes. "That's good, thanks," and more movement from behind the storage units, "Use my belt. Pull it tight."

"Who is that?" Janet asked. "What sonofabitch shot you, and what do we do?"

As he stood listening, he heard Ben say, "I think I know who it is." Then, louder, "Mosie, is that you?"

He shook his head. "Right, kid. Too smart for your own good." In the darkness of the range, it was only the two NYU students far away from the world they knew.

"Mosie?" He heard Janet react. "You mean he's

the—?"

No need to hurry this task. "Where did I get you, kid?"

"In the shoulder," Ben said from behind the lockers. "Hurts like hell."

"A little too far for a silencer, I guess. I'm not as steady as I used to be."

"I'm not complaining," Ben said. "I'm still breathing."

"Only for a while, kid." The boy and girl were whispering, but he couldn't understand what they were saying. "I'm sorry 'bout this, Ben."

"We don't have to do this, Mosie." It sounded like the kid got to his feet. "We could go across the state line for a beer. My treat."

"I wish I could, Ben." Then, "You're not thinkin' of tryin' for the car, are you?" It was an obvious, but unwise choice. "You wouldn't make it."

"At this point, we're exploring all options." Mosie sighed. "No cell phone service out here?" More whispering between the two, "Mosie, I'm asking you not to do this."

"You pulled it all together, kid. I tried to get you to walk away." Then, he realized a tear crept slowly down his cheek, and a knot choked his throat. How long had it been since he'd felt such emotion? "I've run out of ideas, son. You forced me into this dumbass move."

"It won't change anything, Mosie." He knew that. "Maxwell and Ms. Pritchard have filled in most of the holes, and the investigation won't be stopped."

He had to know, "How'd you get onto me? There were plenty other likely candidates."

"Well, the rental car explosion eliminated

Rappart's brother as a suspect?"

Mosie brushed the moisture from his face. "Yeah, another dumb move, but I thought I was hidden. How'd you go right to me?"

"I didn't go right to you. I had several suspects. The palm print on my dad's car..." More whispering from behind the lockers "...too perfect to be a plant, so whoever left the print was the killer. Unfortunately, the sheriff couldn't narrow the candidates enough. I collected several prints and sent them to Elkton." As he listened to Timmons's explanation, Mosie's mind raced in a thousand different directions. "When I was in Kansas, the army said they could help. They're checking the records of local Vietnam vets, yours included. I sent a restaurant glass with your handprint to Elkton." More shuffling in the darkness from the kids' direction. "You won't get out of this, man."

"Too far to back out now, son," he shook his head at the stupidity. "When I saw you with the minister's Bible, I figured you were collecting prints."

"I haven't gotten any results on the prints, but it occurred to me, when we were talking the other day, you knew the first rental car was a Ford."

"What?" he didn't remember.

"You knew what rental car I had driven, but I don't remember it ever being at your place. The news reports didn't mention the make or model. I wasn't sure, but the only way you could have seen it was in the Little Rock garage."

"I can't believe I'm so stupid!" His anger at himself clouded his thoughts. He felt sorry for the kids.

"I'd hoped to find a spent cartridge tonight. That'd get us a search warrant, and I was betting we'd find the

Makarov." Then, another plea from Timmons, "Mosie, there's no point in doing this."

"Dammit, Ben!" Janet's voice had a tone of calm intensity. "I can't get a signal out here," and Ben whispered something.

"Mosie, I suspected you, and there are too many investigators looking now. You'll never get past them."

"You're a smart boy, Ben."

"So, there's no sense in shooting us?"

"Son, my only chance is to pull some money together and disappear, but I can't do that with you and the girl pointin' fingers at me. This won't stop the investigation, but it'll buy me some time." He took a step toward their hiding place. "Sorry, kids."

Suddenly, from the dim he saw Timmons emerge from behind the storage locker. Mosie could see the bandage on his left shoulder, and his arm hung limp on that side. His other arm extended, and he had a pistol in his hand. "You clever punk! Where'd you get a gun?"

"I don't want to do this, man. Put down the weapon."

Ballsy kid, he thought, but could he shoot? "It won't work, son. No turnin' back at this point." The tears on his face were getting heavier. "You're goin' to have to shoot me."

"I will, man. Don't make me do it. Please." Just enough light fell on the kid's face for Mosie to see his emotions, too.

As he lunged toward the spotter's station, trying to gain cover, he brought the Makarov up and fired. He missed, but the two reports from the kid's weapon were true, and he felt the rounds tear at his stomach and chest. His dive for cover stopped, his knees gave way, and he fell. As he lay on the ground, he could taste the dust and blood in his mouth, feel the small stones digging into his face, and the dampness of the earth made him colder. He tried to roll onto his back, but could only make it part way.

Immediately, the kid kneeled beside him, taking the Makarov and throwing it away. "Janet, can you drive up the road until you get a signal. We need an ambulance." He extended the keys, but she hesitated and even in the night, Mosie could see the contempt on her face. "Janet!" Ben insisted, and she took the keys.

"Come with me." Her eyes did not move away from him on the ground. "You're bleeding, and I can get you to a hospital. We can send someone back for Mosie." The smell of blood and the New York princess had a ruthless streak in her.

"I won't leave him here," and Mosie could not understand the kid's motivation. Anyone else would let him die in the dirt. This boy, wounded himself, was concerned for his father's killer. "Hurry, Janet!"

"Watch him, Ben! I don't trust him." She hurried down the walkway toward the parking area.

Ben turned him onto his back, and using his good hand, he tried to stem the blood flow. "You're wastin' your time, kid." Ben didn't say anything, so he continued, "Where'd you get the gun?"

Now, it was the kid's turn for heavier tears. "I got it from a Syrian professor."

Mosie didn't understand, but it didn't matter. "Where'd you learn to shoot?"

"My dad taught me. Actually, he never fired a weapon after returning from the service. As a child, I showed interest, so he took me to a local range for lessons."

"Someone did a good job teachin' you." He struggled getting his breath, and the ground felt very cold. "Your father must have been a good man, kid."

Ben was crying, now. "Why? Because I know how to kill someone? That's not a test of quality, you bastard. You know how to kill." Mosie heard him catch his breath.

"Say what you want, Ben. It won't matter in a minute, or two." A sharp pain tore through his gut, and he lost his words. He coughed, and the taste of blood increased.

"I'm not interested in spitting on even you, Mosie."

"It was a stupid play, kid," he gasped. "Sorry 'bout your dad." It seemed like midnight—so very dark. "I've killed, and regret jus' two." He didn't have enough breath to tell about the innocent rice farmer in Nam. "One was your dad." His breathing grew shorter. "Too little, too late, I guess."

"Did you kill my professor, too?" Timmons seemed to spit the words. "I need to know."

He tried to shake his head, but couldn't find the strength. "No, not me, kid. But, I know the gentlemen who did. My job was to get you. "

The kid spoke through his tears, "Dammit, Mosie! Why'd you get into this?"

He struggled to catch his breath. "My ideals aren't as righteous as your, son. I did it for money. Men always go for the money. You need to remember that, son. It's not over, kid. Follow the money," he whispered.

"Hang on!" Timmons said. "Janet will bring help."

"You've done good, Ben, but watch your back

from here. I don't want to be your rice farmer." More coughing ended further explanation.

Vaguely, he felt Ben increase the pressure on his wounds. "Shut up, man. Stay with me. Help is coming."

Another hard cough, and the blood and spit choked him. He struggled to clear his throat. "I know you don't believe in such, son, but when you get to your final destination, look me up." He felt the pain leaving his body as he whispered, "I'll buy you a beer."

Chapter Forty-One
Under Investigation

"Stay with me, man!" In the darkness Ben could see the cold stare from the man's eyes. He lifted his right hand from the wound and realized the blood had stopped gushing from the old man's chest. Ignoring the hurt, his shortness of breath, and the pounding of his own heart, he pressed two fingers against the man's throat, searching for the carotid artery. After perhaps a half-minute, he removed his hand, sat back on the dirt, and looked at the motionless body. Squeezing his left shoulder, he tried to subdue the pain as he rested on his back, stared up at the stars, and tried not to cry.

He felt a warm, sticky substance down his left side, and he was so cold. Was he home? No, he remembered Arkansas in the middle of summer, and he felt tired. He closed his eyes and tried to ignore the ache

"Ben! Ben!" Janet's voice startled him. A bright light shined in his face, jarring him back to awareness. "I couldn't get a signal, but Mr. Pittmann will help us."

"Pittmann?" He tried to shake the fog from his brain. "Mosie? Can you check on—?"

"I'm sorry, son." A man's voice came out of the darkness. "He's dead."

"Can we get him to the car?" He could hear the concern in Janet's voice.

"No, we'll throw him in the back of my truck, and

get him to the hospital. You stay in the back with him and keep pressing his wound."

"Mr. Pittmann," Ben said, "I need to talk with you."

"Yeah, I know, kid. Not now. Let's get you to a doctor."

Ben felt hands lifting him off the ground. Then, the feel of the cold metal surface jarred him as Pittmann and Janet loaded him into the cargo area of a pickup truck. "I need to talk with you."

"Get in there with him, Miss. Tell him I'll give you my life insurance receipt. You can make sure he gets it." Timmons heard the tailgate latch. "If we haul ass, it'll still be fifteen minutes to the hospital. Don't either one of you bounce out." The jolt of the truck door slamming jammed his injured shoulder, and made him wince. Next, came the rev of the engine, and as the vehicle sped off, he heard the loose stones and gravel against the undercarriage of the vehicle.

The scent of Janet's perfume filled his nostrils, and he felt her arms around him, but it offered little comfort as the jarring ride quickly rendered him unconscious.

****

Thursday morning, a nurse woke him with his medication. He swallowed the two pills with a sip of water, and nodded thanks. As he rolled over, hoping to go back to sleep, he saw Janet dozing in one of the bedside chairs. Beside her in another chair, his mother, Connie Timmons, looked unkempt, uncomfortable, and anything but gubernatorial. Perhaps it was the strangeness of the location or maybe, the strength of the narcotics, but it took him a moment to recognize where he was. He lifted his right hand and touched the heavy bandage on his left shoulder.

Tuesday night when Mosie died, Janet and Pittmann rushed Ben to the hospital. The rest of the evening remained a blur. Apparently, a Makarov inflicts a hell of a wound, and it'd taken several hours of surgery to stop the internal bleeding and repair the damage to his shoulder. He touched the bandage, again.

Wednesday saw a steady stream of visitors to his hospital room. Sheriff Rappart took his statement about the events at the firing range. Christina Turner questioned him for the newspaper and the wire services. Reverend Kinson sought some absolution from Ben, and failing that, took the opportunity to pray for his salvation. His mother arrived mid-morning without her staff. And he was surprised when Dean Epstein visited mid-afternoon. Other investigators from Little Rock and Elkton wanted to talk with him, but the doctors asked them to delay until Timmons grew stronger.

He stirred, and Janet opened her eyes, stretched and looked around the room. Spotting his mother still sleeping, she whispered, "What time is it?"

"No idea," he said. "I can't find my iPhone, and apparently, hospitals have something against clocks in the rooms. I could turn on the television."

"No, you'll wake your mother." Then, she asked, "How are you?"

He shrugged on his good side without further explanation, "I could eat."

"Okay," she said, getting out of the chair. "I'll see about breakfast." As she rushed from the room, he thought how pretty she was—even after a night spent in a hospital chair.

"I like her, Ben," his mother mumbled. "What's up

with you two?"

"It's too complicated to explain, Mom."

His mother sat up in the chair and tried to smooth the wrinkles from her slacks. "Oh, your sister keeps me advised. She thinks you and Janet are too traditional." She yawned and rubbed her eyes. "The doctor said we could move you home, tomorrow. I've arranged transportation with a medical staff. It's a long drive, but we can stop whenever necessary."

"I think I'll be okay," he said. "Janet's going back to New York. She's returning the car to Little Rock later today."

"Last day in Powhatan. I'm glad you're getting out of here."

"Well, I do have some legal issues." He remembered Mosie. "I still need the district attorney to release me to travel."

"Just a formality," she said. "You defended yourself, and saved Janet, too."

"Then, why does it feel like vengeance?" he murmured.

"What?"

Just then, Janet walked back into the room. Behind his classmate, Rappart, Turner, and the Pritchard women followed. "They're serving breakfast in a few minutes." She pointed to his visitors. "I told them you were feeling better." She rolled her eyes.

He looked at the group, "I'm sorry we don't have enough chairs." Ben watched old Ms. Pritchard walk around the bed and sit down in the chair Janet had vacated. Tonya stood beside the policeman with Miss Turner in the back. "Mother, this is Ms. Pritchard and her granddaughter, Tonya. And of course, you know the sheriff and Miss Turner. They were both here yesterday."

"It very nice of you to visit." His mom touched the arm of the grandmother as a gesture of gratitude.

"Not at all," the old lady replied. "We've grown fond of your son." Ben recognized the lie, but it did render his mother speechless.

Rappart said, "I've heard from your hometown police. You'd sent some items for fingerprintin'. The drinkin' glass had a match to the print on your daddy's vehicle. I assume Mosie's?"

"Yes, it was."

"You already knew that," Rappart said.

"I did," Ben replied. "My cousin called me last night with the results."

Rappart asked, "How many more of our citizens did you submit for criminal examination? Me?"

"I'd rather not answer that without the advice of counsel," he replied, causing the officer to chuckle aloud.

"I could call your attorney, but I have the feelin' his fingerprints are in Indiana, too." Ben did not respond, causing the policeman to laugh even more. "That's what I thought." He took a step closer for emphasis. "The investigation can't be stopped. Obviously, a full-blown conspiracy existed with Mosie as the trigger. I'd bet he killed Matthew, too."

Ben watched Tonya and Ms. Pritchard. While he appreciated their visit, he knew their primary concern was to learn whatever he had discovered. "I'm glad it lets your brother off the hook, Sheriff. Good for you."

"Thanks to you, kid."

"Any chance to reopen your brother's case?" Ben

knew the answer.

"Nothin' I can see," he replied. "His wishes were to be cremated, so ashes are all we've got."

"Any clues about the other participants?" Janet asked. "How'd Mosie plant the palm print, for instance?"

"We're not sure," answered Powhatan's top policeman. "It's likely he bribed someone in state records."

"How would he do that?" Janet continued. "Aren't the files secured?"

"Well, sure they're secured," Rappart said. "The criminal database is ironclad. Not so much state employees." Behind the sheriff, Miss Turner was taking notes on a pad of paper.

"That's reassuring," Janet's sarcasm was apparent. "I'm sure the computer terminal and password will be identified and that person found. How about the masterminds of this scheme?"

"Well, I've got a pretty good lead," Rappart replied. "It'll take some chasin' down, but I'm on it."

While Ben listened to Janet and Powhatan's head policeman, his eyes went back and forth between Tonya, Ms. Pritchard, and Miss Turner. "I'm glad to hear it, sir. I'm sure there's a solution in our futures."

"How about you, Mr. Timmons?" Ms. Pritchard asked. "I assume you're returnin' to Indiana to recuperate? Have you put your demons to rest over this issue?"

"I have some legal issues in this town," he answered. "Can you update me, Sheriff?"

Rappart took a small step forward. "Well, based upon the evidence we've recovered and Miss

Sharpton's description of events, I'm not holdin' you. You've got some enemies in these parts, and they'd like to make more of the shootin'." He paused with his explanation, but did not look at Tonya. "The DA agreed to delay the preliminary hearin' until you've recovered, and no one here is goin' to delay your trip home."

"How about Mosie's family?" Timmons asked. "Has anyone done anything about funeral arrangements?"

"My god, Ben," Janet sounded upset. "He did try to kill us."

"I agree with Janet," his mother said. "He killed your father, Sheriff Rappart's brother, and he tried to kill you two kids. I don't give a damn if they leave him out with the garbage."

Ben did not reply to either of the comments, and Rappart said, "I don't think he had any family, son. He's a retired vet, so the military will bury him."

"My grandmother inquired about your intentions beyond your recovery?" Tonya asked. "Can we bring an end to this vendetta?"

Timmons looked at Tonya and then, turned to Ms. Pritchard. "Mosie was the trigger, but I haven't found the person who sent him."

"Do you have any leads, son?" The sheriff took another small step forward.

"Isn't that your job?" Ben could tell Tonya tried to be casual with the inquiry, but she failed.

Rappart looked at Tonya with equal contempt. "I'm just usin' every available resource, Miss. The boy's done a pretty good job up to now."

Ms. Pritchard leaned forward and raised her hand to quiet Tonya. Ben thought she was trying to defuse the situation. "I'm still your likely suspect, young man?"

Maybe, it was the pain pills, or maybe, he'd tired of the mystery. He shook his head and failed to hide his sadness. "In spite of what you said to me the other morning, ma'am, I've tried to keep an open mind." She didn't respond, so he continued. "I conducted a search of phone patterns between Arkansas and Indiana around the time my father died." He didn't want to reveal Narayan's role in his search.

"How in the world did you do that, son?" Rappart looked at him with awe. "You'd need warrants for that information." It was obvious he realized the idiocy of his statement, so he fell silent.

"Is that an admission you've committed several felonies?" All attention turned toward Tonya. "I'm sure the DA will be interested in that disclosure."

"Hush, Tonya, and let the boy talk," Ms. Pritchard sounded irritated. "Go on, young man. Obviously, you think you found somethin'."

"Dammit, Ben," his mother interrupted. "I agree with Tonya. You can't go in and out of protected systems with immunity. Do you realize what I'd have to do, if you're arrested for corporate espionage?"

Timmons didn't feel a need to respond to his mother's question, either. To Ms. Pritchard, he said, "When I identified the likely pattern of calls, I looked for the owners of the phones. Unfortunately, the Arkansas numbers were to burn phones, apparently purchased with the intent to hide their existence."

"So, what did you find?" Ms. Pritchard asked.

Ben looked at Janet, and she signaled him to continue. "I discovered a pattern of calls to my grandfather's care facility." He paused a moment, watching for a reaction. "Someone used my grandfather as part of the scheme, and yes, ma'am, I assumed you. His mind had almost gone by that time, and he'd only talk to someone he knew—someone who knew his history and could relate to him." He watched as the old lady's mind worked overtime. "At first, I thought it had to be you, ma'am."

Ms. Pritchard remained silent, so Rappart asked the question. "What do you mean 'at first', son? You don't still believe it?"

Ben's eyes remained on Ms. Pritchard. "The night my father died, there were several phone calls from Northern Indiana to Arkansas within minutes. The only number I could identify was my grandfather's, so I worked on locations of the other phones." Now, he turned his gaze to Tonya. "Triangulation pinpointed one phone in the area of the murder. That would be Mosie."

"My god!" his mother jumped up from her chair. "Lewis was involved in Jack's death. I've got to make a call. My god, we've got to start damage control." Connie Timmons rushed from the room, while the others stared in shocked surprise at her actions.

"You must forgive my mother," Ben apologized. "She's an important figure in Indiana politics."

He turned back to Tonya Pritchard.

"Why are you looking at me?" she asked. "It's very annoying."

"Ma'am," he addressed Ms. Pritchard. "My granddad made a call to a burn phone in Arkansas, and a minute later, that burn phone called Mosie."

"I don't have a burn phone, young man." Now, Ms. Pritchard watched Tonya, also. "I've never had use for such a thing."

"On the evening of my father's murder," Ben said, "Susan reacted to his hesitation.my grandfather called an unidentified phone located in Fayetteville. Isn't that where the University of Arkansas is located?"

"Holy shit!" Rappart blurted out. "Forgive my language. Can you prove any of this, son?"

"Tonya," Ms. Pritchard said, "Is any of this true?"

"Hush, Gran," she barked. "He's talking for his own benefit, or to impress his girlfriend. He can't prove any of it, because it wasn't me."

Instead, he spoke to Tonya. "When I first saw the results of the search, I believed you were involved. I thought you'd used my grandfather in your scheme by pretending to be your grandmother?"

"It wasn't me, and I don't have to sit through this!" Timmons recognized her attempt to hide her fear with defiance. "You can't prove any of this. It'll never hold up in court, and you just killed your only link. If any of this fiction spreads, you'll regret ever being born."

She turned to leave, but her grandmother stopped her with a comment, "We can manage this, Tonya."

"It doesn't need to be managed," she pleaded with Ms. Pritchard. "Gran, I've tried to protect you throughout, but I'm not involved in murder."

The old woman turned to Ben. "I believe my granddaughter, young man, and I'll use all my power to protect her."

"Tonya's right, Ben," Rappart added. "It's strong, but circumstantial. I'm not sure they'll convict on just that."

"I didn't do it!" Tonya begged.

"We believe you," and now, all eyes turned toward

Janet, who had moved close enough to Christina Turner to read her notes. Realizing the conversation had paused, Janet addressed the gathering. "Oh, when I first saw the pattern of calls, I assumed it had to be the granddaughter. Who else could it be?" Ben watched his classmate turn and look into the eyes of Ms. Turner. "Then, I remembered your award on your office wall."

The reporter looked confused. "My journalism award? What are you talking about?"

Janet glanced at Ben before she continued. "A very prestigious award given by the University to the state's top journalist, and I noticed the banquet was the same night that Ben's father died. You were in Fayetteville that evening, Ms. Turner."

The room fell silent, and everyone waited, but the reporter did not reply. After a moment, it was Tonya who spoke, "You bitch!" She seemed like she wanted to attack Christina, but refrained. After another moment, she said, "You're fired!"

"Wait," the policeman said. "You believe Tonya didn't do it, but you think Tina did? Why?"

Without allowing a response, the unemployed reporter said, "Why, indeed. None of this can be proven. I'm just as guilty, and just as innocent, as Tonya. Good luck getting any of this into a courtroom." She turned to leave. "Without a job, I guess I don't need to be here."

"You forgot about Howard Parkington and Tim Brickley." Ben's statement caused her to delay her exit.

"Who?" she asked.

"The two people in the airport garage," he said. "The Little Rock police are already connecting the dots, and before he died, Mosie gave me some good advice."

"And what would that be, Mr. Timmons?"

"He told me to follow the money." She turned and walked out of the room without responding.

"Shit, kid!" Rappart sounded concerned, but also amused. "You do have a way with women, and boy, did I get played." He seemed embarrassed by his last statement.

Ben ignored the officer and continued to look at Ms. Pritchard. "I'm sorry, ma'am."

"Sheriff," she said. "Will you give me a moment with Mr. Timmons?" Rappart looked at Janet. "Miss Sharpton can stay, too. Tonya, go with the sheriff." With that, the two left the hospital room. Ms. Pritchard looked at Ben, and he could see the sadness in her eyes. "We talked about this just a few days ago, Ben. It seems so long ago."

"Yes, ma'am."

She took a very deep breath, and then, she sighed. "Ms. Turner's right, son. You'll never get any of this to a jury."

"Yes, ma'am," he acknowledged. "I know you'll protect your family by any means."

"How do you know it wasn't Tonya?"

Ben glanced at Janet, and she gave him a reassuring wink. "Whoever played my grandfather had to know details. I guessed you hadn't told your secrets to your granddaughter, so she'd have a hard time convincing anyone. I needed another suspect, and Mosie provided it."

"How'd he do that?" Ms. Pritchard asked.

And just that quickly, Ben realized how tired he had grown of the entire mess. "Before he died, he told me men did it for the money. I didn't understand until I realized my other suspect was a woman. There had to be other reasons than money."

He saw the realization in her face, and she turned to stare out the door. Under her breath, she said, "I guess she did love him." She patted his arm, and then rose from the chair to leave. At the foot of the hospital bed, she paused and turned back toward him. "You'll still need to be careful," she said. Then, before she left, "Your daddy would have been proud."

Epilogue

Sunday afternoon in New York, and the first warm March day brought real signs of spring. Benjamin Timmons sat on a wooden bench in Washington Square Park, reading a book, while around him, activity filled the landscape. In the distance musicians played guitars and sang folk songs from the '60s. Animal lovers walked their dogs or threw peanuts to the park squirrels. In a far corner, a competitive game of bocce ball attracted several enthusiastic watchers.

Janet Sharpton's head rested in his lap as she dozed in the warm sunshine. He paused his reading to lightly stroke a few locks of hair, and as he did, a middle-aged man, wearing a brown bomber jacket, approached. "Mr. Timmons?" Janet opened her eyes.

Ben recognized his Syrian benefactor. "It's good to see you, Dr. Hameed."

Now, Janet sat up to give the man some room on the park bench. "Hello, Professor. How'd you know we were here?"

"Actually, Ben's roommate told me. Nice to see you, Ms. Sharpton," and Hameed waved at Janet. "The roommate couldn't hide his concern about my ethnicity. Not too many Arab friends in your circle, I take it?" He laughed at his own comment.

"I've had all kinds of visitors since we last talked, sir. In this great melting pot called New York, my roommate probably didn't notice your heritage or culture. He's just tired of the traffic in and out of our apartment." As Hameed took his seat, Ben continued, "I've tried to contact you through your embassy, but they couldn't put me in touch with you. I wanted to return the Beretta."

"Not to worry, young man. My gift to you." Hameed took a moment to look at the park crowd. "I'm sorry you had to use it."

"Thanks for that," Ben said. "To what do we owe the pleasure of your visit?"

"My backers and I have a selfish interest in you and Miss Sharpton," he said. "We'd like to see the economic model completed. Will you two consider accepting our assistance?"

"The model is the property of NYU," Janet answered. "We'll never get their permission to resurrect the project."

"Surely, there are ways around such obstacles?"

"No, sir," Ben replied. "Janet's right. Besides, the project stands as a testament to the work of a group of very gifted students. We're two months away from graduation, and most of them have their lives planned. We'd never be able to get such a group together, again."

"I fear you two are selling yourselves short."

"Thanks for the compliment," Janet said. "However, the value of the model depends upon its independent construction by an economics class at NYU. With your assistance, or that of any foreign government, it loses its credibility. By accepting any such help, we'd destroy its value."

"Too bad," Hameed said. "You might be right.

Will your class be able to live with the knowledge that the architects of 9/11 got away with their scheme?" Ben and Janet remained silent. "And your efforts in Arkansas, young Ben?"

"You've been following the story?" He'd grown tired of such discussions over the months, but he didn't want to offend Dr. Hameed.

"It's been a fascinating tale for almost a year, and we've followed you closely. I understand the television networks want to add to your fame, but I haven't seen either of you on the air." Hameed leaned closer to Janet. "How are you holding up under the pressure?"

Janet shook her head, "I'm just a bit player in this scene. Ben's the star, so you'd have to ask him."

"I'm not interested in such fame," Ben said. "I won't grow my reputation on the tombstones of others."

"Very honorable, young man!" A football bounced past them, and for a second, they were distracted as a student retrieved it. "I've monitored, with great interest, the events in Arkansas. It's been a good fight to watch from a distance. I understand the police in two states are prepared to arrest the mastermind behind the scheme?"

"No, sir," he said. "Two women involved, and circumstantial evidence points to both. The young woman comes from a wealthy family, and her grandmother has great power. It's been a long fight, but the authorities haven't found enough to arrest either. I've heard rumors that the other woman fled the area."

"I don't believe they'll ever sort it out—the blindness of some women," Janet said, causing Ben and Dr. Hameed to chuckle. "What?" she asked.

Ignoring her challenge, Hameed asked, "And

Maxwell? You have him in jeopardy, too? I've heard rumors of a presidential pardon, because of his efforts after the attacks, but Cohen is delaying, because there might be murder in the background?"

"That's my uncle, but I don't have any details of those negotiations, sir," Ben confirmed.

"Wouldn't it be wonderful to get his cooperation on the project? Any chance of that?"

"Ben has an insurance policy that might encourage him," Janet said, but Ben shook his head to quiet her.

"What insurance policy?" Hameed looked from Ben to Janet and back. Neither of them answered, so Hameed got to his feet and prepared to leave. "I've talked to NYPD. Not much progress on Abby's murder, either."

"A few clues, but progress is slow." The words hurt Ben as he said them.

Hameed gestured at the park's activity. "It's a beautiful day in the city," he said. "Miss Sharpton, what are your plans after graduation?"

"I've been accepted to Harvard law," she said.

"Congratulations." The professor sounded pleased. "Your parents should be very proud. And how about your future, young Timmons?"

"Northwestern Florida University invited me to assist with an economic study about the Gulf oil spill. That will be my summer, and assuming my legal issues are resolved, I'll be in England in the fall. I've been named a Rhodes Scholar."

"Very impressive," Hameed said. "I wish you both good fortunes." Then, before he walked away, he said, "There's an Arab proverb that says you should judge the quality of a man by the reputation of his enemies."

Ben smiled. "Janet's family has a similar expression."

"If there's truth in those words, Mr. Timmons," the Syrian responded, "you walk among kings."

"I know you mean that as a compliment, sir, but I'd prefer my old anonymous life."

"Ah, young man," Hameed said, as he walked away, "I know such a path no longer exists for you. Allah's plan goes forward."

A word about the author...

As a teenager, I wanted to be a writer. In college at Indiana University, I studied journalism. However, I switched my concentration to business. I have a bachelor of science in business, an MBA, and I'm a licensed CPA in two states.

In 2010 with two partners, I purchased a meat-and-seafood distributorship in Panama City. We completed the deal by using a large portion of our life savings and a huge bank loan. The business was totally dependent upon the tourist industry.

Whenever a business is purchased with leverage (debt), the new owners must understand the business must be grown. Without growth, the new debt load will destroy the business.

We closed the deal on February 3, 2010. On April 20, 2010, British Petroleum blew up the Gulf of Mexico, destroyed the tourism business in our first year of ownership, and adversely impacted the industry for the next several years. Any chance we had to grow the business disappeared with the fireball over The Deepwater Horizon oil platform.

You might imagine the stress we were under. As a means to maintain my sanity during the business battles, I turned to writing. It took my mind off our troubles, and gave me a much-needed release.

From Sacred Ashes is a labor of love, stress, battle, emotional drain, and frustration. I'm proud of my novel. The creation of this book saved my sanity, and may save my life.

Thank you for purchasing
this publication of The Wild Rose Press, Inc.

For questions or more information
contact us at
info@thewildrosepress.com.

The Wild Rose Press, Inc.
www.thewildrosepress.com

CPSIA information can be obtained
at www.ICGtesting.com
Printed in the USA
BVHW061105060120
568694BV00025B/1585/P

9 781509 229987